Readers have fallen for the Cornish Girls

T0337129

The Cornish Girls series:

Wartime with the Cornish Girls
Christmas with the Cornish Girls
Courage for the Cornish Girls
A Mother's Hope for the Cornish Girls
A Wedding for the Cornish Girls
Victory for the Cornish Girls

Betty Walker lives in Cornwall with her large family, where she enjoys gardening and coastal walks. She loves discovering curious historical facts, and devotes much time to investigating her family tree. She also writes bestselling contemporary thrillers as Jane Holland.

A New Hope for the Cornish Girls is the seventh novel in Betty Walker's heart-warming series.

BETTY WALKER

A New Hope for the
Cornish
Girls

avon.

Published by AVON
A Division of HarperCollins*Publishers* Ltd
1 London Bridge Street
London SE1 9GF

www.harpercollins.co.uk

HarperCollins*Publishers*
Macken House, 39/40 Mayor Street Upper
Dublin 1
D01 C9W8

A Paperback Original 2024
1
First published in Great Britain by HarperCollins*Publishers* 2024

A catalogue copy of this book is available from the British Library.

ISBN: 978-0-00-871511-3

This novel is entirely a work of fiction. The names, characters and incidents portrayed
in it are the work of the author's imagination. Any resemblance to actual persons,
living or dead, events or localities is entirely coincidental.

Typeset in Minion Pro by HarperCollins*Publishers* India

Printed and bound in the UK using 100%
Renewable Electricity at CPI Group (UK) Ltd

MIX
Paper | Supporting
responsible forestry
FSC
www.fsc.org
FSC™ C007454

This book contains FSC™ certified paper and other controlled
sources to ensure responsible forest management.

For more information visit: www.harpercollins.co.uk/green

For my son Dylan, who's just starting out as a novelist. Be bold and enjoy the journey!

CHAPTER ONE

April 1946, Porthcurno, South Cornwall

It was a beautiful spring day and Sheila Newton was in tears in front of her husband's grave. 'Oh, Arnie,' she sobbed, dragging a hanky out of her sleeve. 'We was barely married five bloomin' minutes … Why d'you have to go and die on me, you silly darlin' old curmudgeon?'

She had walked down to the churchyard with her daughter Violet and her son-in-law Joe and their young daughter Sarah Jane because, as she'd told the others over breakfast, 'Ain't it glorious today? Let's gather spring flowers and lay them on Arnie's grave. He always loved this time of year.' At Joe's sidelong look, she'd insisted defensively, 'I know, he was forever complaining about one thing or another, bless him. But he had a soft side too, did my Arnie. He just never let other folk see it. But he didn't fool me, despite all his argy-bargy and moaning about the war and the government.' She had cleared away the breakfast dishes, bustling about the farmhouse kitchen with restless energy. 'Oh, Violet, I do miss

Arnie something dreadful. I know it's been over six months since he passed, but it ain't getting any easier.'

'Then we'll take a walk down to the churchyard,' her daughter had agreed, nudging her husband, who'd been out in the fields since six and was just finishing his second breakfast. 'You can spare an hour, can't you, Joe, to come with us?'

'Eh?' Joe pushed back his flat cap to scratch his forehead, caught his wife's stern eye, and nodded. 'Oh aye, but just an hour, mind. Them new Land Girls can't be left to their own devices too long or we'll have gates left open and all sorts.'

Sheila's other son-in-law, Ernest, had also agreed to come with them, though only as far as the village. 'I fancy a longer walk myself,' the widower had told them cheerily. 'Need to stretch my legs after sitting behind a desk all week.' He worked at Eastern House, an international listening post located a stone's throw from Porthcurno's sandy beach, which had served as a top-secret government installation during the war. 'I love my job but these long hours don't leave much time for fresh air and exercise.'

So they had walked down the track from Joe's farm, perched high above the seaside village, gathering a few pretty flowers from the hedgerows along the way. With a wave, Ernest had peeled off along a grassy path at the bottom of the hill, walking stick in hand, striding out for goodness knows where. And once at the churchyard, Violet and Joe had wandered away among the graves with Sarah Jane, leaving Sheila alone with her husband.

Having spread a square of folded canvas on the damp grass, Sheila had knelt there to tidy the grave. In her capacious handbag she'd brought a small trowel for weeding and a cloth to wipe down the marbled plaque on the headstone.

Once she'd finished her work, she placed the spring flowers below Arnie's name and dates, and sat back with a sigh.

It was then that she discovered she was weeping. She hadn't meant to. Arnie had said, in the last days of his sickness, 'Now, Sheila, don't you waste any salt on me. I've lived a long life, and though I haven't always been a churchgoer, I'm confident I'll see those pearly gates rising before me at the end. So there's no point crying, because I'll be in a better place.' He'd managed a wink, despite his ill health. 'Or there'll be questions asked, let me tell you.'

That was something people had always missed about Arnold Newton. His unexpected optimism. Maybe he hadn't been the most popular man in the village, but as keeper of the local shop since long before Sheila and her daughter had moved down here from Dagenham, east of London, he'd been well known and respected.

Years ago, while running her busy caff in Dagenham, Sheila had been widowed for the first time, and then had lost her eldest daughter Betsy to the Blitz, finding herself left to look after her two granddaughters, Alice and Lily, with only Violet's help, who'd been unmarried at the time.

Leaving Sheila behind in Dagenham, Violet had taken young Alice and Lily down to Cornwall in '41, and not just to escape the bombing. The girls' father, Ernest Fisher, had enlisted early in the war but been reported missing. Being a native German speaker, his disappearance had sparked rumours among their neighbours that he'd defected to the other side, and Violet had been keen to remove the girls from all the nasty whispers and suspicions. Since the end of the war, Ernest's heroism had become plain. Sheila's son-in-law had been a spy, risking his life for years behind enemy lines, and now was happy to be working in Porthcurno, where he was able to visit his daughter Lily in nearby Penzance, now married with a child.

Following Violet and the girls down to Cornwall later had been intended as a temporary measure for Sheila, after heavy bombing forced her to close the caff. She herself was of Cornish birth, having been born not far from Penzance and moving to the London area with her parents while she was still a child. But she'd never expected to find love again in quiet Porthcurno, nor to settle permanently in Cornwall, far from the busy capital. But Arnie had insisted on courting her, and after a year or so, she'd finally given in to his nagging and let him kiss her. After that, there'd been nothing for it but to marry the man.

Sheila dabbed away a tear and sniffed. 'So, Arnie,' she said, addressing the headstone as though he could still hear her, which just maybe he could, 'I'm sorry it's been a while since I came to see you. And I've a good deal of news for you, love. I was ill over the winter. Nothing too serious; no need to worry. Just a nasty bout of bronchitis. But I'm better now, apart from a wheeze now and then.'

Spotting a dandelion she'd missed, she tugged it laboriously free from the soil, root and all. 'The war's been over a good six months now, but you'd be forgiven for thinking we was still fighting the Jerries, because rationing ain't much better. It might even be worse, depending on what you want. And your shop is still closed. Mr Boyce brings a handcart into the village once or twice a week, selling veg from the farms here about. But it ain't the same as having a proper shop.' She sighed. 'I know you meant well. But I wish you hadn't left it to me because I don't bloomin' know what to do for

4

the best. Sell it to Mr Boyce like he keeps asking, maybe? Or find someone to run it for me?'

Catching a burst of high-pitched laughter, Sheila turned her head to see Violet and Joe swinging Sarah Jane along the neatly kept path towards her, and felt a burst of impatience. She'd been thrilled when Violet had finally married in her late twenties, and even more so when little Sarah Jane had come along. But Joe's farm, while a loving family home, felt a bit overcrowded these days, and she often wished she could spend more time alone.

She blew out a breath, realising she'd better hurry if she wanted to tell Arnie all the news before being interrupted. 'Joe took on another new girl at the farm. Her name's Tilly. Nice girl, if a bit scatterbrained. Oh, and the pig's had another litter. You've never seen so many curly tails and pink trotters …' She laughed, and then blew her nose again. 'Oh, Arnie, I miss you so much.' Her heart stuttered, and she banged herself in the chest, determined not to let grief get the better of her. 'Now, what on earth am I supposed to do with your shop?'

But before any divine inspiration could strike her on that score, Violet and Joe arrived, and Sarah Jane tottered forward with her arms held out. 'Gramma, Gramma … I can skip!'

'Bless you, of course you can, my love,' she said kindly, and struggled back to her feet with Joe's help.

Puffing a little, she bent to collect the little square she'd been kneeling on and folded it under her arm. 'I brought the shop key with me,' she went on. 'I'd like to sort out a few things while we're down in the village. It'll be boring work though. You should take Sally … I mean, *Sarah Jane* back up to the farm and leave me to it.'

5

She'd forgotten how Violet hated anyone calling her daughter by the affectionate 'Sally', though it came more naturally than 'Sarah Jane', which was such a bloomin' mouthful.

Violet took her arm with an affectionate smile. 'Don't be daft, Mum. We're not leaving you alone, especially today of all days.'

Sheila stared at her daughter. 'Gawd blimey, I've a brain like a colander … I clean forgot.' No wonder she'd woken up thinking of Arnie that morning. Turning to her husband's gravestone, she kissed her fingertips and then touched them to the stone, adding softly, 'Happy birthday, Arnie, wherever you are.'

Arnold Newton's shop stood halfway up the hill in the village of Porthcurno, a converted fisherman's cottage with a shop below and living quarters above, though Arnie had always sat in the snug back parlour between customers. Sheila unlocked the door and opened it, pushing aside a small heap of letters that had accumulated since her last visit some months previously. Bending to collect the post, she felt a stab of guilt again. She'd been neglecting her duties as his widow and now owner of this property. But the ready tears brimming in her eyes reminded her why she'd stayed away so long. Because the memories of happier days with Arnie were too much to bear. The grief was still so raw …

'I suppose I'll have to open all these later and find out who they're from,' Sheila said, tucking the letters into the large pocket of her jacket. Straightening, she took a few steps into the dim interior, coughing as Violet and Joe traipsed in after her. 'Blimey, look at all the dust in here … I'll have to come down with my pinny and headscarf soon and give this place a proper cleanout. I thought I'd just do some sweeping and sorting today.' She glanced round at her daughter, who was looking wistful. 'Now, Vi, I don't need you to hold my hand while I do this. You and Joe should take Sarah Jane up to the farm. I'll be here at least an hour or two.'

'I want to help, Mum,' Violet said stoutly, grabbing the broom from behind the shop counter. 'Joe needs to get back to work, so he can take Sarah Jane home. I'll stay here with you.'

Sheila didn't argue. Truth was, she didn't much fancy being left on her own in the shop. Not without Arnie there. She would only spend the whole blessed time weeping. And that wouldn't do anyone any good. At least with Violet there, she'd be less inclined to get soppy over Arnie's old belongings.

Joe hoisted his small daughter onto his shoulders. 'Come along, Sal—' he began cheerfully, before stopping abruptly upon catching Violet's frown. He hurriedly corrected himself. 'I mean, Sarah Jane … Let's see how Pinky's piglets are coming along, eh?'

Pinky was the name of Joe's prize-winning sow, whose recent litter of twelve healthy piglets was the talk of the village.

Sarah Jane clapped her tiny hands in delight as she swayed back and forth on her father's shoulders. 'Pinky!'

'See you later then, love,' Joe told his wife. He touched a calloused finger to his cap as he smiled at his mother-in-law. 'You too, Sheila.'

'Ta ta, Mama,' Sarah Jane declared happily, waving from her precarious perch. 'Ta ta, Gramma.'

Once they'd gone, Sheila took a deep breath. 'Right, I'm starting in the parlour.' She gave Violet her bravest smile. 'I need to sort out that big chest of papers. I've no bloomin' idea what I'll find in there, but I can't throw anything out without making sure it's not important.'

'Oh, Mum,' Violet said with soft sympathy, giving her a quick hug. 'Are you sure? I can deal with his old papers if you'd like to sweep up instead. I don't want you getting upset again.'

'I won't get upset.' It was a dreadful whopper, for Sheila could already feel a tear trickling down her cheek. But she stuck her chin in the air. How she felt weren't nobody's business but her own. 'I promised Arnie on his deathbed that I'd do what's right and sort out his things. So, if you want to make yourself useful, you can sweep the shop and clean the shelves. Though I still say you should be wearing a headscarf.' She dragged out her hanky again, pretending to blow her nose, when in fact she was wiping her eyes. 'Blimey, them shelves are so dusty, me eyes are waterin'.'

With a reluctant laugh, Violet let her go. 'Whatever you say, Mum.'

Before she could make a spectacle of herself by bursting into tears again, Sheila hurried into the parlour and pushed the door shut behind her.

The first thing that met her eyes was the sight of Arnie's old green wool cardigan draped over the back of the rocking chair.

Sheila stood a moment, remembering Arnold, large as life, rocking back and forth in that chair as he told tales of the past.

Her husband had served in the Great War and had enjoyed sharing stories of that time, the grimmer the better. 'These young whippersnappers,' he used to say, 'they don't know how bad it was for us back then. All the mud and the shells … Ah, them were dark days all right.' And her son-in-law, Joe, formerly in the Royal Navy, had always listened respectfully, even though he'd lost his leg in action, poor man, and had had a false one fitted.

With a sigh, Sheila turned to the battered wooden chest under the window where Arnie had kept his papers.

'Blow me,' she muttered, throwing back the lid to reveal complete disarray, old photographs stuck in with official-looking papers, ancient school reports, Christmas cards and so many letters. There was no telling at first glance what should be kept and what thrown away.

As someone who preferred order over chaos, Sheila was half inclined to tip the load into a sack for burning. But her promise to Arnie nagged at her. Besides, there might be something worth keeping in this mess of paper and dusty knick-knacks.

Using a cushion to save her knees, she began to rifle through the chest, putting photographs aside, as well as anything that looked official, and taking a few minutes to peruse each musty old paper before deciding whether it could be chucked on the fire or kept for further inspection. It was a lengthy task, but not without a few moments of humour or nostalgia. She chuckled once or twice, glancing through letters from his grandmother to the younger Arnie, warning him not to lose his head over some Penzance girl and to remember to wash behind his ears, and smiled over a faded photograph of Arnold looking strong and handsome in his prime. Ah, he'd been good-looking in his youth, and she wished she'd known him then. But he'd been a gloriously irreverent and amusing man even in his later years when they'd met and courted. Neither of them had been spring chickens but she'd hoped they would grow older together, with many adventures still to come … Life was so cruel sometimes.

She didn't regret a single day of their short marriage though. After resisting his advances at first, she had found love and contentment with Arnold, and knew she could never feel the same again for another man.

One of the items she retrieved from the chest was a cracked china figurine of a dolphin. She turned it over in her hand, frowning. Then she remembered where it had come from. It was a little knick-knack Arnold had bought for her on their first trip to Bude, a town on the north coast of Cornwall.

They'd gone to Bude to visit her clever granddaughter Alice, who'd been working up there during the war, doing something top secret. Now she and her beau Patrick were engaged to be married and back in London, both working for the government. It was all 'hush-hush' work, as her widowed son-in-law liked to say. And since Ernest himself had been absent throughout the war, spying for Britain, he would presumably know.

Somehow this souvenir of Bude had ended up in Arnie's chest of odds and ends.

Violet came in, broom in hand, looking puffed out, a streak of dirt on her cheek. 'Mum, do you need me to sweep in here as well? Or should I wait until you're finished with that chest?'

'Look at this, love,' Sheila exclaimed in return, holding up the china dolphin. 'Arnie bought it for me when we went to Bude. Do you remember? We had such a lovely day with Alice. That was when we took the bridesmaid's dress over to her for a fitting, because she couldn't be spared from her war work to come home. Oh, such a fuss she made over that dress. Didn't like the lace flounces or the sleeves.' Sheila shook her head, recalling her wonderful wedding day to Arnold. She had never felt happier than at that moment, walking up the aisle to become Mrs Arnold Newton. 'I thought Alice looked a treat in the church though, with her hair swept up and that lovely bouquet of flowers … She done me and Arnie proud.'

'You're not crying again, are you?'

'So what if I am? My poor Arnie deserves a few tears shed over him, don't he?'

'I suppose so.' Violet took the china dolphin and smiled down at it mistily. 'Yes, I remember this. He was always buying you little gifts, wasn't he? You made a good choice there.'

'You never said a truer word.' Sheila wiped away her tears.

They were interrupted by a loud knocking at the door of the shop.

'Who on earth can that be?' Sheila struggled to her feet and brushed down her pinafore dress. They both peeked out into the empty shop to find a man clad in a tweed jacket and trousers in the doorway, a wiry terrier running about his feet.

Sheila didn't know his name but recognised him as a friend of the vicar's.

'Good morning, Mrs Newton, Mrs Postbridge. My apologies if I disturbed you, ladies,' the man said politely, taking off his cap and giving them both a nod. 'I saw the door open and thought I'd come and ask when the shop will be up and running again.'

'You can ask, but you won't get an answer.' Sheila saw her daughter's surprised glance at this short reply. But she felt unreasonably annoyed by his enquiry.

Goodness, her husband had barely been gone six months

11

or so. And all the locals cared about was when they might get their fruit and veg back. And their baccy and sweets too, no doubt.

'Nothing's been decided yet so if you don't mind …' She bustled over to shoo him out into the street.

The man was still protesting as she shut the door on him, the bell set above the frame clanging noisily.

Violet gave an embarrassed laugh. 'Mum, you can't speak to people like that. Poor man … He was only asking.'

'Only asking, my elbow.' Sheila pursed her lips, adding tersely, 'Ain't none of his business. Besides, I haven't decided what to do with the shop yet. I wish people would stop badgering me.'

Her daughter regarded her steadily. 'You want my opinion?'

'I'm sure you'll give it to me whether I want it or not,' Sheila muttered rebelliously.

'You should sell up. I'm sure that's why Arnold left you the shop. So he could provide for you after his death.'

Scandalised by this, though she knew perfectly well it was what Arnie had likely intended, Sheila flung back at her, 'Yes, and a fine thing it would be if I was to sell this place to the highest bidder like it means nothing. My husband ran this shop for donkeys' years. I can't just sell it.'

'Well, what else are you meant to do with it?' There was exasperation in Violet's voice, and Sheila couldn't blame her. She knew she was being stubborn and contrary but couldn't seem to help herself. 'You can hardly run this place yourself, Mum.'

Of course she couldn't. Not at her age. Why, she was sixty now. Or thereabouts, at any rate. She'd stopped keeping count at sixty, as it no longer seemed worth the bother.

Besides, she knew nothing about keeping a village shop.

'Oh, can't I?' Sheila replied all the same, stung by the implication that she was past the age of being useful. 'I'll remind you, my girl, that I ran our caff in Dagenham a good five years, and nobody would have dared tell me I wasn't up to the job back then.'

Violet blinked. 'A caff ain't a shop.'

'Folk come in and buy things, and sometimes we have a good old natter. Where's the difference?'

'Now you're being ridiculous. Brewing tea and baking cakes ain't the same as selling fruit and veg, plus all the store cupboard produce. There'd be suppliers to deal with, and goodness knows what else. Besides, Arnie was down here most days. We'd never see you up at the farm, and who would help with the cooking or mind Sarah Jane when I'm about my chores?' Violet shook her head and went back to sweeping. 'It simply ain't possible and you know it.'

Sheila bit her lip and returned to her task of clearing out Arnie's chest. She was aware of a nagging sense of disappointment. But her daughter was right. She was being silly and obstinate as usual. Run a village shop indeed!

Only now she'd thought of it, that foolish idea wouldn't go away. And she did miss the good old days at the caff, chatting away in her white pinny and cap, bending an ear to juicy local gossip and passing it on. Sixty and a bit weren't so very old, after all. She might not be as steady on her pins as in younger years, it was true, but her brain was still every bit as sharp, and she'd been brought up near Penzance and knew some of their Cornish ways at least … So why *shouldn't* she run a little village shop like this one?

CHAPTER TWO

Since the farmer and his wife had gone out for a walk, and the other Land Girls were up in the top field, Joan hung lazily over the iron gate into the pig pen and clucked her tongue at the row of wriggling pink piglets feeding on the sow's underbelly. As she watched, one of the piglets, jostling to get the best spot, fell sideways out of the scrum and stumbled about in the muddied straw, lost and squeaking, its tiny snout rooting in vain for the teat.

Concerned, she clambered over the gate to scoop it up in her arms, placing the piglet back among its brothers and sisters so it could feed. 'There you go, piggy,' she said with satisfaction, and wiped her hands on the mustard-coloured breeches that formed part of the Land Army uniform.

Standing back, Joan watched as a dozen piglets fed together on their mother Pinky with fervent concentration, and found herself wondering whether any of them ever felt lonely in that crowd.

Joan had asked herself that question many times when working at an ammunitions factory near Manchester, having nothing in common with her fellow workers except drudgery and the woes of restrictive rationing. There'd been a certain camaraderie among the factory girls. A sense that they all knew why they were there and were proud of doing a man's job while the men themselves were fighting overseas. Yet she'd still felt lonely at times.

When things had gone badly wrong, she'd been hospitalised, and then permitted to transfer to the Women's Land Army, receiving her draft papers to this quiet part of Cornwall with a sense of relief. The factory up north had been noisy and dirty, and after she'd been assaulted by a drunken soldier at a party, her nerves had given way entirely. The shock of that assault had given her nightmares and left her wary of men, even though she knew they couldn't all be that bad where girls were concerned. Her recovery had been slow, leading some to mock her for being too fragile. 'There's a war on – harden up!' more than one well-meaning nurse had told her during her hospitalisation. And she had tried, heaven knows.

Now the war was over, thank goodness, and she was twenty-three years old, a grown woman. Yet the Land Army marched on, dreary and monotonous, and rationing remained a fact of life. Many men were still overseas, including her younger brother, Graham. She missed him so much, it hurt. But at least she'd escaped the hellish factory and now spent her days toiling on the land instead. It was hard work, but she loved the fresh country air and the amazing views. And she had never minded getting her hands dirty. Not when it was good clean earth under her fingernails, not grease and filth from the ammunitions factory.

The very thought that she'd been making something

designed to kill had filled her with dread. She'd always been aware that there must be a girl like her in a factory in Germany, making weapons and ammunitions that might one day take her brother's life.

Sighing, Joan raised her face to the blue sky. Spring sunshine was a welcome sight after the long cold winter, encouraging her to imagine that better days might lie ahead.

Ever since Mr Newton's death last autumn, life at the farm had been strangely dark and grim, compared to all the fun they'd had during the war. Yes, fun. Everyone had felt such a sense of purpose, especially towards the end, mucking in and doing their bit for King and country. Violet, the farmer's wife, had kept them all amused with her pithy East End sayings, and her way of keeping her husband Joe in check. And when news of D-Day had come and later, victory, Violet's widowed mum Sheila Newton had insisted on celebrating with a 'knees-up' as she'd called it. Dancing, games, paper hats, home-made wine, and Joe's dogs howling along to the singing … The memory made Joan smile.

But everyone had assumed life would change once the war was over. That things would soon be back to normal. Rationing would end and people would be free to go about their daily lives.

Instead, it seemed they were still working for the war effort long after the war had ended.

Of course, with so many soldiers being kept overseas, women were still needed to till and plant the soil, harvest crops and tend to animals. So the Land Girls had not yet been relieved of their duties. And many women volunteers were still in their positions too. Plus, food was scarce, so rationing had remained strict.

It was like being at war, but without that unifying sense of purpose, she considered unhappily. She didn't mean to feel sorry for herself. But sometimes, the days just seemed to drag on endlessly …

A cheerful shout split the quiet air, and she turned to see Farmer Postbridge trudging up the track from Porthcurno with his small daughter perched on his shoulders.

As Joe reached the farm gates, he swung the child down and allowed Sarah Jane to totter on her own towards the farmhouse. He raised a hand in greeting to Joan, removed his cap to wipe his forehead, and continued on his way.

Hurriedly, Joan climbed over the pig pen gate and picked up the heavy bucket of chicken feed, guiltily aware she'd been neglecting her duties.

But before she could scurry away, Sarah Jane spotted the bucket and rushed towards her, crying, 'Chicky! Chicky!' with flushed enthusiasm.

Joan crouched to steady the little girl before she could stumble over the uneven cobbles. 'Yes,' she agreed with a ready smile, 'I'm just about to feed the chickens. Would you like to help?' She glanced up at Joe as he approached. 'If she's allowed, that is?'

'Try and stop her,' the farmer said easily, and ruffled his daughter's fair hair. 'You love the chickies, don't you?' His mild gaze rose to Joan's face as he hesitated. 'Would you mind bringing Sally into the kitchen after to wash her hands, and maybe fetch her a cup of milk too? I've a few things to tend to in the barn.'

As usual, Joe Postbridge had addressed his daughter as Sally, though he rarely did so in front of his wife, who insisted rigidly on calling her Sarah Jane, as she'd been christened.

It had become a frequent bone of contention between the married couple, Joan had noticed with amusement. A strange one too, for the farmer readily gave way to his wife on most other issues.

'That dratted tractor … It's on the blink again and we'll need it tomorrow.' Joe scratched his head. 'Sorry to lump you with the girl, but my wife's still down in the village with Sheila.'

Grinning, Joan shook her head. 'I don't mind at all, Mr Postbridge. I'll look after your daughter until your wife's back. Don't you worry.'

He replaced his cap with a look of relief. 'That's kind of you, Joan. Thank 'ee.' And with a few muttered words to his daughter, reminding the little girl to mind her manners, he limped away to the barn.

Joan watched the farmer with sympathy. He'd served in the Navy during the war, she'd been told, and had lost his leg when his ship was hit. But his false leg never seemed to stop him doing whatever he wanted. All the same, she could understand why he was glad to have Land Girls on the farm to help out. There were four of them now. Young Tilly Coombes had arrived just after Christmas, and although it used to be a squeeze in the attic rooms set aside for their use, since Joe and Violet's niece Alice had moved back to London, the girls were only sharing two to a room now.

'Right, put out your hands,' she told Sarah Jane, and the little girl obeyed, her eyes bright with excitement.

Gently, Joan sprinkled chickenfeed into her open palms, some of it dropping through to the cobbles, and laughed as Sarah Jane instantly dashed forward to toss it wildly at the chickens, who ran about clucking and pecking at the ground.

'Chicky! Chicky!' the child cried in delight, clapping as she watched them.

Joan scattered the rest of the feed for the chickens, making sure to save a few last handfuls for Sarah Jane, but was interrupted in this task by the other Land Girls arriving back from the top field, all three in mud-flecked mustard breeches and green jerseys, though only Caroline was wearing her standard issue taupe jacket today.

Caroline Ponsby came first, trudging along with hands thrust in her jacket pockets, her expression distracted as Selina and Tilly chatted behind her. Selina Tiptree was wearing her hat tilted to protect her face from the spring sunshine, always keen to avoid freckles, and her fair hair was knotted in a long plait that hung over one shoulder. Tilly Coombes was the youngest at eighteen, and clearly the newcomer to the team, as evidenced by her still-neat uniform with no rips or patches. She was wearing her hat correctly, the string knotted tightly beneath her chin. She was a slight girl with clever green eyes and curly red hair worn fashionably short, and an infectious laugh. Joan had liked her instinctively from their first meeting.

Smiling, Joan waved in greeting, though instantly she was reminded of her earlier question … How was it possible to feel so lonely when surrounded by people? Because she did feel lonely at the farm. And yet she was on reasonably good terms with the farmer and his wife, and with the other Land Girls.

The problem, she suspected, was that she struggled to make conversation with the other residents at the farm, their tastes and interests being so different from hers. Tilly had been impressed by the watercolours Joan liked to paint whenever she had a few hours' spare time, but had confessed to not being very artistic herself. And Caroline, seeing her keenly knitting, had asked if she would teach her the craft, which Joan had agreed to do, though she guessed Caro had only asked out of pity, knowing how rarely the others involved Joan in any of their activities.

As for Selina, she'd barely spoken to Joan in recent weeks, her head no doubt full of plans for her wedding, which she claimed would take place this summer once her soldier beau was home from France. After that, Selina intended to give up work altogether, having plans to start a family as soon as possible.

Joan wished her well with it. Though as she'd personally never met anyone who could inspire her to become a wife and mother, it was hard to be as enthusiastic as Selina clearly expected.

Selina eyed her sideways. 'Been lumped with little Sarah Jane, have you?' she asked, her tone not altogether friendly. It had been clear from Joan's first day at the farm that Selina was top dog. And although Joan had gone out of her way to avoid antagonising her, Selina nonetheless seemed to view her as a threat. 'It suits you. You look very … maternal. Doesn't she, Caro?'

Caroline said nothing.

Joan returned the bucket to the stand outside the kitchen door and took Sarah Jane back inside with her as Farmer Joe had instructed. The other Land Girls followed.

'Nothing wrong with that,' she said calmly, kicking off her boots and trying not to let Selina's comments make her uncomfortable. 'I like looking after children. They're good fun.' With a quick smile, she sat Sarah Jane on the empty draining board to clean her up. 'Ready?'

Sarah Jane nodded, raising her chin as Joan dampened a flannel and wiped her face and hands. The little girl squirmed but didn't try to escape.

'I'm pushing off upstairs to read a magazine.' Caroline headed out of the kitchen, hands still deep in her pockets.

Joan looked after her in surprise. 'Something wrong with Caro?'

'Nothing worth mentioning.' Cutting herself a slice of raisin cake, Selina gave a sniff of disapproval. 'She got in a huff when I told her Johnny and I are planning to honeymoon at Lyme Regis. Though I don't know why that should upset her. Not exactly Paris, is it?'

Tilly took Joan's place at the sink, a thoughtful look on her face. 'I doubt anyone would be keen to spend their honeymoon in Paris. Not for a good few years, at any rate. The Germans must have left the city in a right state after they retreated.' Tilly soaped her hands vigorously, gazing through the window at the sunlit farmyard. 'Anyway, Caroline only said she was bored of hearing your plans for the wedding,' she added, glancing back at Selina, a defiant note to her voice. 'I wouldn't call it *a huff*, exactly. You do talk about Johnny quite a bit, Selina. No offence.'

Carefully drying Sarah Jane's hands with a clean tea cloth, Joan hid her smile. She tried never to be confrontational with Selina, knowing how strong her personality was and disliking arguments. But Tilly was clearly made of sterner stuff. A self-confessed tomboy, the younger girl came from a large family with several older siblings. No doubt it had left her unafraid to pick a fight.

'Well, I never …' Selina gasped, hands on hips, glaring at Tilly. Joan noted that she didn't blaze into a row over the comment though. Perhaps she could sense that Tilly would give as good as she got. Instead, she merely stomped away after Caroline. 'I'll wash my hands upstairs. I don't have time to stand about gossiping. I need to write a letter to Johnny.'

Once the door had closed behind her, Joan threw Tilly a warning look. 'Selly can be quite sharp when she's crossed,' she said softly, just in case Selina was still hanging about in the hallway. 'Best be on your guard with her.'

'Oh, I'm not scared of Selina,' Tilly replied airily. 'She reminds me of my eldest sister, always throwing her weight around and talking the loudest to stop anyone else getting a word in edgeways. I learned early on that you can't give an inch or people like that will take a mile. Besides,' she added with a quick glance at Joan, '*someone* has to put her in her place.'

Was that a reprimand? She filled a mug with milk for Sarah Jane and sat her down at the kitchen table. 'I prefer to stay out of arguments,' Joan replied frankly. 'They give me a headache.'

Tilly just shrugged.

Joan, who had noticed a haunted look on Selina's face in recent weeks, wondered if the little spat she'd just witnessed stemmed from something that was worrying Selina, not from a vexatious temperament. But she didn't press the point.

'I'm sure your mummy will be home soon,' she reassured the little girl, who was kicking her feet under the table and blowing bubbles into her milk in a bored, irritable fashion.

'Gramma?' Sarah Jane queried, head on one side.

'Yes, and your gran too. Though it's a long climb up that

steep hill in the sunshine. I imagine your gran is taking it slowly. But they'll both be back soon,' she insisted. 'Now, drink your milk. You need milk to grow big and strong. So stop blowing bubbles in it, there's a good girl.'

Sarah Jane shot her a distrustful look but said nothing, meekly sipping her milk.

'Selina's right about one thing,' Tilly said in an offhand manner, grabbing a handful of oats from the round-bellied container on the kitchen table and heading for the outside door.

'What's that?'

'You're good with the little uns.'

Speechless, Joan turned, staring round at her in surprise. When Selina had said something similar in the farmyard, it had sounded like an insult. But she guessed from Tilly's smile that she'd meant it as a compliment.

Slipping on a pair of clogs, Tilly hurried out into the sunshine, calling over her shoulder, 'I'm off to see Barney,' as she disappeared across the yard.

Barney was the shire horse that Joe had acquired to work on the farm when the tractor was either awaiting repairs or busy on another job. He was a vast grey with great feathery hooves and tail, but surprisingly placid in temperament. Little Sarah Jane was too scared to go anywhere near the horse, who must have seemed like a giant to her. But, like Tilly, Joan occasionally sneaked the horse a wizened apple from last year's store, or a handful of oats. And she'd seen the other Land Girls doing the same when they thought nobody was watching. Especially Selina, who apparently came from a horsey family and missed being able to ride.

Moments later, the kitchen door swung open and Sarah

Jane jumped down from her chair with a shout of joy. 'Mamma! Mamma!' she cried, tottering across to her.

'Hello, poppet. Joan been looking after you, has she?' Violet Postbridge smiled down at her bouncing daughter, then unpinned her hat and gave Joan a friendly nod. 'I spoke to Joe in the barn. It was very kind of you to mind her. Do help yourself to a slice of raisin cake, love.' She crouched to speak to her daughter. 'Would you like a slice of cake, Sarah Jane? Gran baked it, and you know her cakes are always the best.'

Not surprisingly, Sarah Jane readily agreed to cake.

'I'll cut us both a slice,' Joan murmured, fetching plates and the cake knife.

'Thanks, love. Only a tiny portion for Sarah Jane, mind,' Violet told her, hurrying to the sink to wash her own hands. 'Don't want to spoil her appetite.'

Sheila Newton limped into the kitchen. 'Blimey, I swear that bloomin' hill gets steeper every time I climb it.' She looked flushed and there was perspiration on her forehead, but she gave Joan a wink. 'You're a good girl, ain't you? Looking after our Sally for us.'

'Her name is Sarah Jane,' Violet snapped over her shoulder.

'Yes, all right, love … Sarah Jane. My mistake.' Behind Violet's back, Sheila gave Joan another wink and laid a finger to her lips. Dragging off her own hat, she hung it lopsided on the coat-stand, still puffing noisily. 'Phew. This is what comes of never walking down into the village like I used to when Arnie was alive. I'm out of condition.'

Hurriedly, Joan pulled out a kitchen chair for the older lady and received a breathless mutter of thanks.

'And this is why I should reopen the shop,' Sheila went on,

addressing her daughter as she sat down. 'Think of all the exercise I'd get, walking up and down that hill every day.' She fanned hot cheeks before reaching into her bag for a comb to tidy her dishevelled, silvery hair. 'Why, I'd be ready to enter the Olympic Games by the end of the summer, I daresay.'

'Don't talk rubbish, Mum,' Violet exclaimed, and then caught Joan's eye. With an embarrassed smile, she withdrew an envelope from her jacket pocket and held it out to Joan. 'I almost forgot, love, we ran into the postie on the way up from the village. She gave us a letter for Selina. Will you pass it on when you next see her?'

'Of course. She's in her room. I'll be heading up there in a jiffy.' Joan glanced at the envelope and recognised the handwriting at once. It was from Selina's fiancé, Johnny. Another love letter, no doubt, which they would all be forced to listen to as Selina read it out loud. She was thoroughly enjoying being the only one to have a fiancé, seeming to think this made her superior to the others.

Personally, Joan didn't mind being unattached. It made life easier. Besides, being engaged hadn't made Selina any happier. In fact, the worry of all their complicated wedding arrangements seemed to have got her down. But this letter would probably cheer her up in no time.

'Ah, young love ...' Sheila sighed, folding her arms across an ample bosom. 'I remember when Arnie and me fell in love. What larks, eh? I couldn't think of nothing else for months.'

Sarah Jane ran to her gran, holding up the last fragment of cake that Joan had cut for her. 'Cake, cake!' she chanted before cramming it messily into her mouth.

'That was hardly "young" love, Mum,' Violet remarked.

Throwing her daughter a sharp look, Sheila brushed cake crumbs off Sarah Jane's face and dress. 'All right, Miss Hoity-Toity, maybe we weren't neither of us young. But we *felt* young. And what would you know about it, anyway? Nobody knows what goes on between two people. And don't you forget it.' Sheila's face became mutinous. 'My Arnie would have wanted me to take over running the shop. To preserve his legacy. So that's what I'm going to do. Even if it kills me.'

Amazed by this, Joan glanced at Violet speculatively.

Sure enough, the farmer's wife did not look amused, and since her husband had just come into the kitchen at that moment, she complained bitterly to him that her mother was behaving irrationally. 'I want you to speak to her, Joe,' she said, quite as though Sheila wasn't right there in the same room. 'She needs to shake that silly notion right out of her head. She's too old to be running a shop. Tell her, Joe.'

Joe Postbridge looked from his wife to his mother-in-law in dismay. 'I'd rather not get involved, if it's all the same to you, love,' he told his wife and edged towards the snug, where he liked to sit with a pipe and his feet up between work shifts.

'You get back here, Joseph Postbridge,' Violet began but was interrupted by her mother.

'This ain't nobody's business but mine, Vi, so you can leave poor Joe out of it.' Sheila hoisted up her granddaughter to sit on her knee. 'I've made up my mind and that's that.'

Deciding this was a good moment to slip away upstairs, Joan left the Postbridges arguing among themselves. Upstairs, she saw the light on in the little washroom Joe had rigged up for them and heard Caroline humming as she took a stand-up wash.

Knocking on the door of the room that Selina shared with Caroline, she pushed it open without waiting for permission, as none of them really bothered with such things, and was taken aback to find Selina with her face buried in a hanky, her shoulders slumped, sitting dejected on the edge of her bed.

'I'm sorry,' she stammered, beginning to back away, 'I'll come back another time.'

'No, no,' Selina cried in a muffled voice, and wiped her face. Her eyes looked very red. 'Hayfever starting early, I expect. I'm fine, honestly.' She blinked, apparently only just registering that Joan was in the wrong bedroom. 'Did you want something?'

Joan held out the letter that Violet had given her. 'Some post has arrived for you. I think it's from Johnny.'

Jumping up, Selina almost snatched the envelope from her hand. 'Thank you.' She gave her a direct look. 'I'll see you at tea, then.'

Taking the hint, Joan gave the other Land Girl a perfunctory smile and retired to her own bedroom, two doors down. There, sunshine pooled on the wooden floor and lit up the sloping attic ceiling, and yesterday's spring flowers that she'd brought upstairs and arranged in a vase smelt sweet and fresh, like the fields and meadows above Porthcurno.

She changed out of her uniform, took out a sketchpad and pencils, and began to work on a new sketch of the piglets feeding on their mother in a bed of straw.

Soon, the distractions and worries of being in a group of people who didn't always rub along together perfectly began to fade away, and the space inside her head became peaceful and silent.

27

But Joan knew this peace couldn't last forever. Because it never did. She could take refuge in being alone like this, while still feeling isolated and wishing for company, or she could spend time with others whose petty quarrels and differences fretted at her nerves. There seemed no solution to her dilemma. It was as though she was missing some vital piece to the puzzle of her life, and had no idea where or how to find it …

CHAPTER THREE

As soon as the door had closed behind Joan, Selina grabbed up her penknife and slit open the letter from her fiancé, her heart thumping with nerves. It had been some time since Johnny's last letter, and although she knew there could be many reasons for his long silence, her spirits had begun to flag in recent days, fearing that something might have happened to him.

There was also a nagging suspicion that his attachment to her was not as strong as it had once been.

For some months, Johnny's letters had lacked that spark that had made her heart sing in the early days of their relationship. The first year they'd been apart, his letters had often made her blush, some of his comments not fit to be read aloud even to her friends. Lately though, he had kept to dull news of regimental movements and local information, signing off with a simple *Johnny*, instead of something more affectionate.

Johnny was still overseas, of course, with his regiment, the brave lads all working hard to put things right in France now the war was over. But he had promised faithfully that they would be wed on his return, and had even said she could begin to plan the event if she wished.

No doubt the long delay had made him glum too, that was all. And she could hardly blame him. It was easy for two people to stay in love when they could see each other every other month or so, but she hadn't seen Johnny since his last official leave over six months ago, when he'd hitched a lift to Porthcurno to see her for one magical evening before disappearing again.

That visit already felt like a lifetime ago.

His lengthy absence from Britain had surprised her, for he'd assured her earlier that the troops would be allowed home for Christmas, perhaps for as long as three days. But then he'd written to warn her not to expect him, saying his permission slip had not come through.

Sometimes, lying in the dark, a silly fear would nag at her, that her darling Johnny had told a little fib. That he had in fact been given leave for Christmas, but had visited his parents instead, and not told her.

Yet why would he do that? It was such nonsense. Johnny loved her and she loved him, and the only thing that might be causing a problem was the blasted army, who had so far refused to allow him home to marry her.

Of course, if he'd decided to see his parents instead of coming all the way to Cornwall to spend a few hours with her, that was understandable. But she would have liked the truth.

Worse, it wasn't possible even to check on his story. They had met right here in Porthcurno, where he'd been stationed as a guard on the listening post that had kept information flowing smoothly in and out of Britain during the war. But his home was in Kent. Where exactly, she had no idea. Johnny had often sworn that he would take her to Kent when he got back from France, to meet his parents and siblings before they tied the knot. But he'd never shared his parents' address with her.

Still, her darling had written now. And that would have to suffice.

Seating herself below the attic skylight, Selina tucked her feet under her knees and unfolded the single sheet of paper she'd found in the envelope. His letters were usually two sheets at least. Surely this must be a very short message, then. The date when he could come home and finally marry her, perhaps?

Dear Selina,

I'm sorry that I haven't written in such an age. But I did not have the heart to write before. You see, what I have to say will hurt your feelings. And I wish I had better news. The thing is, I've changed my mind about getting married.

Please know, it's not your fault. You have been a wonderful fiancée. But I've met a girl here. She's French, but she speaks very good English, and we've been seeing quite a bit of each other recently. I'm awfully sorry and I know this will upset you, but I've had to ask her to marry me, and she's said yes, and that's all there is to it. Maybe one day you will forgive me.

I wish you all the best in the world.

Johnny

Selina felt curiously numb, her body frozen despite the sunshine. A splash of something wet struck the date on the sheet of paper and trickled down, blurring the ink below.

She was crying, she realised, but didn't move to wipe her eyes.

Stunned, she re-read the letter several times, the cruel words echoing in her mind. Then she gave a howl of furious agony, crumpled the letter into a ball, and flung it across the room with all the violence she could muster.

I've met a girl here. She's French, but she speaks very good English, and we've been seeing quite a bit of each other recently.

Collapsing onto the bed, her face buried against the hard bolster pillow to muffle the tell-tale sounds, Selina sobbed until her sides ached and her eyes were sore.

I've had to ask her to marry me.

There was only one thing that could mean. He and this French girl had been … intimate. And now she was expecting his baby. So getting married had been the only honourable solution.

Maybe one day you will forgive me.

She would never forgive him, Selina promised herself bitterly. Nor trust another man with her heart.

Never, ever, ever.

And what on earth could she tell the others? She'd been boasting about her engagement to Johnny for ages, and discussing the plans for her wedding and her honeymoon with anyone who would listen. She knew they were all heartily sick of the topic but lately it had become an obsession. Perhaps this was why, she thought miserably. She'd been so nervous about Johnny's increasingly few-and-far-between letters that she had grown ever more feverish about the wedding, determined to nail down every detail as perfectly as she could. And now the whole thing had crumbled beneath her …

Selina groaned, rolling over and burying her face in her hands. She was never going to live this down. The Land Girls might pretend to be sympathetic, but she knew they'd be laughing as soon as she was out of earshot. As for Violet and Joe … Well, the Postbridges were kind people, and she knew they would never laugh, but it was still so humiliating. Her fiancé was going to marry another woman. A woman he had clearly made pregnant. It was as shameful as it could possibly be.

Fresh tears ran down her cheeks. She didn't want to lie. Yet how could she admit the truth without breaking down and making a complete fool of herself in front of everyone?

Hearing Caroline on her way back from the washroom, Selina sat up hurriedly and rubbed her hanky across damp cheeks. It was futile though. There was no way to hide the fact that she'd been sobbing her heart out. Still, she could trust Caroline, couldn't she? Apart from the odd spat, they'd been friends ever since the two of them had joined the Land Army and ended up at Postbridge Farm together. All the same, she was too embarrassed to admit the full truth.

Perhaps it wouldn't be a lie if she simply omitted the most awful part of the story.

'Golly, it makes such a difference, washing all that mud off …' Dressed in a bathrobe and still vigorously towelling her hair dry, Caroline stopped dead in the middle of the room as her astonished gaze locked on Selina's face, which no doubt bore the marks of half an hour's wild sobbing. 'Goodness, whatever's wrong? What's happened? Oh, you poor thing …'

Without waiting for an answer, Caroline dashed forward and threw her arm about Selina's shoulders, giving her a quick squeeze. 'You can tell me. I won't breathe a word, however bad it is.'

Selina pointed across the room to the crumpled-up letter, which now lay forlornly beside the chest of drawers they shared. 'I … had a letter from … Johnny. We … We're not getting married anymore.' Her voice wobbled and she drew an unsteady breath before hurrying on. 'There's nothing I can do about it. Looks like he … he was the wrong man for me.'

'Oh, Selly, I'm so sorry. That's rotten luck.' Caroline grimaced. 'But you're right, Johnny can't have been the right man for you, can he? Or he wouldn't have called it off.'

Selina swallowed hard. She wanted to tell Caro about the French girl he'd met. And the shameful acknowledgement that he'd had no choice but to marry her. But the wound was still too raw.

'Exactly.' She sat up, dabbing at her eyes with the now sodden hanky. 'I shall just have to … to forget him, shan't I? And at least we hadn't booked the church or the honeymoon hotel. All my arrangements were only on paper.'

'Then you can tear those stupid plans up and throw them in the bin,' Caroline told her stoutly.

'Yes, that's what I'm going to do. Right now, in fact.'

Selina jumped up, found the notebook where she'd listed all her wedding arrangements and ideas, her hopes and dreams for the future, and ripped out the pages she'd been so fervently scribbling on for the past few months. These she scrunched up viciously and threw across the room after the dismal letter from Johnny.

'I'll take them all down to the kindling basket later,' she

declared, her voice a gasp. 'Violet can use them as twists to light the fire. That … That's all they're good for.'

'That's the ticket.' Towelling her hair again, Caroline gave Selina an encouraging smile, though it was clear she was still concerned for her friend's well-being. 'Feeling better?' When Selina gave a jerky nod, she smiled and bent to the chest of drawers to fetch clean clothes for herself. 'I'd better get dressed. It'll be teatime soon.' She shot Selina a cautious look over her shoulder. 'Are you planning to tell everyone else? Tonight, I mean. Or will you wait?'

Selina hugged herself. Now the news had truly sunk in, she felt miserable and rather chilly. She certainly wasn't looking forward to seeing everyone's faces when she explained about the broken engagement. But now that Caroline knew the truth, it would be ludicrous to keep it hidden from the others, even for a day or so.

Besides, if she tried to keep it quiet, it would soon look as though she was embarrassed to admit what had happened. And though she was, she didn't want anyone else to guess her inner sense of humiliation. She would just have to be brave, that was all.

'Yes, of course.' Selina pushed her chin in the air. 'I've nothing to be ashamed of.'

Though if that were true, why did she feel so empty and hurting inside?

At dinner, Selina helped lay the table as always, her face averted whenever anyone looked her way. She had checked her reflection in the washroom before coming downstairs and knew that her cheeks were pale and blotchy, and her eyes red-rimmed, a sure sign that she'd been crying. But she was not ready to answer any questions until everyone was seated. That way, she wouldn't have to repeat herself. Bad enough having to make the announcement to the whole household, without missing anyone out and having to say it all over again.

Mrs Newton, sharp-eyed as ever, broached the subject first. Her knife and fork hovering over the rabbit stew that she and Violet had prepared, Mrs Newton looked directly at Selina and asked, ''Ere, Selina, love ... You look bloomin' awful. Was it that letter that come for you today? I don't want to pry if you'd rather not say, but ...'

Slowly, Selina put down her cutlery and swallowed her mouthful of food. Nervously, she glanced up and down the long kitchen table, aware of everyone's gaze on her face.

'Yes, it was a letter from my fiancé, Johnny. I'm afraid to tell you that ... Well, the thing is, he's broken off our engagement. So, there isn't going to be a wedding after all.' She had intended to say more but her voice wavered and she fell silent, tears pricking at her eyes as she stared dully down at her dinnerplate.

Never had rabbit stew looked less appetising.

A hubbub of voices broke out around the table. Joe swore under his breath and was reprimanded by his wife. Tilly exclaimed, 'What? But that's *horrible*!' Caroline muttered something supportive from beside her, and Joan said clearly above the noise, 'I'm so sorry to hear that, Selina.'

Tutting furiously, Sheila Newton shook her head. 'Well, I never ... Young men can be stupid, you know. Maybe he'll come around in time.'

'I don't think so,' Selina admitted miserably, still not looking up. Something deep inside forced her to add in a rush, 'He's going to marry someone else. A French girl. He didn't tell me her name but ... I believe she may be in the family way.'

Silence met this appalling admission. Then Tilly, who was still only eighteen, gave a little gasp as she belatedly worked out what Selina meant, and whispered, 'Golly,' behind her hand.

Joe swore again, and this time Violet said nothing.

'Sounds to me like you're better off without such an irresponsible young man,' Mrs Newton said wisely, and continued eating. In between mouthfuls, she added indistinctly, 'Some fellas can't keep their hands to themselves ... Oh yes, you can wait a long time for the right one to come along ... I was lucky with my two husbands. Proper gents, both of 'em, gawd rest their souls.' She gave a gusty sigh. 'Pass the salt, Joe, there's a dear.'

Joe did as instructed as everyone began commiserating with Selina at once, their voices beating at her in a wave of sympathetic murmurs and apologies. Selina managed a wan smile, thanking them in a small voice, then struggled to finish eating her stew without giving way to the tears building up inside again.

At the end of the meal, collecting the dirty plates with Tilly's help, Violet Postbridge paused beside her seat. 'Didn't you say you have a sister, love? You told us you'd written to her a few months back to tell her about the wedding.'

'That's right. Bella. She was widowed in '44. Her husband Sebastian was wounded in Normandy, soon after D-Day. They hoped he might recover but he died of an infection a few months later.' She saw Joe's look of surprise, for she had never discussed her family with them before. 'Her letter telling me about it went astray, so I missed the funeral.' She paused, feeling unaccountably guilty. 'She has three children.'

'How awful,' Mrs Newton muttered, shaking her head. 'Poor lambs.'

'*Three kids*? Your sister must have married young,' Violet said, blinking.

'Bella's quite a bit older than me,' Selina explained. 'Thirty-nine next birthday.'

'You should write and tell her about Johnny,' Violet advised her.

Selina felt even more miserable. She couldn't even manage a smile as she said, aware of everybody listening with interest to this exchange, 'The thing is, we don't really see eye to eye. Not since she got married herself. I doubt she'd even care.'

'Of course she'll care!' Violet peered at her over the stack of dirty plates. 'You should never lose touch with a sister. I lost mine in the Blitz and there's not a day goes by that I don't think of her.'

'Oh yes, my dear Betsy, my first-born,' Mrs Newton agreed, her eyes misting. 'She gave us Lily and Alice before she departed this world. Such lovely girls. But I don't 'alf miss Betsy.'

'Write to your sister,' Violet advised Selina sternly. 'Even if she don't reply, you'll know you've done the right thing, eh? When things go wrong, there's nothing like family to support you.' Hurrying to the sink, she threw back over her shoulder, 'Though we're here for you too, love. If you'd like a finger or two of my mum's home-made gin, there's still some left in the bottle. That'll take you out of yourself in no time, I swear.'

'Aye, if that's what you call being flat on your face on

the kitchen floor,' Joe mumbled, but lapsed into silence on catching his mother-in-law's eye.

Selina choked, half laughing, half crying. It was strange, but she did feel less wretched now that she'd admitted the whole sorry fiasco to the household. These people might not be family, but they were friends. Still, the idea of writing to her widowed sister was not one that appealed. She and Bella had not got along in a long time. Missing Sebastian's funeral had not been her fault – her sister's letter had genuinely gone astray at the time – but she knew from Bella's brief note afterwards that her sister had assumed the worst, that she simply hadn't been bothered to turn up.

All the same, Violet was probably right. Perhaps it was time to try again with her sister.

After sharing some sloe gin with the Postbridges after supper, Selina took paper and a pencil out to the barn, where she could work quietly and without interruption. There, she sat in the fading light to work on a draft of her letter to Bella. She sucked on the end of her pencil, trying several times to explain what had happened between her and Johnny. In the end she gave up, and decided to pen her sister a simple note, explaining that their engagement was off and there would be no wedding. Further details didn't seem necessary.

Besides, she couldn't bear the idea of her sister triumphing over her failure. Growing up motherless and under the care of a father with fragile health and little interest in his daughters, Bella had hooked her beau early on and married him without delay, not long after their father died. Her husband, Sebastian March, had been a shy Oxford academic, and Bella had wasted no time in persuading him to make a home in Cornwall once they were married, where they could start a family in peaceful rural surroundings.

Although she and Selina had grown up in Oxford, a student city of narrow lanes and ancient colleges, Bella had been eager to leave those familiar surroundings, especially once she'd learned that Sebastian's family owned a large Cornish manor house on the fringes of Bodmin Moor. No doubt she'd yearned to play lady of the manor. Once her new father-in-law had passed away, leaving her husband everything he possessed, she must have got her wish.

When Selina had been posted to Cornwall as a Land Girl, she had written to let her sister know. But Bella had not replied. Perhaps she'd been too busy, raising her young family and looking after her husband. The only contact between them until Selina's engagement had been a brief note from Bella to let her know that her husband, by then an officer in the British army, had been wounded in action in France. Then had come that awful misunderstanding over Sebastian's funeral, and when Selina had belatedly heard from her sister again, she'd written back with condolences at once and an apology for missing it, but had heard nothing since. Perhaps Bella had been so offended by her absence at the funeral, she'd decided never to speak to her again.

But Violet was correct – wouldn't be right not to inform her only flesh and blood about something so important, even if Bella never responded.

Given how little contact there'd been between them, Selina was amazed to receive a response from her sister only a few days after she'd written to her.

'It's postmarked Bodmin,' Mrs Newton remarked, passing her an envelope over lunch later that week. 'That will be from your sister, I daresay. You see? There's nothing like family when there's a crisis.'

At the stove, Violet turned to study her, and even young Tilly leaned forward to peer at the envelope with undisguised interest.

'Excuse me.' Selina left her lunch half eaten and hurried away into the sunlit farmyard for privacy, keen to read what her sister had written without so many curious eyes on her.

Dear Selina

I'm so glad to hear from you at last, though I'm dreadfully sorry about your news. That young man should be ashamed after what he's put you through. I know this will be little consolation now, but it may turn out to be a blessing in disguise, since he was clearly not a good choice of life partner. Let us not think of him again.

As you know, I was unhappy when you didn't come to Sebastian's funeral. But I should not have written to you as I did. I know the post has not been reliable since the war and I do accept that you were unaware of his passing. I hope you can forgive me for that, and for not keeping in touch since that time. It seems incredible to me now that we never invited you to visit us here at Thornton Hall, and I apologise for my coldness, for which I have no excuse.

Now for some difficult news of my own. A few months ago, I went to Dr Ford over a lingering cough and various aches and pains. I fully expected him to give me a pick-me-up tonic and send me on my way. Instead, he insisted on hospital tests, and these showed tumours in both my lungs. You'll remember, perhaps, that I contracted tuberculosis as a child, and was very unwell for almost a year. The doctor thinks this may have weakened my lungs, and made it easier for the tumours to take root. Either way, I'm afraid he's given me a rather grim diagnosis. There's nothing to be done and I only have months to live.

I know this will come as a terrible shock. I've been struggling with it myself, and haven't yet had the heart to tell the children. Peter is thirteen, and will inherit the estate when he comes of age. I've been holding the estate in trust for him since Sebastian's death. Poor boy, he's barely got over his father's passing. Now I'm going to leave him and my two girls too. Jemima is eleven and a clever, capable girl. But Faith is only four and still needs a mother. I dread to think how my littlest one will cope when I die. Just thinking of it leaves me cold with fear. But I have to face the truth. I'm not going to be here to watch them grow up, so I need to make provision for them now.

My dearest Selina, I know we've been estranged for many years, and that's mainly my fault, but please don't blame the sins of the mother on my children. I beg of you to please come and live with us during this dark time, and to stay on after I've gone. The children have a nanny, and the estate should continue to pay her wages, and the same is true for the housekeeper, so you would not be run off your feet. But it would soothe me to know my own sister will be here to care for my three children when the worst happens.

The estate goes entirely to Peter at eighteen, and the girls both have allowances when they reach their majority. You would receive a small allowance for living at the hall, plus housekeeping money, so you would not be out of pocket either. It would all be administered by our family solicitor, Mr MacGregor, who is an excellent man. You can trust him with anything. I know you are still working as a Land Girl, but once it is clear that you have children to look after, you should be released from your official duties.

Please don't fail me, dear sister. With all my love,

Bella

She dropped the letter to the cobbles, her fingers numb, her mind reeling … Her sister Bella was dying? And wanted Selina to live with her and her three children on Bodmin Moor?

Bella had been like a mother to her once, their own mother long dead, and their father having become sick when Selina was barely six, while Bella herself had only just turned eighteen. No doubt the responsibility of looking after her sister had become too much in the end, for she'd married Sebastian after their father's death and vanished to far-off Cornwall, leaving Selina in Oxford with an elderly aunt. Looking back, Selina could understand Bella's desire to start her own family and build the kind of close-knit home life they'd missed out on when growing up. But at the time she'd been deeply hurt. Her aunt had often complained about Selina's behaviour, but if she had been a demanding child at times, it wasn't all that surprising, given how lost she'd felt without her big sister.

43

Now Bella was only months away from death herself, and calling on Selina to perform much the same duty for her as she'd done when their father had died.

It seemed too cruel and impossible.

Besides, Selina thought with a stab of guilt, she knew nothing about being a parent. She wasn't even sure she liked children. Most of the kids she'd known, like the three evacuees they'd housed at the farm during the war, had been noisy and annoying …

Yet now her sister needed Selina to take on responsibility for her *three* children. It was almost a deathbed wish.

How could she refuse?

CHAPTER FOUR

Hearing a brisk knock, Sheila bustled to the shop door and opened it to let Mr Whitney in, along with the bright May sunshine. 'You're early,' she told him, not without a hint of accusation. She still had her work pinny and headscarf on, and a broom in her hand, and had intended to make herself more presentable before his arrival. 'I was just sweeping up behind the counter. I cleaned off all the shelves and it's left the floor in a dreadful state. Well, you'd best come in.' She eyed the man's dirty boots, and he paused before wiping them on the boot scraper outside. 'I'll put a brew on. Then we can sit down for a nice chat in the back room.'

Mr Whitney was apparently a man who could ensure the shop was regularly supplied with seasonal fresh fruit and veg, plus eggs and dairy and so on, from all the farms thereabouts that had supplied Arnie's shop before his death. She had found his home address in one of Arnie's dusty ledgers behind the counter, and had sent him a note explaining what was required and asking him to meet at the shop for a discussion.

It had taken her four drafts to get the note right, despite being only five or six lines in length. But she'd not run a business in so long, she'd forgotten how to phrase things, and she wanted to start off on the right foot. In particular, she was keen to come across as professional, though not stuffy with it. That wasn't the kind of businesswoman she'd been back in Dagenham. She preferred to keep things friendly and informal. So long as suppliers brought in what they were supposed to and everyone got paid on time, or accepted tick where required, depending on what Arnie had always called 'supply and demand', then why insist on paperwork in triplicate?

Mr Whitney looked like a farmer himself, and indeed during their brief chat about Joe's farm and her family in general, he admitted to keeping a goat and some chickens. He removed a tweed cap to reveal a bald head, and shook hands with her. Then they sat down in the cosy back room for a cup of tea. The 'back room' was basically just an extension of the kitchen, with an old-fashioned wooden settle and a table and chairs, plus the armchair where Arnie had always sat while waiting for customers to jingle the bell over the door.

It had torn her heart out to remove Arnie's tatty old rocking chair, and replace the stained antimacassar draped over the back of the armchair, a few silver hairs still pressed into the fabric where his dear head had rested. But if this was to be a fresh start, that meant putting her own mark on things. So, a brand-new armchair cover had been put in its place, a sturdy, blue-patterned cotton that would wipe down easily if it got dirty.

Over tea and biscuits, she thrashed out a deal with Mr Whitney and the gentleman declared himself happy with the arrangement, shaking her hand again. They then lapsed into idle local gossip until Violet appeared at the door, looking narrow-eyed at Mr Whitney, who promptly remembered another appointment and took himself off.

'I'll bring the first deliveries in a fortnight, Mrs Newton,' he told Sheila on his way out, adding a wink that she'd never seen him give her husband. 'We'll soon have this shop back in business. Though I'll miss my chats with Arnie, that's for sure.'

'Oh, I can chat as much as he ever did,' Sheila shot in response, with a gurgle of laughter. '*Sheila can talk the hindleg off a donkey,* my husband used to say, bless his soul.'

After Mr Whitney had gone, she closed the shop door with a smile and turned to find her daughter glaring at her, arms folded across a heaving chest.

Sheila's heart sank. She knew that look.

'Your face looks like a slapped bottom,' she remarked. 'Small wonder you scared him away, poor man, with such a sour look. He probably thought you were about to snap his head off.'

Violet said nothing but her foot tapped menacingly.

'Go on, spit it out,' Sheila urged, her heart thumping. 'Let's hear what's bothering you. Because I can see you'll burst if you don't share it.'

'I hope to goodness you won't be having any "chats" with that man, Mum,' Violet exclaimed at last. 'You've barely known him five minutes and the two of you are flirting like nobody's business.'

'Flirting?' Sheila's bosom swelled. 'Excuse me? Who on earth do you think you're talking to?'

'My mum, that's who!'

47

'And I'll thank you to remember it. I'll speak to whomever I choose,' Sheila told her with dignity and clucked her tongue, struggling not to let loose with a stream of angry words that would probably mean Violet never spoke to her again. And that would be awkward, given that they lived under the same roof. 'Blimey, I've never heard the like. I'm trying to reopen the shop and here you are, warning me off chatting to people I need to do business with.' She took an unsteady breath. 'You'll be dropping in soon to tell me not to talk to the *customers*.'

'That's not the same, Mum, and you know it.'

Stubbornly, Sheila shook her head. 'No, I don't have a bloomin' clue what you're going on about.'

Already a tall woman, Violet drew herself up even taller, a hoity-toity look on her face. 'That man—'

'Mr Whitney.'

'Mr Whitney, then … He was a sight too familiar for my liking, that's all.'

'Now you listen here, Miss Know-It-All, you may have helped me out in the caff back in the old days, but you don't know the first thing about running a business. Not a business where you've got to deal with *people*. It's not about the price of fruit and veg. It's about the customers. If they get a smile and a little natter, they'll come back and buy more in future.'

Sheila saw her daughter's brows rise and added testily, 'Not that that's why I like a little chat now and then. I'm not all about money. That caff I ran in Dagenham, that was about *community*. It was a place where people could go to talk to each other, air their grievances and say what's what. I never judged any of 'em, any more than I'll judge someone coming into this shop with an opinion. I'll listen and yes, maybe I'll have an opinion of me own, but I won't say who can speak and who can't. Because this is still a free country, see? We won the war so we could stay free.' Her final words burst out in a rush, 'And if I want to have a bloomin' natter, you ain't going to stop me.'

'I don't want to stop you having a natter, Mum,' Violet insisted, looking flushed. 'I just don't want you getting married for a third time.'

Sheila stared at her daughter in astonishment. 'You *what*?'

'I saw you flirting with him. It's indecent at your age.'

'You'd best get out of my shop this minute, Violet Postbridge, otherwise I don't know what I'll do.' Sheila's voice shook with fury. 'But you won't like it, I can promise you that.'

'For goodness' sake—'

'I said, out!'

With an angry shake of her head, Violet marched out of the shop. Trembling, Sheila shut the door behind her and locked it, then stormed back into the kitchen to wash up the cups from Mr Whitney's visit. But she was in a blazing mood.

How dare Violet? Her own daughter, talking to her like she was a child. How bloomin' dare she?

It took a long while for her temper to subside, and she managed to crack a perfectly good china cup against the tap before it did.

Later, as she was locking the shop door, a woman came up behind her in the street, asking breathlessly, 'Hello, how d'you do? Mrs Newton, isn't it?'

Pocketing her keys, Sheila turned and looked the woman up and down. She was a pale, skinny little thing in her mid-thirties, with untidy ginger hair that looked like it hadn't been combed in days. She wore a faded frock without even a cardigan, and heavy clogs on her feet, so she hadn't come far. A baby lay cradled in one of her arms and a chubby-faced toddler in a blue smock was perched on her hip, rubbing grimy hands together as he stared bolt-eyed at Sheila. Two more small children ran about her in the street, squealing and giggling, while a fifth child leaned against the grassy bank opposite, a boy of about fourteen with a pudding basin haircut and a surly expression. All five children had been blessed with the same crop of ginger hair, so there was no mistaking whose children they were.

'Yes,' she agreed, adding cautiously, 'How d'you do?'

'Oh, very well, thank you. I can see you're busy and I'm sorry to disturb you, only I heard Arnie's shop was opening up again, and I was hoping to talk to you about getting some work.'

'I see. And who might you be?' Sheila demanded, a mite flustered by this unexpected request.

'I'm Mrs Treedy. I clean up at the vicarage twice a week.' The woman shook hands with Sheila awkwardly, hampered as she was by children. 'Pleased to meet you.'

'Likewise, I'm sure.' Sheila shook her head. 'Look, I'm sorry. You can see for yourself, the shop's empty – I'm still waiting on my first delivery – besides which, I won't know for several months if I can afford to hire any staff.' She saw dismay on the woman's face and added more kindly, 'For yourself, is it, love?'

'That's right.'

'But you already clean at the vicarage?'

'Well, that is, I used to. Only the vicar's wife … She doesn't need a cleaner anymore, she says.'

'Gave you the push, did she?'

'I didn't do anything wrong,' Mrs Treedy said hurriedly.

'I'm sure.'

'But that's why I'm looking for work. Only there's not much to be had hereabouts.'

'No, though I shouldn't think you'd have much time for a job.' Sheila frowned. 'Not with all them little uns to care for. Who looks after the babies while you're at work?'

'I used to take them with me when I was cleaning.'

Sheila studied the two youngest children dubiously. One barely looked weaned. 'I'm sorry, love. I can't have kiddies underfoot, running about and making a racket while we're working …'

'Oh no, I wouldn't bring them into the shop.' Mrs Treedy's face brightened. 'My boy Jack there,' she went on, indicating the surly youth with a jerk of her head, 'he'd look after them. I always leave them with Jack if I'm to be gone a few hours. He's a nice lad and the kiddies like him.' She hesitated, meeting Sheila's gaze frankly. 'To be honest, we need the money.'

'I'm not surprised, with so many mouths to feed … But I'm afraid I don't have nothing available for you.'

'Please, Mrs Newton.' Mrs Treedy swallowed, her eyes shiny with tears. 'I'm a hard worker and I'll do anything. Sweep up, wash windows, clean out the veg crates. I'm not proud.'

Sheila didn't know what to say. She recalled women coming to the caff in Dagenham before the war, asking for work, and how difficult it had been to turn them away. She'd always hated having to say no, especially knowing how much difference a few pence extra a week could make to some families. But given the shop wasn't even open yet, and she had no idea how much trade there'd be in a tiny village like Porthcurno, especially now the war was over and the listening post had lost its protective camp of soldiers, she wasn't in any position to be promising work to villagers, however hard up they might be.

'I'm sorry, Mrs Treedy, but there it is. Good day.' With an apologetic smile, she hurried up the hill, too embarrassed to look the woman in the face again.

Halfway up, she stopped to take a breather, and glanced back. The woman was trudging away along the village street, children still running about her. The boy Jack followed more slowly, kicking a stone along the road, his hands in his pockets. He and his mother both looked dejected.

Fourteen? Most lads his age took the bus to and from Penzance School every day, so she was surprised he'd managed to come home this early on a school day. The younger ones would be attending the local primary school, of course, which was nearer at hand. But maybe the boy had already left school in hopes of getting a job. Many children did leave school at fourteen these days. Times were hard now the war was over and there was less support for families.

Noticing the woman's slumped shoulders, Sheila felt wracked with guilt again. There'd been something close to desperation in Mrs Treedy's face.

Yet what could she do?

'You need to develop a thicker hide, my girl,' she told herself grimly, turning to tackle the steepest part of the hill that led to Joe's farm. 'Because now you're opening a business again, that woman may have been the first to ask for work, but she won't be the last.'

Halting wearily at the back door of the farmhouse to remove her dusty shoes, Sheila heard raised voices inside. Pushing the door, she found Joe and Violet glaring at each other across the kitchen, though the couple fell silent as soon as she walked in.

Joe bent to thrusting wood into the range and Violet washed her hands savagely, looking flushed and argumentative.

Sheila hung up her hat, eying the handsome meat and potato pie she'd made before leaving home that morning, which was now stood on the table covered with a fly mesh, and said lightly, 'You not put that pie on to heat yet, Vi? We'll be sitting down late for supper if it don't go in soon.'

'I'm getting around to it, Mum,' her daughter replied with a snap, but fetched a tray for the pie and put it in straightaway.

Sheila filled the kettle and put it on the range to boil. 'I'm having a brew,' she said conversationally, aware of bristling tension in the room.

'I need to go and check on Sarah Jane,' Violet said shortly. 'She'll have finished her nap and be up to no good by now.' With that, she left the kitchen, stamping upstairs with her usual dainty tread.

Sheila looked round at Joe, who'd shut the fuel door on the range and was studying its highly unreliable temperature gauge. 'What was all that about?'

'It's Selina,' he admitted, looking troubled. 'She's moving on. That means we'll be down a Land Girl coming into the summer season.'

'Selina's leaving?' Sheila was surprised. 'But why? Because of that business over her fiancé?'

'I don't know the ins and outs of it. All I know is, I said we need another Land Girl to replace her, and Violet isn't keen. She says we've too many mouths to feed as it is. The government gives us an allowance per girl, but with how tight things are, Vi's not sure we can keep making ends meet. She says I can't apply for another Land Girl, and that's final.'

'Vi's just fussing. She'll come around.'

'I'm not so sure.' He pulled a face. 'And with young Tilly not fully trained up yet, I don't know how I'll cope. It's a big farm for a man with one leg.' He banged his stick against the false one, which gave a hollow clang.

Sheila made the tea and popped a cosy over the teapot. She didn't know how he'd cope either.

'It's a pity Selina's leaving,' she mused. 'I'll miss her about the place. Oh, I know she puts on airs and graces, and she's got a sharp tongue when someone rubs her up the wrong way, but she's a nice girl and a hard worker.' She fetched down mugs and poured a dash of milk into each. 'Well, we must have a farewell supper for her. I'll bake a cake. But what kind? Jam sponge or something fancier? What do you think, Joe?'

When Joe didn't respond, she turned to find the kitchen empty.

'Talking to meself,' Sheila muttered with a grimace, and sat down to nurse her cuppa and dream of how Arnie's village shop – her shop, now – would look once it was stocked and open for business again. Truth was, she was a little scared of what the future might hold. But she'd got used to being afraid during the war, and she'd be blowed if she would let fear stop her.

CHAPTER FIVE

It was late May and the weather had turned unbelievably gorgeous, Joan thought, with bees buzzing everywhere in the sunshine, and the sea a bright silver glitter only a short way off from where she was working. She and the other Land Girls had spent the morning in the top field, wrestling with an old fence that Joe had asked them to repair. He'd brought the new wood up in his tractor, along with poles and fencing withies, and other necessary equipment for making fresh holes at intervals to bury the fence posts in. Then the farmer had left them to it, hurrying back down for an appointment with the vet, who'd been called out to check on one of the smallest piglets, who had developed breathing issues, poor thing.

The girls had donned thick gloves and separated into two teams, Tilly and Joan creating holes for the fence posts at strictly regulated intervals, while Caroline and Selina sunk the long poles into place afterwards and hammered them home. Later, the more intricate work of weaving the fencing from pole to pole would begin.

It was a laborious job but had to be done. Recently, Farmer Joe had caught lambs straying from the top field towards the cliffs and, having lost at least one lamb to the sea below, had decided to put a stop to his livestock wandering so freely.

The girls had taken a break from their sweaty work, lying on their backs on a carpet of coarse grasses, staring up into a blue sky where seagulls arched and soared.

Caroline had thoughtfully brought a bottle of lemonade and a small picnic to keep them going. Having eaten two slab-like triangles of brown bread and cheese, and drunk her fill of fizzy pop, Joan closed her eyes and concentrated on the sounds of nature around them.

She was almost nodding off to sleep when the quiet was broken by Tilly exclaiming excitedly, 'I say, look … There's a man!'

This extraordinary remark brought them all sitting up at once, staring in the direction of her pointing arm.

Sure enough, a man was heading their way. As he came closer, Joan saw that he was quite young, maybe in his early twenties. He was wearing baggy brown trousers with his shirt sleeves rolled up, a tweed jacket draped over one arm and a leather satchel slung across his chest.

The young man climbed gingerly over the low stony bank of grass that had been the previous barrier to the lambs escaping, and trod towards them. With a shy smile, he dragged off his cap, saying, 'Hullo … I'm awfully sorry to disturb you, ladies. But there's a lamb stuck halfway down the cliffs and I'm not sure what to do about it.'

Caroline scrambled to her feet, frowning. 'Thank you for coming to tell us. Did you notice if the lamb's mother was anywhere in sight?'

'I didn't see the mother sheep, I'm afraid. I only hope she didn't fall off the cliff. That would be too awful.'

Tilly smothered a giggle. Joan glanced at her, hoping she was laughing at the young man's posh manner of speaking and not the prospect of the ewe's sad demise.

Selina made a dismissive gesture, chewing on a stalk of grass. 'Just leave it. You can't go climbing down to rescue a lamb, that would be far too dangerous. Anyway, it will probably climb back up on its own.'

'Maybe, but we should probably go and see for ourselves.' Caroline shielded her eyes against the strong sunlight as she studied the young man. 'How far down did it fall?'

He scratched his head before returning the cap to cover his short fair hair. 'Not too far. Maybe ten feet?'

'Caro, we don't have time for a rescue mission. We've only just finished putting the posts in,' Selina pointed out irritably. She'd received bad news from her family, apparently, and this had left her in a terrible mood. Joan sympathised, of course, but did she have to make everyone else uncomfortable? 'Joe will be furious if he comes back and finds us all gallivanting about the cliffs.' Selina gave the young man a direct look. 'The vet's due to call about now, so you'll catch Mr Postbridge if you walk straight down to the farm and tell him yourself.' She pointed towards the distant farmhouse, though only the roof could be seen in a dip below trees, thanks to the undulating nature of the field. 'He'll come and rescue the lamb once the vet's gone, mark my words.'

The young man looked conflicted, glancing back over his shoulder the way he had come. 'I can't just leave it like that. What if the lamb was to fall while I'm gone fetching help?'

'Suit yourself.' Selina got to her feet, brushing grass off her mustard-coloured breeches. 'We've got work to do, sorry.'

The others trudged back to the fence and began sorting out the long, flexible withies that would be woven from post to post to create a strong barrier. Joan turned to follow, but caught the young man looking at her hopefully. It was hard to ignore the pleading in his gaze. He had such pleasant blue eyes. She got the feeling he was the sort of person who would never tell a lie. Or, if he did, would give himself away by stammering or blushing fiercely. As she suffered from an excess of truthfulness herself, she felt an instant sympathy with him.

'I'll come and look, if you like,' she offered impulsively. 'Maybe we could try and rescue the lamb together?'

He grinned, his face transformed, at once friendly and approachable. 'I say, that's awfully kind of you. Though I wouldn't want to put you in danger. Maybe I should climb down while you keep watch. That way, if I fall into the sea, at least you'll be around to bear witness to it. And maybe fetch help.'

Joan readily agreed to this plan, and hurried after him across the wild stretches of grass that led to the cliff's edge. Belatedly remembering the others, she turned to call over her shoulder, 'I'll be back soon, don't worry.'

Selina and Tilly were involved in sorting out lengths of withy into piles, so didn't look around at her shout, but Caroline raised a hand, looking after her.

'Sorry to tear you away from your work,' the young man said. 'I'm Arthur, by the way.' He held out a hand, and she shook it. 'Arthur Green.'

'Joan Fletcher.' Together, they climbed the stony, grass-

58

covered bank that used to keep the lambs from wandering but was now too eroded by the weather to do a good enough job. On the other side, she fell into step beside him. 'I'm a Land Girl, in case the uniform hadn't given it away. What do you do?'

'Not very much these days,' he said awkwardly. 'I went over to help liberate France, but got myself injured and had to be sent back.'

'You must be frightfully brave,' she said, unable to imagine having to fight for her country but convinced it must be horrible and terrifying in equal measure.

'Hardly,' she thought he muttered, but couldn't quite be sure, the noise of the sea growing steadily louder as they drew nearer the cliffs.

'My brother's still over there,' she told him. 'I shouldn't worry about him, I know – the war's been over long enough, and he's probably not in any danger – but I can't help it. Not when he's so far away.'

This admission had got his attention. 'What's his name?'

'Graham.' She added shyly, 'He's only two years younger than me, so hardly a kid. But our parents are no longer with us, so we only have each other now. I'd hate to lose him.'

His gaze searched her face keenly, then he gave a curt nod. 'Perfectly understandable. But I think it's safe enough now. Not like in those first few weeks after D-Day. It was pretty bloody back then, to be honest.'

They had reached the cliff's edge, and Arthur stopped to point down to where he'd seen the fallen lamb. Sure enough, peering over, Joan saw a tiny lamb trapped on a ledge some distance below the clifftop, just as he'd described.

'Oh, poor thing!' There was a narrow track down to the

ledge, barely more than an indentation in the coarse grasses, weaving between outcrops of rock and stopping a little way short of where the lamb stood bleating piteously. 'But my goodness, you'll have a job fetching it. You might be able to reach it safely. But how can you climb back up and carry a lamb at the same time?'

His look of consternation told her that he'd not thought of that. Then his brow lightened. 'I'll put the lamb in my satchel. It should just about fit, and as long as it doesn't wriggle too much, I should still be able to use both hands to climb.'

'It's worth a try.' Dubiously, Joan watched as he emptied out his satchel onto the grass. To her surprise and delight, the bag contained a sketchpad, a tin of pencils, a few tubes of paint, some paint brushes and a palette for mixing.

He saw her wondering stare and grinned. 'I fancy myself a bit of an artist,' he explained, checking the satchel was completely empty before strapping it across his chest again. 'I've been walking along the cliffs for the past week, trying to find a good spot where I can paint. That's why I was out here and saw the lamb. I hope Farmer Postbridge won't be too annoyed at me crossing his land, but the views from here are quite glorious.'

Enthusiastically, she agreed, adding, 'I'm sure Joe won't mind. Especially as you'll have helped him save this lamb. He's lost a few over the cliff in the past. That's why we're putting the new fence up. To stop them wandering.'

Removing his cap, Arthur handed it to her. 'In case it blows off. I'll be damned if I'll lose my favourite cap to the sea.'

At the foot of the rocks, the sunlit tide was dragging across shingle, salt thick on the air. Clutching his cap to her chest, Joan watched in trepidation as the young man began to clamber down the barely visible track towards the ledge. Several times, his foot skidded on loose stones, and her heart leapt as she thought he might tumble to his death. But he always seemed to recover himself just in time, continuing more cautiously, groping for rocks or grass tufts as he made his slow way down.

Finally, he reached the ledge and, although she'd feared it would be startled and dart away, the lamb quite sensibly allowed him to pick it up and place it, with a few kicks and struggles, in his leather satchel. He then managed to fasten one strap of the satchel, the young animal's forelegs hanging out as it bleated for its mother. Though goodness knows where the ewe had gone, Joan thought unhappily. It was impossible to see past the rocky outcrops to the shore below.

With the lamb safely anchored in his satchel, Arthur began to ascend the cliff with fierce concentration.

'Do be careful,' Joan called down, no doubt unnecessarily, but she couldn't help herself. She felt so concerned for his safety. Before he'd gone down, it had struck her as a not too difficult climb. But now, seeing how precarious each handhold was, she felt a terrible foreboding that he would fall. Somehow though, he struggled to the top, the wind winnowing his fair hair and a steadily increasing grin on his face. The lamb was still in its protective satchel, for all the world like a baby kangaroo in its mother's pouch.

With profound relief, Joan helped him up and back to his feet. 'Well done.' She handed over his cap. 'What now, do you think? Should we take the lamb back to the field and let it go?'

'I'm afraid one of its back legs looks to be injured, probably from when it went down the cliff in the first place.' He stroked the lamb's head, who seemed to have lapsed into a terrified stupor now its long ordeal was over. 'Didn't your friend say the vet was due at the farm?'

'Yes, what a good idea. I'll walk down with you.'

'That's very kind.' He hesitated. 'If you're sure you're not needed up here?'

She probably was needed, but Joan felt sure the others could cope without her for half an hour. 'There's a shortcut, but you can easily miss it if you don't know the way. I wouldn't want the vet to leave before he's had a chance to look at the lamb.' She smiled. 'Besides, you need someone to carry your sketchpad and paints. Since your satchel is out of commission.'

He saw the sense in this, and as soon as she'd gathered together his painting gear, most of the smaller items fitting into the capacious pockets of her Land Army jacket, and tucked the sketchpad under her arm, they set off together. It was too hot to wear her jacket, so she carried it over her shoulder, while he draped his own jacket over the head of the lamb, as they feared it might suddenly recover from its torpor and try to escape the satchel.

Together they hurried along the breezy clifftop to the track that led around the large top field, rather than walking straight across it. This was much quicker than navigating the field, and they were soon approaching the farm.

'Whereabouts do you live?' she asked, fearful that he might disappear after dropping off the lamb and she would never see him again. It was a strange realisation that she didn't want that to happen. She so rarely felt like that towards someone she'd only just met, especially a young man. She only hoped he wouldn't take her question the wrong way.

He answered her easily enough though. 'Out towards

Trethewey, about three miles from Porthcurno on the way to Sennen. But lately I've been spending more time than usual in the village, sorting out the late Sir Malcolm Castleton's private collection of books. His son Geoffrey was at Eton with me and intends to sell his father's library to help the estate. The house fell into disrepair during the war, you see, and Geoff says the family can't afford to fix it up. So they're selling whatever they can to fund the repairs.'

'That's so sad.'

He shrugged. 'Geoffrey was never a big reader. I don't imagine he cares a stuff for old books.'

'But you do?' Joan glanced at him curiously. 'And you went to Eton?'

'For my sins.' He laughed, then sobered at once. 'Not that I've done much by way of studying since then. The war put paid to my university career and the best I've been able to do since is potter about, dusting off books and cataloguing them for sale.'

'It's probably harder work than you're making it sound,' she said, noting the strain in his voice.

'It's lonely work, for sure.' He paused, stopping at the stile to let her climb over first. 'I say, you wouldn't fancy giving me a hand, would you? Do you like books?'

'I love books,' she admitted. 'I'd like to help, but I don't think I can be spared from my work. It's spring now and Joe needs all the help he can get around the farm.'

He looked downcast but nodded. 'You're right. Forget I asked.'

Forget I asked.

Goodness, how could she? Because she dearly wished she could say yes to his invitation. How wonderful that would be, to spend hours sorting through books in a well-stocked private library …

She led him across the cobbled yard to the pigsty where she could see Joe deep in conversation with the vet, both men leaning over the gate as they studied the piglets and their mother.

'Though maybe I could come over for an hour or two on my afternoon off,' she added quickly before she could change her mind, 'if it's not too far to walk.'

'Honestly? Would you?' Arthur looked delighted. 'It's The Grange, the big house down the lane past the vicarage. A bit of a hike from here, I suppose. Do you have a bicycle?'

'No, but I could borrow Mrs Newton's.' The farmer's mother-in-law had bought herself a second-hand bicycle a year before, when her husband Arnie was ill, so she could cycle down to the shop a few times a week to make sure customers could collect what they had ordered. But she had found the saddle too uncomfortable and had soon gone back to walking. The bicycle itself was now rusting away in a corner of the barn and would need oiling and its tyres pumping up, but Joan couldn't believe that Sheila Newton would say no to her borrowing it.

The lamb struggled and Arthur stopped halfway across the farmyard, gently removing his jacket and stroking its small white head. 'When's your afternoon off?'

'Thursday.' She hesitated. 'Though I've already promised to go into Penzance with the other girls this week. We go to the pictures together when something good's showing.'

'What's on this week?'

'*The Bandit of Sherwood Forest*.'

He grinned. 'Enjoy a good swashbuckler, do you?'

'Well, they're usually more fun to watch than all these war pictures.'

'And a little less close to the bone,' he agreed, his face sombre again.

'But maybe the following week?' she suggested shyly.

'That would be perfect. I'll make sure I'm at The Grange after lunch next Thursday then, to let you into the house.' He saw her frown and added quickly, 'There's rarely anyone else about, you see. Geoff's based in Germany with the Foreign Office and the housekeeper keeps herself busy during my visits. I hope you won't mind being alone with me?'

The embarrassed enquiry in his eyes made her smile. What a gentleman he was. 'I'll manage,' she said firmly, and turned to introduce him to Joe, who was looking surprised to see a young man with a lamb in his satchel in the farmyard. 'I'd better get back to the fencing job now,' she added, shaking Arthur's hand, 'or the others will never forgive me for leaving them to do all the work. Goodbye.'

As she trudged back up to the top field, Joan found herself smiling. Imagine thinking she'd be worried to be alone with him in a library. He must be very well brought up, or he wouldn't have mentioned it. Eton-educated too. She sensed there was nothing snobbish about him though.

Perhaps a few hours spent pouring over musty old volumes with Arthur Green would be just the thing to raise her spirits.

CHAPTER SIX

Just as Selina had finished stripping the linen off her bed for washing, the door to the attic room opened and Caroline stood there, staring at her from the doorway. Her friend looked awful, blotchy-cheeked and red-eyed, which wasn't surprising, as Caro hadn't stopped crying for hours.

'I'm sorry to disturb you,' Caro said in a disjointed voice, hesitating on the threshold. 'Are you all packed now?'

'Yes, I just need to fasten my bag.'

Selina eyed her friend with concern. The previous evening, Violet and Mrs Newton had thrown a farewell party with cake and home-made gin, but Caroline had been unable to join in the general laughter and anecdotes of Selina's time at the farm, sitting glumly through the festivities. Now she seemed no more reconciled to Selina's leaving than last night.

'Do you really have to go?' Caroline asked, a hanky pressed to her mouth.

'You know I must. My sister needs me. I can't say no.'

'But you and Bella have hardly spoken in years. You told me once you had nothing in common with your sister.'

'That's true.' Selina dropped the rolled-up dirty linen into the wash basket, trying to stay patient with her friend. She had not gone into detail over her sister's illness when announcing her departure, only indicating how serious it was. Joe had immediately agreed to let her go, hearing that her sister was unwell, and his wife had agreed, insisting that family was more important than anything else. But Caroline was clearly still not convinced. 'But, as I already told you, Bella is sick. To be honest with you, the doctor says she's dying.' The words still struck her as somehow unreal. Her sister dying? It was too horrible to contemplate. 'So it's my duty to be with her, and to help her children if I possibly can.'

'*Dying*?' Caroline gasped, turning ashen. 'I had no idea. That's awful. I'm so sorry. Poor, poor Bella. I wish you'd told me before. Why didn't you?'

'Because it's a family matter. Private.'

'Yes, of course. Though I could have supported you … You must have been so unhappy.' With an effort, Caroline wiped her eyes, watching as Selina turned to fasten the straps on her travelling bag. 'Will you ever come back to Porthcurno, do you think?'

'I doubt it.'

With a sharp cry, Caroline battled yet more sobs. 'Oh, I'm sorry … I meant to be brave. But I don't think I can bear it. We've been friends so long.'

Wiping away a tear of her own, Selina told her kindly, 'I know Joan is a bit of a dry stick. But Tilly's a nice girl, even if she hasn't been with us long. And she'll be taking my bed once I'm gone, so you'll have her for company, at least.'

'It's not the same.'

'Honestly, Caro, I had no idea you'd be this upset.' Selina

frowned, at a loss how to comfort her. 'You didn't cry like this when Penny left the farm. Or Violet's niece, Alice, when she took that job in London.'

'That's because I … didn't like Penny and Alice … the way I like you.' The words tumbled out in a wild, disjointed fashion, muffled by a hanky. When Selina turned to look at Caro in surprise, there was despair on her friend's tear-stained face. 'Alice and Penny weren't *special*.'

'Goodness me … I mean, thank you.' Touched by this unexpected show of devotion, Selina put down her bag. It was true that neither of them had rubbed along that well with Penny, but Caroline had been friends with Alice, despite her not being a Land Girl like them. 'Let's have a proper hug, shall we? Then I really must dash or I'll miss the bus. My train leaves Penzance at three o'clock sharp, and I've arranged to be picked up at Bodmin station when I arrive.'

'If there's ever anything I can do to help … You will write, won't you? Please say you'll keep in touch.'

'Of course I will.'

Caroline flung her arms about Selina and hugged her tight, her face buried in her shoulder. 'Dearest Selly … Oh, I can't bear it!' With a cry, she broke off and ran from the room.

Selina stared after her friend in frowning concern but knew she couldn't delay leaving any longer. Fearful of missing her bus, she carried her bags downstairs, encountering Violet in the kitchen with a drowsy, pink-cheeked Sarah Jane nestled on her hip.

'You off then, love?' Violet gave her a fumbling hug. 'I'm sorry to be losing you, Selina. And I know Joe is too, for all he never says a word. You've been a good worker.' The little girl shifted, showing pearly white teeth as she yawned. 'I'm afraid I can't see you off as I need to take Sarah Jane up for a nap.' The farmer's wife tiptoed up the stairs, whispering over her shoulder, 'Tatty-bye then, love. Write to let us know you got to your sister's place safely. Or I daresay Caro will be fretting for Britain.'

The farmyard was reassuringly empty after all the tearful farewells, though Selina could hear the other girls' voices and the rumble of Joe's laughter, no doubt as Tilly cracked a joke.

Glancing back, she saw Caroline's face at an upper window, watching her leave. Guilt flooded her and she raised her hand in a quick wave before turning away. Despite pangs at leaving Postbridge Farm, her home for so many years during the war, she was soon tripping lightly down the hill as the track descended between hawthorn-thick, insect-jewelled hedgerows in the spring sunshine. Not so long ago she'd hurried down this steep hill to post her last letter to Johnny, sure she would soon be his wife … Now all that was over, and she was leaving Porthcurno forever.

It was a fresh start, she reminded herself, pushing away that bitter-sweet nostalgia. Not an end but a beginning.

Besides, Violet's homely advice at dinner the other night had been right.

In times of crisis, nothing was more important than family. And Bella and her children were her only family now.

It was early evening when the train finally pulled into Bodmin station. The platform was busy and Selina stood for several minutes, bags in hand, looking up and down in search of someone who might be waiting for her. Her sister had written to say she would send someone to the station to collect her, but perhaps it hadn't been possible.

She was just beginning to wonder whether buses to the moors ran that late, and how she would manage if nobody appeared, when a middle-aged woman in low heels came hurrying towards her along the platform. Her face was heavily powdered, her lipstick scarlet, a patterned headscarf smoothed over a neat bob of silvery hair. Her expression was harassed as she looked Selina up and down before reaching for her case. 'You'll be Miss Tiptree, I imagine. You're the spitting image of your sister. No, Miss, let me carry that one. You've had a long journey. Anyway, I've a car outside.' She bustled away with Selina's bag, turning at the station exit to add abruptly, as an afterthought, 'I'm Mrs Hawley, housekeeper at Thornton Hall. The mistress sent me to fetch you.'

The car turned out to be old and battered, the seats and windscreen dusty, dried mud in the footwell. Mrs Hawley drove very quickly through the narrow Cornish lanes, occasionally leaning on the horn when whizzing around blind bends. The sky was a murky grey as the evening headed into a spring twilight, yet the housekeeper seemed oblivious to any danger. Presumably she thought the headlights of any oncoming vehicles would be visible long before they collided with them. But what about pedestrians? Or bicyclists? Or errant sheep?

Thankfully, the lanes were mostly empty, apart from a tractor parked on the verge beside a field, and a woman foraging in the hedgerows who turned to stare as they approached, belatedly waving a hand when she recognised the driver.

The housekeeper kept up a steady stream of remarks about the weather they'd been having on the moor and the guest room she'd prepared for Selina, sometimes pointing out landmarks that passed before Selina had time to properly register them. She had a broad Cornish accent, even more pronounced than Joe's, and spoke out of the corner of her mouth. Thankfully, it wasn't too hard to follow what she was saying, except when she mentioned local place names, some of which were clearly in the Cornish language.

As they left the main road from the station, Selina wound up the car window and drew her cardigan closer. 'How far is the house?'

'Oh, not far now. About three miles past Cardinham Woods.' The housekeeper said this with great authority, perhaps assuming that Selina knew where these woods were, and could therefore picture the distance quite easily.

'Woods? I thought the house was on Bodmin Moor.'

'So it is,' Mrs Hawley agreed comfortably, changing to a low gear as the lane steepened. 'The woods are at the edge of the moor. But you'll see.' She sounded puzzled. 'Have you never been to visit your sister before?'

'I always meant to,' Selina told her defensively. 'But I was busy with war work. I was a Land Girl down at Porthcurno much of the war, and stayed on after because of labour shortages.'

'It's shocking, the shortage of workers. We can barely even get groundsmen at the hall.' Mrs Hawley paused. 'I'm sorry if it sounded like I was prying, Miss. I only started work at the hall last year, so I didn't know you hadn't been here before.'

The lane climbed laboriously towards a summit. At the brow, the land seemed to open up like a picture book, and Selina sucked in a breath at the stunning vista before them.

Greenish-brown moorland rose and fell into the distance, bare outcrops of rock here and there, with the occasional glint of water. A few stunted trees clustered together in dips and hollows, and along drystone walls that presumably served as boundaries in a place where grasslands rolled relentlessly to the horizon. It was a bleak and barren landscape, exactly as it had seemed that one time Joe had driven them all to the north coast, so they could witness a former Land Girl, Penny, marrying her fisherman in Bude.

And yet, glowing gold in the last of the sunlight, the moors were almost magical too. A place where anything might happen …

Mrs Hawley had seen her staring. She slowed for a broad gateway and a track signposted to Thornton Hall. 'Ah, it's quite a sight, the moor. I came up from Hayle, down near Penzance. I was in service there before the war, and then worked as a nurse for a spell. Last year, a cousin of mine in Bodmin wrote to tell me there was a housekeeping position available at Thornton Hall for someone with nursing experience.' She drove more cautiously along the bumpy track, which was quite overgrown in places. 'When I first saw the moors, I couldn't believe my eyes. Such a beautiful sight, especially in summer. I could see at once why it brings the walkers and campers down from that London.' She glanced at Selina assessingly. 'Do you like to walk, Miss?'

'Call me Selina, please. And yes, I do like walking. Though I'm not terribly athletic.'

'If you go out alone, never cross the moors after dark. Or if a heavy mist is coming down. Before leaving, be sure to tell one of the staff which direction you're planning to take. And always carry an umbrella. The weather changes very quickly on the moors. You can set out on a sunny afternoon and be drenched within fifteen minutes.'

'Goodness.' Selina was about to add something about not being so keen a walker that she'd bother going out on a rainy afternoon, but fell silent, staring as they rounded a corner on the bumpy track and she saw Thornton Hall for the first time.

It was a tall, old-fashioned building with ivy-covered walls, dark slanting roofs, and many windows reflecting a grey sky. Thin scarves of smoke trailed from several high chimneys, dissipating in the air. It was a much more substantial building than Selina had expected to find out here in the middle of nowhere. The grounds were large too, wild grasslands ending in a gloomy knot of trees that bordered the house and gardens. Bedraggled sheep grazed in the distance, and a group of moorland ponies could be seen trotting up a slope below them, their rough flanks half hidden behind heaps of bracken.

She blinked, trying not to gape at the sheer size of the place. 'How many rooms does the hall have?'

'Seven bedrooms, three large reception rooms, plus a study or two, a library, and a billiards room. Then there are the kitchens, though I daresay you won't be bothering yourself with them. I do most of the cooking, though I have an assistant who helps with meals and cleaning. She doesn't live in though, so she'll have gone for the day by now.'

This tallied with what her sister had written in her letter, that Selina would not be expected to take on many domestic duties. All the same, it was a vast place. A library? And a billiards room too? Although their family had been quite well-to-do, she and Bella had grown up in an ordinary-sized suburban home on the outskirts of Oxford. Certainly nothing on this scale.

No wonder her sister had been so keen to marry Sebastian,

despite his dull conversation and worthy academic air. As she recalled, Sebastian's mother had died when he was young, while his father had been seriously unwell at the time of Bella and Sebastian's wedding and succumbed not long afterwards, leaving everything to his son. Yes, her sister had done very well for herself indeed.

Though now, given her fragile health, she doubted that Bella saw her luck in the same light. Even with staff to help maintain such a large house, it must feel more like a burden.

'And there's a nanny too, is that right?'

'Her?' Mrs Hawley snorted under her breath. 'Yes, there's a nanny. Too young, if you ask me. She lets those children run wild while she sits with her feet up, smoking and reading magazines. It's not right, especially now Mrs March spends most of her days in bed and can't be expected to keep a track of such goings-on.' Her lips were pursed disapprovingly. 'It's not my place to say this … but I'm glad you've come to Thornton Hall, Miss Tiptree.'

Selina smiled, deciding not to comment further until she had met this nanny.

The front entrance was very posh, curved white stone steps leading up to a set of elegant double doors, but Mrs Hawley parked round the back in what must once have been the stable yard. Getting out of the car, Selina heard a horse whinny softly, saw a dark gleaming head poke out of a half-door, and realised the stable block was still in use.

As they walked through an archway into the kitchen garden, three children came tumbling out of a low doorway towards her but stopped dead on seeing her.

Her sister's children, presumably. Heading the trio was a serious-looking fair-haired girl in a brown-patterned dress and sensible shoes whom Selina guessed to be eleven-year-old Jemima. An adorable child with short blonde hair and chubby cheeks in a pink smock, who was clearly four-year-old Faith, was holding her hand. Behind these two sauntered a lanky smiling youth with his hands in his pockets and dark blond hair brushing his collar. Peter, the heir to Thornton Hall.

'Aunty Selly, Aunty Selly!' the little girl cried, breaking free from her sister's grasp and clapping her hands.

'Hello, Faith,' Selina said, bending to smile at the girl. She straightened, eyeing the other two more warily. 'And you must be Jemima and Peter. Yes, I'm your Aunty Selina. I take it my sister warned you that I'd be coming to stay?'

'Mother said you were coming to *live* with us,' Jemima corrected her, solemnly shaking her hand. 'I'm very pleased to meet you, Aunty Selina. Or do you prefer Selly? Mother said she always called you that when you were children.'

'Selina or Selly, I answer to both,' she assured her, smiling.

'And is it right that you'll be living with us from now on? Not just visiting?'

Something in the girl's anxious voice struck a chord in Selina, taking her back to childhood days when she'd been stricken by the fear that she was all alone in the world.

'Yes, I'll be living here.' Selina turned to the boy and shook his hand too. 'Nice to meet you both.'

'Back inside, you lot,' Mrs Hawley insisted, shooing the children back into the house. As they disappeared, she turned to Selina, saying conspiratorially, 'Young Peter was enrolled at Marlborough School, but came home when his mother fell ill. He and Jemima have a tutor who calls twice a week to take them through their lessons. The nanny looks after the two girls otherwise, but Peter has the run of the house, since he's just turned fourteen and hardly needs minding.' Chatting away, the housekeeper led Selina along a dim, echoing corridor and up a short flight of steps into a wood-panelled hall. The children were nowhere to be seen by then, though Selina caught a burst of laughter in the distance. 'I'll show you up to your room now, Miss Tiptree, and then take you along to see Mrs March. Your sister's been poorly today, otherwise she would have come to meet you at the station herself.'

Upstairs, Selina was shown into a large pink and white bedroom with an adjoining washroom and walk-in closet. The bed was huge, and although the furnishings were old-fashioned and even tatty in places, it was still like something out of a fairy tale.

After years of hard labour in the fields, sharing an attic room, Selina could not quite believe that this was to be her home from now on.

'I hope this room will suit you.' Mrs Hawley placed her bag on the ottoman at the foot of the bed. 'I'll let you wash, and come back in ten minutes. Then I'll need to go down and put supper on. I'm sorry not to be able to show you around the house properly. Maybe tomorrow?'

'Don't worry about me,' Selina told her politely. 'This is wonderful, thank you.'

Once she was alone, Selina looked around in silence, stunned by the unexpected grandeur. Peering out of the window, she saw that her room was at the back of the house, overlooking the moors. She stood a moment in dazed appreciation of the view, and then recalled that she was supposed to be making herself presentable.

Grabbing up a clean towel from the pile on the ottoman,

she dashed into the adjoining washroom, where a jug and scented bar of soap awaited her beside a deep sink encased in walnut surround, a mirror mounted above it. To her delight, the water ran hot almost immediately – such a luxury after the unreliable farmhouse plumbing – and Selina soon scrubbed away a few faint smuts from her cheek, one of the hazards of train travel. Then she washed her hands, taking care to clean under the fingernails, and combed her hair into some semblance of tidiness.

At the farm, she had gone about looking almost wild; there'd rarely been any point scrubbing yourself clean when you'd be waking up at dawn the next day to go out into the fields and get filthy all over again …

She was just wondering if she had time to change out of her travelling clothes when Mrs Hawley knocked for her, and she was whisked away to the grander rooms at the front of the house.

Her sister was sitting up against a bank of pillows in a four-poster bed draped with cream lace. She had been reading a book but laid this aside on seeing Selina. 'Darling,' she said huskily, and held out her hands, 'you made it. Was the journey dreadful? Come and sit on the bed. Thank you, Mrs Hawley,' she added as the housekeeper switched on a lamp, for the window shutters were closed to keep out the daylight. 'I won't make it down for dinner tonight. Could you bring something up on a tray instead?'

'Yes, ma'am.' The housekeeper left, closing the door behind her.

Perched on her sister's bed, Selina felt shy and tongue-tied. It had been many years since she and Bella had been face-to-face like this. Her chief memories of Bella were of a healthy, strong young woman with glorious golden tresses down to her waist and firm opinions about the world. Certainly, she would never have dared argue with her sister as a child.

But she barely recognised the woman in the bed as her sister. She looked exhausted, her face drawn and haggard, deep shadows under her eyes. Her hair lay draped over one shoulder, tamed into a braid tied with a ribbon as pale as her skin.

'Well, Selina … Here we are again at last,' Bella said, taking her hands. 'And I'm dying. How ironic is that?'

CHAPTER SEVEN

'In memory of Mr Arnold Newton, I declare this village shop open.' The Reverend Clewson opened Violet's dressmaking scissors wide and snipped the ribbon in two. As it fluttered to the ground, there was a round of applause from the crowd of watching villagers.

The shop was now officially open for business, and the name above the door was hers. *Mrs. S. Newton, Proprietor.*

The signwriter had asked, with obvious disapproval, if she wouldn't rather be known as Mrs Arnold Newton, as was the accepted fashion with married ladies. But Sheila had decided against that in the end. Arnie was gone and she needed to make a go of things on her own two feet now.

But her stubborn refusal to adopt his Christian name didn't change her feelings for her dearly departed husband.

With tears in her eyes, Sheila looked at Violet and they hugged each other. She muttered against her daughter's shoulder, 'This is all for Arnie. I know you disapprove, love, but I'm sure it's what he would have wanted, and I can't let my Arnie down.'

'It's all right, Mum. I understand why you're doing this,' Violet whispered back. There were tears in her eyes too as she released her mum, though she managed a brisk smile. 'I just think it's crackers, that's all.'

'You're a charmer, you are.'

'Oh, come on, Mum. You're not like Arnie. You ain't got the gift of the gab. More like the gift of the jab.' Her daughter laughed at her own joke. 'You'll fall out with your customers within five minutes. And all this having to trot up and down the hill every day? Well, you'll get fit, that's the best I can say.'

Overhearing this, Joe shook his head. 'You should be proud of your mother, Violet,' he said stoutly, braving her sharp glare. 'And if you can't manage the hill every day, Sheila, and don't want to use that rusty old bicycle, maybe it's time you learned how to drive. I'll teach you if you like.'

'Eh?'

Joe cleared his throat, looking embarrassed. 'I've been meaning to get a new van – the old one's always breaking down. It's not much of a runner, granted, but it should get you up and down the hill for work most days.'

'You're giving her *the van*?' Violet's eyes bulged.

'Only once I've got a new one,' her husband told her mildly. 'I thought you'd be happy, love. You're always complaining about the poor suspension.'

Sheila felt as though her heart would burst with happiness. 'Do you really mean it, Joe? You'll let me have the old van once you're done with it?' When he nodded, she gasped. 'That's the best news I've heard all week. I'm so tired, my legs feel like they're about to fall off. Getting them shelves fully stocked has been a job of work.'

'Well, I think it looks smashing,' said a man with a deep

80

familiar voice behind them, and Sheila swivelled in surprise to find George Cotterill and his wife there.

Seeing their old friends, Violet gave a squeak of delight. 'George, on my life … Where've you been? I've barely seen you two since Christmas.' She shook his hand before giving his wife a warm hug. 'Hazel, love. How's the little one? Is she with that wonderful neighbour of yours? I wish I had a neighbour who'd look after Sarah Jane whenever I need to go out, especially now Mum's always down here at the shop.' Her gaze focused on Hazel's prominent tummy. 'Oh my, but I see you two have been busy.'

Sheila chortled, realising that Hazel Cotterill was pregnant again. The couple must've been keeping it quiet. 'Congratulations,' she said, also shaking George's hand and kissing Hazel on the cheek. 'And it's a sound idea … Like I've said to Joe and Vi, might as well have another kiddy while you still have the pram and cot to hand.'

'Sally's enough for us now,' Joe rumbled, looking uncomfortable.

'Sarah Jane,' Violet corrected him.

'If I want to call my own daughter Sally, I will,' her husband insisted, his jaw hardening.

Violet glared at him but caught Sheila's warning look and turned back to her friend without further argument. She knew better than to cause a ruckus in public. Especially at the shop's grand reopening …

They were all soon chatting easily again. Hazel had been a lifesaver for poor Violet when she and her two young nieces, Lily and Alice, had first come down to Cornwall to escape the Blitz. There'd been a dreadful incident at the farm where they'd been staying with Sheila's older sister, Margaret, and her brother-in-law, Stanley Chellew. Stan, who'd been Margaret's second husband and a bit of a bully by all accounts, had behaved very poorly towards young Lily, and Violet had quite rightly taken both girls away for their safety. Only that decision had left them homeless. Thankfully, Violet had just met Hazel at the time, who'd invited Violet and the girls to move in with her and her schoolboy son Charlie.

It had been a squeeze, by all accounts. But it had worked out nicely, with Hazel helping Violet and the girls get work at Eastern House in Porthcurno. George Cotterill had been running the top-secret communications base there, in the early years of the war. He'd been sweet on Hazel since childhood, though she'd still been married at the time and had discreetly kept her distance. But then she'd lost her husband in action soon after discovering she was pregnant again. To everyone's relief, George had proposed and gladly taken on the raising of Hazel's lovely baby daughter as his own.

'When's this one due, then?' Sheila asked now with a wink.

Hazel, a shapely brunette with a pillbox hat and a generously cut smock, smiled indulgently up at her husband. 'This will be a late July baby.'

George grinned. 'Unless he or she comes early.'

'Well, I can always ask Lily home for the summer. That's what she does best, ain't it? Delivering babies.' Violet was laughing but Sheila knew she was not entirely joking.

Sheila's granddaughter Lily, now a married woman with a child of her own, and a midwife too, had been a new trainee nurse in St Ives when Hazel, heavily pregnant, had gone on a visit there. There had been an air raid, and Lily and Hazel had been cut off from the others for the duration. Hazel had taken a bad fall and gone into labour unexpectedly, but young Lily had kept her head and delivered the baby. By the time the doctor arrived on the scene, Hazel's little girl, whom she'd named Lily, after her deliverer, had been happily asleep in her mother's arms.

Most of the villagers who had gathered for the reopening were now milling about inside, and Sheila realised with a start that she needed to be behind the counter.

'Oops, I'd best get my pinny on,' she muttered to Violet and almost ran into the tiny, crowded shop. 'Excuse me … Pardon me … If I could just squeeze past, Madam.'

Finally, she reached the counter and sidled behind it, dragging her work apron over her head and tying the belt in a double bow at her waist. The vicar's wife was already at the head of the queue, impatiently waiting to be served. 'What can I do for you, Mrs Clewson? What's that? An ounce of lemon sherbets? Yes, I'll fetch that for you at once.'

Her heart thumping, Sheila turned in sudden panic to survey the jars of sweets laid out in a neat row, just as they had been in Arnie's day. For a moment, her vision blurred and she couldn't find the lemon sherbets. Her trembling finger trailed across the elegant black and white labels … Aniseed Balls, Black Jacks, Flying Saucers, Dolly Mixture, Liquorice Allsorts …

She wished Arnie was there to help her.

Then, almost as though she could hear his voice in her ear, and see him pointing at the correct jar, she reached up and removed the correct jar from the shelf. Her hand still shook a little as she unscrewed the lid and tumbled out a few handfuls into the weigh scales, but her heart was no longer pounding quite so heavily. She checked the amount, then slid the weighing scoop into a brown paper bag and swung it around twice to tie the corners tight.

All exactly as she'd seen Arnie do a thousand times.

'There you go, Mrs Clewson,' she said more confidently. 'And some baccy for the vicar's pipe? Right you are.'

As she fetched the tobacco, glancing out through the window, she spotted her daughter still chatting to Hazel, while Joe and George stood in the doorway, also deep in conversation. The three remaining Land Girls had come down for the opening ceremony and were giggling as they flicked through women's magazines on the news shelf. The vicar himself was at the centre of the shop, nodding solemnly as he listened to Mrs Pearson complain about a stray dog digging up her spring bulbs. The village shop, so cold and desolate only a few weeks ago, was once again full of noise and laughter and a sense of people coming together.

Sheila grinned, turning back to the vicar's wife with the tobacco in hand. 'There you go, love,' she said, and saw Mrs Clewson's shocked expression.

Had she just called the vicar's wife 'love'?

Oh well, she thought, biting her lip as Mrs Clewson paid and returned to her husband, no doubt to whisper in his ear that the new shop owner was an odd sort who didn't know her place. She might as well start as she meant to go on because, as Arnie had always said, there was 'no use teaching an old dog new tricks'.

Besides, she felt at home here, behind the counter in her work apron, already smiling at the next customer in line, ready to tot up her goods on the newly refurbished till. Maybe it was fanciful, but she did feel as though Arnie had been there in spirit just now, guiding her hand to the right sweet jar, steadying her nerves, showing her how the job was done.

Yes, she'd done the right thing by reopening this little shop and not selling it. When she lost Arnie, she'd thought that she might as well have died too. That her life was over and buried in that churchyard along with him. Instead, she'd been granted a new lease of life.

It was nearly an hour before the crowd of villagers began to thin out. Now only her friends and family remained, with a few stragglers, like the vicar. If you could call the Reverend Clewson a straggler, Sheila thought, with a hurriedly quashed gurgle of laughter. His wife had left soon after the 'love' awkwardness, and Tilly and Caroline had walked back to the farm on Joe's instructions, as he disliked leaving the place untended for any length of time. But Joan had remained and was now chatting to a young man outside the shop.

Seeing her glance that way, Violet sidled up with Sarah Jane on her hip to mutter in Sheila's ear, 'That's the young man who rescued the lamb. Joe just told me. His name is Arthur Green and those are his parents over there, talking to the vicar.'

'He looks like a nice boy,' Sheila said cautiously.

'Apparently,' Violet continued, ignoring this, 'his parents are very well-to-do. I only hope he's not sweet on Joan.'

Astonished, Sheila stared at her daughter. 'So what if he is? It's not just birds and bees that enjoy the spring.'

'I'm not thinking of kissing and cuddling.' Violet gave her a withering look. 'We've already lost Selina. And Penny before that. We can't lose another Land Girl.'

Sheila laughed, shaking her head. 'The poor lad's only

talking to her. Not proposing marriage. Blimey, love, you've got some imagination.'

'I've got eyes, that's what I've got,' Violet told her darkly.

Sheila caught her daughter's arm as she turned away. 'Hang on a tick,' she whispered, checking that Joe was not within earshot. 'I wanted a word with you about Sarah Jane. You can't keep taking me and Joe to task over calling her Sally. It's a lovely, affectionate name and suits her better while she's so little, bless her. Anyway, you shouldn't argue with Joe about it so much.'

Violet shook her arm free. 'I'll ask you to keep your nose out of my marriage, Mum.'

'You won't have a marriage much longer if you don't stop badgering the poor man over nothing,' Sheila said sharply, then sighed, seeing Violet's stubborn glare. 'Leave him be, love. Joe's got a lot on his plate at the moment. And yes, maybe it's not my business,' she added, 'but a mother's got a right to give her daughter advice when she sees something wrong.'

Violet bit her lip, watching her husband through the shop window. 'Well, maybe I have been a bit harsh with him lately. But I called her Sarah Jane because—'

'You thought it sounded posh.'

Violet blushed. 'Well, why shouldn't I try to raise my child to something better than what I had?'

'Ta,' Sheila said, feeling affronted.

'Oh, Mum, it weren't your fault, raising us in a place like Dagenham, and I know you done your best, especially after Dad died. I'm not saying Sally sounds common either, but …' Violet's shoulders slumped and she shook her head. 'Gawd, I'm sorry. I've been a right nag about this, haven't I?'

'Don't be silly, love. We've all had a tough time of it recently, and I can handle a bit of back-biting. Just make sure you ain't taking it out on Joe. Men can be funny about things like that. Oh, come here …' Sheila gave her a quick hug. 'Don't hold on so tight, that's all. The war's over. It's all going to work out, you'll see.' She wasn't convinced of that herself, yet what could she do but reassure her daughter?

Nodding, Violet wiped away a tear and hurried outside to join her husband.

Sweeping up behind the counter for the next few minutes, Sheila straightened with an aching back to find Joan's young man's mother waiting patiently to be served. 'Sorry, missus, didn't see you there … What can I do for you?'

'I don't think we've met properly, but I'm Mrs Green. We live out on the road to Trethewey.' Tall and elegant in a beige woollen skirt suit with a cream blouse under the matching jacket, the woman shook her hand across the counter. 'Congratulations on reopening the shop. We're all very happy to see it blossoming again. I'm sure you'll do a marvellous job.' She paused, her smile fading. 'I'm very sorry for your loss. Mr Newton was a real asset to the village and is terribly missed.'

'Thank you.'

'I was wondering, Mrs Newton, if it might be possible for you to order a book of knitting patterns? Ordinarily, my husband runs me into Penzance once a month and I pick them up there. But it would be more convenient if you stocked them.'

'Some of them magazines have knitting patterns.' Sheila pointed them out, blinking at this unusual request.

'Yes, I did have a quick flick through. But they're quite limited in scope. If you were to stock a whole book of patterns here, I could just buy the ones I needed, as I do when we visit the fabric shops in Penzance.'

A whole book of patterns just for one customer to browse? It sounded rather expensive, Sheila thought, but gave the lady a hearty smile. 'I'll see what I can do, Mrs Green. Perhaps you could call back in a week or two when I've had a chance to speak to my supplier.'

'Of course. And good luck with the venture. Things have gone rather quiet in the village since the end of the war.' Mrs Green glanced across the valley to where the roof of Eastern House could just be glimpsed above the treetops. 'When all the soldiers were camped here, Porthcurno bustling with troops, I longed for the peace and quiet we used to have before the war. But now …' She smiled wanly. 'Well, it's silly of me, but I miss it. Do you know what I mean, Mrs Newton?'

Sheila gave a sympathetic nod. 'Can't say I disagree with you, Mrs Green. This place was certainly more alive during the war. And to think, we had a top-secret base right here in this village—'

'Hush!' Looking shocked, Mrs Green hurriedly put a finger to her lips. 'We're still not meant to talk about it. The war may be over, but you never know.'

Sheila pursed her lips; she didn't want to offend anyone else on her first day, so merely smiled and nodded. 'Of course. Forget I spoke. Good day to you, Mrs Green.'

When the Greens and their son Arthur had walked away to their car, Sheila turned to Violet. 'Well, the reopening seemed to go well enough. But I'm puffed out now. How about we put a brew on and sit down, now it's quiet?'

Violet agreed, and turned to Hazel and George Cotterill,

asking if they too would like to stay for a cup of tea. But George had to return to work at Eastern House, where he still ran the communications centre, and Hazel had to drive back to rescue their neighbour, who'd been left looking after little Lily. Joe made his excuses too, walking back up to the farm with Joan, since they had a list of jobs 'as long as both my arms', he told them with a grimace.

Soon, the shop was empty.

With a gusty sigh of relief, Sheila shut the door and sat in the back with a cuppa, chatting to Violet. While they talked, Sarah Jane played with a tea-set in Arnie's old armchair, pretending to give her rag doll a cuppa too. Arnie had made that rag doll himself to put in her cot as a baby, Sheila thought, watching her granddaughter absent-mindedly.

'It was marvellous how many turned out,' Sheila said proudly. Then she heard the bell tinkle as the door to the shop opened. 'Blimey, that must be another customer. Though I suppose I'll have to get used to this sitting down and getting up lark. No rest for the wicked, eh?'

'I'll see to them, Mum,' Violet said, beginning to get up.

'No, you've got your hands full with Sarah Jane there. Anyway, I need to get used to being in demand. Arnie loved it. So I'd better try to enjoy meself as well, eh?'

With a wink, Sheila downed the dregs of her tea and hurried through to the shop.

There was a woman in a hat studying the magazines, her back turned to Sheila, but it wasn't Mrs Green come back for another browse of the knitting patterns. This woman was shorter and more sturdily built, in a brown woollen dress and low heels.

As the woman turned to face her, Sheila recoiled in shock.

'Blow me,' she exclaimed, winded by this spectre from her past. 'What on earth are *you* doing 'ere, Maggie?'

It was her older sister, Margaret Chellew. Only she wasn't a welcome visitor. She certainly hadn't been invited to the grand reopening of the village shop today. She hadn't been invited to Arnie's funeral either. Nor to Sheila's wedding.

The truth was, Sheila hadn't seen her sister in years. Not since her husband Stanley Chellew had tried it on with young Lily in the haybarn while Violet and the girls were staying on his farm. Later, when Sheila had finally arrived in Cornwall, Margaret had come to see her in Porthcurno, hoping to make peace. But when Shcila demanded an explanation for what had happened, her sister had refused to listen to the truth, blaming the whole incident on the innocent girl instead, while Stanley sat like a stone in his truck and never said a word.

Now here her sister was, turned up in the shop like a bad penny, a stubborn glint in her eye, facing Sheila down, bold as brass …

Well, what a bloomin' cheek!

'Hello, Sheila,' her sister replied, sticking her chin in the air with a stubborn look that Sheila knew only too well. 'Can we have a chat?'

Before Sheila could say a word, Violet was striding past her to throw open the shop door. 'Out,' she snapped at her aunt, her face flushed with temper. 'You're not welcome here, Aunty Margaret. And you know why.'

Margaret's chin rose even higher. She kept her eyes on Sheila. 'Are you going to let your daughter talk to me like that?'

'I am,' Sheila said, though her voice faltered. Violet was right. What her sister's husband had done was beyond forgiveness.

Margaret turned to leave but stopped beside Violet. 'I'm sorry about what happened. I didn't realise what Stanley had done at the time. I thought Lily was just making trouble.'

'Out,' Violet choked, her eyes ablaze.

'I've left him,' Margaret threw back at her, her voice shaking.

'What?' Sheila stared, and even Violet fell silent.

'You heard.' Her sister swallowed. 'You were right about him, Shee. He's a bad lot. Not just because of what he done to your Lily, but other things too. Drinking, seeing other women … And he hits me.' She pulled aside the greying hair hanging close to her cheek to reveal the traces of what must have been an ugly bruise. Violet gasped, but Sheila wasn't surprised. 'He's got a hard hand when he's drunk.'

'So you left him?'

'Oh, I broke a pot over his head first.' Margaret's eyes flared with sudden anger. 'Stanley didn't like that. He took off his belt and beat me with it. Black and blue, I was.'

Violet swore under her breath.

'A friend's letting me sleep on her sofa, but it's a tiny place and I've no money to pay for bed and board. Only my ration book.' Margaret met Sheila's eyes. 'You know how it is around here, Shee, trying to get work in the country … There's not much for someone my age. I've farming experience a-plenty, but none of the farmers round here would dare take me on, not when they might have Stanley pay them a visit.' She paused. 'Then I heard you'd opened up this shop again.'

Violet's eyes bulged. 'You're not expecting *Mum* to give you a job?'

'All right, that's enough now, Vi,' Sheila said, gesturing Violet to return to the back room. 'Sarah Jane's calling for you.'

Violet's thin brows arched in disbelief but she took the hint and left them to it.

'You'd better go, Maggie,' Sheila said briskly, ushering her out of the door. 'I'm sorry about what's 'appened between you and Stanley. But it don't change what you did.'

With slumped shoulders, her sister turned to leave, but slowly. She stopped in the doorway, looking into Sheila's face with a sorrowful expression.

'Blood's thicker than water, Shee,' Margaret reminded her. 'What Stan did was wrong, I know that now. But I'm still your sister. And I need help.'

Perhaps it was stupid to be moved by the plea in her sister's voice, but she couldn't help it.

With a hurried glance over her shoulder, Sheila whispered, 'Come back another time, when Vi's not here, eh?' Seeing relief on her sister's face, she added fiercely, 'I ain't promising nothing, mind. Violet's right, what your Stan did was unforgivable. You're lucky I'm even standing here, talking to you. But if you come back this day next week, around closing time, we can have a chat. All right?'

Then Sheila shut the door, hoping to goodness she hadn't just made the worst mistake of her life.

CHAPTER EIGHT

Joan wasn't terribly good at cycling but now it was June, the fine weather made the hard work of pedalling enjoyable at least. 'Whee,' she cried on the downhill stretches, the wind lifting her hair, but groaned on the upward slopes and often stopped to admire flowers in the hedgerow while catching her breath. Porthcurno was quite a hilly place, so by the time she reached the track leading to the Grange where she was due to meet Arthur on her afternoon off, she was breathless and a bit shiny with perspiration. Still, she bumped along the uneven track with enthusiasm, admiring the impressive exterior of the Grange, a building which was clearly over a hundred years old, and the neat gardens bordering the drive. Although the owner was still in Germany – according to Arthur – he clearly kept on staff to maintain the house and gardens.

Stopping outside the creeper-covered front entrance, she leaned her borrowed bike against the wall and rang the bell. While she was gazing about the place with interest, a window was almost immediately thrown up on the first floor and she saw Arthur poke his fair head out of the window.

He lifted a hand in greeting, asking with a grin, 'Shall I come down and let you in, or would you rather climb up the creepers?'

'I doubt they'd take my weight.'

He laughed. 'I'd better come down then. Just a tick.' And with that, he disappeared.

Soon, the front door swung open and Arthur stood there, smiling. She greeted him shyly, for although she'd insisted at their first meeting that she wouldn't mind being alone with him at the Grange while they sorted out the library, she was a little nervous. Which was silly, as she'd met plenty of boys before who were on the handy, impudent side. And Arthur wasn't like that at all. He had an honest, clean-cut air, and she trusted him instinctively.

'I'm glad you came,' he admitted, closing the door after her. 'The library's upstairs. This way. Oh, don't mind the cat. She belonged to Geoff's late father. Pining for the old man, I imagine.' He waited while she stopped to pet the animal, who had come forward with curious eyes. The cat was a tortoiseshell with large glowing eyes, who began to purr as soon as Joan stooped to stroke her. 'Probably got fleas too.'

'Of course you don't have fleas, do you? What a horrid boy to say such a thing.' Joan scratched behind the cat's ears and was rewarded with deeper purring. 'You're a beauty. Though it must be boring for you, poor thing, hanging about an empty house all day.'

'The housekeeper looks after her. And once or twice she's come up to the library to keep me company. Scratches at the door and meows until I let her in.' As they went up the stairs, the cat followed, and he laughed. 'Like that, see?'

'What's her name?'

'Shelley.' He saw her quick look and nodded. 'Yes, after the poet. Bit of an odd choice, perhaps. But the library's crammed with poetry.'

Joan bit her lip, trying not smile. 'I expect it's more because she's a tortoiseshell.'

'Oh, good grief.' He was blinking in surprise at the cat, who had trotted ahead of them. 'You're right, of course. What a duffer I am. Bit slow on the uptake, I'm afraid.'

They passed a few open doors, and Joan, peering curiously inside, saw furniture draped in covers to protect against dust and sunlight. The windows were also shuttered or had curtains drawn to keep out any rays that might fade fabrics and wallpaper. The rooms looked sad and empty, and their footsteps echoed emptily along the landing. But when they entered the library, she found it a much more welcoming space. There, the shutters had been opened and sunlight was streaming in, dust motes spinning in the air. Books lay scattered across the tables and in uneven, leaning stacks, large gaps yawning in the bookshelves from where they'd been withdrawn. There were loose sheets of paper lying about too, with mysterious lines and squiggles on them. She paused to examine one more closely, and guessed that Arthur had been attempting some form of inventory. But his methodology was suspect, for his lists were not in alphabetical order, either by title or author. She said nothing, however, for perhaps he had some secret methodology, which he would soon divulge.

It was a long room, with free-standing bookcases as well as shelves lining the walls. Four diamond-patterned, lead-lined windows let in the light. And on each deep windowsill stood an austere stone bust. She recognised one august head at least. 'Shakespeare,' she murmured, stopping beside that familiar head.

The cat jumped up on the windowsill and waved her tail in Shakespeare's face.

Arthur gave a snort of laughter. 'Not a fan of the bard, I suspect.'

Laughing with him, Joan turned on her heel, taking in the intimidatingly high shelves opposite, which came equipped with a sliding ladder so that one could reach the top shelves.

'What a marvellous room,' she breathed, her heart thumping with excitement at the sight of so many books. Her reading at the farm had been frustrating so far, limited to the few books she could borrow monthly from Penzance Library. 'You're so lucky to have been given access to all these. Have you made a good start on sorting them out?'

He looked awkward. 'To be honest, I've been slacking off a bit lately. All this fine weather … I've been taking walks and reading more than anything else.' He shuffled his feet, not meeting her gaze. 'This kind of job would be better for someone who doesn't like books. I'm hampered by having to open the damn things to find out what's inside, and then I get lost in them. Do you know what I mean?'

'Funnily enough, yes. But I promised I'd help. So perhaps you'd better explain your plan, and what exactly all these squiggles mean.' She nodded to one of the loose sheets of paper. 'Is it a code?'

'Code?' He looked blank. 'That's my handwriting.'

'Oh.'

'And I don't have a plan, as such. I pull out the books that look oldest … The leather-bound volumes with gilt lettering on the spine, you know. Then I note down the title and author.

I thought maybe I could sit down later and categorise them. You know, into poetry, classical literature, linguistics and so on.' His voice tailed off and he scratched his head. 'Not much of a method, is it?'

Joan was astonished. 'You went to Eton, didn't you?'

'Yes, but as you can see, I didn't learn much there. To be honest, I'm pretty rotten at organisation. It's what's inside the books that I enjoy, not the librarian side of things. Don't have that sort of brain, I suppose. More poems and ballads than, erm, quantum mechanics.' His mouth worked in self-deprecating humour. 'Whatever on earth *that* means.'

She laughed, finding him amusing. 'All right, here's an idea. You carry on doing that, and I'll sort them out into categories as you finish each sheet. In fact,' she added, turning to the pack she'd slung over her back on leaving the farmhouse that afternoon, 'I can use this.' She rummaged in the backpack for her black notebook and a pencil. 'I bought it last week in Penzance, expressly for this job.'

'I say, Joan, you are a simply marvellous girl.' His brow had cleared. Turning with an eager smile to the shelves, Arthur dragged out a few calf-bound volumes at random, blowing dust off each one as he did so. Choosing one, he flicked through marbled endpapers to the old-fashioned title page. 'Goodness, this is an old one. Blount's *Glossographia*, 1661. Looks like an early English dictionary. I bet it's worth a packet.' Laying it carefully aside, he noted down the details on one of his loose sheets. 'I suppose that comes under the heading of Languages.'

'Sounds like it, yes.'

Dutifully, she opened her new notepad and began to draw a few columns freehand. At the head of the first column, she wrote 'Subject'. Next column was 'Title'. And the third column was 'Author and Date of Publication'. She hesitated over whether to squeeze in a fourth column for publisher, but decided there wasn't enough space. Besides, she could note that down under publication date if necessary.

While the cat sat on the desk beside her, purring and kneading steadily at the sleeve of her cardigan, Joan lined ten pages in this way, with space on each page for at least ten or twelve titles to be listed. On the first three pages, she wrote 'Poetry' in large letters at the top. On the next few, she wrote 'Classical Literature' – judging by the abundance of Greek and Latin titles on the shelves, it would be a large category. Then came 'Language', under which the *Glossographia* would presumably be listed. She left the next few sheets blank, in case other categories occurred to her as they went along.

Finally, she gathered Arthur's loose notes, and painstakingly began to transcribe the scribbled details into her notepad, so that any poetry collections were listed under the 'Poetry' heading, and so on.

They passed several hours in this pleasant manner, chatting about subjects as varied as the weather, Shelley's killing sprees with mice and rabbits, the general frustrations of rationing, and where Arthur had been stationed during the war.

He told her entertaining anecdotes from his basic training, and they were soon laughing like old friends. Joan, who'd not had so much fun in years, was ecstatic that she had made such a wonderful new acquaintance, for apart from being scatterbrained at times, she couldn't detect any faults in the young man.

As the afternoon wore on into early evening, the sun

disappeared and the room grew chilly. Perhaps noting how Joan was struggling to read her own writing, not to mention having to button up her woolly cardigan, Arthur turned on the overhead lights as well as a two-bar electric fire set discreetly in an alcove.

'It can get a bit nippy here in the evenings. I usually try to get home before dark, though only because my mother fusses if I don't.' He saw her glance surreptitiously at her watch. 'I'll walk you back to the farm, if you like. What time do you need to return?'

When she spent her afternoon off with the girls in Penzance, they were rarely back in time for supper, so fended for themselves on their return to the farmhouse. Caroline and Tilly had gone into Penzance without her today to visit a friend and she doubted they would even be back yet. The last bus from Penzance would be due into the village in just under an hour, and though it was often late coming back, she calculated that she should have time to catch up with the girls as they walked back to the farm.

His offer of accompanying her home left her secretly pleased though. She had dreaded cycling back on her own in the dusk. Not that anything untoward was likely to happen to her in a quiet spot like Porthcurno, but she had a lively imagination and would often glance with suspicion at dark shapes in the hedgerow or looming ahead on the narrow Cornish lanes, even though her rational mind told her they were probably just trees and shrubs.

'Not for another hour at least,' she told him, and was surprised to feel her heart beat faster at the thought of spending more time alone with Arthur. With the electric fire glowing beside them, the library was cosier than before, and she had to admit to enjoying the musty smell of old books and the rustle of pages being turned.

'In that case, I'll nip down to the kitchen and see if I can find us some bread and cheese. And maybe some tea?' Arthur eyed her, hesitant. 'Unless you'd prefer something stronger to drink?'

She laughed, shaking her head. 'Tea would be fine, thank you. And bread and cheese sound heavenly too, if you're sure they won't be missed?'

'Oh, Mrs Penhallow never lets me go hungry,' he assured her, 'and you're my assistant now, so that means she'll have to feed you too.'

Arthur hurried away on his mission, and when he returned some fifteen minutes later, he was accompanied by the housekeeper, carrying the tea tray.

Mrs Penhallow was a stout, smiling Cornishwoman who greeted Joan cheerfully and without any hint of disapproval at her being there. She was clad soberly in grey with a white lace-trimmed apron over her dress, and keys dangling off her belt in the time-honoured fashion of housekeepers. She seemed to know all about the Land Girls and Joe's farm, and gave a nod of appreciation when mentioning the village shop that Mrs Newton had recently reopened.

'We're all very glad to see the shop open again at last. There's a man with a barrow who comes round but it's not the same.' Mrs Penhallow paused. 'One shouldn't speak ill of the dead, but I found old Arnie a little brusque in his manner. He always kept the shelves well stocked though, God rest his soul.'

'I'm sure Mrs Newton will too,' Joan assured her.

The housekeeper smiled. 'Well, m'dears, I'll leave you to

your books. Though I can see I'll need to do some dusting in here tomorrow,' she added, coughing as she left the room.

Arthur and Joan grinned at one another.

After their bread and cheese was finished, and Joan had gulped down the last of her tea while finishing up her notes, they decided to call it a day. Arthur insisted on walking back with her to the village, where they only waited five minutes before the last bus from Penzance came trundling into view.

Tilly and Caroline jumped off the bus, studying Arthur Green with smirks of undisguised curiosity. Perhaps seeing this, he didn't stay long, merely shaking Joan's hand and muttering that he'd be pleased to see her again the following week, if she was free on the Thursday. Then he hurried away in the opposite direction, no doubt on his way home.

'Goodness, you sly thing,' Tilly said in a rush when he was no longer in earshot. Her green eyes sparkled. 'Did you have a *date*? You never breathed a word to us about meeting a *boy*. In fact, I distinctly remember you saying something about having an errand to run in the village.'

'Must have been an interesting errand,' Caroline remarked, her gaze on Arthur as he trudged away into the dusk.

Joan was glad of the gathering gloom; it meant they wouldn't be able to see the blush in her cheeks. 'Now you're just being silly. It really was just an errand.'

Tilly tossed back her red hair, laughing. 'Oh, come on!'

'No, honestly. Don't you remember him? He's the one who told us about the lamb falling over the cliff. We got talking on our way down to the farm, and I said that I like reading, so he asked if I'd help him with a private book collection he's trying to sort out.' She hated the thought that they'd got the wrong idea about her and Arthur. 'That's all I've been doing this afternoon. Looking through books with him.'

'Whose private collection?' Caroline was frowning.

'A local bigwig called Sir Malcolm Castleton. He died recently and now his son wants to sell his library, so Arthur's been helping him work out which books might be valuable. Their home is on the other side of the village.' Carefully, she didn't mention that the 'son' was away in Germany.

Caroline nodded. 'I remember that house. We went there once when Selina and I were flogging tickets for a charity auction. It's big. Very posh.'

'A *posh* errand, then.' Tilly was still laughing.

'Arthur's not posh,' Joan said desperately. 'Not really. He … He's only there as a favour to his friend, who hates books and reading.'

'Well,' Tilly said, 'I see now you must have been thoroughly bored, locked up in a library all afternoon with that dreamboat.'

Dreamboat?

Joan glanced over her shoulder but Arthur was no longer visible. She supposed he *was* quite dreamy. But of course she had only gone to meet him out of curiosity and because she loved books. And since he hadn't laid a finger on her the whole time, and had been perfectly polite on the way back into the village, she had to assume he had no special designs in asking her to help out. He was just a nice young man. Or so she told herself.

As the hill steepened, Tilly and Caro fell into step together, arms linked, while Joan pushed the bicycle.

'And are you going to spend your next afternoon off with him?' Caroline asked, breathing heavily at the exertion.

'I haven't decided yet,' Joan replied in lofty tones, though that wasn't true. She did like Arthur and had every intention of meeting him again next Thursday, come hell or high water. But she wasn't about to admit that to the other Land Girls. 'Maybe. Maybe not. I'll see how I feel next week.'

The other two laughed, and after a moment, she joined in. Suddenly, the world didn't seem quite as dull and boring as usual.

When they got back, they discovered the farmhouse in uproar. Mrs Newton seemed to be providing most of the uproar, though Violet was also bashing noisily about with sud-covered pots and pans in the sink, and Joe was holding forth with uncharacteristic loudness as they entered the house.

Mrs Newton turned on seeing them come in and waved a piece of paper in the air. Her face was flushed, her grey hair dishevelled as though she'd dragged her hat off without bothering to comb her hair afterwards.

''Ere, girls, look at this. We've 'ad a letter from London. Our Alice … She's getting wed at last. To that lad of hers, young Patrick. Bloomin' marvellous news, ain't it?'

'And about time too,' Joe grumbled, with a disapproving shake of his head, 'the way those two have been carrying on together.'

Violet turned to glare at her husband. '*Carrying on*? I'll thank you to remember that's my niece you're talking about, Joe Postbridge.' Her voice sharpened. 'Besides, they ain't been living together in London, if that's what you're tryin' to suggest. Stop putting wicked ideas in the girls' heads.' She looked at the Land Girls seriously. 'Pay no attention to Joe. Patrick has his own digs, and Alice is living with a very nice

103

family in London, picked out specially by her dad. Nothing untoward about it at all.'

Right on cue, as though he had heard himself mentioned, the door from the snug opened and Alice's dad, Ernest Fisher, strolled into the kitchen, a rolled-up newspaper tucked under his arm and a wry smile on his face. He was rarely at the farm during the day now that he was working full-time at Eastern House, helping George Cotterill out with goodness knows what … Presumably the communications devices Joan had overheard Violet and her nieces discussing once or twice, machines they'd seen housed in tunnels behind the listening post during the war, when they'd worked there as cleaners. It was an open secret at the farm that Ernest had worked in Intelligence during the war …

Mr Fisher saw the Land Girls standing hesitantly on the threshold and nodded to them. 'Evening, ladies,' he said pleasantly, and wandered across to place an empty tea mug on the draining board for Violet to wash. 'I'm afraid you've walked into a minor family disagreement. My daughter Alice is getting married and would like to come back to Porthcurno for the ceremony. Only Joe here is worried that people will talk.'

'Only because everyone will be wondering why two young people who went away together to London months ago aren't married yet,' Joe pointed out in his slow way, not raising his eyes from his tea mug. 'It's your Alice I'm thinking of, Ernest. Yes, and Sheila too.' At this, he looked up directly at his mother-in-law. 'Now you're running the shop, you don't want tongues wagging in the village, do you?'

'They'll be wagging about nothin', Sheila Newton muttered,

hands on her ample hips, her expression fierce, 'and I'll tell 'em so.'

'Aye, but Porthcurno's a small place and folk do gossip,' Joe reminded her unhappily. 'They might say nothing to your face. But they can still make you feel bad.'

'I catch a single blighter gossiping about my granddaughter,' Mrs Newton promised him shrilly, 'and I'll give 'em what for, no mistake. Alice is a good girl, and Patrick's a nice, well brought up lad. There's been no funny business. And it's quite proper she wants to tie the knot here in Porthcurno. Where else would she do it, but with her family all around her? Yes, and her friends too,' she added, nodding towards the Land Girls. With an air of awful restraint, she passed Mr Fisher the letter. 'Ernest, you're the girl's father. Write back and tell her yes, we'll book the parish church for later this summer, and we'll lay on a nice spread here at the farm after the wedding.' Then she stamped out of the kitchen, snapping over her shoulder, 'Blimey, Joe, it's 1946. Anyone would think Queen Victoria was still on the bloomin' throne the way you go on sometimes.'

Once she'd gone, Violet stood drying her hands on a tea towel, clearly embarrassed by her mother's outburst. 'Did you have a nice afternoon off, girls?' Without waiting for an answer, she turned to refill the kettle and set it on the range. 'I'll put a brew on for you, how's that?'

'Thank you,' Caroline said wanly, 'but I'm quite tired, Mrs Postbridge. I'm going straight up to bed.'

'Without any supper?' Tilly demanded, staring after her friend in amazement, but Caroline had already disappeared. 'Well, I'd love a cup of tea, Mrs P,' she said with a shrug, hanging up her coat. 'Caro and I had a great time in

105

Penzance. Though Joan didn't come with us, did you?' she added, turning with a wink to Joan.

Violet glanced their way, surprised. 'Why was that, Joan?'

'Oh, she was seeing a boy,' Tilly announced while Joan said nothing, standing in horrified silence, her heart thumping at this betrayal of her confidence. But perhaps the younger girl wasn't aware that her afternoon with Arthur ought to have been kept a secret. Tilly was only eighteen and not very discreet.

Violet's eyes bulged. 'A boy?'

Even Joe was looking their way now, his thick brows knotting together. 'Eh? Which boy?'

'I … I wasn't *seeing* him, precisely,' Joan stammered, aware of everybody staring at her now. She felt heat in her cheeks and twisted her hands together awkwardly. 'Not the way Tilly's making it sound.'

'What were you doing with him, then?' Violet demanded, almost as though she were Joan's mother.

Hot-cheeked, Joan was tempted to tell the farmer and his wife to mind their own business before following Caroline up to bed. It was what Selina would have done in her place. But she was a polite girl and didn't want to make a scene. Besides, getting upset would only confirm their suspicions that she had something to hide.

'He asked me to help out with a job, that's all.' Briefly, she explained what they had been doing at the Grange. 'Then he walked me to the bus stop, and I came back with the girls.'

'Are you talking about the young lad who brought the injured lamb down to the farm the other week?' Joe asked, and glanced round at Violet, who bit her lip.

'Yes, Arthur Green.' There was a horrid silence and Joan's

blush deepened. She was confused by their unexpected reaction and didn't know what to think. 'What is it? Why are you looking at me like that?'

'Yes, what's wrong?' Mr Fisher asked, a sharp curiosity in his face.

'It's not our business to say …' Joe began cautiously, but his wife interrupted him.

'Of course it's our business, Joe. The Green's son … Arthur, is that his name?' Violet took a deep breath when Joan nodded. 'Thing is, love, there's been some gossip in the village about him … It seems something happened to that poor lad in the war. Nobody's sure what exactly. But he … he came back not quite right.'

'I beg your pardon?' Joan couldn't believe her ears.

'I'm sorry to be the bearer of bad tidings,' Violet told her, more gently. 'And I don't know the ins and outs of it, it's true. But next time he asks for your help, you tell him no thanks.'

Angrily, Joan began, 'I don't see—'

Violet shook her head, frowning. 'No, Joan, listen to me. Steer clear of the Green boy, all right? Joe and me, we're responsible for your welfare while you're living under our roof, young lady. And you're not to see that boy again, do you hear? Not if you know what's good for you.'

CHAPTER NINE

Summer weather, it seemed, was highly unpredictable on Bodmin Moor. But Selina soon settled into her new life at Thornton Hall with its bleak but beautiful views of moorland all around, the bracken-thick slopes often drenched with showers before the hot sun came out again. Her daily routine generally consisted of sitting with her sister every day after breakfast to read the newspaper together and discuss the lamentable state of British politics. She would also listen to Bella's worries about the children, whose emotional well-being greatly occupied her mind, and try to allay her fears.

After lunch, which she ate with her sister whenever Bella was well enough, the afternoons were her own. Selina went for a stroll across the moorland once or twice a week, trying not to venture too far in case she got lost on that vast expanse with so few landmarks to guide her home. And sometimes she would sit in the garden or alone in her room, and read hardbacks borrowed from Bella's shelves, mostly romantic and historical novels, which she enjoyed immensely, even though she wasn't usually much of a reader.

Occasionally, she popped her head around the door of the nursery, which doubled up as a schoolroom when the tutor was there, hoping to make friends with the children. The two older ones were friendly but remained politely distant, and she often caught a wary look in Jemima's eyes. They both knew that their mother was very ill, but perhaps were unaware that she was dying. She wondered uneasily when her sister would break the bad news to them.

By contrast, little Faith was always enthusiastic to see her, and Selina often rescued her from the stuffy nursery and took her into the large gardens, with plenty of room for the carefree little soul to run about and play in the sunshine. There was a swing hanging from an old tree and Faith would beg Selina to push her back and forth on it, though never too high.

They also had two cocker spaniels, who ran about barking whenever the children were playing outside. Selina wasn't much of a dog person, but she became grateful for their company on some of her longer walks, especially since the spaniels knew their way home even when she was horribly lost.

Not having to get up at dawn and tramp into the fields or struggle with fencing or recalcitrant sheep or any of the other livestock that Joe kept on his farm, or sow seeds and harvest crops, and trudge home at night bone-tired and covered in mud, was such a change that she felt almost shell-shocked at first. She would wake to full sunlight and scramble out of bed in a panic, fearful she must be late for her shift and wondering why on earth nobody had woken her. Then, her heart pounding, she would recall that she was no longer at Postbridge farm, no longer a Land Girl.

It was wonderful to be free. But it was also boring. She would know a moment of utter blankness after lunch, realising that she had nothing to do and nowhere in particular that she had to be. She was simply not accustomed to occupying herself without somebody telling her what she should be doing. At last, she asked her sister if there were any jobs that needed to be done about the house.

Initially, Bella refused, insisting that she was a 'guest'. But as the days crept past and she grew more ill, Bella gave up and asked Selina to undertake various tasks. Some were simple and easily achieved, such as bringing the children to see Bella in the afternoons, or passing on some instruction to their nanny or the tutor. But others were more challenging. Once, she asked Selina to write a letter to the solicitor, Mr MacGregor, asking him to visit the house at his earliest convenience. And after his prompt visit, she began to tell Selina more about their closest neighbours, and even asked Selina to draw up a list of such people with a few details beside each name.

'You want me to write down a list of names?' Selina had asked, perplexed. 'Happily, whatever you like. But what's it for?'

Her sister had succumbed to a coughing fit, which took some minutes to pass, then said faintly, 'For my funeral, of course.'

Selina had stared, and her hand had trembled as she took down the names and details that her sister suggested. It felt too horrible to have finally bonded with her sister again, after years of estrangement, only to be losing her to this dreadful sickness. It was unfair. Yet there was nothing to be done. And at least these little tasks gave her something to occupy her mind rather than dwell on this cruelty.

One day, her sister decided that she was well enough to host a small dinner party. 'No, I can manage,' she'd told Selina when she protested, concerned for her fragile health. 'All I need do is sit at one end of the table, and you and Mrs Hawley can do the rest. Besides, these will be friends and neighbours. They won't expect me to put on a show. They all know I've been unwell.' She paused. 'Though they don't all know that I'm dying, of course.'

Not wishing to upset her, Selina agreed to organise everything with Mrs Hawley's help. She sent out invitations to the guests, using her sister's address book, and even borrowed one of her sister's evening dresses for the event itself, not owning anything even remotely respectable enough for a dinner party. The only celebrations they'd ever held at the farm had been Mrs Newton's knees-ups whenever there was a birthday, or some great breakthrough in the war had occurred, and even then, few of them had bothered changing out of their everyday clothes. She had even attended Alice's birthday party once in her Land Army uniform, and probably with mud on her face as well. Nobody had said a word. It wasn't that kind of place.

Besides which, there had been a war on, and such niceties had seemed ridiculous and petty. Not when the country could be invaded by Germans at any moment. In those days, they had seized their pleasures where they could and celebrated with home-made gin or wine, though it burnt their throat and made their eyes sting. Those had been different days.

But now the war was over, and she was living in Thornton Hall, and her sister was clearly a person of some importance in the district.

So evening dress it had to be, coupled with her only pair

of heels. Selina piled her blonde hair up in a chignon and applied make-up, and clipped on dangly earrings as an afterthought. Looking in the mirror, she barely recognised herself. She hadn't bothered with such finery since the late thirties, when there had been so many dances and parties to attend, and she'd still lived in hope of attracting some young man and marrying him. Anything to escape the dreary boredom and confinement of her aunt's home, to fall in love as her sister had done …

The long, grinding years of the war, topped by Johnny's cruel betrayal, had put paid to those dreams. And now Selina was so much older. Twenty-seven. Her late aunt would definitely have termed that age 'on the shelf'. After that terrible letter from Johnny, she had accepted it was too late for her, that she would never now marry. 'And thank goodness,' she told herself, thoroughly jaded by the idea of love. Those unhappy games of will-he, won't-he were over for her, and she didn't miss the heartache they'd brought.

Dr Ford was the first to arrive for the dinner party and he went straight in to sit with Bella, who had come down early and was taking a tonic before the strain of dinner. Minutes later, the family solicitor arrived and Selina went out to greet him in the hall, discreetly leaving her sister with the doctor.

'Good evening, Mr MacGregor.'

The solicitor was a soft-spoken but highly intelligent man of business. His first name was William, but although he had quickly told her to call him William or even Bill, Selina did not feel comfortable addressing him as anything but Mr MacGregor. He was a bachelor in his early forties, and she could tell from his smile and sidelong looks that he found her attractive. So being overly friendly towards him might give the man the wrong impression.

It wasn't that she didn't like the solicitor. But she was still smarting from Johnny's behaviour in marrying another woman behind her back, and she couldn't see herself ever trusting a man to do the right thing again.

'Miss Tiptree.' Mr MacGregor shook her hand and handed his hat to Mrs Hawley with a pleasant smile. 'Am I the first? Promptness is a sin of mine, I'm afraid. Ingrained through years of habit.'

'No, Dr Ford arrived a few minutes ago,' she reassured him.

'Ah.' The solicitor held her gaze longer than was entirely comfortable before glancing towards the drawing room. 'The estimable Dr Ford is here tonight, is he?'

'Would you care for a glass of sherry, sir?' Mrs Hawley indicated the drawing room. 'Mrs March is already downstairs.'

Thanking her, Mr MacGregor waited until the housekeeper had taken his hat and coat away before turning to Selina. 'Your sister is well enough to eat dinner with us, then? I must admit, I'm surprised. I had assumed you would be presiding over dinner.'

'My sister is determined to play hostess tonight, despite her poor health.' Selina couldn't prevent a note of disapproval creeping into her voice, and had to remind herself not to encourage him by being too friendly. 'Shall we go through?'

She poured a small sherry for herself and one for the solicitor, and perched on the edge of the seat to listen as the others chatted. She felt too nervous to join in, waiting for the other guests to arrive. When the bell finally rang again, she put down her sherry and hurried into the hall in time

113

to see Mrs Hawley showing in a pleasant-looking man and woman, who looked so alike they were clearly siblings.

These two, Selina guessed, must be Mr Cameron Bourne and his unmarried sister Helen, their nearest neighbours on the moor. She had seen their house on her walks, for Bourne Cottage was only a mile or so from Thornton Hall, a large eighteenth-century cottage nestled in a sheltered hollow at the edge of scrubby woodland.

'Hello,' she said, going forward with her hand outstretched. Her voice was high with nerves. 'How do you do? I'm Selina Tiptree, Bella's sister. I'm very glad to meet you.'

'Hello, I'm Helen,' the woman said with polite restraint as she removed her coat and shook Selina's hand. She was tall and spindly, her long, silver-grey evening dress cinched at the waist by a wide, silver-fringed belt that only emphasised her slenderness. Nut-brown hair was swept back from a high forehead and set in soft rolls about an angular, dark-eyed face. She looked to be in her thirties. 'And this is my brother, Cameron.'

Her brother was younger by a few years, but with the same dark hair, peaked above his broad forehead, and large, expressive dark eyes that came to rest on her face with a strange shock of familiarity. She almost felt they must have met before. And yet she was equally sure they had not.

'How do you do, Mr Bourne?'

'Very well, thank you, Miss Tiptree. How do you do? But please, call me Cameron.' He also shook her hand, his grip firm and deliberate. However, he didn't immediately release her hand, gazing into her eyes as though he too felt that odd sensation of familiarity. 'So you're Bella's mysterious sister.'

'Mysterious?'

'Don't mind my brother,' Helen Bourne said, her voice sharp, almost a reprimand. 'Cameron's only messing about. It's just … Well, your sister never mentioned your existence to us before, and we've known her ever since Sebastian brought her home as a young bride. So we were naturally astonished to hear that her *sister* had come to visit.' She was looking Selina up and down in a barely surreptitious manner. 'But no doubt it's because she's been unwell. You've come to nurse her back to health, perhaps? You look like a nurse.'

You look like a nurse.

Selina stood speechless, out of her depth. It was true she wasn't as well-to-do as her sister had become when she married Sebastian March. But she hadn't expected to be *attacked* by one of her sister's closest neighbours at this dinner party. And what else could that catty little speech be but an attack?

To her relief, Mr MacGregor rescued her, coming into the hall at that very moment and saying, 'Good evening, Cameron, Miss Bourne. Good to see you again. How are you both?' After they'd shaken hands and exchanged a few pleasantries, he asked, 'Cameron, did you ever get your car fixed? I meant to ask you about it.' They wandered into the drawing room, the two men falling into an easy conversation about cars, while Miss Bourne gave Selina a chilly smile.

Pouring their guests a small glass of sherry each, Selina found herself more angry than upset. Yes, she hadn't married into wealth and position like her sister. Yes, she had spent the last few years working on a farm. But that didn't give anyone the right to look down their nose at her the way Helen Bourne had just done. At least she had been working for the war effort, while her sister had been bringing up children.

What had Miss Bourne done during the war? Not worked on the land with her bare hands, that was for sure …

For her sister's sake, however, she remained polite, and handed out the sherries with a fixed smile.

Four other guests arrived over the next half hour.

The next two were pleasant, elderly sisters, one a wealthy widow and the other her companion, who lived in a large house in the centre of Bodmin. Dr Ford introduced them to Selina as 'philanthropists' who cared for art and music. They spoke of a classical concert they had hosted recently and suggested that Selina could visit them in Bodmin town the next time they held such an event. She smiled politely when the widow asked what her favourite music was and had to restrain herself from saying, 'American band music', sure they would look down their noses at her for such populist taste.

Just as Mrs Hawley was asking if she should delay dinner, the doorbell rang again, and she let in Mr and Mrs Knowles, a portly man in his fifties and his much younger wife. Apparently, John Knowles had met Deirdre at one of Bella's parties back when she and Sebastian March were first married. It was clear that Bella was quite fond of Mrs Knowles, for the two sat together and chatted quietly while the others were talking local politics.

As the guests finally headed towards the dining room, Bella tugged on Selina's sleeve to hold her back, whispering in her ear, 'What's the matter, Selly? I saw your face back then … Did Helen say something to upset you?'

'It's not important,' she muttered.

'If she did, pay no attention. Helen's never liked me and doesn't bother to hide it. A bitter spinster, that's what Sebastian used to call her.'

'What do you mean?'

'Oh, she was in love once but it came to nothing. Now she lives with her brother and nobody will have her, according to gossip.' Bella's smile was brittle. 'Remind me later and I'll tell you all about it.'

Selina shot her a puzzled look, wondering why on earth Bella had invited the woman to dinner. But she was more concerned by how tired her sister was looking, so merely smiled and supported her in to dinner.

Dr Ford sat at one end of the table, in the place Sebastian would presumably have taken, and Bella sat at the other end, smiling wearily. The room was large, too large really for such a small dinner party. The extending table itself could easily have seated twenty. However, Selina had watched Mrs Hawley and her assistant removing some of the table leaves earlier to make it shorter, so the setting was more intimate. She sat opposite Mr MacGregor, with Cameron Bourne on her right, and the wealthy widow to her left, as per her sister's seating arrangement.

For much of the meal, she was uncomfortably aware of Miss Bourne's occasional spiteful glances her way, but resolutely kept her own gaze either on her plate or directed towards those around her.

The men spoke mostly about the war, explaining their own roles in the recent conflict for her sake, as the newcomer. Dr Ford had not been called up, being 'too old in the tooth,' as he put it laughingly, but had worked at hospitals in the district, tending to locals and wounded soldiers alike. Mr Knowles had been unable to enlist, having a lazy eye, so had enrolled as a fire warden instead, while his wife Deirdre had made bandages at a local textile centre, when not caring for their young twin sons.

It seemed that Mr MacGregor had served in the local regiment, as had Cameron, both apparently coming through unscathed. However, it was obvious from mysterious comments dropped by the doctor that Cameron had endured a few issues during the war, and these had allowed him to understand the problems some young men faced on coming home. Selina was too polite to enquire further, and no more was said about it, so she pushed aside her curiosity and concentrated on her sister instead.

Conversation over dinner was lively and not too serious, which suited Selina. Her own spirits had begun to flag in recent days, the loneliness and isolation of Thornton Hall weighing heavily on her, compounded by the fear of what horrors might lie ahead. Selina smiled and laughed in all the right places. But her nerves were stretched thin. She feared that at any moment she might embarrass herself by bursting into tears, without being able to explain why.

As they finished dessert, Bella tapped her spoon against her glass, and conversation died away, everybody looking towards her.

Dr Ford's smile faded, but he gave his patient an encouraging nod.

Selina's hands balled into fists in her lap.

'My dear friends and neighbours,' Bella began, 'I have something important to tell you, and a favour to ask.' She halted, and took a sip of wine, breathing heavily. 'The fact is, I'm dying. There's no hope, as Dr Ford will tell you, and I have mere weeks left. I don't know how many but I'm taking each day as it comes.'

'Good God,' Cameron exclaimed, his brows drawn together in shock.

His sister gasped. 'You poor dear thing. I'm so sorry.'

The elderly ladies said nothing but glanced at each other knowingly, as though they had already guessed Bella's sad news.

Bella managed a wavering smile. 'The favour I would like to ask is this … Will you please help and support my sister once I'm gone? She's going to stay on, you see, and care for the children. We haven't always been friends, my sister and I, but the finality of death has a way of making you see things differently. So I'm asking you to make my sister welcome at Thornton Hall and to lend any support you can in the days following my …' She couldn't quite finish, raising her napkin to her lips as a coughing fit shook her frail form. By the time she'd recovered, there were tears in her eyes. 'I hope I can count on you all to be there for Selina and my children.'

'Of course,' Helen murmured, gazing at Bella sympathetically.

'Yes, yes,' the sisters said in unison.

Mr Knowles and his wife also agreed heartily.

'You have my solemn oath,' Cameron said, looking deeply moved. 'Sebastian was my closest friend and I know what I owe his widow.'

Bella smiled faintly. 'There, Selina, didn't I tell you? They are the best friends and neighbours in the world. You won't have a thing to worry about.' She rose from the table, her gait unsteady. 'Now I must say goodnight. I'm afraid I'm rather tired.'

Selina got to her feet too, meaning to assist Bella to bed, but her sister shook her head.

'No, please stay with my guests,' Bella insisted. 'Mrs Hawley is waiting to help me upstairs.'

Left alone, Selina looked round at the others helplessly. She felt more like running after her sister than staying to exchange small talk with strangers. But if the war had taught her anything, it was that one could get through even the darkest moments simply by gritting one's teeth and getting on with it.

She took a deep breath. 'Coffee and brandy, anyone?'

'Excellent notion,' Mr MacGregor agreed, and gave her a reassuring smile.

CHAPTER TEN

Sheila poured tea into her best china cups, nodding towards the plate on the table. 'Help yourself to a slice of sponge cake, Margaret,' she said, perhaps a little gruffly.

It had been a hectic day at the shop, with a delivery arriving late afternoon that had worn out her bad knee, and then she had been cashing up when she'd spotted the figure of her sister looming in the doorway. Now she'd brought out the best tea service from Arnie's old sideboard, for goodness knows what reason. Her sister wasn't a best tea service visitor. She was a chipped mug person, assuming she was offered a sip of bloomin' tea at all.

Sheila gave a gusty sigh and shook her head at her own nonsensical thinking. Ever since she'd agreed to sit down for a brew with Margaret, she'd been regretting that rash decision. Yes, they were kin, but her sister had behaved so badly.

Lily would no doubt return later in the summer for Alice's wedding, and the fact that Sheila was back in touch with her attacker's wife would upset the poor girl and cause uproar in the family. And uproar was the last thing Sheila needed right now.

'Thank you.' Margaret took a thin slice of sponge cake and nibbled on it. She'd never had as much of an appetite as Sheila, even back when they were kids. No doubt because of that, and her thrifty ways, she wasn't as broad in the beam as Sheila. 'Though you called me Maggie when I visited you before.'

'Eh?' Sheila covered the teapot with a knitted cosy. 'Oh, yes … Well, you called me Shee,' she pointed out. 'Long time since anyone did that.'

'Don't you like it?'

'I'm a bit long in the tooth now to be anything but plain Sheila,' she said flatly, and drew out the chair opposite her sister. She'd locked the shop door and put up the closed sign, so there was no danger of them being interrupted. 'Listen, I know I said you could drop by for a cuppa. But there's nothing I can do. After what happened with Lily, Violet would be furious if I helped you.'

'And she's got good reason,' Margaret surprised her by saying. 'I closed my eyes to what Stan was like. I let him get away with—'

'Don't!' Sheila closed her eyes, swallowing. 'I can't bear to think of it. My poor granddaughter …'

After a brief silence, Margaret went on more quietly. 'I didn't try to help Violet when she took the girls away either. I should have put my foot down, made Stanley give them money towards new lodgings. Or driven her into Penzance, so she could speak to the evacuation housing officer.' There was a faint flush in Margaret's cheeks. 'Instead, I let my own niece walk out of there with those two girls and all their luggage, and not a blessed word said.'

'Violet did the right thing.'

'I know she did.' Margaret paused, peering at her. 'She's like you, Sheila. She always does the right thing.'

Sheila picked up her cup of tea, her gaze on the tablecloth. 'Don't you go buttering me up, Maggie, like you used to when we was kids and you wanted summat. I ain't a child no more, and we ain't proper family now. Not the way that word's meant.'

Margaret gave a muffled gasp.

Shooting her a glance, Sheila was horrified to see her sister crying. She put down her teacup and sat in shock. Margaret wasn't the crying sort. She didn't even cry at funerals.

'I'm sorry, but I … I've got nothing left to my name,' Margaret choked. 'If I can't turn to my own sister … God help me, Shee. Do you need me to beg? Because I will. I'll get down on my knees right here and beg if I must.' Margaret was staring at her, tears coursing down her cheeks. 'If you don't help me, I might as well be dead.'

For once in her life, Sheila didn't know what to say.

Two days after Margaret's disturbing visit, Sheila was still undecided. She knew offering to help her sister would cause no end of ructions with her daughter, but what made her dilemma worse was not feeling able to ask Violet's advice, for fear of the row that it would cause. She hated feeling like the weight of that decision rested on her shoulders alone …

She was at the vegetable rack, selecting a big leafy cabbage and some broad beans for a posh-spoken lady, picking out the best beans while she chatted about rationing and how strict government regulations were, when she caught a movement out of the corner of her eye.

Turning, she saw a grubby hand reach through the open doorway and grab a large pork pie she'd just unwrapped on the counter, ready for slicing into saleable portions.

''Ere, what d'you think you're doing?' she gasped.

But the thief had already darted out of the shop, taking the pork pie with him, before she'd even finished her question.

'Oi!' Furious, Sheila thrust the paper bag of broad beans at the lady she'd been serving, and hobbled as fast as she could across the shop.

But it was no good. She'd been up and down the cellar steps so frequently in recent weeks, fetching up heavy goods stored down there, that she'd put strain on her gammy knee, which was now hot and achy. It needed a good day's rest, which was impossible, given how busy the shop was keeping her. Not being as quick on her pins as usual, by the time she was standing in the village street, hands on hips, glaring up and down the hill, there was beggar all sign of her thief.

'Well, I don't believe it,' Sheila puffed angrily, limping back inside. 'Did you see that? Someone just swiped my pork pie. A great big 'un too. Cost me a pretty penny, that did. The supplier only dropped it off this morning.' Fuming, she collected the leafy green Savoy cabbage she'd picked out for the lady and carried it to the till, placing it alongside her other purchases. 'You might expect that kind of carry on in Penzance, but here in *Porthcurno*?'

'I couldn't agree more.' The customer placed her bag of broad beans on the counter and began rummaging in her plaid-covered shopping basket for her ration book.

'What am I meant to do now, eh?' Sheila weighed the broad beans and began stabbing at the heavy metal keys on the till, not paying much attention to what she was doing.

She kept seeing that grubby hand reaching in through the door, and wished she'd been quicker and caught the little blighter. 'I promised the coalman, Bert, a slice of that pork pie for his dinner tonight. He was coming in after work to collect it. Now I'll have to disappoint him.'

Sheila felt close to tears, and so discombobulated by the whole episode that she tore out the ration coupons very poorly, undercharged the lady for the four off-ration bottles of milk stout she was also buying, and was too flustered to correct her mistake.

'And I didn't even get a good look at the little sod,' she complained, knowing it was no good going to the police with so little information.

'Didn't you?' The well to-do lady, whose name Sheila didn't know, arched thin eyebrows at her. 'He's well known in the village. I'm surprised you didn't recognise him.'

'I didn't bloomin' see the rascal, he was in and out so fast.' Sheila frowned. 'Who is he, then?'

'Mrs Treedy's eldest boy, Jack. He's always been a troublemaker. Got himself thrown out of Sunday School when he was only eight years old, and that's quite an achievement. Reverend Clewson is a strong believer in compassion and turning the other cheek.' The lady chewed on her lip. 'Still, it's true you can hardly blame the boy.'

'Oh, can't I?' Sheila muttered rebelliously, helping to pack her basket.

'Mrs Treedy lost her husband in the war and likely has no income beyond her widow's pension. And with so many children … It's a shame.' The woman pursed thin lips. 'But stealing is not only a crime, it's a sin. So we can't be *too* forgiving, can we?'

Sheila, who wasn't sure she believed in sin, though she certainly believed in crime, abruptly remembered who this lady was. Another of the vicar's cronies from the big posh houses beyond the village. She was also a regular churchgoer, unlike Sheila, who rarely bothered with church now that Arnie was no longer there to keep her company. Not that Sheila disapproved of prayers, in the general way, and she loved hymns, belting them out as loud as she could. But all that kneeling in a draughty old church played havoc with her joints.

'Jack Treedy,' she repeated bitterly. 'Yes, I know who you mean, and I've seen the lad hanging about the shop. Not buying anything, of course. Just waiting for me to be distracted, so he could dash in and pinch summat.' Sheila took a deep breath and tried to calm down. It was only a pork pie. But she knew something had to be done about it. Or he'd soon be back for more loot. 'I'll have to close the shop and pay a visit to his mother. If I go now, maybe I'll get me pie back. Assumin' he ain't gobbled it already, that is.'

Sending the lady on her way with hurried thanks, Sheila dragged on her hat and cardigan, and then locked up the shop, not even bothering to remove her work apron and clogs, as she didn't expect this mission to take long.

With a nod to a passing farmer on his tractor, she marched downhill and along the narrow, overgrown lane where a cluster of old cottages crowded together, higgledy-piggledy, out of sight of the main road. She knew from listening to local gossip that the Treedy family lived along that lane, and soon realised she'd tracked down her quarry on spotting two barefoot girls in pinafore dresses playing hopscotch in the dust outside one of the more unkempt, ramshackle cottages.

'You not at school?' she asked the older girl sharply, and was given a blank stare before the child ran inside the house, dragging her giggling younger sibling behind her.

'Mam! Mam!' the child piped in a high-pitched voice. 'Visitor for you.'

Mrs Treedy herself appeared in the doorway, smoothing down dishevelled hair, a stricken look on her face as she realised who her 'visitor' was.

Yes, missus, Sheila thought crossly, folding her arms across a heaving chest. *You may well look scared.* Why, the woman was no better than horrid old Fagin in that Dickens story, sending kids out to beg and steal for her.

'Your boy Jack just stole a pork pie from my shop,' Sheila said without preamble.

'Jack?' Mrs Treedy called over her shoulder, not taking her eyes off Sheila. The boy slunk up behind her in the doorway and she glanced down at him. 'Mrs Newton says you stole something from her shop. Is that true?'

The boy shrugged, looking away.

'Go and get it,' his mother told him, and he disappeared, coming back with Sheila's pork pie. Her face fell on seeing it. 'You idiot … Give it back to her.'

A surly look on his face, Jack trudged across the yard to hand back the pie. Sheila took it, saying nothing. She was still angry, but embarrassed now too.

As the boy tried to slip past his mother, Mrs Treedy told him shrilly, 'Don't you ever let me catch you stealing again, you hear?'

There was no more to say on the matter. Sheila had her pie back and it looked untouched.

Sheila turned away. But Mrs Treedy hurried after her. 'I'm

sorry, Mrs Newton. You won't tell the police, will you?' There was desperation in her voice. 'Jack … He's a good lad, at heart. And he was only trying to help me out.'

'By stealing?' Sheila stared at her.

There was a high flush in the woman's cheeks, facing down that stare, and her mouth trembled as she said stiffly, 'I do my level best to put food on the table every day, to stretch the ration book as far as it'll go, but me and Jack often have to go without so the little ones can eat. I expect he was hungry, that's all. And maybe he thought a nice big pie like that one would feed the whole family, with gravy and veg on the side.' Her gaze dropped hungrily to the pie in Sheila's hands. 'He did wrong and he'll make it up to you, I swear. I'll send him round to clean the shop windows tomorrow, how's that?'

Me and Jack often have to go without so the little ones can eat.

Wracked by guilt, horrified at the thought of the widow's children going hungry while she marched away with her huge pork pie like a trophy, Sheila came to a decision.

She thrust the pie back towards Mrs Treedy. 'Go on then, take it.'

Stunned, Mrs Treedy gaped. 'What?'

'You heard me, love. You can take the pie and welcome. I'll not have you and your kids go hungry while I've a big dinner waiting for me up at the farm.' She kept holding out the pork pie and eventually Mrs Treedy took it, though the woman still looked doubtful. 'You can still send your boy round to clean the shop windows though. In return for the pie. That would be much appreciated.'

'Thank … Thank you.' Mrs Treedy drew the pie close, sniffing at it in dreamy amazement. 'Bless you.'

'Well, enjoy your dinner.' And with that, Sheila stamped back up the lane and towards her shop. The whole way, she was thinking, *what a soft touch I am. Giving away that bloomin' huge pork pie! I'll never make my money back on it now.* But deep down she knew she'd done the right thing.

What she didn't understand was why it was necessary. The war was over, wasn't it? The grief and hardship they'd all suffered during those dark years ought to have come to an end when the soldiers had laid down their arms and the bells had rung out for victory. Instead, it seemed that some people were still struggling to feed themselves and, judging by what she'd seen of Mrs Treedy's ragged children, to clothe themselves as well.

There was a hill walker with a backpack and stick waiting impatiently outside the shop for it to reopen.

'It ain't right,' she muttered, unlocking the door and glaring at the man. 'What did our boys die for, eh? So that folk back home could go hungry? It ain't right, I tell you. This country's going to the dogs.'

'Quite so,' the man stammered, producing a ration book from his backpack. He pointed to the sweet jars behind the counter. 'Aniseed balls, please. Two ounces. And do you have any pear drops?'

CHAPTER ELEVEN

Joan woke from dreaming, alone in the grey light of pre-dawn now that Tilly had moved in with Caroline next door. Suffocating and shaken, she threw back the covers, gasping for air.

In her nightmare, she'd been pushed up against a wall while a man in uniform pawed at her and slobbered wet kisses over her face.

But it was less of a nightmare and more of a memory. In the early years of the war, she'd been working in a factory, far from friends and family, and excited by the promise of alcohol and dancing at a Christmas party after months of dreary, repetitive work.

She'd been dancing with her friends when soldiers on leave had rolled in off the street. They'd clearly been drinking but seemed merry enough with it. So she'd danced with a few of them, enjoying herself for the first time in ages. She'd been drinking too and the next thing she knew, one of the soldier boys had pulled her away from her friends and was kissing her in a corner. Not just kissing either. His hands had been all over her.

She'd pushed at the man's chest, crying out for help. Thankfully, another soldier had pulled the drunken man away, sending him sprawling. Otherwise, goodness knows what might've happened, under cover of all that maddening noise and music.

Joan sank back against the pillows, tormented.

What had Violet said about Arthur Green? *Not quite right.* And she knew what that meant. That Arthur had come back from war shell-shocked, suffering mental distress. Of course, it was almost commonplace these days for soldiers to come home in a state of anguish. But Violet had made his condition sound like more than that.

On impulse, scrambling out of bed, Joan rummaged for paper and filled a pen with fresh ink.

Dear Arthur, she wrote hastily, and then stopped, sucking the end of her pen.

How to ask a man if he had been badly affected by the war without risking offence? The last thing she wanted was to upset him.

I can't see you this week, she began carefully, heart thumping, but knew before she'd even finished those words that she couldn't obey Violet's injunction never to see him again. The mere thought distressed her. Besides, why should she? She was a member of the Women's Land Army, not Violet and Joe's employee. The couple had no right to tell her who she could or couldn't meet outside work times. And Arthur should be allowed a chance to prove himself.

But maybe next Thursday instead?

Her heart lightening, she went on to remind him how best to organise the books in the library, and suggested a time they could meet.

131

Yes, it was a revolt against Violet's strict rules, and she did feel guilty about it, but what the eye doesn't see, the heart can't grieve over, as Mrs Newton might have said. What harm could it do to see Arthur Green again, after all? Just the thought of his smile soon had her lips curling upwards, that horrid nightmare forgotten …

All week, she toiled harder than ever at the farm, trudging up and down the deep soil rills with the other girls, scattering seed and pulling out any weeds she spotted. Usually, she found this repetitive work boring, but now she barely noticed time flying past, her mind engaged in thinking up ways to broach the delicate topic of Arthur's time in the war …

On Thursday afternoon, the three girls walked down the steep hill to the Penzance bus together, as planned. But, as soon as the bus trundled into view, she gave the other two a cheery wave and skipped off.

'Not a word to Violet, all right?' She couldn't believe what she was saying. It wasn't like her to misbehave. But it had to be done if she wanted to keep seeing Arthur.

'Mum's the word, cross my heart and hope to die,' Tilly shouted after her, crossing herself fervently. 'Have fun with Arthur!'

Caroline simply giggled, the two girls clutching each other with undisguised amusement as they boarded the bus to Penzance, heading for the shops.

It was a long walk, and a hot afternoon, but Joan couldn't have borrowed the bicycle again as that would have alerted Violet to her intentions. Cautiously, she also skirted the village shop, in case Mrs Newton happened to be looking out of the window. Once free of this danger, she strode on past the green, heading for the distant church and the lane beyond it.

When she reached the big house, Arthur was sitting on the front step, waiting for her, dressed in his usual baggy trousers with a white shirt and brown tie, sleeves rolled up to the elbow. He jumped up with a grin, his tie flapping, saying, 'Hullo, I was beginning to think you wouldn't make it again.'

'I'm sorry I'm late. Did you get my note last week?'

'Yes, thank you.' He smoothed back the fair hair that had flopped over his forehead. 'It was a pity you couldn't come. But I muddled through and managed to follow your scheme. Still plenty more to do up there, if you're game.'

'It's such a lovely afternoon though,' she said shyly, glancing about at the beautiful gardens that lay in full sunshine. 'Maybe we could go for a quick walk before we start work?'

His brows rose but he readily agreed. 'There's a nice rhododendron walk this way,' he said, leading her round the back of the house, where lichened stone steps led down to a path shaded with towering rhododendrons, their deep-pink, red and white flowers hanging about them like coloured lanterns. It was cool and intimate down there, out of the sun, the sky barely visible above thick foliage, like walking through a secret passageway …

'Oh, this is lovely,' she exclaimed.

'Isn't it?' Arthur seemed pleased, ducking his head and brushing aside a low-hanging branch for her. 'I often come down here when the house gets too stuffy. I love all those old books, but sometimes you just need to clear your head, don't you?'

This gave her an opening she couldn't ignore. 'Yes,' she said softly, and stopped, looking up into his face. His smile was so open and friendly that guilt assailed her. But with Violet's words still ringing in her ears, she pressed on, warmth in her cheeks as she stammered, 'That is, I *think* I understand what you mean. I've felt like that in the past. When things get too much for you,' her gaze searched his face, 'and when other people don't know what you've been through, that makes everything so much worse.'

His smile had faded, his brows tugging together. 'I suppose so.'

'Especially if people *talk*.'

There was a moment's stillness, then Arthur turned away and walked on a few faltering steps. 'Yes, I see,' he said in a choking voice.

She didn't follow, her heart thumping. Had she said too much? He was clearly upset. The one thing she'd been hoping to avoid.

His hands had clenched into fists by his sides, his bearing stiff. Trepidation filled her.

'I'm so sorry if I've said something to upset you,' she whispered, abruptly remembering Violet's warnings and wondering if she should return to the house.

They were all alone out here … Was it possible that he was *dangerous*?

His head had been bowed, but Arthur straightened at this, turning with what seemed a pitiful effort at a smile. 'No, no,' he insisted in bracing tones, and relaxed his hands, thrusting them into his pockets instead. 'Good Lord, no … You could never upset me.' His voice cracked, but he cleared his throat and squared his shoulders. 'Please, just ignore me.'

They strolled on along the rhododendron walk together,

134

but at a slower pace. He was solemn now, his gaze bent on the ground.

She couldn't stand it. 'Arthur, what's wrong?'

'Nothing, nothing.'

'Oh, please don't lie. Not to me.' Urgently, she caught at his shirt sleeve and they stopped again. 'I thought we were friends.'

'We are,' he told her doggedly.

'Then be honest with me. Even if it's not easy.' She bit her lip, seeing a flash of agony in his face. 'I'm sorry. But the thing is, Violet said something … The farmer's wife, up at Postbridge Farm. She said …' Joan had meant to be straight with him, hoping for the same courtesy in return, only she couldn't go on, seeing his fierce expression.

'Yes, what did she say?' he demanded.

Joan hesitated, more cautious now, not wanting to betray Violet's trust. 'I'm not sure if I should—'

'Please.' He swallowed and closed his eyes, a spasm passing over his face as he repeated more softly, 'Please, Joan.'

If he had spoken harshly, she would have turned and run, and probably never agreed to see him again. But there was such a terrible despair in that one repeated word that it left her defenceless.

'Violet said you'd come back from the war a changed man. That you … That you weren't *quite right*.'

Arthur sank his face into his hands and groaned, bending over.

'I'm sorry,' she whispered.

He stayed bent over for a good minute, causing her concern for his well-being, then finally straightened, shaking his head. He took a few deep breaths before managing a crooked smile. 'Don't be, please. It's not your fault. It's mine, in fact. That damn war …' He stopped himself with a visible effort and looked away, hands thrust in his pockets again. 'Look, I'll walk you home, if you'd like. You don't need to come inside. I'll quite understand.'

'Go home?' Shock gripped her as she realised what he meant, what he was thinking. 'I don't want to go home.'

'But—'

'I'm not scared of you,' she burst out, and saw his tortured stare return to her face in wonder. 'That wasn't why I asked. Oh, hang it all. I only asked about your past because I wanted you to know that I understand.'

'You do?' He sounded puzzled now.

'It's not the same, I know. Could never be the same.' She struggled through her confused thoughts, groping for the truth of the matter. 'I've never been to war, for a start, so it's not in any way equal. But things have happened to me that …' She ground to a halt, breathless, unable to go on.

For a few brutal seconds, she was back in that dark noisy room, the burly soldier's hands pawing at her. She could almost smell his breath, taste the cigarette smoke on his lips, feel the crushing weight of his body as she fought in vain to push his bulk away …

'I suffer from nightmares,' she choked out, her chest tight. Their gazes locked together in a welter of understanding. 'The same nightmares every time. When I wake up, my heart's beating so fast … and it hangs over me all day. I don't find it easy to talk to people. Everyone assumes it's because I'm shy but that's not true. I can't help it but—' She couldn't go on.

'But you're trapped in it. No escape.'

'Yes,' she breathed.

'Oh, Joan …' His voice had deepened in sympathy. Gently, he placed a hand on her shoulder, the same way he'd soothed the nervous lamb in his satchel with a touch. She felt a blooming of new strength inside, even though he'd barely touched her. 'What happened? Are you able to tell me?' His astute gaze searched her face. 'What did he do to you?'

The simple knowledge that he understood her pain without needing it explained was enough to release a weight from her mind that had been crushing her for years. She wasn't strong enough to push any further into that nightmare memory though.

'I want to tell you, honestly.' Tears sprang to her eyes as she shook her head, stammering, 'But I can't.'

'Of course not.' Arthur stepped back, his hands in his pockets again. His gaze rested on her face, soft and undemanding. 'Well, let's go inside, shall we? I'll rustle up a pot of tea and a slice of Mrs Penhallow's cake, and we'll go back to cataloguing those musty old books. No more said about this.' His smile was encouraging. 'How's that?'

She returned his smile, feeling better at once. It was as though helping her with that past pain had eased his own. And she felt the same.

'Golly, sounds fun,' she managed to say, with a jerky nod of her head.

He turned on his heel, looking about speculatively, then plucked a deep pink rhododendron bloom from the thick rustling foliage and tucked it behind her ear.

'There,' he murmured, smoothing back her hair. 'Now you could be Persephone herself.'

She blushed, shivering at the touch of his fingers against her cheek. 'The goddess of spring?'

'Exactly.' He grinned. 'Though I'm no Pluto. Only tea and cake on offer here, no pomegranate seeds, I promise.'

Joan gave a gurgling laugh, not sure where to look.

They walked back up to the house together, shoulder to shoulder under the low-hanging rhododendrons, hands close but not quite touching. The world was sparkling after last night's rain, the back windows of the grange dazzling her with reflected sunlight. She could smell salt and even hear the soft, distant whisper of waves on the white sands at Porthcurno beach, the air was so still.

She wished that she could have been more open with him. She had never told anyone else about the horrible events of that night, too wracked with shame even to admit what had happened. Also, women were often blamed for things men did to them, even when they'd done nothing wrong or had merely been too trusting. And yet with Arthur, mentioning that deep-buried episode had felt so natural. Perhaps she ought to have explained everything. But he hadn't seemed to need the details, understanding instinctively. *What did he do to you?* Nor had he pointed out the difference between the horrors he must have experienced on the battlefield and her own barely comparable upset.

She had found a friend at last, she thought in wonder, aware of an inner lightening of her burdens. No, not merely a friend, Joan corrected herself, drawing the fresh Cornish air deep into her lungs. A kindred spirit.

CHAPTER TWELVE

It was a beautiful day in early June, the sun soft on the moors, when Bella reached the end of her life's journey. Selina knew she would remember that dreadful day for the rest of her life. Hearing from Mrs Hawley that Bella had worsened during the night, she hurried there soon after rising to find her sister in a bad state, gasping for breath, a high flush in her cheeks. The doctor was called but there was nothing to be done, except to ease Bella's pain as best they could. At around noon, the doctor suggested solemnly that the vicar should be called, and one of the gardening boys was sent running for him.

'My children … I must see them …' Bella rasped in a hoarse voice, her desperate gaze seeking out Selina's. She was slumped, resting against a bank of pillows, for she'd asked to see out of the window and across the moorlands in her last hours.

'I'll fetch them to you, ma'am.' Mrs Hawley, who had been tidying Bella's bedlinen, hurried away at once.

While they waited for the children, Selina held her sister's hand. 'I wish I'd come to you sooner. That I'd known about your illness earlier …' Choking with tears, Selina bowed her head, unable to go on.

But her sister's limp fingers stirred within hers. 'That was my fault,' Bella whispered. 'I should have kept in touch.' There was silence for a while, then her sister stirred at the sound of her children running up the stairs. 'They need love, Selly … You will love my little ones, won't you? Swear to me.'

'Of course.' Tears were running down Selina's cheeks. 'I swear it on my life. I'll love them like they're my own.'

Her sister seemed satisfied by this, and as the door burst open, she struggled to smile, rasping in a dreadful whisper, 'Come to Mummy, my darlings.'

Selina watched helplessly over the next few hours, as the children came and went, sitting with their mother at times, then hurrying downstairs for a meal, then returning with anxious stares and pale silences. Jemima sat tense and wide-eyed. Peter's eyes brimmed constantly with tears. Only little Faith didn't know what was happening to her mother. Yet even she understood that everything was about to change for them, sobbing her heart out as she lay nestled against her mother, listening to the hollow drag of her breathing.

Bella passed away in the early hours. It was not an easy death, but fortunately, after a final farewell, Selina had taken the decision to send the children to bed. She knew it would leave a lasting scar on those children to witness their mother's demise, and hoped she was making the right decision. So each child kissed Bella on the cheek and then wept bitterly as Mrs Hawley took them away for the last time.

Bella was beyond words by then, though there was still intelligence in her eyes as she kissed her children goodbye.

Once they'd gone, she turned her gaze to the doctor and his bottle of morphine.

In the silence that followed their departure, she lay more quietly, as though resigned to the end, perhaps even keen to end her suffering. The doctor administered a large dose of morphine, and Bella sighed, lapsing into a coma-like sleep. Selina dabbed at her forehead and cheeks with a damp cloth, and held her hand, speaking to her in a soft voice, reassuring her sister how much she was loved, and that she would soon be seeing Sebastian again.

Then it was over, and Selina was free to weep at last. The doctor felt for her sister's pulse, then nodded. 'She's gone. I'm very sorry for your loss, my dear.'

Somehow, Selina found the strength to thank him, and to dry her eyes, before stumbling away to snatch a few hours' rest before she had to face the children. She fell asleep at last through sheer exhaustion, grimly rehearsing the words she would need to say to her nieces and nephew in the morning.

The first week after her sister's death was a blur of sleepless nights and frantically busy days, mostly spent making arrangements for Bella's funeral. Putting notices in the local and national papers, informing friends and family and neighbours, some of the more personal notes having already been dictated by Bella herself while she was still able. Selina spoke with the solicitor on several occasions, and sat silent and depressed through the reading of her sister's Last Will and Testament. For this, Peter and Jemima were also present, along with a few others who were receiving small legacies.

On the day before the funeral, Selina decided to take some time for herself, to walk in the grounds in hazy sunlight and recall her own childhood, when her much older sister had been like a mother to her after they'd lost their parents.

She had penned a short letter to Caroline at Postbridge Farm, outlining everything that had occurred since she'd come to Bodmin Moor, and asking her to let Violet know that her sister had died, and that she would definitely not be returning to Porthcurno. She could have handed this letter to Mrs Hawley to put into the post, but decided to post it herself instead. There was a small postbox set into the wall of a house a few miles away, and it was a lovely afternoon for a walk. And perhaps she would find some peace in the solitude of the moors.

She had posted her letter and was on her way back to Thornton Hall, her face tilted to the sun, recalling long summer days on the farm and how she might have been out in the fields since dawn if she were still there. Instead, her only duties involved keeping track of the older two children once they'd finished with their tutor, little Faith spending much of her day with the nurse. She had not spoken much to Martha, the nanny, a sallow-faced girl with elaborate hair, who often dressed inappropriately for her job, with a hemline shorter than it ought to be and clothes too small for her generous form. But Selina saw something of herself in the younger woman, a desperation to be noticed that had led to that dreadful situation with Johnny. So she said nothing, and tried not to respond to Mrs Hawley's tutting shakes of the head whenever Martha turned up in some provocative outfit. The girl would learn in time, and Selina didn't feel it was her place to comment. Not as a relative newcomer to the household. And it wasn't as though she was Martha's employer.

Though, she considered carefully, was she not Martha's employer now? If not, then who was? The solicitor had been tasked with paying household bills and staff wages until Peter came of age, but he was hardly overseeing the household as Selina had been asked to do as part of her 'duties'. It was a grey area, so she could theoretically be seen as the nanny's employer, at least in terms of being in a position to have her dismissed. This added responsibility came as a shock. She'd only been the legal guardian to her young nieces and nephew for a few days, and was not yet accustomed to that unexpected burden. Now it seemed she might have power to hire and fire at Thornton Hall, or at least to advise the solicitor on such matters. For he had so far deferred to her judgement where the funeral was concerned, not making any decisions himself. But he would surely also do so where the household was concerned. For Mr MacGregor knew little of what happened there on a daily basis.

Summer heat had burnt off the clouds and the sunshine was finally radiant when a car drew alongside Selina with a toot of its horn.

She nearly jumped out of her skin, so deep in her thoughts she hadn't even heard a vehicle approaching, and turned to find a young man behind the wheel of a swish-looking car, its hood folded down for the good weather, sun glinting off the chrome and metalwork.

'Hullo,' he said with a smile, jumping out and removing his cap politely. 'Did I startle you, Miss Tiptree? I'm awfully sorry.'

It was Mr Bourne, their closest neighbour on the moor. She hadn't seen the young man since the evening of the dinner party, when Bella had admitted to her terminal condition, though he and his sister Helen had written a note of support soon after, and had swiftly replied to the funeral notice with their heartfelt condolences.

'No need to apologise, I was miles away. Head in the clouds as always,' she assured him shyly.

'Need a lift?' he asked.

'Oh.' She suddenly realised his car was headed in the same direction. 'That's very kind, but …'

'But you'd like a chance to get a proper walk on such a glorious day?' He nodded at her awkward hesitation, stripping off a leather driving glove and thrusting out a hand to her. 'Of course. It's good to see you, anyway. And my condolences again.'

Glad that he didn't seem offended by her refusal, Selina smiled and shook hands with him. 'Thank you. Are you off somewhere nice?'

'Hardly. Some stuffy business meeting at the bank in Launceston.' He saw her frown at the name of the town, and grinned. 'Next big town on the way to Exeter. The old capital of Cornwall. Not a huge place but it has a good market and some nice ruins. An old Norman castle, you know?'

'Sounds … fun.'

Cameron laughed at her uncertain expression. 'Mouldy ruins not your sort of thing?' He replaced his cap. 'They have a few dress shops too, if that's more up your alley. And a good tea shop or two. Maybe I could take you for a drive there one day?' Taken aback by this offer, Selina stammered something incoherent, and he hurriedly added, 'Sorry, I didn't mean to embarrass you. I just thought … given your loss, you might fancy a day away from the house.'

'That's very kind of you,' she began, meeting his friendly gaze with a smile, and felt a shock of recognition at the look on his face. She had seen that same expression on Johnny's face too often not to know what it meant. Cameron Bourne found her attractive. And while at any other time she might have been flattered, and even interested in return, for he was hardly a dud in the looks department, the sudden racing of her heart warned her that she was in danger.

Her hands turned clammy, curling in to press fingernails deep in her palm. The last thing she wanted was to lurch straight from Johnny's betrayal into another disastrous crush.

At once, her intended acceptance turned to another refusal. 'But the thing is, I'm so busy at the moment, I'm afraid I couldn't be spared for such a long drive. The children ...' She let that sentence drift away with an apologetic look.

'Oh Lord, yes. Sebastian's poor children ... You're right, they must need their aunt badly just now.' Cameron climbed back into the car, not meeting her eyes again. He fiddled with the gear levers. 'You know I served with Seb in France. He was a damn good sort. When he died, I ...' With a sudden grimace, Cameron stopped and shook his head. 'Well, I'm sure you don't want to hear any more depressing stories. War's over and we all need to look to the future now ... Isn't that what they say?' He threw her a brief smile. 'I'd better let you get on. Maybe we could take a drive out together one day? Somewhere closer than Launceston.'

'Maybe,' she agreed in a non-committal way, and stood back as he drove on with a wave of his hand. 'Oh, all my best to your sister,' she called after him, belatedly remembering her manners.

But Cameron had already accelerated away in a cloud of dust, along the winding country lane that led past Thornton Hall onto the wild desolate beauty of Bodmin Moor.

Selina kept walking, her steps hurrying now. Perhaps she ought to have accepted his offer of a lift. She'd been away longer than planned, according to her wristwatch, and the children might need her.

But that brief encounter with Cameron Bourne had given her much to think about. Bella had managed to tell her more about Helen Bourne's past the day after the dinner party. Sebastian March had been the younger of two sons, and his brother and heir to the property, James, had once been sweet on Helen. It had all ended in tears when the two families argued about a land boundary issue, and James, perhaps naturally, took his father's side in the dispute. He'd snubbed Helen publicly, humiliating her and deepening the chasm between their families. Then James had died in a riding accident, breaking his neck during a moorland hunt, and by all accounts Helen had been heartbroken.

There'd been bitter enmity between all parties for a few years after James' death, but then Sebastian's father had died, swiftly followed by Mr Bourne. And Bella herself had urged her new husband to make up with the younger Bournes, finding it uncomfortable to be at war with their closest neighbour. The disputed boundary had been ceded to the Bournes, and peace had reigned between them ever since …

Except that Helen had never quite regained her 'bloom' according to Bella, and it was whispered locally that she would never marry now, preferring to keep house for her bachelor brother.

Bella's solemn funeral took place at Bodmin Parish Church. Afterwards, there was a wake at Thornton Hall. For the wake, Selina had gratefully left most of the arrangements to Mrs

Hawley and her kitchen assistant, and so merely had to shake hands with guests and murmur, 'Thank you so much,' a few dozen times to kind expressions of condolence.

Like her, all three children had wept at the graveside. But while Selina had hugged the two girls, one on either side, Peter had stood apart, stiff-backed, trying manfully to hide his tears. The boy might only be fourteen, but he was clearly determined to act older than his years now he was the man of the house. And if that helped him cope with his grief, why not?

After the wake, Selina left the staff clearing up and took the two girls up to the nursery before their bedtime. There, she sat on the floor as though a child herself, playing with building bricks and china dolls to keep them company, while the nanny looked on disapprovingly. To her surprise, Peter didn't vanish straight off to his own bedroom, as she'd half expected, but stayed with them, exclaiming over an old train set he'd forgotten since his nursery days, and running it enthusiastically over a circular track also unearthed from the toy chest.

When it was time for Faith to go to bed, Peter tidied away the train and track, shook Selina's hand in an adult manner, and disappeared off for 'a walk in the grounds'.

It was coming on to rain by then, but she didn't stop him going. Young Peter was an orphan now and his life would never be the same again. She remembered how she herself had suffered following the loss of both her parents. The boy needed time alone to get used to his new reality and she didn't intend to interfere with that process.

The younger children would need more help to get through their grief though. Dismissing the nanny, she tucked

Faith into bed herself and even sang a nursery rhyme that she recalled her own mother singing. Jemima, listening in surprise, told her, 'That's the same song Mummy used to sing to us at bedtime too. How did you know?'

That almost broke her heart.

Once Jemima had finally gone to bed, and Peter was back inside and safely accounted for, Selina wandered through the empty downstairs rooms in the slow, lonely hour before suppertime.

Cameron and Helen Bourne had invited her to dine with them, no doubt intending to spare her an evening alone after her sister's funeral, but she'd declined, deciding it was better to get used to being alone. Mr MacGregor had also offered to stay and keep her company, but again she'd politely refused. She still suspected the solicitor's motives and didn't want to give him the false impression that she was interested in anything beyond mere friendship.

'Your dinner's on the table, Miss Tiptree,' Mrs Hawley said, finding her at last in the drawing room, where she'd turned on the radio for a little company. Her look was sympathetic. 'Would you like me to bring the wireless through so you can listen to music while you eat?'

'Thank you, that would be lovely.'

Once Mrs Hawley had returned to the kitchen, Selina sat on her own, spoon in hand, peering into her soup.

She didn't recognise the music on the wireless but it was soothing and helped dispel the silence. At least it wasn't a presenter droning on about food rationing or how things were going with the rebuilding of London and other major cities in the wake of the Blitz.

She looked about at the empty seats on each side of the

long dining table and wondered idly about inviting Caroline to visit. That would be fun. Except that Caroline would be needed at the farm all summer, she reminded herself. Land Girls couldn't just take holidays as and when they chose. The only reason she'd been released from her own work was because she had children to care for now.

But perhaps her friend could be spared for a few days … It would be good to see Caro again, and hear all the gossip from Postbridge Farm and Porthcurno.

Putting down her spoon. Selina burst into scalding tears, and was still weeping helplessly when she heard Mrs Hawley's firm tread along the passageway, no doubt coming back to collect her empty bowl and present her with the main course.

Hurriedly, she seized her napkin and dabbed at her wet cheeks and eyes.

'It was delicious but I'm afraid I couldn't finish it all,' she babbled as the housekeeper came in. 'I'm sorry, I don't know what's happened to my appetite.'

Mrs Hawley looked at her with soft eyes. 'You've just lost your sister, Miss. Of course you've no appetite.' She took away the half-eaten soup, and replaced it with a plate of cold mutton with new potatoes and spinach. 'Tomorrow will be better. Besides, you need to eat. Your sister would have wanted you to keep your strength up, wouldn't she?' She paused, adding temptingly, 'It's roly-poly with custard for pudding tonight.'

Selina managed a shaky smile in return. 'Roly-poly with custard? How delicious, I haven't had that in yonks. Thanks ever so, Mrs H.'

The housekeeper was right, she thought, left alone once more with her modest supper and a fresh cup of tea;

tomorrow would be better. And she did need to keep her strength up. She could hardly look after those three children properly if all she did was sit around blubbing and feeling sorry for herself.

Throwing aside the napkin, Selina squared her shoulders and began to eat.

CHAPTER THIRTEEN

Sheila was spooning hot oats into breakfast bowls when Caroline came into the kitchen looking pale and red-eyed. ''Ere, what's up, love?' she asked with a frown, scraping the last of the porridge oats into her own bowl. Not quite a full helping maybe, but she'd been picking at the lemon sherbets and pear drops lately, bored in the long, dreary intervals between customers at the shop, and needed to watch her figure. 'You look like you lost a shilling and found a sixpence.'

The Land Girl took an envelope from her pocket – the letter she'd received in yesterday's post, by the look of it, and laid it on the table beside her bowl. 'Dreadful news from Selly,' Caroline mumbled, sitting down with slumped shoulders and downcast eyes. Sheila thought she'd never seen the girl so miserable since the day her friend had left. 'Her sister's died.'

'Oh no,' Violet exclaimed, setting the brimming milk jug down so hard it spilt on the table. 'Poor Selina ... So soon? Why, it feels like barely five minutes since she went off to Bodmin.'

'Aye, that's bad news,' Joe agreed heavily, tucking into his porridge with a hearty appetite.

Having put the dirty pan to soak in cold water, Sheila poured a little cream into her bowl, along with a dollop of honey. A soul still had to eat, she thought defensively.

'Remind me, how many kids did her sister leave behind?' Violet was asking, stirring a small amount of porridge into some cold milk for Sarah Jane.

'Three,' Caroline said, staring down at her breakfast without touching it. 'And the youngest only four years old.'

'Oh, poor lambs,' Violet said feelingly. She turned to fuss with her daughter's bib as the child sat kicking chubby legs back-and-forth in the high chair. 'I couldn't bear to think of my little Sarah Jane left all alone without her mum.'

'It's very sad, but you should still eat up, Caroline,' Sheila said stoutly. It was well past dawn, and the Land Girls were due out in the lower fields with Joe soon, to check the growing crops for weeds and pests. It was a back-breaking task that often took most of the day. 'I know you're unhappy about your friend but you won't help anyone by wasting away.'

Tilly snorted, presumably at the idea of Caroline, who'd always been on the big-boned side, wasting away. But she lapsed into silence when Sheila shot her a quelling look.

'Talking of wasting away,' Violet said with a frown, pointing her spoon at Sheila's bowl, 'what size portion d'you call that, Mum? I've never seen you eat so little. That wouldn't keep a sparrow alive.'

All eyes turned to Sheila.

Embarrassed, she replied testily, 'Don't fuss, Vi. I'll have a pasty for my lunch. That'll do me, and handsome.'

She laid aside her spoon, having already emptied the bowl. Perhaps her breakfast had been on the meagre side, she thought, licking her lips and gazing hungrily around as the others continued to eat.

Ernest strode into the kitchen with a briefcase and stopped to study the breakfast table. 'Porridge again, is it?'

Sheila looked at her son-in-law suspiciously but there was no hint of accusation on his face. 'It's cheap,' she said flatly, 'and we've no bacon. Not until them piglets grow a little bigger.'

Joan sucked in a sharp breath, looking round at her wide-eyed, and even level-headed Tilly shuddered.

Sheila shook her head pityingly, taking a gulp of lukewarm tea. What on earth did these girls think the pigs were for, if not eating?

'I'm afraid there's no porridge left.' Violet half rose, grimacing. 'Would you like me to find you something else?'

'No need,' Ernest said, grabbing his coat and hat. 'I'm on the early shift today, so I'll eat in the canteen at Eastern House, assuming I get time.' He ruffled Sarah Jane's hair and strode out on his way to work with a nod to everyone else.

Ernest rarely talked about what he did down at the listening post in Porthcurno but since they'd grown accustomed to such secret work during the war, nobody dared ask for details anyway. It was still miraculous to Sheila that Ernest had come through the war years unscathed, given he'd been a spy in foreign territory all that time, as a native German speaker. The tragedy was that he'd been away from home when they'd lost his wife Betsy, and with everyone thinking he was 'missing, presumed dead' – the government's official story for his disappearance – her grieving granddaughters had wrongly believed they were orphans. She could see the reasoning behind it now, but blimey, them had been tough years for Alice and Lily. For all of them, indeed.

At least Ernest had chosen not to go back to London after the war, preferring to be nearer Lily and his young grandson Morris in Penzance. He'd been a good father since his return, Sheila had to give him that.

'Would you like some of my porridge, Mrs Newton?' Caroline offered wanly. 'I'm not sure I'm going to finish it.'

'Very kind but no thanks,' Sheila insisted, rising to freshen the teapot with some hot water. 'The truth is, I'm trying to watch my weight.' As a chorus of protests – and a rumble of laughter from Joe – broke out behind her, she confessed, 'I've been helping myself to the sweet jars at the shop, ain't I? Now my waistband's too tight, that's all.'

'Mum!' Violet looked shocked.

'You could get into trouble doing that,' Joe remarked placidly. 'Rationing regulations being what they are. I recall Arnie having to account for every last bean to the ration officer.'

'Blimey, Joe's right,' Violet breathed, going pale. 'You'll have to make it up, Mum. Or you could be done for fraud.'

'A jailbird mother-in-law.' Joe reached for his tea mug with a quirk of his mouth. 'Don't fret, Sheila, I'll visit you in jail. And bring you a file in a cake, if I remember.'

Tilly snorted again. Seeing Violet's glare, the girl got up hurriedly to carry her bowl to the sink.

'That ain't funny, Joe,' his wife snapped.

Joe raised bushy brows. 'What makes you think I was joking?'

'Fiddlesticks.' Sheila thought guiltily of the pork pie she'd given to Mrs Treedy. But she shouldn't have to account for her actions to anyone, least of all her own daughter, she thought impatiently. 'Nobody's goin' to cart me off to the magistrates over a handful of missing sweeties.'

Thankfully, little Sarah Jane dropped her spoon at that moment and began to wail, so that Violet had to turn to comfort her daughter, while Joe stared glumly into his tea.

Sheila worried the couple must be having problems, for they were increasingly short with each other, and in public too. But Sarah Jane was still keeping them up nights, so that might also account for it.

Joan, who'd asked Caroline earlier if she could read Selina's letter, handed it back with a sympathetic look. She was a serious girl and rarely smiled, though she spoke up in company more often these days than she used to. Sheila thought it was good to see her coming out of herself. 'Will you go and visit her on Bodmin Moor, Caroline? I see she asks if you've any holiday leave coming up.'

'I'd like to.' Caroline looked hopefully across at Joe, who shook his head.

'Sorry, can't spare anyone. Not when we're so short-handed.'

Caroline's face fell.

Feeling sorry for the girl, and glad of the distraction, Sheila asked quickly, 'What about after Alice's wedding? I daresay things will be topsy-turvy around then, Joe, so you won't notice one body less about the farm.'

'But won't Selina be coming back for the wedding too?' Tilly pointed out.

'Yes, she wants to be at the wedding,' Caroline agreed, her gaze still on Joe's averted face. 'But I could go back with her afterwards. Just for three or four days. It would mean ever so much to me, Mr Postbridge. Selly's had such a hard time lately, she badly needs a friend to talk to. She's

155

lost her sister, and now she's got three grieving children to look after …'

Violet glanced at her husband. 'Joe?'

There was a wealth of meaning in that one word.

'I promise to work ever so hard when I get back,' Caroline added in a small voice. 'Cross my heart and hope to die.'

'Well, when you put it like that … I suppose I could spare you for a few days after the wedding,' Joe grumbled. 'Seeing as how it's apparently a matter of life or death.'

'Oh, thank you so much, Mr Postbridge, I won't let you down. I'll be back before you've missed me,' Caroline said eagerly.

'I doubt that.' Joe pushed aside his tea and got up, peering out of the kitchen window. 'Well, time to get moving. Come on, girls. We've a full day's work ahead, and it looks like it might rain later, so we'd best get out there while the weather's still with us.'

When they'd all pulled on their boots and trooped out of the kitchen, Violet bent to wipe her daughter's porridge-encrusted face, then began to clear away the breakfast things. 'So, how's the shop going these days, Mum?'

The question sounded deceptively innocent.

'Perfectly fine, thank you,' Sheila said, and turned to the sink. 'I'll wash these dishes before I head down into the village, shall I? To save you a job later.'

'Thanks.' Violet rolled up her sleeves to wipe down the kitchen table, the pungent smell of her home-made vinegar and baking soda cleaning mix filling the air. 'Aunt Margaret not shown her face again, I take it?'

Sheila sucked in a breath, hands plunged deep in soapy water. Thank goodness Vi couldn't see her guilty expression, she thought. 'Erm, your aunt? Goodness me, no. You saw her off last time, good and proper.' She rinsed suds off the bowls as noisily and hurriedly as she could. 'Blimey … is that the time? I'll be late opening the shop at this rate.'

'Do you need me down there today?' Violet asked, wiping her hands clean before turning to pick Sarah Jane up out of her highchair.

'Oh no, love. I'm getting along just fine on me lonesome,' Sheila assured her, and hoped to goodness that Vi wouldn't think to spring a surprise visit on her.

It was just as well, Sheila thought, puffing as she hurried down to the shop, that her daughter didn't know about Margaret having asked for work. Not just asked but been given it.

'For a trial period of one month,' Sheila had told Margaret as firmly as she could, aware that it might be harder to fire her sister than hire her. Blood, as her sister had rightly said, was thicker than water. And the older Sheila got, the more she missed having people around her who'd known her when she was young. She and Maggie knew things about each other. Nothing important, only the silly little things siblings knew that nobody else did. But that had to count for something, didn't it?

Margaret had spent an afternoon at the shop a few days before, learning how to work the till and deal with ration books. Sheila had intended to tell her family that she'd offered her sister work, but, in the end, she'd decided to leave it for now, in case things didn't work out between her and Maggie. That way, nobody would be any the wiser.

Having given her sister a spare key, she found the shop open by the time she arrived, with Margaret already behind the counter, chatting away merrily as she boxed up a Victoria sponge for the wife of one of the parish councillors.

'Be sure you only charge Mrs Bottomley half price,' Sheila told her sister, taking off her hat as she bustled in. When the lady threw her a grateful smile, she added quickly, 'Them cakes is still good and tasty, Mrs Bottomley, don't worry. But they were made two days ago, so you shouldn't be paying full price.' She put down the large cake tin she'd carried in under her arm. 'I've two fresh here, if you'd prefer today's batch.'

Mrs Bottomley smiled, shaking her head. 'I'm perfectly happy with a half-price cake, thank you, Mrs Newton,' and gave Margaret the correct change. 'Good day to you both,' she added on her way out of the shop.

Margaret looked at Sheila anxiously. 'You don't mind, do you? Me opening the shop early without you, that is. I wasn't sure if you'd been delayed, you see. So I thought it best to make a start. And you did give me a key.'

'Now, Maggie, don't get worked up over nothing. Of course I don't mind. That's why I gave you the key in the first place.'

'Right.' Her sister looked relieved. She prised off the lid of the large cake tin and carefully removed the two Victoria sponges, setting them neatly side by side on the counter, with a fly cover over each. 'Ooh, they look delicious. You're ever so good at baking, Shee.'

And you, my girl, are ever so good at buttering me up, Sheila thought. But she said nothing. It felt strange to be doing her sister a favour, when for most of their lives, the boot had been on the other foot. Strange but satisfying. Though, to tell the truth, she was glad enough of the company. Now the novelty of running a shop had finally worn off, it meant she'd have someone to chat to when there were no customers to serve, or to hold the fort while she took herself off for a walk.

As she checked the coins in the till drawer, and made a note of the total in Arnie's old cash ledger, her sister hovered. 'Yes?' she said at last, raising her head. 'What is it, Maggie?'

'Have you told your Violet about me yet?'

'I ain't found the right moment,' Sheila admitted with a grimace. 'But I shall, when the time's right. Not that it's any of Vi's business, mind. This is my shop and I'm in charge here. If I say my sister can work the counter, it's not Violet's place to stick her oar in.' She paused, suddenly uneasy. 'Though you won't tell her I said so, will you? There's no need to be causing trouble.'

'I wouldn't dream of it, Shee.'

After work that afternoon, once Margaret had returned to the friend's house where she was staying until she could afford proper digs, Sheila set the shop sign to 'Closed', and walked across the valley to the churchyard under grey skies. She was clutching a bouquet of lilies that were on their last legs, not having sold. Shame to throw them out, she'd thought, wrapping them in a twist of paper. Not when they'd do nicely for Arnie's grave. Never one to waste surplus either, he would have appreciated the sentiment.

There were two elderly draymen in the village, delivering kegs to the pub, noisily rolling each barrel down the ramp behind the truck and shouting to each other. One of them whistled as she passed, the cheeky beggar, and she gave him a sharp look. But at least it was peaceful and still in the graveyard. Sheila passed through the gates and wandered the short rows of headstones under the watchful gaze of a stone angel. Stopping at Arnie's grave, she placed the lilies in pride of place, and sat on the grass, which was thankfully still dry, the threatened rain having held off so far.

'Well, here I am again, love,' she said conversationally. 'This time I have some proper news for you. Not just village tittle tattle. So buckle up.'

Pausing now and then to pluck a few daisies from the grass and thread them expertly into a chain, Sheila told her late husband all the latest news from the shop, including the theft of the pork pie, leaving out none of the details, for Arnie had always enjoyed a good tale well told. After she'd laughed herself to tears, even though it hadn't been that funny at the time, she dried her eyes and expressed a wish to help people like Mrs Treedy. She did feel a little uneasy at having taken on her sister at the shop, and not Mrs Treedy. But she couldn't have left her own sister to starve now, could she? All the same, guilt pricked her on to wonder how best she could help that unfortunate woman and all her brood …

'Nobody's looking out for folk like Mrs Treedy,' she told his headstone, 'that's what worries me. Oh, they get a few handouts from the government. But that's no way to live, is it? Now the war's over, most of 'em seem to have been forgotten about. And that ain't right.'

At that moment, an idea popped into her head, and Sheila's voice faltered as she stopped to consider it. What if she could help them struggling people, not with a pork pie here and a handful of sweets there, but with more substantial, long-term help? How about if she could somehow use her position as shop proprietor to encourage better-off villagers to help those in need? Modest it might be, but Arnie's village shop had always been the heart of the community. Her husband had held summer fete raffles there, selling tickets from behind the counter, and sometimes a Christmas collection for charity too, and both had been well-subscribed. Now she was running the shop, there was no reason why that tradition of charitable giving shouldn't continue. Though a raffle couldn't hope to solve such a major issue, she thought gloomily, as costly prizes would have to be donated, plus it would be a one-off event.

'I'd dearly like to do something to make their lives better. Though I don't have a bloomin' clue what,' she admitted, feeling defeated. 'All pie in the sky, I daresay. Oh, I wish you was here to advise me, Arnie.'

Perhaps she could have a chat with Margaret about it though. Two heads were better than one, weren't they?

Coming to the most problematic part of her news, she told him about her sister coming to work at the shop, and how she was keeping Margaret's presence hidden from Violet and Joe for the time being. Her late husband would never have understood her decision, given how the two sisters had been at daggers drawn while he was alive.

'No doubt you'll think I'm barmy, love. But times change, don't they? And who have we got but family, when all's said and done?' She got up at last, brushing grass off her skirt. 'Maybe it won't work out. And maybe it will. But it's good to have someone in the shop who can take over when I need five minutes' break or to put my feet up in the back room with a nice cuppa.' She laid the ragged daisy chain along the top of the headstone, touched her fingers to her lips and transferred the kiss to the stone. 'Bless your soul, Arnie … I love you dearly and I'll come again soon. Tatty bye, my darlin'.'

As Sheila turned to go, she realised there was a gentleman doing much the same as her a few graves down, standing under an old sycamore, apparently talking to the air. He had silver hair brushed back and was dressed nattily in a tweed jacket and smart tie. He'd been picking old leaves and blossoms off the headstone in front of him, where a rose bowl held pink rosebuds, freshly cut by the look of them.

Taking another few steps in his direction, she stared at the man's profile in disbelief.

'Blimey,' she whispered. 'It can't be …'

She and her sister had been born down here in Cornwall while old Queen Vic was still on the throne. They'd lived in a row of rural cottages not far from Penzance, where they'd gone to school. But their parents, both East Enders by birth, who'd moved down to Cornwall after their marriage in search of greenery, had later returned to Dagenham, on the eastern outskirts of London, where her father had been offered work as a mechanic during the Great War.

Her sister, having just left school at the time, had stayed behind to marry her first husband, Fred, deaf to their mother's entreaties.

Sheila, on the other hand, had willingly left Cornwall, for she'd had her heart broken by a young man with 'more hair than sense', as her mother had put it, and was keen to start afresh somewhere new. Until she'd moved back to Cornwall during the war, partly to escape the bombing, but also to be reunited with Violet and her granddaughters.

Now here he was again … the man who had broken her heart all those years ago.

The old gent looked her way, and his eyes widened. Eyes from a distant past she'd all but forgotten. 'Good God,' he said, staring back at her, and removing his hat in a daze. '*Sheila*?'

''Ello, Bernard,' she replied hoarsely, and her heart gave a funny little hop, which she put down to indigestion. 'Small world, ain't it?'

CHAPTER FOURTEEN

It was porridge yet again for breakfast on Sunday. As Joan spooned stodgy mouthfuls of grey goo into her mouth, she flipped over the pages of a hardback hidden in her lap, squinting down to read the lines printed there. Unfortunately, she was so intent on the poem she was reading, a tiny blob of porridge escaped her spoon and landed on the book.

'Oh, golly,' Joan muttered, dropping her spoon in the bowl and dragging a hanky from her sleeve. Carefully, she wiped the splodge of porridge off the page, and grimaced at the stain left behind on the thin paper. She hoped to goodness it would disappear as it dried.

'What have you got there?' Violet asked, pausing behind her as she collected the empty bowls. Her frown deepened. 'Are you reading at the table?'

'Leave the girl alone,' Joe grumbled, pulling on his boots at the other side of the kitchen. 'If she wants to read at the table, that's her own business.'

His wife flashed him a look but said no more.

Sheila Newton, getting up from the table with her empty

163

bowl, peered across at the book that Joan had now laid open on the table to dry. 'Is that a novel? I've read a few in my time. Historical romances, that's what I like. With great big strappin' heroes.'

Tilly giggled.

'Mum!' Violet tutted and shook her head. 'You shouldn't go putting ideas in these girls' heads.'

'Oh, there's no harm in it. Blow me, Vi, you never used to be so prudish,' her mother commented and gave Joan a wink. 'What's the book, then? Show us the title.'

Embarrassed, all eyes on her, Joan held up the hardback. 'It's a selection of Keats' poetry.'

'Eh? Who?' Mrs Newton looked blank.

Ernest, at the far end of the table, put down his mug of tea. He was wearing glasses to read yesterday's newspaper, apparently also immune to Violet's rules about reading at the table. 'John Keats. He was a poet in the early half of the last century. Known as one of the Romantics.'

'I like the sound of the Romantics. Though poetry was never my thing.' Mrs Newton looked pensive. 'We had to learn a poem by Kipling when I was at school. Now, how did it go? "If you can keep your head when all about you are losing theirs …"' She hesitated.

'"And blaming it on you,"' Ernest completed the line for her.

'That's right. Now that's the kind of poem I enjoy. One that makes sense and has good rhymes and an easy rhythm. Same as all the best hymns.' Mrs Newton gave Joan's book a dubious nod. 'This Keats fellow … Is his stuff like that?'

'Not particularly,' Joan admitted, aware of heat in her cheeks as she was once again the centre of attention. 'He writes about nightingales and Grecian urns.'

'Talk about historical romance,' Joe quipped, grinning.

'Grecian *what*?' Mrs Newton shook her head and stamped off to the sink with her bowl. 'Rather you than me, love.'

Violet picked up the book and studied it. 'This isn't a library book. Where did you get it?'

'Oh … erm, it was Selina's. She must have left it behind when she went. I thought I'd see what it was like, that's all.' Joan hated lying, yet here she was, doing it again. But the book belonged to Arthur, and she could hardly admit that, could she? Not when Violet and Joe had advised her so strongly against seeing him again. 'I'm holding on to it until she comes back for Alice's wedding.'

Getting up, she caught Caroline's quizzical look and bit her lip. Of course, Caroline had been Selina's closest friend at the farm. She must know that Selina had no great interest in poetry. But thankfully the other girl kept schtum and didn't drop her in it.

Sheila Newton had expressed a desire to attend Sunday service that week, and unusually Violet and Joe had both decided to go with her, taking Sarah Jane in her pram. The Land Girls had been asked if they too wished to go to church. Tilly, who seemed to enjoy spending time with the Postbridges as though they were her own family, had agreed readily. Caroline had politely declined, slipping out for a walk instead. Joan herself had other plans, having arranged a secret rendezvous with Arthur that morning, since they generally had the day off on a Sunday, except when the farm was particularly busy.

Joan waited until the Postbridges and Tilly had set off for church on foot, as was their custom when the weather was good, and then slipped out of the back door of the farm.

Feeling almost giddy with excitement, she headed across the field towards the cliffs. She'd strapped a bag of sketching materials across her chest, for she and Arthur planned to take advantage of the fine summer weather and do some sketching.

She was almost clear of the farm buildings when a whistle stopped her. Shocked, she turned back to find Caroline leaning on the back gate to the farm, watching her.

'Where are you going?' Caro called after her. 'As if I need to ask … You're off to see your young man, aren't you?'

'I just fancied a walk, that's all,' Joan insisted, reddening at yet another lie. Goodness, it was difficult to keep up with all the fibs she was telling these days. Perhaps she ought to have gone to church, after all. Her immortal soul was probably in jeopardy, if such a thing even existed.

'I won't tell on you,' Caroline insisted. 'I know that's his poetry book you're reading. I never saw Selina read a poem in her life. Besides, you only ever take that bag out with you when you're going sketching. And you told me Arthur likes sketching too. So there's no need to pretend you're not meeting him, Miss Fibber.'

Joan hesitated, biting her lip. 'You promise you won't tell?'

'Of course not.' Caroline pouted. 'What do you take me for?'

'He's not a bad lad, you know. Violet's wrong about him. And I … I like him.' She paused. 'Do you understand?'

Caroline nodded, though she seemed rather glum. It struck Joan that the other girl seemed lonely, her shoulders slumped, her mouth downturned. 'It's none of their business who you choose to walk out with. They can't tell us what to do. They're not our parents.'

166

Joan laughed at this. 'You're right, we should stand up for ourselves more. But Violet … I probably shouldn't say this, but she scares me.' They both giggled, then Joan gave her friend a wave and trudged on, calling over her shoulder, 'You'll find someone one day too, Caro. See if you don't. Then you'll be the one sneaking off on a Sunday morning.'

Arthur was there ahead of her when Joan arrived on the cliffs at the appointed time. He had already set up his easel and mixed his paints, in fact, and was pencilling in a rough outline of the cliff edge and the sea beyond. She thought he made a dashing and romantic figure, working at the easel, his fair hair lifting in the sea breeze.

Hearing her approach, he turned and grinned. 'I say, you made it. Well done. Did you have any trouble getting away?'

'None at all. We only work Sundays when there's an urgent job on. Today, the family are going to church, so nobody noticed me leaving. Well, Caroline did. But she won't say a word.' She chose a good spot to sit down, where an outcrop of rock looked flat enough to be comfortable, and unpacked her bag of sketching equipment. 'What marvellous weather,' she added. 'Though it's often a little breezy this close to the cliff edge. I hate it when the paper flaps around while you're trying to draw, don't you?'

'Quite right. That's why I prefer the easel, where I can clip down the paper. Though rain's the worst. Especially when you're working with watercolours and the heavens open partway through.' He raised his face to the sunlight. 'Not much chance of rain today.'

With a pang of envy, she studied his sturdy easel and wooden palette. 'Where did you get those?'

'My mother bought them for me,' he admitted, looking sheepish. 'For my last birthday. She thinks painting keeps me out of trouble. My father's not so keen. Says it's all nonsense and I should get a job instead. But …' His voice tailed off and he bent his head to mixing his paints again.

'I almost never paint outdoors,' she said, wondering what he'd been about to say.

'Really? Why ever not?'

'I don't know.' Joan hesitated, finding the question awkward. 'Too embarrassed in case somebody sees me, I suppose.'

'I used to feel like that. But I fell into the habit of working outdoors when I got drafted. Of course, in France, you never knew when someone was going to take a potshot at you while you were wandering about with a sketchbook.' He added with a grin, 'Now I go out painting all the time and don't think about it.'

'It's easier for men,' she muttered.

He looked puzzled, then grimaced. 'Ah, I see what you mean. Some men can be beasts, can't they? It's such a shame. Still, next time we go out sketching together, you could use the easel to paint while I sketch. That way, I can protect you from marauding males and impudent stares.'

She smiled and said nothing. But it made her heart beat quicker to imagine doing this on a regular basis with him.

It was almost as though he were suggesting a date.

Studying the landscape and sea, he said abruptly, 'Hang on, I'm a bit too close to the edge. I'll move back a few feet.' Carefully, he shifted the easel backwards, the canvas wobbling dangerously. She realised he would be standing behind her now, and glanced back at him over her shoulder. But he was intent on the view. 'That's better.'

They worked in silence for almost an hour. The time flew by, for she found him pleasant company and couldn't understand why Violet had thought him so problematic. At the Grange, he'd admitted more than once to having nightmares and strange thoughts at times, but today he was nothing but a friendly young man with a glittering future ahead of him, if he chose to make the most of his undoubted talents.

'One of the girls who used to live at the farm went to London a while back,' she said conversationally. 'Mrs Newton's granddaughter, Alice. She's coming back to Porthcurno in a couple of weeks because she's getting married.'

'To a local boy?' he asked, wrinkling his brow.

'Funnily enough, no. She's marrying a young man called Patrick. I believe they met in Bude at first, where she was working during the war. In a printing shop, I think it was. Then she went off to London and managed to get herself shot—'

'Good God!' he interrupted, his gaze flying to her face. 'Shot? You can't be serious?'

'I'm entirely serious. She was shot in the shoulder. And the man she was with that night was killed. It was a tragedy. Alice was never the same again, if you ask me.' Feeling his gaze on her face, Joan studied her sketch with critical eyes and then added a little more shading to the foreground. 'Anyway, she came back wounded from London towards the end of the war and started work at Eastern House instead. The listening station? All hush-hush, you understand.'

'Golly, that sounds awfully exciting. So this girl lived at the farm with you?'

'Along with her father, yes. Though her father Ernest only

turned up towards the end of the war.' Joan bit her lip, unsure how much to reveal of Alice and her father's background. 'It's probably safe enough to say this, now the war's done and dusted, but I think he was a spy. He was working behind enemy lines in Germany, by all accounts. And I think Alice was training to be a spy too. When she got shot in London, I mean.'

'I say, what an amazing story.' Arthur was staring at her keenly now. 'But who's this Patrick that she's marrying, then?'

'He used to work with her at Eastern House. They went to London together.' Joan stopped, embarrassed. 'Though Violet wouldn't like me telling you that about her niece. She thinks people will gossip because Alice and Patrick aren't married yet. But nobody cares about that sort of thing anymore, do they?'

'No, very old hat. Good luck to them both, that's what I say.' Arthur lowered his paintbrush and took a step back to study what he'd done. His expression was serious. 'There, that's the basic thing finished. When it's dry, I'll go over the details again. Make it better.'

'May I see?'

He hesitated, then said, 'Of course.'

She wandered across to admire his painting and stopped with a gasp, a hand at her mouth. 'Oh!'

Arthur had painted her into the picture. His original sketch had shown only the cliff and the sea beyond. Now she was there too, seated on the outcrop of rock, bending over a sketch book with a pencil in her hand, and her hair flying everywhere. That was why he'd moved his easel further back from the edge, she realised belatedly. To put her in the landscape.

'I wish you'd told me. Look at my hair … It's a mess.'

'That's what I like about it,' he said earnestly, a smile playing on his lips as the sea breeze whipped her hair about her face. His gaze met hers. 'Honestly, Joan, I think you're the most dashed good-looking girl I've ever met.' He pulled a face. 'Sorry, I probably shouldn't have said that. But there it is. Do you mind awfully?'

'I … I don't know,' she mumbled, looking away.

There was a short silence.

Then Arthur burst out, 'I'd like to kiss you …'

Her heart thumping violently, Joan took an instinctive step backwards as he reached for her. It was one thing to go painting with him, and even to spend hours poring over books with him in the library at the Grange. But she wasn't sure she felt ready for *a kiss*.

'I wish you wouldn't,' she said quickly.

'Very well.' His paint-stained hands fell back to his sides at once. 'I won't, then. Not if you don't want me to.' But she thought there was a look of disappointment on his face. Seeing that, she felt sorry for him. But feeling sorry for a chap didn't mean she ought to let him kiss her, did it? That would be very muddled thinking.

'I should get back,' she said quietly, turning to collect her sketchbook and pencils. 'Church will be finished by now and they'll be wondering where I am.'

That wasn't quite true. She doubted the busy Postbridges would even notice her absence. But Caroline might miss her, and she knew where Joan had gone today, and with whom. It would be deeply embarrassing if Violet asked where Joan had gone and Caro let the cat out of the bag, forgetting her promise not to.

Without another word, Arthur began to pack his paints away. He unfolded the easel and put it under his arm, carrying the canvas gingerly by the edges, as it was still damp.

'So, your friend Alice is coming back to Porthcurno for her wedding,' he said conversationally, as though he'd never offered to kiss her. 'I imagine that will be quite an event.'

Joan smiled. 'Oh yes, the Postbridges and Mrs Newton have been planning it for weeks now. There'll be a do for her and Patrick afterwards at the farm. Would you like to come?'

'I haven't been invited,' he pointed out.

'I'm not sure there have been any formal invitations. Word's just gone around the village for friends to turn up and celebrate with us.' She blushed. 'And you're my friend, so why not?'

He said nothing but looked uncertain.

Slowly, weighed down with equipment, they walked down the steep track together towards the farm. Sheep were bleating in the top fields, a summer breeze rippling through sunlit grasses and hedgerows. Up above, seagulls soared and cried in a soft blue sky. Joan always thought the gulls sounded so unhappy and alone up there, high above the earth. Though 'greedy gannets' was what Mrs Newton called them, and always shooed the birds away whenever she saw them flap down and go pecking around the farmyard in search of missed seed from the chickens.

They reached the little muddy dip where the track diverged, one side leading down to the farm and the other continuing along the cliff edges, and she stopped there.

'I can go on alone from here. See you later?'

'Let me walk you back to the farm,' Arthur insisted,

heading down the track ahead of her. When she didn't follow, he turned, surprised. 'What is it?'

She felt bad, especially after having insisted he would be welcome at Alice's wedding. 'It's probably best if we're not seen together,' she admitted. 'They'll be back from church by now and you know what the Postbridges are like.'

'Yes, I understand.' He stared down at the mud ruts on the track, scuffing his shoe tip with them. 'Maybe I'll go back up the cliff then. Carry on painting for a while. The wind's died down anyway.'

There was something in his face that she didn't like. It made her uncomfortable. As he went to move past her, she put a quick hand on his arm. 'No, come on … It's none of their business who I spend time with. Forget what I said. We can walk down to the farm together.'

They were standing very close. A smile tugged at his lips and the gloom lifted from his face. 'I say, do you mean that?'

'Of course.' She tugged on his sleeve. 'Hurry up though. I don't want to miss my lunch. Mrs Newton makes the most bang-up Sunday roasts.'

Together, they hurried down the track, parting at last at the farm gate. Joan was uncomfortably aware of Violet peering out of the kitchen window, but kept her face firmly turned away.

'I enjoyed myself today. Thank you for the company. I think you're a smashing painter.' Standing on tiptoe, she pressed a quick kiss to his cheek, just a friendly peck, then she backed away, saying hurriedly, 'Well, goodbye. Maybe I'll see you on Thursday afternoon. At the Grange.'

'I look forward to it,' Arthur said huskily, clearly taken aback by that peck on the cheek. 'Goodbye, Joan.'

After he'd gone, she trudged slowly back to the kitchen door to find Violet standing there, hands on hips, glaring at her.

'Wasn't that the Green boy? The one I told you to steer clear of?'

'Yes,' Joan told her defiantly, her chin in the air. 'What of it?' She stepped past Violet into the porch, pulling off her boots with a nonchalant air. Her heart was thundering fit to burst, but she was sick of being told what to do by a woman who wasn't her boss or related to her. 'It's my free time, and it's a free country, and I'll see whomever I like, thank you very much, Mrs Postbridge.'

Joe, standing in the kitchen doorway, cap in hand, gave a short laugh but said nothing. She thought she caught a flash of admiration in his eyes.

'Well, I never!' Violet gasped, staring after her.

But Joan paid no attention.

CHAPTER FIFTEEN

Some weeks having passed since Bella's funeral, the household at Thornton Hall had fallen into an uneasy but predictable routine. The children spent time with their tutor or nanny in the mornings, and roamed the grounds in the afternoons, when the weather wasn't too hot. Selina sometimes walked out with them, taking the dogs too, and would point out the names of flowers and trees, and tell them anecdotes about their mother's childhood. She talked of Oxford's dreaming spires, where she and Bella had grown up, becoming a little tearful with nostalgia at times.

And yet what was there to be nostalgic about? She and Bella had never been close like Alice and Lily Fisher seemed to be, the age difference between them being too great for that kind of warm sisterly relationship, and Bella had also taken on a mother's role with her. They still seemed like halcyon days though, long before the war, before her sister had married and gone away. She'd enjoyed a carefree life back then, Selina realised with hindsight. She had thought herself lonely and abandoned by her sister when she married, but would gladly swap that loneliness for the weight of responsibility she bore now, and took every opportunity to snatch some time alone.

There was a wooden swing under the comfortable shade of a beech tree, just out of sight of the hall, and Selina had taken to visiting it occasionally. She liked to sit on the swing and read a magazine or simply contemplate her life in solitude.

One day, the post brought an envelope bearing Caroline's messy handwriting. That afternoon, excited to hear all the latest gossip from Porthcurno, Selina sat on the swing under the high, leafy beech tree and opened the letter.

Dearest Selina,

It feels like ages since I last saw you. How are you coping since your sister's death? It must be so hard; my heart goes out to you. I hope you're getting plenty of help from everyone there. Suddenly being landed with three children sounds like a nightmare. Everyone here was very sad to hear the news about Bella, by the way. Violet and Joe and Mrs Newton send their condolences. As do I, of course.

But I have wonderful news. You're still coming to Alice's wedding, I hope? Because Joe has agreed to let me take some time off afterwards. I thought perhaps I could come back to Bodmin with you. You did ask if I could visit you, so I hope you won't be too cross at me for suggesting it.

Could you write and let me know how you're getting here, so we can travel back together? Joe has only allowed me four days' leave, but I'll try for a week if I can wrangle it. I can't wait to see Thornton Hall and the lovely gardens you've described, and to hug you again, my dear friend. Life at the farm has not been the same since you left. I miss you quite dreadfully. So please say yes.

In your last letter, you asked how things were going at the farm. Do you remember that posh boy who told us about the lamb going over the cliff? Well, you'll never believe this, but him and Joan have been courting. Violet nearly blew a gasket when she found out. She said he's not been right since the war and Joan mustn't go near the boy again. But of course Joan paid no attention. You know what a stubborn mare she can be. Though I'd never have guessed she'd go behind Violet's back like that. But still waters run deep, don't they?

As for Mrs Newton, she's got a bee in her bonnet over folk in the village who are struggling to make ends meet. Some boy swiped a pork pie from her shop, and when she chased after him, she found him living in a filthy hovel with his mum and a parcel of brats dressed in nothing but rags, or so Mrs Newton told us. She wants to do something about it. Raise some money somehow, I suppose.

Violet's furious, of course. She says her mother's taking too much on and will make herself ill. She's probably right. But you know Mrs Newton. Once the old bird has got the bit between her teeth, there's no stopping her.

Final bit of news. Remember Hazel Cotterill? She had her baby earlier than expected and it's a boy. They've christened him Richard, though everyone's calling him Dickie for short. She brought him to the farm yesterday for Violet and Mrs Newton to coo over. He's got red cheeks and such a round comical face. But I suppose babies are always funny looking. I can't see myself ever wanting to have one, can you?

Anyway, I'd better dash to give this to Mrs Newton for the post. Joe wants us out in the fields again today, weeding for Britain. I swear my back is breaking. I was stung by a hornet too the other day and got a lump on my arm the size of an egg. You would have laughed to see me running about shrieking my head off, making a complete fool of myself as usual. But it stung like Billy-oh.

I miss you madly and can't wait to see you. Counting the days now.

Love always, your friend, Caroline xxx

Smiling at her friend's haphazard style of writing, Selina read the letter through several times, laughing out loud at some of the passages.

She was taken aback to learn that Joan was defying Violet in order to see a boy, especially since Joan had never shown much interest in boys before. But Caroline was right. It was the quiet ones who surprised you the most. As for Mrs Newton – or Mrs Sheila Hopkins, as the Land Girls had known her before she married her shopkeeper, Arnold – none of that news surprised her. Violet's mother always had some mad scheme up her sleeve. And now that Selina was having to grapple with household accounts herself, albeit with Mr MacGregor and Mrs Hawley's help, she'd discovered first-hand just how much it cost to feed the staff at the hall as well as the three children and herself, even with the help of ration books.

Things had been difficult during the war. But they'd all muddled through together, expecting things to return to normal once hostilities had finally ceased. Back to the way life had been before the war. Instead, Britain was in a worse state than ever, and nobody had any money to fix it. Least of all the government, it seemed.

She dashed away a tear at the thought of seeing Caro again. She hadn't realised how much she'd been missing her friend since leaving Postbridge Farm. But now, cut off from the world and mourning her lost sister, she found herself missing Caroline's cheerful, non-judgmental presence.

Yes, she would make arrangements for Caroline to visit the hall after she went to Porthcurno for Alice's wedding. Though she hadn't even thought about her own travel arrangements so far, her head too full of grieving children and household costs.

Suddenly, the memory of Cameron Bourne in his dashing car, offering to take her out for a drive one day, came back to her. But she banished the idea at once. She couldn't ask a neighbour to drive her all the way from Bodmin to Porthcurno, and especially not an unmarried man. It was out of the question. Besides, such a journey would cost a fortune in petrol, which was still under rationing restrictions, though if they pooled fuel supplies, it might just be possible. She'd spotted some fuel cans stored in one of the outbuildings while exploring the grounds, though they were probably kept for emergency use only. Perhaps she could ask the old head groundsman about them.

She worried what Cameron Bourne would make of such a bold request. He might assume she was interested in him romantically, and that would never do. Nonetheless, it would save her a very dull and lengthy train and bus journey from Bodmin to Porthcurno, and back again.

Folding the letter back into the envelope, she returned to the house across the lawns, still mulling it over …

Jemima and Peter came running across the sunlit lawns as she reached the hall. 'Aunty Selina,' Jemima cried, her face a blotchy mess of tears. 'You said we could take Faith into the garden after lessons today, now the rain has stopped. Only Martha is absolutely beastly and won't let us. She says it's too hot.'

Hugging her niece in dismay, Selina said uneasily, 'It is rather sunny. We need to be careful that Faith doesn't get sunburnt.'

'There, Jemmy, what did I say?' Peter kicked a stone viciously away into undergrowth. 'I knew she'd side with the nanny. Grown-ups always stick together.'

'Oh, come on, Peter, that's hardly fair,' Selina protested. 'I'm not siding with anyone.' She gave him an appeasing smile, which he ignored. 'Don't forget Faith isn't even five years old. She can't take strong sunshine like you and Jemima. Perhaps you could wait until later when the sun's lower in the sky?'

'But Faith has tea earlier than us and goes straight to bed after her bath,' Jemima pointed out tearfully, rubbing at her eyes. 'Martha will complain if we take her out of doors when she's meant to be eating her tea.'

'In that case,' Selina told them both diplomatically, 'I'd better speak to Martha about changing Faith's teatime, maybe just this once.'

She couldn't get used to all these rigid rules for the children. It seemed unnatural to her. At Postbridge Farm, the three evacuee kids that Violet and Joe had housed for most of the war had kept their own hours without much interference. Indeed, she recalled often having to complain to Violet about how late they stayed up some evenings, making a hellish racket in their attic room when the exhausted Land Girls were trying to sleep.

Now that she was her nephew and nieces' legal guardian, perhaps she should relax some of the stricter rules governing what the three children could and couldn't do. At the very least, she could change the ones that made no sense. Who was there to stop her, after all?

Peter raised his brows at this suggestion. 'Good luck with that.' And without another word, he sloped off in the direction of his treehouse, a wonky platform of ropes, planks and tarpaulin constructed high among the leafy branches, where even Jemima was rarely invited.

Gloomily watching her brother disappear between the trees, Jemima slipped a sticky hand into Selina's, looking up at her with a sniff. 'I hate Martha.'

This was going too far, Selina decided. 'No, you don't,' she told her niece firmly. 'She's your nanny, and I'm sure she's only doing what she thinks is right for your sister. Now, be a good girl, and tell Mrs Hawley I'd like to speak to Martha in the study right away.'

Jemima opened her eyes wide at this, but dashed off to obey, looking almost enthusiastic. No doubt she hoped that her strict nanny was about to receive a grand ticking off.

Hands sunk in her dress pockets, Selina wandered into the house after her niece, feeling a certain apprehension at having sent for Martha in such a lofty manner. She wasn't used to being in charge of anyone and it felt awkward. But there was no one else to make such changes, was there? Of course, she could have sent Jemima straight up to the nursery in search of Martha. But she knew her niece was intimidated by the nanny, and indeed Selina was not entirely confident herself about confronting the young woman on her own territory. But Mrs Hawley made a useful intermediary, and Martha would surely not ignore any summons that came through the housekeeper.

Selina loved the study, which her sister had never seemed to use, the room having been mostly Sebastian's domain. It had a lovely view over the rose garden and the misty hills beyond, and was cosy, book-lined and wood-panelled. She wasn't a big reader but liked the look of the leather volumes on the shelves. Besides, the room held two deep, oxblood leather armchairs beside the fireplace, and she suspected it would make a perfect den during chilly winters here on Bodmin Moor.

Though she was trying not to think that far ahead. Her dearest Bella had not been gone long. Contemplating a long winter in this house, plus the years ahead until Peter reached his majority – and indeed beyond that, for she doubted Peter would want to look after his younger sisters once he'd inherited the estate – was more than she could bear. For now, she was content to live one day at a time, not looking too far into the future.

Some time passed before there was a knock at the door, and Martha entered without waiting for permission. The young woman stood with her arms folded, the door still ajar, glaring at her as though Selina were the one who'd done something wrong. Selina took a deep breath and told herself not to lose her temper. No doubt Martha was suffering too, having just lost her employer. Perhaps she was feeling insecure and needed reassurance, not a telling off.

'Thank you for coming so promptly,' Selina said politely, glancing over the young woman's shoulder. 'Would you mind closing the door?'

Martha hesitated, then closed the door as instructed. 'I've left the little girl with Mrs Hawley,' she said, without any attempt at deference, and nodded to the clock on the mantelpiece. 'It'll be time for her tea soon.'

'That's precisely what I wanted to speak to you about.' Very deliberately, Selina sat in one of the leather armchairs, leaving Martha to remain standing. Her heart was thudding, and she felt queasy. She'd never been in a position like this, where she was forced to take someone to task over a behavioural issue. It was one thing to have a spat with another girl, especially over a boy, which had happened often enough during her time at the farm, but it was quite another to reprimand a member of staff. And she did feel quite nervous about it. But she'd been on the receiving end of Violet's sharp tongue once or twice when things had gone awry, and tried to copy that lady's majestic air of authority.

'The thing is, Martha,' she began, 'I'd like to relax some of the rules around Faith's schedule. She's nearly five now and old enough for a later bedtime. Also, I don't believe she's had much schooling, has she? It's high time she learned her letters and numbers.'

Martha stared at her balefully. 'Her mother didn't hold with teaching children their letters and numbers too young. She said it was bad for their brains.'

Selina was perfectly sure her sister had never said any such thing. It was clear that Martha was jealously holding on to what little power she had as head of the nursery. Once Faith started taking lessons instead of playing with toys all

183

day, the nanny would be at a loose end, and no doubt feared being sent to help Mrs Hawley with housework instead.

But there was no point upsetting the girl by being too frank with her. As Violet had often said back at the farm, 'You catch more flies with honey than vinegar'.

'Be that as it may,' Selina replied carefully, 'I'm planning to teach her. And she can eat her supper with Jemima and Peter from now on, and take her bath a little later too.' Her hands tightened on the arms of the chair, aware of the nanny's fulminating gaze on her face. 'Does Faith possess a sunhat?'

Martha's lips tightened. 'Yes, but she's always dragging it off.'

'I see. Well, would you be so kind as to put it on her head and let Jemima take her into the gardens for a little fresh air and sunshine? I'm sure if she's only out for half an hour, there can be no harm done.' She rose to her feet to indicate that the conversation was at an end. 'Perhaps you could watch them, to be sure Faith keeps her sunhat on.'

'Yes, Miss.'

There was an awkward silence. Selina mustered her most magnanimous smile and said, 'You may go now, Martha.'

Once the nanny had gone, Selina sank back into the chair and buried her face in her hands. It was surprising how hard she'd found that exchange.

'Oh, Bella, I wish you were here … I don't know if I can do this.'

But she had to manage somehow, didn't she? She'd made her sister a solemn promise to look after her children and love them as though they were her own. It seemed she would need to harden up if she was to keep that promise and not let petty tyrants like nanny Martha rule the household.

Straightening up with a sigh, she gazed grimly about the room, hunting for something to distract her from her worries. There was a small ornate wooden chest on the floor next to the other armchair. She had a feeling that she'd opened it once and found knitting inside. That might be one way of passing the time, she thought.

Kneeling beside the chest, she opened it and did indeed find wool and needles inside, plus a few old pattern books. Removing these, she realised the chest was still not empty. There were three black leatherbound notebooks in its base.

Taking out the first notebook, she flipped it open to see her sister's handwriting, neat and elegant as ever. Some of the pages were dated. After reading half a page, she realised with a start that this was a journal. Her sister's diary, in fact.

Taking out the other two notebooks, she found they were also full of dated entries in the same handwriting. And the earliest dates harked back to the time of Bella's wedding to Sebastian.

Clutching the notebooks to her chest, Selina hesitated, biting her lip. These were her sister's private journals, perhaps never intended for others' eyes. She ought to burn them. Or put them away for when Bella's children were old enough to read them. But she did neither, and knew herself tempted to take the journals up to her room and read them herself, away from prying eyes.

After all, her sister was gone. What harm could it do?

CHAPTER SIXTEEN

Sheila was down in the cellar, sorting out tinned goods, when her sister came to the door at the top of the stairs. 'There's an old boy in a suit to see you. Says his name's Bernard.' Margaret's voice was high with astonishment. 'And I think I remember him from years back. Bernard Bailey ... Wasn't he sweet on you when we were youngsters?'

'For gawd's sake, Maggie ...' Straightening so quickly she almost banged her head on the low ceiling, Sheila hissed back, 'Tell him I'll be right up. And keep your bloomin' voice down.'

As soon as her sister had vanished, she smoothed down her hair, snatched off her work pinny, took a breath and hurried up the cellar stairs.

Bernard was standing over the local newspaper on the counter, reading the front page with apparent interest, but he turned when she appeared and took off his hat, saying smoothly, 'Hello again.' He looked her up and down, a twinkle in his eye that had Sheila worried she might have cobwebs in her hair or a run in her stockings. 'You know, I almost thought I'd imagined seeing you in the churchyard the other day. Yet here you are again, large as life.'

''Ere, watch who you're calling large,' she told him, but added a crooked smile, so he'd know she wasn't being serious. Her heart was beating rather fast, but she put that down to having raced up the steps so quickly. Her sister was watching the two of them with great interest, but Sheila ignored her. Maggie could take a flying jump if she was busy putting two and two together and making sixpence.

'Would you like to come through to the back room?' she asked in her most polite voice, intimidated by his smart appearance. 'I was due a half-hour break, anyway,' she fibbed, shooting her sister a look that warned Maggie not to contradict her. 'We can have a nice chat and catch up on old times.'

'If you're sure I'm not interrupting your work.' With a nod to Margaret, he followed her through to the back of the shop, murmuring, 'Isn't that your sister, Maggie? I remember her from the old days. She married ... Oh, what's his name? Local farmer. I've seen him down the pub quite a few times lately.'

'Stanley Chellew,' Sheila said, trying not to visibly grind her teeth. She closed the door so her sister couldn't overhear what was being said, then waved him towards the table while she put the kettle on. 'They're still married. But separated.'

'I'm sorry to hear that. How long has that been going on, then?'

Always happy to gossip, Sheila gave him a pithy summary of how her sister's marriage had foundered, while fetching the best china, cutting them both a slice of tangy ginger cake, and making the tea. 'I never liked Stanley,' she admitted in a low voice, 'the miserable so-and-so. And he was very badly behaved towards my granddaughter, Lily. I've never forgiven him for that, and I never shall.' She poured the tea. 'Good riddance to bad rubbish, eh?'

Bernard raised his cuppa. 'And so say all of us.' She watched in approval as he sipped the tea in a quiet, gentleman-like fashion, not slurping or spilling any in the saucer like Arnie used to do. She'd loved her husband dearly, but his eating and drinking habits had driven her almost wild at times. Then he set his china cup down carefully. 'Sheila … I mean, Mrs Newton … This tea is delicious. You're a miracle worker.'

'It has been said,' she replied airily.

He smiled.

Seated opposite each other, they nibbled on the ginger cake and politely discussed the weather, and then how the country had changed since before the war. She'd been worried his attitudes might be too posh these days for her and she would feel bored. But the old Bernard was still there, his eyes twinkling, his funny anecdotes soon making her lose her inhibitions.

That business with Mrs Treedy kept returning to plague her though, and eventually she couldn't hold back.

'When we met in the churchyard,' she blurted out, 'and I told you my trials and tribulations with this shop, you said you might have some ideas for me. Ways to help some of the villagers with these hard times we're facing.' She narrowed her eyes, scouring his face. 'Did you mean it?'

Bernard laughed. 'Never one to mince words, were you, Sheila? Do you mind me calling you Sheila?' He grimaced. 'I saw the marriage notice in the paper, but I still can't picture you as Mrs Newton, sorry. Much as I admired Arnold for the good work he did for the community in his later years, I don't think he deserved you.'

'I won't hear a word against my Arnie,' she said in a rush, and felt her chest tighten with upset. 'All right, maybe he weren't as posh as you. But his 'eart was pure gold. And I loved him.'

'In that case, I apologise.' He sipped his tea again, his look thoughtful. 'It's true, he did like to look out for the people of Porthcurno. And it seems you'd like to carry on in the same tradition.'

'Will you help me if I do?'

'Of course.' He smiled, that twinkle back in his eye, and she had to remind herself that he'd dumped her, not the other way around. There was no call to be thinking soft thoughts, just because he'd lost his spouse too. 'You think I'm posh? An old boy from Cornwall?'

'You're posher than me,' she said frankly.

'That only goes as deep as the suit.' Bernard nodded to his smart togs. 'My wife Eugenie's influence. She had such ambition for me. Sadly, I couldn't live up to her dreams. But I did my best.'

'I recall you was always good with words at school. What did you end up doing?'

'Journalism. I worked on the local rags in Penzance at first, then moved to Exeter. I was even in Bristol for a spell. Served in the war too – the Great War, that is – and came back with a few unsightly scars, but my spirit intact.' He grinned. 'Bit long in the tooth for the second shout, I'm afraid.'

'You were lucky, then. We lost so many bloomin' men in this last war. Yes, and women and children too, in the Blitz, and gawd knows what else.' She shook her head sadly. 'I don't know how this country'll ever recover.'

'This new Labour government is a start. But legislation

can take years to enact. In the meantime, Britain needs people like *you*, Sheila, people who are willing to stand up and do something to help their community.' He tapped the table decisively. 'So, what do you intend?'

'To be honest,' she admitted, 'I can't for the life of me work out what's for the best. Should I start a fund to help the poor folk out? Run a tombola? Maybe a jumble sale at the village hall? But what about afterwards? I can't just go round their houses like bleedin' Santa Claus, handing out a few bob here, a tenner there.' Sheila gave a gusty sigh. 'And what if they get offended and tell me to sling it? I'll look a proper Charlie then, won't I?'

'Yes, I quite see that. It has to be done properly.' Settling back, Bernard crossed one leg comfortably over the other, balancing his hat on his knee. 'In my opinion, you ought to speak to the Parish Council.'

Sheila stared at him, taken aback. 'You what?' She'd only ever heard Arnold speak in scathing terms of the Parish Council and didn't see how it could possibly help her cause to approach them. *Bunch of stuck-up toffs and turnips*, was what Arnie had dubbed them, despite having been one himself at one point. 'I dunno about that. Parish Council? They wouldn't be interested in talking to the likes of me.'

'I only recently moved back to Porthcurno,' he explained, 'after Eugenie died. I don't think you ever knew her, did you?' When she shook her head, he went on wistfully. 'She was born near here but was sent away to a boarding school, you see, so we didn't meet until she was in her twenties. Her family still have a plot here in the churchyard, so that's where she was laid to rest, and I came back to Porthcurno to be … Well, to be near her.' His keen eyes searched her face. 'You understand, don't you? You were visiting your Arnold's grave when we met the other day.'

She nodded, her eyes misty.

'When I settled back here, I was retired. I've always been a busy person, so I soon found myself at a loose end. I stood for the Parish Council and was elected unopposed. They're always desperate for new council members, with so many men still away on the continent.'

'Sorry, but what can the council do?'

'They hold the purse strings for the local area,' he pointed out. 'If there's money in the kitty that can be put aside for families in need, the council will know what's in the coffers and what can be spared. They also understand how to organise the collection and distribution of funds,' he added with another wry smile, 'without anyone getting offended.'

'But I told you, they won't listen to the likes of me.'

'You won't know until you try. Anyway, I'll be there to introduce you. I'm a councillor, remember.'

'I don't know …' She was deeply uncomfortable at the idea of having to speak in public. 'No offence, but what do all you toffs on the council know about poverty?'

'I wasn't well-off until I married Eugenie,' he pointed out gently.

'Well, maybe not you … But I don't have time for all that malarkey. I've got my granddaughter's wedding this weekend. We've got family and friends arriving from all over. The house is at sixes and sevens over it.'

He studied her for a moment. 'I never figured you for a coward, Sheila.'

'I beg your pardon?'

'You heard me. You're scared, so you're avoiding it. Yes,

maybe talking to the council isn't what you're used to. But you're running this shop now. You're a respected member of the village community.' He leaned forward, his gaze boring into hers, impossible to avoid. 'And if you want to help those people, you're going to have to stand up and speak out. The council has its monthly meeting a week on Thursday. Will you be there, or won't you? I'll be chairing the meeting. I can put you down under Any Other Business.'

Sheila folded her arms, huffing. 'I suppose there's no point me saying no, seeing as how you're determined to railroad me into it.'

He sat back, smiling. 'I always suspected you were a person of conscience. I'm glad to see I was right.'

'Conscience, my giddy aunt ...' But she felt ridiculously pleased at this compliment. 'Got time for another cuppa, Bernard?'

When Sheila returned to the farmhouse late afternoon, she found the place in an uproar. There were two cars parked in the farmyard, and she could hear a child crying somewhere inside. Someone had also put the wireless on loud, with big-band music drifting out of the open kitchen windows. When she opened the back door, the first thing to meet her eyes was a hand-painted banner hung across the kitchen rafters, that read: CONGRATULATIONS, ALICE AND PATRICK. Little squiggles that were clearly meant to be wedding bells and flowers decorated the banner on either side of these words. The kitchen seemed to be crowded with people, and she hesitated on the threshold, feeling her heart thump with surprise. But she was soon seized by her tall, fair-haired eldest granddaughter and given a resounding kiss on the cheek.

'Gran!' Lily was beaming, her cheeks flushed with pleasure.

'Blimey, love,' Sheila exclaimed, giving Lily a tight squeeze in return. 'You nearly gave your old gran a heart attack, jumping on me like that. And what on earth's going on in here? Looks like we've been invaded.'

'The old place is a bit full, ain't it?'

'Oh, but it's wonderful to see you again.' She held Lily out at arms' length. 'Gawd, look at you. You're the picture of 'ealth.'

'It's all this fresh air I keep getting. Tris has me out on the farm most days, teaching me how to look after the sheep.' Her granddaughter laughed at Sheila's horrified expression. 'It ain't as bad as it sounds. Morris comes too sometimes. He loves riding on the tractor with his dad.'

'Bless his little soul. I hope Tris keeps bloomin' good hold of him. Dangerous things, tractors.'

'We're always careful,' Lily assured her. 'Aunty Violet told me you've been opening the shop most days. How's it going?'

Sheila bit her lip. She hadn't yet told anyone about her sister working there, and Lily would be devastated if she knew, given how wickedly Margaret's husband had behaved with her. 'Oh, don't mind about that now. Let's talk about you, love.'

'No, I want to hear all about the shop. You're so brave, taking it on in Arnie's place. I meant to drop in today and have a look around,' she added blithely, and Sheila's heart leapt as she realised how close she'd sailed to disaster that afternoon. If her granddaughter had turned up and seen Maggie there … But the girl was rattling on, oblivious to Sheila's guilty stare. 'Tristan and I arrived early with Robert and Demelza, so we thought we'd drive down to pick you up and save you the walk home. But then Hazel and George

Cotterill turned up with their own little Lily, and their new baby, Dickie, so I had to stay for a chat and to admire the baby. They've just taken them both to see the pigs, along with the Land Girls.'

'Oh, baby Dickie's a sweet one, ain't he? Though he came a few weeks earlier than expected and poor Hazel was in labour two days with him, did she say? I think she was soon wishing you were around to help, love, after you delivered their first so easily.' They both had a chuckle. 'But who's Robert?' Sheila frowned. The name was familiar, but she couldn't place it.

'You remember Robert, Gran … He's my brother-in-law. Demelza's husband.' Lily turned, nodding towards the two young men deep in earnest conversation at the kitchen table. One was ginger-haired Tristan, so the other one had to be Robert. The young woman beside him, also with a shock of gingerish hair and freckles, was cradling a chubby baby in a pink smock and chatting excitedly to Violet, who was wiping Sarah Jane's face while the girl wriggled and tried to escape. 'That's their baby, Teresa. Noisy little thing. Quite a set of lungs on her. But adorable, of course.'

'Of course,' Sheila agreed, adding in a whisper, 'He's the Quaker, is that right? The hero.'

'That's the one, yes.'

Robert Day had refused to fight in the war, declaring himself a conscientious objector. But he'd earned a George Cross all the same, as an ambulance driver, risking his life on the battlefield to rescue wounded soldiers under heavy fire and take them by ambulance to the field hospital.

'A little help here, Joe?' Ernest muttered, standing on the top rung of a wobbly stepladder as he struggled to tie the congratulations banner in place. Joe sidestepped a dancing child to hold the stepladder grimly in place. 'Thank you.'

The small child staggering around the kitchen table, clapping his hands and crooning tunelessly to the band music, was Sheila's great-grandson, Lily and Tristan's little boy Morris, who was nearly two and a half now. He was big for his age, with a lively intelligent face, and the trademark reddish hair, though not as bright as his father's.

'My, your little Mo's growing quicker than a beanstalk,' Sheila said admiringly.

'He's a handful, for sure,' Lily agreed, eyeing her child ruefully.

'I didn't know those two were coming to Alice's wedding too. So who's looking after the farm?'

Since the recent death of Tristan and Demelza's father, the four young people had been running his sheep farm on the outskirts of Penzance. Sheila wasn't sure what she thought of two couples living together, especially now they both had a child. But if it suited them …

'Tristan's aunt is holding the fort, with some help from friends. We'll only be away a couple of days anyway, just long enough for the wedding and to see Alice and Patrick off on their honeymoon. Then we'll be dashing back to Penzance, I'm afraid.' Lily gave her an apologetic smile. 'I'm sorry it's a flying visit. But the livestock won't look after itself.'

'Of course not. And I'm delighted to see you at all. But where's the bride-to-be herself? She's not here yet, I suppose?'

'I think Alice is due any minute. Though Patrick won't be staying long. Apparently, the Cotterills are putting him up until the wedding. Bad luck to see the bride before the wedding night, and all that.'

Sheila went to say hello to Tristan and little Morris, now sitting on his dad's knee, still clapping his hands to the music. 'This one will be a drummer when he grows up, mark my words.' When she'd kissed both on the cheek, Sheila shook hands with Robert and Demelza. 'You've all been given a cuppa, have you?' she asked, glancing at the mugs on the table.

'Violet's been looking after us brilliantly,' Robert said in the deep, calm voice she remembered, and then turned to applaud Ernest as he came gingerly down the ladder, Alice and Patrick's welcome banner having been fixed in place. 'Well done, you two.'

'I didn't do much.' Joe grinned, folding up the stepladder and putting it away under the stairs. 'Though we got it up just in time, I'd say,' he said, nodding to the kitchen door.

Sure enough, they could hear an engine straining up the steep hill to the farm.

'Alice!' Lily shrieked, and ran out to greet her sister.

Demelza passed her baby to Sheila with a wink. 'You'll look after her, won't you, Gran?' she asked with an innocent expression before following Lily outside.

Sheila wasn't Demelza's grandmother, but she didn't mind being an honorary 'Gran' to the young woman, given that her granddaughter had married Demelza's brother. And she liked being Gran to everyone. It was a comfortable title.

Still, she mused, gazing fondly into the baby's wide eyes and admiring her wisps of strawberry blonde hair, she had rather enjoyed revisiting her youth today, chatting with Bernard Bailey in the back room of the shop. Margaret had teased her about it afterwards, of course. Said all manner of foolish things, as though the two of them had been up to no good together over that cup of tea and slice of ginger cake.

Guiltily, Sheila recalled how much she'd enjoyed her little chat with Bernard, barely giving Arnie a second thought until after she'd waved goodbye to her old friend. *You're a respected member of the village community,* he'd told her, and she'd been pleased as punch. Even so, it wasn't right for her to have been smiling like that at another man, she told herself sternly. She was still mourning her husband, for gawd's sake.

Nonetheless, as she'd told her sister afterwards, their meeting had been purely business. Bernard was going to help her speak to the council, and the council would apparently help her raise funds for the villagers down on their luck, the ones who barely had two shillings to rub together. And it was no use saying the Labour government would sort it all out because those things took time, and meanwhile families were starving and children walking about barefoot.

The thought of going barefoot gave her an idea. Perhaps she could ask villagers to donate unwanted clothes and footwear in reasonable condition, rather than simply money. In these days of ongoing restriction, with everyone still forced to tighten their belts, suggesting a clear-out of drawers and wardrobes for items they no longer used might meet with more favour than asking outright for money.

In the absence of proper help from the authorities, she could even start the ball rolling herself. There were several dresses and skirts in her room that no longer fitted her, and although it might hurt to donate Arnie's Sunday best to the fund, his old clothes and hats were no use to anyone just sitting in her room and maybe it was time to let him go …

'That's a very serious face,' Robert said, coming to relieve her of his baby daughter. 'I hope Teresa hasn't disgraced herself,' he remarked, sniffing the pink-smocked baby suspiciously.

'Bless her, no. I was just thinking about the government.'

'Good God.' Tristan, trying to keep his own child from running out of the door after the others, shook his head. 'This is a celebration, Mrs Newton. No politics allowed.'

Lily's dad, Ernest, stopped in passing and threw them both a quizzical look. 'What? No politics? What kind of a party is this?'

'One without fisticuffs,' Tristan said wryly, and finally let go of Morris, who had been wriggling fit to burst. Morris dashed to the door and Ernest hurried after him, followed by the boy's father.

A few minutes later, Alice and Patrick, flanked by their family, grown-ups and little children alike, were bundled into the kitchen, and for a while Sheila couldn't hear herself think, as everyone burst into applause, along with shouts of 'Congratulations!' and 'Here's to the happy couple!'

Alice, not quite as tall as her sister Lily, was looking slimmer these days and surprisingly elegant, despite having chosen to squash her fair hair down under a white straw hat. But then Lily had filled out since producing a child, and Sheila saw nothing wrong in that. She wondered if Alice and Patrick were also considering starting a family straightaway. She knew the young couple were ambitious though, and suspected they might want to wait a few more years until Alice felt ready for a baby. Back in her youth, of course, married women had almost never worked, but these were different times …

Patrick looked more mature too, smart in a clean-cut suit jacket and long trousers. He stood about grinning while everyone cheered, turning a stylish hat in his hands. Sheila thought she detected the hint of a moustache, and guessed he was growing one to look older, for his face was still a little boyish.

Sheila knew Violet had felt awkward about her niece not being wed and had been keenly telling everyone the two were only working together, not *living* together.

Well, they were about to tie the knot now. And good luck to them.

Ernest put an arm about his daughter on one side, and about his future son-in-law on the other, and drew them both towards him. 'Welcome home, kids. And congratulations.'

Everyone cheered even louder at this, and the men stamped their feet until the kitchen rafters rang with the noise of their drumming.

'My poor ears,' Sheila groaned, clapping her hands over them until the hubbub had died down. Then she hugged Alice. 'My beautiful, clever Alice. We've all missed you, love.' Then she hugged her grandson-to-be, Patrick, who looked awkward and embarrassed as she wished them both well. When Violet and Joe moved in for their hugs too, Sheila bustled to the range to make sure everyone was furnished with fresh tea and her tasty home-made biscuits.

Sarah Jane, sitting on the floor with one of the dogs, was yawning and looked ready for her bed. Poor lamb, she was only two, after all.

'You were a long time coming home from the shop today,' Violet commented, bringing her a tray of dirty tea mugs for rinsing and re-using.

'Was I?' Sheila fetched down a biscuit tin and prised the lid off with the handle of a spoon. 'Well, I'm here now. Is there any cake left?'

Violet eyed her suspiciously but didn't press the matter, not least because Sarah Jane was tugging on her skirt. 'Not much,' she admitted. 'Except wedding cake, and we won't be touching that until after the ceremony.' She bent to her daughter. 'Tired, poppet? Mummy will take you to bed soon. You need some bread and cheese first. And I expect Morris will want some too.'

Hazel and George Cotterill had returned from the pigsty with young Lily and baby Dickie, and were congratulating the happy couple, who both grinned and blushed, for George had been their boss down at Eastern House. The Land Girls had crowded in behind them too, giggling and teasing Alice about her forthcoming nuptials.

Sheila gazed about the kitchen, shaking her head. Her bad knee was beginning to ache again after today's exertions. 'Dinner's going to be like the bloomin' feeding of the five thousand … And where in gawd's name are all these people expected to lay their heads tonight?'

'Don't fuss, Mum. We'll find space, we always do. And Patrick's staying with the Cotterills tonight.' Violet smiled happily, sorting out bread and cheese for the youngsters. 'Our Alice is getting married, Mum. Isn't that wonderful?'

'I never thought I'd see the day,' Sheila admitted, thinking back to the gawky, oddly behaved girl she'd waved goodbye to when Violet had taken the two girls down to Cornwall from Dagenham. 'But she's all grown up, ain't she?' She sighed, remembering her eldest daughter Betsy, who'd died too young. 'I wish your sister could have been here to see her two girls so happy.'

'Betsy's looking down on them right now,' Violet said, her eyes misty. 'I feel it.'

Moved to tears, Sheila hugged her daughter close, and then managed a smile as the kettle began to whistle. 'Stuff the tea. Let's celebrate Alice and Patrick's return with something stronger.'

'Oh no, Mum, not your home brew again …'

Hearing this, Ernest shouted, banging on the kitchen table, 'Yes, your magnificent mother's famous home-made wine! That's precisely what this party needs.'

Alice groaned, burying her face in her hands.

Laughing, Sheila hobbled off to fetch her home-made sloe wine.

CHAPTER SEVENTEEN

'How do I look?' Joan asked Tilly, performing a shy twirl for her on the attic landing. She was wearing flats to Alice's wedding because she didn't own a pair of heels, and hoped nobody would think any the worse of her for not clopping along like an unsteady horse on this special occasion, which was how she usually felt when walking in heels. But she'd taken up the hem on a pretty yellow and white dress that Selina had given her when she left, saying it was too long to be fashionable and had never suited her colouring anyway. The dress might not be practical for work on a farm, but it did set off Joan's dark hair nicely and was surely perfect for a summer wedding.

'Smashing,' Tilly said enthusiastically, and did a quick twirl of her own, grinning. 'What about me? I haven't been to many weddings, so I wasn't sure what to wear.'

'You look lovely.' Tilly was wearing a simple green dress that hugged her figure and brilliantly complimented her red hair and green eyes. But, with pearls about her throat and bold scarlet lipstick, she looked quite the thing. 'I always feel so awkward in a dress these days. It's being a Land Girl, I suppose. You get used to those horrid mustard breeches, don't you think?'

'I loathe the colour but I do love wearing trousers,' Tilly admitted. 'Even if a man in the village did mistake me for a boy the other day. But I was striding along, whistling, hands in my pockets,' she added. 'So maybe he had a point.'

They both snorted with laughter, but turned as Caroline came stiffly out of the end bedroom. She was barefoot and still in her slip, looking pale and gaunt.

Tilly gave her an anxious look. 'Are you all right, Caro?'

'I feel awful,' Caroline complained, wrapping her arms about her waist. 'I wish I didn't have to dress up and look smart today. I'm not in the mood. Do you think Violet would be very angry if I wore my Land Girl uniform to the church?'

'Yes,' Tilly said frankly, and propelled the other girl back into the attic bedroom they shared. 'Right, let's lay everything out on the bed so you can try things on in turn. Then we'll choose which outfit looks best on you. Now, don't scowl … It'll be fun, just like a fashion show.'

'Must I?' Caroline groaned.

Joan would have left them to it but the other girl looked truly miserable. 'Come on,' she said encouragingly, and started dragging clothes out of Caroline's drawers and tossing them to Tilly to lay on the bed. 'It's either this or face Violet's wrath.' She lowered her head, bunched her brows together, and glared at the other girl for all she was worth. 'Is that what you want? The Violet Postbridge stare?'

Caroline burst out laughing. 'Oh, when you put it like that … All right, so what should I try on first, Tilly? Because I don't have a clue.'

It took half an hour, but finally they picked out a suitable outfit for Caroline to wear, which was an earthy brown skirt that just skimmed her knees, coupled with a frilly white blouse. Some of Tilly's borrowed jewellery and make-up made the ensemble less plain, but it was clear that Caroline's wardrobe was extremely limited when it came to party clothes.

'I look like a waitress,' Caroline moaned, staring at herself in the mirror.

'In that case, I'll have a bottle of Champagne and a slap-up dinner,' Tilly announced in a faked posh voice. 'Hurry up, my good woman, and bring us a tray of cocktails while you're about it.'

Caroline tried to look cross but failed miserably, and all three of them fell about laughing. Until they heard Violet shouting up the stairs.

'Are you girls ready yet? We're all waiting down here. You need to get to the church before us, because Joe and I will be waiting here with Alice until it's time for her to leave. The bride always needs to get there last, see?'

They hurried downstairs and found George Cotterill waiting by the car with all its doors open. 'Hop in, girls,' he told them briskly, 'I'll be driving you down to the church, then coming back for Alice and her dad.'

Everyone else seemed to have left already. There was no sign of Alice, who was no doubt still with her gran, enduring last-minute adjustments to her dress.

When they reached the church, they found villagers milling about, hoping for a glimpse of the bride, and mixing with the wedding guests, who were all dressed very smartly in hats and suits, standing about in the sunshine, chatting. The Reverend Clewson was already ushering people inside to take their seats, while everyone was doing their level best to ignore his breathless pleas.

Caroline gave a sudden cry and lurched forward at the sight of Selina waiting near the church. 'Selly,' she breathed, her blue eyes wide, shimmering with tears again. 'I ... I wasn't sure you were going to make it.' She threw her arms about her friend and the two girls hugged. 'I've missed you so much. Thank you, thank you for coming.'

'I couldn't have missed Alice's wedding,' Selina said, laughing as she disengaged herself from Caroline's embrace. She was looking remarkably swish in a navy-blue dress cinched at the waist by a broad belt, with silvery earrings that dangled and immaculate make-up. She'd had her hair cut since leaving the farm, and seemed much older and more serious. But then, Joan considered, she'd lost her sister recently, and such a brutal loss could make people grow up quickly. 'You look very pretty, Caro,' she was telling her friend. 'And you're wearing make-up. Good show.'

'The other two helped me,' Caroline admitted with an embarrassed air, patting her blonde locks, which they'd smoothed back for her and fixed in place with one of Tilly's decorative hair combs.

Joan hugged Selina too. 'I'm so sorry for your loss.'

'Thank you.'

'I say, who's that with you, Selina?' Tilly whispered, eager curiosity in her voice, and Joan's gaze shot to the young man at Selina's elbow. He was tall, probably in his late twenties, and rather good-looking, with thick dark hair flopping over his forehead and deep-set, intelligent eyes that roamed about their group and the churchyard, taking everything in.

Selina turned to her companion with an awkward smile. 'I'm sorry, I should have introduced you all. This is Cameron – I mean, Mr Bourne, a neighbour of mine. He was kind enough to drive me over here today. I feel bad about it, in fact, as I hadn't realised what a long drive it would be.'

'Good God, no need for that,' the young man insisted, grinning. 'It was a perfect excuse to see what the car could do on the long straights. Helen never lets me drive that fast,' he added with a self-conscious laugh, and then glanced at them. 'Helen's my sister, you understand.'

Joan almost smiled at this telling explanation. Her mind had indeed leapt to the possibility that Helen was his wife, and that Mr Bourne had very improperly agreed to drive Selina to the wedding on his own, despite being a married man.

Now Selina was blushing, clearly tongue-tied. It was all very interesting.

Joan held out a friendly hand, saying, 'Well, we're very grateful to you for bringing us Selina. As you can see, she's been sorely missed. I'm Joan, by the way. And this is Caroline and Tilly.'

He shook hands with them all, and would have said something more, except the vicar pounced on their group and chivvied them into the church. 'Sorry to hurry you, but the bride's arriving,' Reverend Clewson hissed before dashing away.

As the others moved inside as ordered, Joan hesitated in the shade of the church porch, glancing over her shoulder. Violet and Joe were walking quickly towards her with Sarah

Jane toddling between them and Mrs Newton puffing behind in the sunshine. The farmer winked at Joan in passing but Violet told her sharply, 'Alice and Ernest are on their way, my girl. You'd best find a seat.'

'I'll be right behind you,' Joan agreed.

But catching a glimpse of George Cotterill's black car pulling up outside the church again, she waited curiously and soon saw Alice emerge, shaking out the folds of her lovely, full-skirted wedding dress.

Her father came round to take his daughter's arm, also looking very smart in a dark suit and tie, and the two smiled at each other. Witnessing the intimate look they exchanged, Joan felt an immense sadness, thinking of everything she'd lost with her father's early death. But there was also a great sense of joy welling up inside for Alice, who was looking absolutely radiant. As she ought to on her wedding day …

Several latecomers brushed past Joan into the church, and as she flattened herself against the wall with a muttered apology, she spotted a lone figure lurking in the churchyard, half hidden behind a vast wych elm.

It was Arthur Green.

Seeing that she'd spotted him, he raised a hand and grinned.

Joan found herself smiling back at him, and even risked a quick wave. She felt a sudden urge to dash across and say hello to him. Not wanting to spoil Alice's big moment though, she slipped into the church instead.

She was surprised though. Arthur had insisted he wouldn't be coming to the wedding, not having been invited, but perhaps he had stopped out of curiosity to see the bride arrive, as so many other villagers had done, clustered about the grassy churchyard as Alice and her father made their way into the church.

It was a lovely wedding service. Joan, who rarely went to church, found herself enjoying the ritual of it all, the prayers and time-honoured words, and the beautiful hymns they sang. Mrs Newton sobbed throughout, quite noisily at times, which made young Tilly bite her lip and giggle in little stifled gasps until tears ran down her cheeks. Violet wept too, but more quietly, while Joe merely looked proud and a little uncomfortable in his best suit.

Alice's older sister Lily was seated in the front pew alongside her husband, her brother- and her sister-in-law, both women struggling with a child throughout the service. Demelza's baby girl cried lustily from time to time, while young Morris, sitting on his mother's knee, cooed and pointed and exclaimed. Violet's daughter, two-year-old Sarah Jane, also sitting beside Lily, was surprisingly well behaved on this occasion.

The church was full, but by some miracle everyone stayed respectfully still and silent while the happy couple recited their vows, the ladies sighing with happiness when the groom bent his head to kiss the bride. Though he didn't have to bend it far, Joan thought with an inner smile, for Alice was almost as tall as her bridegroom.

To her amazement, as a glowing Alice and Patrick made their way to the vestry to sign the register, Joan tasted salt and realised that she too was crying. The church organist was playing a stirring tune, however, and she did love music. So she put her sudden extreme happiness down to that, not wanting to admit even to herself that she'd been moved by the wedding ceremony.

'I suppose they'll be going back to London now,' Tilly whispered beside her, waiting impatiently for the bride and groom to re-emerge. 'They only came back to Porthcurno so all their friends and family could come to the wedding.' She hesitated. 'Well, Alice's family, at least.'

'Patrick's family are here too,' Caroline said, leaning forward. She nodded towards the other side of the aisle, where most of the villagers were sitting. In the second pew back, they could see a stern old gentleman and a small, grey-haired woman also waiting for the bride and groom to finish signing the register. 'They're not his *parents* though,' she explained in a whisper. 'He was orphaned, Alice said. So those must be distant relatives. Or maybe the people who brought him up? I'm not sure. Sad though, isn't it? Alice has such a big family, and he only has those two.'

'But he has Alice now,' Joan pointed out, and again blinked away a tear. Her eyes seemed to be watering quite copiously. Maybe it was all the dust she could see spinning in the soft beams of sunlight that crisscrossed the old church.

Alice and Patrick finally re-emerged, walking hand-in-hand down the aisle and out into the bright day. Her maid of honour was Penny, a former Land Girl at the farm who'd come over specially that morning from Bude, where she lived with her husband, John. It seemed only yesterday that Joan and the others had driven over to Bude for *her* wedding. Now she was her friend Alice's maid of honour.

Too young to be a bridesmaid, Sarah Jane had been made a flower girl instead, and with her cousin Lily's help, the little girl tottered out behind Penny and the bride and groom, hauling a wicker flower basket almost as big as herself.

'Oh, will you look at that? Too, too sweet …' Selina

whispered along the pew, her voice cracking as she dabbed at damp eyes with a hanky. 'Honestly, I don't have a clue why I'm crying … How ridiculous.' Her mascara was running, Joan noticed.

'Me neither,' Joan admitted in a croaky voice, and rummaged for her own hanky. No doubt her make-up was a mess too. Though she hadn't put any mascara on, thankfully, as it wasn't really her thing.

'I know. She's just a … a … a flower girl,' Caroline gasped in agreement, her own eyes overflowing.

Tilly jumped up with a wild laugh. 'Oh, come on, you bunch of watering pots, or we'll miss the photographs.'

But Joan could tell by the younger girl's brimming eyes and flushed cheeks that she too had been blubbing.

Outside in the sunshine, everyone was clustered about the bride and groom, throwing rice and congratulating them, while George Cotterill manfully tried to herd everyone together for family photographs. He had recently bought a smart-looking Box Brownie and so had been designated chief photographer for the event. Undercover of this chaos, Joan discreetly slipped away to speak to Arthur, who was still leaning against the giant wych elm at the back of the churchyard.

'How was it?' he asked, straightening up.

'I thought I'd be bored stiff,' she admitted, putting away her hanky before he realised she'd been crying. 'But it was rather lovely. And such a pretty church.'

'I used to go brass rubbing when I was younger,' he told her. 'Before the war, you know. I'd cycle around all the churches between here and Penzance, and some of them are quite charming. Though I've never been much of a churchgoer myself either.'

'I didn't think you'd still be here when we came out,' she admitted.

'Do you mind?'

'No, I'm glad,' she said shyly. 'Does this mean you'll be coming back to the farm with us once the photographs have been done?'

Arthur thrust his hands into his pockets, watching the wedding party over her shoulder. 'I was just waiting to talk to you. I'm not sure I'd be welcome up at the farm. The Postbridges don't think much of me, you said.'

'All the same, I'm game if you are.' She gave him an encouraging smile, though her heart beat faster at the thought of Violet's reaction. Perhaps it would be better to forget it, but then she wouldn't enjoy the afternoon as much, not if Arthur couldn't be there with her. What did that mean? That she had a crush on him? She felt her cheeks warm under his searching look. 'It's your choice, of course. If you'd rather go home—'

He shook his head.

'So come up to the farm,' she said lightly. 'I think we're all walking up. And if Violet gives you the cold shoulder, we'll just slip away somewhere … Take some sandwiches and beer, and sit on the cliffs. They can't stop us seeing each other,' she added, 'and we shouldn't let them try.'

Arthur caught her arm as she turned away. 'Joan, wait. When you say, *seeing each other*, d-does this mean … What I'm t-trying to ask is …' He winced with frustration at his own stuttering. 'Good grief, I can't even say the simplest thing.'

'Does this mean what?' she prompted him.

'That you and I are … walking out together?' He pulled a face at his own hesitancy. 'Courting? However you want to put it.'

Her blush deepened. 'I suppose it does, yes. Assuming you aren't averse to the idea?'

Now it was her turn to wince. Goodness, how pompous that had sounded, Joan thought. But he didn't seem to notice, shaking his head.

'No, of course not.' He smiled, nodding over her shoulder. 'Look, the bridal party is heading back. We should probably go.'

Walking together, she and Arthur followed the other wedding guests on foot through the village and up the steep hill towards Joe's farm. It was quite a trek, and since they were talking the whole time, they soon fell behind. By the time they reached the farm, celebrations were already going on noisily inside. Someone had brought a fiddle and was scraping away with a lively tune. Through the windows she saw people dancing and could hear Mrs Newton singing at the top of her voice.

She hesitated on the threshold, glancing back at Arthur, who was clearly reluctant to go inside.

'It's rather crowded in there. Shall I fetch us beer and something to eat?' she asked, smiling, 'That way, we can sit in the field until later.'

'You mean, once Violet and Joe have drunk so much they won't notice me among the guests?' His look was ironic.

Joan couldn't help laughing. He seemed to have a direct link into her thoughts. She ought to have been alarmed by that, for she was a private person and rarely shared her opinions with other people. But there was something about Arthur … She sensed that her most secret thoughts would

212

be safe with him. Perhaps that was fanciful. But she couldn't help feeling it.

'Wait here,' she whispered, and slipped into the kitchen.

Unfortunately, it was some time before she was able to escape the party again. Weaving her way through wedding guests, Joan was twice snatched into an impromptu dance, once with Ernest Fisher, who whirled her around the kitchen table like a Dervish. Then Alice herself inexplicably drew Joan into a dance with her new husband. 'How are things?' Alice shouted over the music, swaying as she tried to dance with both Joan and Patrick at the same time. Her face was flushed, her blue eyes rather too wide. But then, it was her wedding day. Why shouldn't the bride be enjoying herself? 'I meant to sit down with you last night … but there were so many people. Are you Land Girls happy? Joe told me he's been struggling with only three of you. He's hoping our boys will come back from Europe soon. But Dad says he's living in cloud cuckoo land. Dad says the soldiers won't be demobbed for ages. Too much rebuilding to be done out there, he says. Whole cities in turmoil, everything bombed to hell. So it looks like we'll need you girls out on the land for a few years yet.' She shouted all this in Joan's ear, who was desperately racking her brains for an excuse to slip away. She didn't want Arthur to think she'd abandoned him.

'I'm happy enough,' she told Alice, raising her voice to be heard above the incredible noise in the kitchen. 'So I don't think Joe has to worry. Congratulations, anyway.' She hugged Alice and Patrick, and joined their hands together. 'You too should be dancing together, not with me as a spare wheel. You make a lovely couple and I wish you all the best.' With that, she grinned and dashed away.

Finally she battled her way out of the kitchen with some provisions and a cloth tucked under her arm that they could use to protect themselves from the grass. Arthur helped her carry the beer bottles and small hamper she'd grabbed.

In a good spot, where the field was fairly even and free from stones, Joan spread out the cloth, only then realising it was too small for the two of them unless they sat close very together. She blushed, meeting his eyes. 'Sorry.'

'Not to worry, we'll just squeeze up,' he said, after a tiny hesitation.

They sat hip to hip, gazing down on the farmhouse and the green valley of Porthcurno beyond. Music drifted up towards them, along with bursts of laughter and conversation. It was an idyllic summer's afternoon with not a cloud in the sky, only a few seagulls circling overhead. Joan kept a wary eye on them, fearing one might suddenly flap down and seize their sandwich triangles.

'This sausage roll has real pork in it,' Arthur commented, blinking as he bit deep into crumbling pastry. 'Mmm.'

'Joe sent one of the pigs to slaughter.' She caught his horrified expression and added quickly, 'Not any of the young piglets or their mother. It was one from the last litter. Alice nicknamed him Macbeth.'

He swallowed his mouthful. 'Funny name for a pig.'

'Yes, he was a bully. Never really fitted in.' She devoured her own sausage roll with pleasure. Throughout the war they'd been forced to eat such horrors as 'mock turkey', and although rationing was still in place, some of the regulations had recently been relaxed and her joy in eating was coming back. 'Though he's making up for it now.'

Arthur stared at her, then flung his head back with a bark of laughter. 'You're a dark horse, Joan.'

She bit her lip and then giggled too. She'd made the joke without really thinking. Thankfully, he seemed to share her sense of humour.

'I wish Joe and Violet knew you better,' she said impulsively. 'I'm sure if they did, they wouldn't be so—'

'If they knew me better, they'd be even less likely to want us courting.' Arthur removed the caps from the beer bottles. 'Drink?'

She took the proffered beer bottle. 'But why?' She couldn't understand what he meant. 'You told me you had nightmares. That's hardly a criminal offence.'

He looked across the valley. 'But sometimes I get the nightmares when I'm awake.' Catching her puzzled expression, Arthur bent his head, playing with the beer bottle. 'It's hard to explain. But this … Us being friends, I mean. Or more than friends. We shouldn't be doing it.' He turned his head and she was mesmerised by his gaze and the way his chest gently rose and fell as he breathed. 'It's unfair of me to be spending time with you. Because it can't last.'

'But if you like me and I like you, where's the problem?'

'Oh, Joan …' Putting down the beer bottle, he touched her cheek. The world seemed to hold still, the distant sea a whisper drowned out by the roaring in her ears as he leaned forward and set his lips against hers. Her eyes closed instinctively, and she sat in a trance as Arthur kissed her.

His mouth was firm and persuasive, and he pulled Joan closer, holding her tight. Her heart was pounding by the time he lifted his head. But it was nothing like the last time she'd been kissed. Now, she felt safe and loved.

Neither of them spoke for a moment, staring at each other. Then she said huskily, 'Goodness.'

Arthur smiled.

They sat together like that, cuddling and talking in murmurs, until the afternoon had slipped into evening and Joan began to feel cold. Arthur shrugged out of his jacket and placed it about her shoulders.

'It's late. You should go inside.' It was full dark and the music was not so loud now.

'But Joe said there'd be fireworks. I want to see them.'

'Fireworks?' Arthur looked uneasy.

'It's all right, he moved all the livestock to the top field or shut them in the barn so they wouldn't be upset by the noise and lights. Look, there's Alice's dad coming out now. It must be time.'

She could see Ernest Fisher, his face lit up by a torch beam, moving carefully about the farmhouse garden to check the pots of earth where he'd placed fireworks earlier that day. Guests began piling out to watch the display.

'Come on,' she urged him, jumping up. 'Let's get closer. Don't worry, nobody will recognise you in the dark.'

Arthur followed her reluctantly down past the farm buildings to the edge of the watching crowd.

She gasped with delight, clapping her hands as the sky was lit up with bright cascading colours, silvers and golds and shimmering reds, starbursts of light that illuminated the whole farm.

'Isn't it marvellous?' she cried above the deafening pops and bangs.

When Arthur didn't answer, but gave a horrible groan instead, she ran back to him in alarm. He was clasping his head, bent almost double, and making such a bloodcurdling noise, she thought he must be ill.

'Arthur? Are you all right?'

But he didn't seem to know her anymore. At her voice, he straightened and bared his teeth. '*You*,' he said hoarsely, and swore at her, glaring. 'You're torturing me … You want me to kill them. To kill them all. But I won't do it, do you hear? I won't bloody do it anymore.' His nostrils flared, eyes wide with fear as he suddenly recoiled, staggering violently. 'Get away from me!'

Then Arthur fell to the ground, writhing in the dirt and gurgling deep in his throat as though he were dying.

CHAPTER EIGHTEEN

Selina had snagged her summer dress on a gooseberry bush in the farmhouse garden, which was mostly laid to veg rather than flowers, where Joe and Ernest were busy setting off fireworks. The display was a lovely thought for Alice's wedding, given the expense and difficulty of getting hold of fireworks. They'd been banned altogether during the war, she recalled, as the light could have guided enemy bombers to their targets too easily, not to mention alarming civilians into thinking an invasion was taking place. But these days there were no restrictions except cost.

There wasn't much room to admire the display though, a few dozen wedding guests having crowded into the warm darkness of the garden, and now she'd stumbled against the thorny embrace of a gooseberry bush.

Carefully, Selina untangled her skirt from the thorns, taking care not to prick her fingers. At least a pulled thread shouldn't be too much of a disaster, she considered. She'd run up the dress on Mrs Hawley's sewing machine, cannibalising one of her sister's old frocks rather than wasting precious ration coupons on something new. So any loose threads would be an easy fix.

As the first rocket whizzed into the sky, she stared expectantly upwards, sighing at the glorious explosion of light brightening the dark … 'Ah.'

Cameron, beside her, murmured, 'Damn noisy things.'

'Pretty, though.'

She flashed him a quick smile. Had she done the right thing, asking Cameron to drive her all the way down to Alice's wedding in Porthcurno? It had been a cheeky request, even given that she'd provided most of the fuel for such a long journey. But had she given him the wrong idea?

Though perhaps she'd asked deliberately, intrigued by glowing reports she'd read of the young man in her sister's earliest journal. Life at Thornton Hall had been so busy lately, she'd barely had time to read more than a few entries so far. But she'd caught Cameron's name among references to Sebastian and his friends and neighbours, as her sister had made a home for herself as a new bride on Bodmin Moor.

She was a little light-headed, Selina realised, and also unsteady on her feet. Tilly had been plying her with Mrs Newton's home-made gin for the past hour or so, which now came in several different flavours, all of them equally violent. To her relief, Joan had agreed to bunk up with Caro, Tilly and Selina tonight, leaving her own room free for Cameron. He'd claimed he could sleep in the car, but Selina was sure that would be awfully uncomfortable. Some of the other guests who were staying in the village overnight were being housed above Mrs Newton's shop, while some rooms in the farmhouse were having to accommodate two or even three times their usual quota. But for most guests their stay was only for one night, so everyone seemed perfectly happy to squeeze up.

She probably shouldn't have drunk so much. But then she would never have agreed to dance, and that had been one of the highlights of her evening so far. The kitchen table had been removed to leave space for dancing, with a scattering of chairs around the room for any older guests or those who'd had too much to drink. During a lull in the dancing, Mrs Newton had set her foot on a stool and played the spoons on her knee, something her late husband Arnie had always done at parties, and then talked politics loudly with Joe, Ernest and a silver-haired man nobody seemed to know, but whom Selina had heard Mrs Newton introduce as 'an old school friend of mine, Mr Bailey'.

It felt strange to be back at the farm after weeks at Thornton Hall. She had grown used to the spacious, comfortable surroundings, and to having time to call her own, wandering in the gardens or reading when not spending time with her sister's children.

Being back in Porthcurno reminded her of how hard she'd worked here. Long years of back-breaking labour, often out in the dark before dawn and in all weathers, achieving tasks she'd never have considered possible before the war had driven her to join the Land Army. But oh, the fun she'd had too … The friends she'd made and the high jinx, tricks played on each other, like the time she and Penny had balanced a bucket of water on the barn door, and Caroline had walked through instead of Hazel's schoolboy son, who'd cheeked Selina and deserved a dunking …

She'd spoken to Penny and Alice for ages in the kitchen earlier. Penny had been full of gossip about old friends, for during the war she and Alice had roomed together in the Cornish seaside resort of Bude. Eventually, Penny had married a local fisherman there. The former Land Girl had come from Bude with her husband, John, and had told Alice everything that had been happening in her absence.

'Florence and Miles have moved to the States,' she'd told them excitedly, before adding for Selina's benefit, who'd been looking puzzled, 'Florence was our landlady in Bude, you understand, and Miles was one of the US Rangers billeted at her boarding house. They fell in love and married just before he had to leave for the D-Day landings. It was so romantic,' she'd gushed. 'Miles was wounded at Pointe du Hoc, so was discharged early, but he's fine now. They've moved to Texas with little Billy and their baby, Hope. Though Hope must be getting on for two now, hardly a baby anymore.'

'Texas?' Alice had looked impressed. 'Blimey, yes, that's where Miles came from, wasn't it? I wish them both well, of course. And it'll be an adventure for young Billy. But I can't quite imagine Florence in Texas. She was so … British.'

And she and Penny had laughed, reminiscing about the old days in Bude, where Alice had secretly been learning spycraft, unbeknownst to everyone at their boarding house, while Penny had been working in a dairy shop.

It was still amazing to Selina how much had gone on behind the scenes during the war. It was as though there'd been another country hidden under the Britain they'd seen every day, but of course people had understood the need for that secrecy. Now they could discuss such things more openly. And yet few people did, perhaps still fearful it might not yet be safe, especially with so many British soldiers still in uniform and in foreign climes, serving their country. As though somehow the British and their allies might wake up to find the hard-won peace had been a dream …

'I say,' Cameron said in her ear, 'I think one of your friends is trying to get your attention.'

Confused, Selina turned from watching the brilliant bangs and lights of the fireworks. 'Sorry?'

It was Joan, who'd come dashing up, and was tugging on her sleeve. 'Selly, come quick … I don't know what to do,' she gasped, barely audible over the applause and chatter. 'It's my friend, Arthur. He's back there and he … he's not well. He needs help.'

Cameron was already heading to the rear of the shadowy garden. He peered over the low wall into the farmyard, then ran through the gate. By the time Selina and Joan caught up with him, he was already kneeling beside a young man on the ground, who was groaning and shaking violently.

'Good God,' Selina exclaimed, 'what's wrong with him?'

'I'm not sure,' Joan said miserably. 'He just started yelling and then fell down like that. But he told me he sometimes has waking nightmares. And Violet warned me not to spend time with him. She said he … he hadn't been *right* since the war. But Arthur's such a good friend, so I … I thought she must be exaggerating.' Joan hugged herself, her eyes wide and frightened. 'This is all my fault. He was fine until I made him come down to the farm.'

'You're all right, dear chap,' Cameron was saying, having helped a visibly distressed Arthur to sit up. He put a comforting hand on the other man's shoulder. 'That's it, that's the ticket … You'll be right as rain in a minute.'

Arthur didn't look 'all right', Selina thought. Indeed, the young man began to sob as yet more fireworks rocketed off into the sky with loud bangs. But she trusted Cameron's judgement. He had been an officer during the war and was clearly used to dealing with a variety of difficult situations.

'Perhaps we should move him indoors,' Joan suggested, 'before anyone sees him.'

But it was too late. Already they could hear voices behind them, and sure enough, Joe came limping through from the garden at that moment, leaning heavily on his cane, a worried-looking Violet at his back, swinging a torch.

'What's going on? What's wrong?' Violet shone the torch beam across Arthur's face and gave a shocked cry. 'What the blazes? Who's that on the ground?'

'It's the Green lad,' Joe muttered.

'Oh, bloomin' 'eck.' Violet dazzled Selina and Joan with her torch instead. 'Had too much to drink, has he?'

'I think it's the fireworks,' Cameron told them grimly. 'He doesn't like them. The bangs and explosions. Brings it all back, see?'

Violet stared at him. 'Brings what back?'

'The war,' Cameron said grimly.

Joan winced.

'But what's he doing 'ere?' Violet rounded swiftly on Joan. 'We told you not to keep seeing Arthur Green, didn't we? Warned you how it would be. But you wouldn't listen, oh no. Thought you knew better than me and Joe.' She hurried forward for a better look, clucking her tongue. But at least she seemed more anxious than furious, Selina thought, and gave Joan's hand a quick squeeze, seeing her friend trembling and on the verge of tears. 'Now look at the state of the poor lad.'

Arthur cried louder at her approach, covering his eyes.

'The torch,' Cameron told her urgently. 'Turn it off.'

Violet gave him another dubious look but obeyed, clicking off the torch, and at once Arthur lapsed into quiet sobbing again.

Joe had disappeared but soon returned with Ernest, who took one look at the young man cradled in Cameron's arms, and nodded.

'Here we go,' he said in jovial tones, helping Cameron get the boy onto his feet again. 'Now, let's get you inside the house. Away from all this sound and fury, eh? That's it, one foot in front of the other. Excellent.' Arthur stumbled but the two men supported him. 'No, you're doing well … We'll soon have you feeling better, my boy.' He glanced back at Joe. 'Can you manage the fireworks without me? There's only a few left to set off.'

'I'll be fine,' Joe assured him, and headed back into the dark garden.

Slowly, Selina followed the men into the farmhouse, Joan trailing behind her. It was dark but she could hear sniffing. 'Hey,' she said, stopping on the threshold to put an arm about the other girl's shoulder. 'He's going to be all right, I'm sure. You heard Mr Bourne, it was probably the fireworks that set him off. I expect they must have sounded like bombs … And who can blame him? I still get nightmares about the war, and I've nothing like his excuse.'

Joan nodded, drying her face with the backs of her hands. 'I can't help blaming myself though. We were sitting up in the fields, and he was perfectly fine. Then I insisted we came down to see the fireworks properly …' She shuddered, whispering, 'Oh, Selina, it was horrible. I've never seen him like that. He's always behaved like such a gentleman towards me. And suddenly he was like a wild animal, yelling and snarling.'

Selina hugged her. 'You poor thing.'

The two men had taken Arthur through into the snug, away from the curious glances of Mrs Newton and her friend, Mr Bailey, who were sitting in the kitchen, catching up on old times, by the sound of it.

Robert, Demelza's husband, appeared. 'Joe says someone's in need of help?' and Selina nodded him towards the snug.

''Ere, what's up with that lad?' Mrs Newton demanded, jumping up as though to follow him. But Ernest came out and closed the door into the snug.

'Sorry, Sheila … Best leave the boy to calm down. He's had a nasty shock, that's all, but he'll be fine in a jiffy.'

'What can I do to help?' Joan asked in a low voice.

Alice's dad paused, studying her. 'Leave him to us. We'll make sure Arthur gets home safely.'

'Isn't there *anything* I can do?' Joan pleaded.

He smiled, shaking his head. 'Good of you to offer but Robert's been a battlefield ambulance man. He's got experience with this sort of thing. And that young fellow Mr Bourne seems to know his stuff too.'

Joan's shoulders slumped and Selina felt sorry for her, knowing how badly she'd be suffering if that had been Johnny while they were still courting. Her friend was no doubt still blaming herself too, even though it wasn't her fault.

'Come upstairs,' she said, taking Joan's arm. 'We can talk about it in Caro's room. I expect the bedding will need to be sorted out anyway. We can chat while we fix up enough blankets and pillows for the four of us girls.'

With one last unhappy glance at the closed door of the snug, Joan agreed and followed her upstairs.

* * *

225

Selina could hardly believe how tiny the attic rooms seemed after a few weeks in her sister's home, their sloping ceilings and dirty skylights almost claustrophobic, while the furniture was ancient and tatty. Had she really slept on this lumpy old mattress, she thought, and made do with a stand-up wash most mornings in this cracked sink with its leaky tap? And yet she'd been happy here, for the most part. It was only after Johnny's long silence, followed by his break-up letter, that she'd begun to wish she could be anywhere else in the world. But that had only been because everyone at the farm had known how badly she'd been treated, and she could no longer handle the humiliation of their pitying looks or hurriedly cut-off whispers whenever she entered a room. They had meant well, no doubt, but it had been with genuine relief that she'd packed her bags and finally cut loose from Porthcurno …

She and Joan found a few spare blankets in the airing cupboard, though the best ones had all been snaffled for the other guests. No extra pillows or bolsters were left, so they decided two of them would have to roll up a towel and use that instead. Joan seemed to settle under the distraction of the task, and was dry-eyed by the time they'd made up two more beds on the floor.

'Mr Bourne's right,' Joan agreed, sighing as she drew up her knees and linked her hands about them, sitting on Tilly's bed, 'it was when the fireworks started that he changed. Those loud bangs and pops … So deafening. It must have thrown him back to the war, somehow.'

'I've heard of that happening to some men,' Selina told her, aware of a guilty relief that Cameron had not been damaged by his war experience in a similar way. She wasn't sure she could have coped with that. Though she and Cameron were only friends. It must be so much worse when it was a boyfriend.

'I don't know how I shall ever face him again,' Joan admitted. 'I should have realised. He was trying to tell me. I see that now. And I ignored him. I didn't understand.' She gave a little gasp. 'He must hate me.'

'Why on earth would he hate you?'

'For bringing this on him … We could have stayed where we were, up on the hill behind the house. Then at least if he'd … changed, nobody but me would have seen him. Now everyone knows.'

'Hardly everyone,' Selina pointed out practically. 'Me, Mr Fisher, Joe, Violet, and Demelza's husband … Oh, and Mr Bourne, who'll probably never come back here again.' She paused, shaking her head at Joan's tormented expression. 'Look, it's a good thing you weren't alone when he *changed*, as you put it. Goodness knows what might have happened if you hadn't been able to call for help.'

Joan stuck out her chin, shaking her head. 'He would never have hurt me.'

'You can't be sure of that.'

'Arthur's not like that. He's … gentle.'

'Do be sensible, Joan. You told me earlier that he was shouting at you … Like a *wild animal*, you said.'

'Only because he was confused. I genuinely don't think he knew where he was or even who I was. Not at the time.' Joan was staring down at her knees, her face abstracted. 'Oh, whatever am I going to do? This is all my fault. And Arthur will never want to see me again after tonight.'

'Maybe that's a good thing.'

'Well, I don't agree,' Joan said stubbornly. 'Though I imagine

Violet will have plenty to say on that topic too. She and Joe are probably talking about it right now.' She gave another unhappy sigh. 'And we'd had such a lovely evening too. We took a picnic up the hill and listened to the music and … and we talked for ages.' She blushed, biting her lip, and Selina had the impression there was something she wasn't telling her. 'Then the fireworks went off and everything was ruined.'

Feeling bad for her friend, Selina went over and hugged her. 'Enough of that self-pitying talk. It could have been worse.'

'How?' Joan looked up, frowning. Then her eyes widened. 'Oh, you mean … That he could have *hurt* himself? Golly, yes, and that might happen yet. His parents are bound to hear about this, and I know they're very protective of him. Maybe they'll forbid him to see me again, just like Violet and Joe did with me. Then we'll have it from both sides.'

'You two sound like a regular Romeo and Juliet,' a voice drawled from the doorway, and Selina looked quickly round to see Cameron there.

She felt immediately happier, which was ridiculous.

'Oh, have you left him? But how is he?' Joan asked, jumping off the bed at once. 'Poor Arthur … May I see him now?'

Cameron shook his head. 'Sorry, Ernest and Robert have taken him home.' He strolled about the small attic room, frowning at the blankets on the floor. 'I say, Alice's dad is a sensible chap. Though he must have nerves of steel. I'm told he was out in Germany for most of the war. Behind enemy lines.'

'Yes, he was, not that anyone here talks about it much. But Alice told Penny ages back, and Penny told Caro, and Caro told me. So, we all found out in the end.' Selina grinned at his shocked expression. 'You know how funny some people are about what they did during the war.'

'Quite right too,' Cameron agreed, thrusting his hands into his pockets. 'Some of it doesn't bear repeating, frankly. I'm surprised you all seemed to have discussed it so freely.' His frown deepened as he noticed Joan's fresh tears. 'I say, no need to cry. That boy will be fine after a good night's sleep. Nothing wrong with him that time and patience won't heal.'

'You didn't see him at the start,' Joan told him, almost savagely. 'Arthur was … Oh, I don't know what he was. But it *scared* me.'

Cameron said nothing to this but looked instead at Selina, changing the subject. 'Fancy a nightcap? Most of the guests seem to have headed home, those who aren't staying the night that is. I'm told I'll be sleeping along the landing here.'

'Yes, next door.'

'I say, have I stolen someone's bed?' He looked horrified. 'No, no, that's not right. I'll sleep on the floor.'

'You'll sleep where you're told.'

He grinned at her firm tone. 'Well, I could do with a last drink before bed. By the way, the family seem to be gathered in the kitchen to say a last goodbye to Alice and Patrick. The happy couple are spending the night down at Eastern House, I'm told, before returning to London tomorrow. They're just waiting for Alice's dad to come back from dropping Arthur home.' He shot Selina an enigmatic smile, though included Joan in the invitation. 'How about joining us all downstairs?'

'Yes,' Selina said firmly, and dragged a protesting Joan from the room. 'Come on, you need a drink. Nobody will blame you for what happened, don't be silly.'

As soon as Joan had been given a drink and seated between Caroline and Tilly in the kitchen, Selina found an excuse to go outside for some 'fresh air', and made sure to give Cameron a meaningful look. Thankfully, he took the hint and followed her after a discreet interval.

It wasn't quite pitch-black outside, for although there was no moon that night, a soft light was shining across the farmyard from the kitchen windows.

'I'm sorry about that thing with Arthur,' she began as Cameron trod towards her across the dirty cobbles, but he shook his head, holding up a hand.

'No need to apologise; it wasn't anyone's fault. These things happen.' He cleared his throat. 'Poor lad. He obviously had a hard time of it out there. I've seen it before, all too often.'

'Will he get over it?'

'Hard to tell. Most do, but an unlucky few don't. I knew one who couldn't stand it anymore and blew his brains out.'

'Oh my God!'

Cameron blenched. 'I'm sorry. That was a stupid thing to say. Forgive me, Selina. I'm sure Arthur won't do anything so desperate.' He paused. 'Besides, he's got your friend Joan to look out for him. She's obviously got a soft spot for the boy.'

'Does that make a difference?'

'It can do,' he said sombrely.

She shivered and he came closer, and abruptly took her in his arms. 'Selina,' he said huskily, and kissed her.

She clung onto his broad shoulders, closing her eyes and her mind too, blocking out any sensible thoughts.

He was a good kisser.

But memories of Johnny soon came back to haunt her and she stiffened in his arms, suddenly unsure, aware that she didn't want to risk being hurt like that ever again.

Cameron pulled back, puzzlement in his voice. 'I hope you didn't mind me kissing you? Should I apologise?'

'No,' she admitted shyly. 'Though it was a surprise.'

His eyes twinkled at that. 'Good surprise or bad surprise?'

'Good, I think.'

Now he laughed outright. But she sensed he was still thrown by such a lukewarm response. 'But you're still not *sure*? Heavens above, I must be doing it wrong.'

Selina was saved from having to elaborate by the arrival of Caroline, who'd come bouncing out of the farmhouse, torch in hand, presumably in search of them.

She felt strangely embarrassed now though, her cheeks heating.

Had Caro witnessed their kiss?

If her friend had seen anything, she didn't comment, much to Selina's relief. 'Ah, there you are, you two,' she exclaimed, running the dazzling torch beam over their faces, and then hiccupped loudly as though she'd had too much to drink. Though no more than Selina, most likely. 'Better come back. We're drinking a last toast to Alice and Patrick.'

'Thanks, Caro. We'll be right there.'

Silently, Cameron squeezed Selina's hand before releasing it, and then turned to her friend with a charming smile. 'I say,' he drawled, 'I believe you'll be travelling back to Bodmin with us tomorrow.'

'Only if you don't mind,' Caroline said awkwardly, shining her light on the way ahead as the three of them strolled back towards the farmhouse.

'Good Lord, no. Why should I mind?' He sounded amused, as though he'd already put Selina's odd reaction to his kiss out of his mind. 'The more the merrier.'

CHAPTER NINETEEN

To Sheila, it seemed an age since the fun and excitement of Alice's wedding, when in fact it had been only a few days. Yet the worry of having to talk to the council had driven all other thoughts from her head …

'Now, we move on to any other business,' Bernard said, as Chair of the Parish Council, and shuffled his papers. 'Ah, yes.' He looked expectantly at Sheila, seated in the front row, who was feeling nervous enough to throw up her tea, which she'd gobbled down hastily on her way out that evening. 'I believe we have a petition from a member of the public, Mrs Newton, whom some of you will know as proprietress of our village shop, following the sad demise of her husband, Mr Arnold Newton. I'm sure we'd all like to offer once more our heartfelt condolences on the loss of your husband, such a well-respected member of our community for so many years.'

There was a rumble of assent around her, and even one 'Hear, hear,' from the back. It was a small parish hall and a little stuffy on this warm summer's evening. Sheila wished someone had thought to open the windows, and felt her heart pounding as everyone looked her way.

The six councillors were seated in an intimidating row at the front of the room. There were usually at least seven, but Bernard had told her they'd been finding it hard to recruit a new councillor since the death of Mr Jackson, a landowner from over Trethewey way.

'If you could stand up, Mrs Newton?' one of the other councillors suggested, an elderly geezer wearing a flat cap and tweed jacket, despite the heat. When she stared, he gestured at her in an imperious way. 'Come on, we haven't got all night.'

Biting back a retort, Sheila got to her feet. She looked about herself uneasily, clutching the short speech she'd written. But as soon as she glanced down at the first line, her hand began to tremble. She swallowed, lowering the paper again. She wasn't about to stand there like an idiot, looking like she was swatting a fly rather than reading a speech. Besides, she had trouble reading without glasses these days, unless she held the print so close to her nose that nobody could see her face, and she'd left her reading glasses at home.

If only she could have persuaded Violet or Joe to come with her. But now that Alice's wedding was over, all their extended family having returned to their own homes, preparations for harvest had begun in earnest on the farm. And Caroline was still absent, having gone off to visit Selina, which meant everyone was working harder than ever. Besides which, they both heartily disapproved of her plan. 'You've got enough on your plate already, Mum,' her daughter had insisted. 'You'll make yourself ill taking this on as well.' And Joe had agreed.

'Good evening, everybody,' she began in a quavering voice, and was abruptly aware how different her voice sounded to everyone else there, not being posh or even Cornish. But that wasn't anything to be ashamed of. She had been born here, after all, even if she'd gained a Dagenham accent after years living there. Bernard Bailey was nodding at her in an encouraging way. 'Thank you for letting me speak at your council meeting tonight. I ain't too good at giving speeches …'

There were a few titters from the audience, and a man behind her cleared his throat noisily, a sure sign of impatience. Her heart began to thud more violently. Why on earth had she agreed to come to this meeting in the first place, let alone to stand up and speak? She wasn't cut out for this malarkey. She'd only just got used to running a shop again and dealing with members of the public. Now here she was, making a fool of herself in front of all these people …

'The thing is,' she went on, groping for what she'd wanted to say, 'being a shopkeeper, I've seen how people are struggling since the war ended. Probably since before the war, to be honest. Back in them days, we closed our eyes to it a bit more. Not our business, was it? But the war taught us to stick together and watch out for our neighbours … To be more of a community, I suppose.' At this, Bernard smiled, tapping his empty pipe on the table, a small sound of solidarity that echoed about the room. Heartened by this, she added, 'Not to mince words, we've got poor people in our village. People who are struggling to make ends meet and put food on the table. Right here in Porthcurno. And we ought to do something about it. Not next week or next year, for gawd's sake. We should do something about it right now.'

As she paused, trying to remember what she'd been intending to say next, and not quite daring to look down at the paper in her hand, someone called out clearly, 'Yes, agreed, but what can we do?'

It was one of the councillors who had spoken, a large, pink-cheeked lady in a flowery dress, probably only a few years older than Violet.

'No one is denying there are poor people in Porthcurno,' the lady went on in her penetrating voice. 'But there's nothing we can do about it, Mrs Newton. Dealing with issues of poverty is not what the Parish Council does. That is the purview of the government.'

'The *pur* ... What?' More laughter around her made Sheila blush. 'Look, if you mean the new government should be dealing with problems like that, I'm sure they will,' she told the lady, maybe a little too forcefully, 'but you know governments ... They don't do nothing in a hurry. Meanwhile, them villagers are suffering. And we could help them. So why don't we?' she pleaded with the room. 'As a community?'

'What precisely are you suggesting, Mrs Newton?' It was the flowery dress woman again. 'That we should hand out largesse to the populace? Go house-to-house with baskets of goods for the great unwashed, perhaps?' She smothered a laugh, glancing at her other councillors. 'The days of *noblesse oblige* are long gone. I'm sure you mean well but most people are too proud to accept charity, Mrs Newton. Indeed, they may consider us interfering do-gooders. And frankly, we had enough of do-gooders during the war. It's high time people were allowed to get on with their own lives.'

'Well, missus, that's all well and good, but I don't agree. Anyway, it ain't a question of handing out food baskets or whatever. I thought we could raise some money for a community fund. Then we could approach a few people, the ones most in need, and ask them to apply for help. That way, nobody need know who's getting extra help.'

'A community fund,' Bernard mused, looking about at his other councillors in the silence that followed. 'Sounds like an excellent idea to me.'

Emboldened by his support, Sheila went on. 'I'm planning to put a poster in the shop window too, asking folk to donate unwanted clothes and footwear in good condition. I'm sure we've all seen them poor little kiddies running about the village threadbare and without shoes, and we can't keep turning a blind eye to them forever … That wouldn't need to be part of the council fund though,' she added nervously, seeing a few frowns. 'I'd be happy to sort out donations at the shop and administer that side of things myself.'

'Hand-me-downs are all very well, but who's going to organise and administer this fund?' the grouchy old man in the flat cap demanded. He took out a large hanky and blew his nose noisily. 'I'm already on the Summer Fete Committee. Yes, and the Harvest Festival Committee too. I can't take on any more work.' He pulled a face, adding, 'My wife would have words if I did.'

'Perhaps a working group?' Bernard suggested gently, 'bringing in members of the public for a wider view of the topic, and to provide liaison with those in need. And while we're discussing this, we're down a councillor since Randall's death, aren't we?' He paused, smiling at Sheila. 'In which case, I propose we co-opt Mrs Newton to sit on the council at the earliest possible opportunity.'

There was an astounded silence.

Sheila stared at him, too stunned to speak. Had Bernard

lost his bloomin' marbles? Her, a councillor? That would be the day.

Flowery Dress stuttered, 'I beg your pardon, Mr Bailey? Did I hear you correctly? Co-opt Mrs Newton? To be *a parish councillor?*'

'Why not?' Bernard shrugged. 'She's been a villager for some years and is a local businesswoman. Arnold himself was on the council for a few years.'

'That's a matter for the full council,' the second woman on the council said, frowning. She was nearer Sheila's age, with steel-grey hair cut short and a neat jacket that matched her hair.

'We *are* the full council, Mrs Brewer,' Bernard countered.

'Point of order, Chair,' one of the other councillors threw in, a thin man who often dropped by the shop mid-week with his wife for sliced meats and cheese, and sometimes a jar of pickles.

'Yes, Tom?'

'Shouldn't we check the rules with the parish clerk first? The council may need to put this appointment out to a proper election.'

'We announced the vacant post last month,' Bernard pointed out calmly, 'and nobody came forward to stand. So, from a technical point of view, you could say an election has *already* been called. But your point of order is worth making, so I'll check with the clerk before moving forward with this. However, in the absence of another suitable candidate, I believe the rules allow us to co-opt Mrs Newton.' He looked at Sheila significantly. 'If she's willing, that is.'

Again, everybody looked at Sheila, who opened her mouth to say no, and then found herself saying, 'Yes, I'm willing.' Her heart leapt at this madness, but she went on stubbornly,

'If that's what I need to do to help people, then I'll become a councillor.'

Bernard smiled. 'Any other comments or objections?'

Sheila glanced about the meeting room, heart pounding fiercely. She expected to see half a dozen hands go up, at least.

But it seemed nobody objected.

'The clerk's laid up with gout,' Bernard continued, making a note on the paper in front of him, 'but I'll go round and see him in a day or two, and report back on what he says for the next meeting. In the assumption that your co-option is in order, Mrs Newton, may I welcome you to the Parish Council?'

Oh blimey, Sheila thought, sitting down again heavily, shaken by the speed of events. Whatever had she gone and done? More to the point, what on earth would Violet say when she found out?

'Have you gone completely barmy?' was what Violet said, staring at her, hands on hips. She shook her head in disbelief. 'You're on the Parish Council? What do you know about being a councillor? How are you meant to fit all that around your work at the shop? Some of those meetings are in the evenings too. It's all very well in the summertime, but what about in the autumn? I can't have my mum wandering the lanes on her own in the dark. Or cycling back and forth. Which means Joe will have to pick you up. Yes, and drop you off. Because I can't. I've got Sarah Jane to look after.'

'Nobody'll need do nothing for me,' Sheila replied, nettled by her daughter's strong reaction. 'Bernard says he'll fetch me down the hill for meetings, and take me back too.' Originally, confessing what had happened, she'd intended to be apologetic and to play down what it would mean. She half agreed with Violet, after all; it was far too much to be taking on. But faced with Violet's sharp words, a contrary spirit urged her to take the opposite tack. 'Any road, it ain't none of your business what I get up to. You're not my mother. In case you ain't noticed, love, it's the other way around.'

Violet pursed her lips. 'Is that so? Funny way you 'ave of showing it … Out till all hours with a complete stranger. I don't know what's going on with you, Mum, but I don't like it.'

'You may not like it, Missy, but you can lump it. This is my life, and I've still got plenty of years left in me. I'm not about to start acting like I'm in my dotage, thank you very much. Anyway, there's another lady on the council about my age. If she can do it, so can I.'

'Well!' Violet turned to Joe, who'd been listening to all this silently while they had a last cup of tea before bedtime. 'What do you make of this, Joe? You're the one who might be called on to ferry Mum about the countryside, if her new fancy man don't turn up one night.'

Fancy man?

Fulminating, Sheila forced herself to bite her tongue. Best let her daughter work out her bad temper without adding fuel to the flame.

Joe rubbed his chin. 'If this Bernard fella's willing to do all the ferrying about, I've nothing to say to it. None of my business, is it?' With that, ignoring his wife's furious exclamation, he got up and began to collect the mugs for washing. 'I'm away to bed now. Early start tomorrow.'

While he was noisily rinsing the cups, Sheila took advantage of the opportunity to escape. 'I'm dead on my feet too. Night, all.' And she hurried away before Violet could dream up more reasons why she shouldn't be a parish councillor.

Next day, she tried to put the whole unpleasant business out of her head, concentrating instead on running the shop. It was delivery day, and Mr Whitney turned up late with the week's supplies, so Sheila and Margaret had to work like the clappers to unpack the crates and get everything stored in the cellar or out on display before the lunchtime rush.

Then a large black Labrador got into the shop in the afternoon and caused chaos, grabbing at food on the counter and knocking over a display with his violently wagging tail, before a red-faced owner turned up, a length of rope in hand and muttering apologies, to drag the unrepentant creature away.

So, it was almost closing time before her mind returned to the thorny issue of becoming a councillor.

She told Margaret what had gone on at the council meeting the night before, and her sister gaped. 'You're going to be a councillor? *You*?' She looked concerned. 'You know, Stan's friendly with one or two of them councillors. I hope he won't make trouble for you.'

'He won't … Though if he does, I'll make sure everyone knows what kind of man he is, treating Lily the way he did.'

'You can hardly do that. Not without exposing poor Lily to gossip,' her sister pointed out, looking shocked. 'I doubt her husband would like it much either, if he knew people were talking about what happened to her before she was married.'

Sheila thought Tristan too nice a man to react like that, but realised her sister was probably right about local gossip. 'It's not fair,' she said angrily, 'that men can behave like that

240

and get away with it, just because they know women don't like their private business talked about.'

'People are funny about anything like that,' Margaret said unhappily. 'I saw a woman in the village the other day. Known her twenty years. I said, "Morning, Barbara," and she looked the other way. Didn't say a single word to me. All because I've left my husband.'

'Silly cow,' Sheila said scathingly.

They were so deep in conversation, neither of them noticed the jangle of the shop door opening until it was too late, and Violet was standing there, glaring at her aunt in astonished outrage.

'What in gawd's name is she doing 'ere?' Violet demanded, striding forward. Then she noticed Margaret's pinny and her eyes widened. 'What on earth? Is she working here? Mum? Tell me you ain't given Aunty Margaret a job.' Her chest was heaving. 'Because if you have, I swear …'

'Yes, I have,' Sheila threw back at her daughter, losing her patience at last. This was her shop, not Violet's. 'And what's it got to do with you?'

'You know what she done to us,' Violet gasped. 'Her and that bloomin' husband of hers. Threw me and the girls out after I told her what Stanley did to our Lily.'

'That's not true,' Margaret said hastily. 'I never threw you out. You left.'

Violet's eyes bulged. 'Was I supposed to stay after what he done? With you calling her a hussy too, and gawd knows what else?'

'I'm sorry I did that. It was wrong of me. But I didn't rightly understand. I thought she was making it up. She was only a girl at the time, and I knew she didn't like us.' Margaret's

241

face was flushed with shame and horror. 'If I'd realised … I'm sorry, Violet. And if you'll give me the chance, I'll say sorry to Lily too.'

'He's still your husband though,' Violet said shrilly.

'Aye, but I've left him. It took me a few years, yes, but I realised in the end what kind of man he is … and I walked out.' Margaret started to weep. 'Please don't be angry. I'm sleeping on someone's sofa, love. If your mum hadn't offered me a job, I'd have nothing.'

'Don't cry, Maggie.' Sheila gave her sister a hug, upset and annoyed at the same time. She glared back at Violet. 'I know what you and Lily went through, and I'm sorry about it, but Maggie's my flesh and blood, same as you, and she came into the shop asking for help. So I gave it her. And if you don't like that, tough.'

Without another word, Violet turned and stalked out, her back stiff.

'I'm sorry, love,' Sheila called after her. 'I was going to tell you, but I knew how you'd feel about it.' She got no reply.

'Oh, this is all my fault,' Margaret wailed, reaching for a hanky and dabbing at her eyes. 'Now you've fallen out with your daughter over me.'

'There, there, we'll get through this,' Sheila said soothingly, though on the verge of tears herself. Pulling out her own hanky, she gave a gusty sigh and glanced at her sister's tear-streaked face. 'You and me together, Maggie, landing ourselves in hot water … Just like old times, eh?'

CHAPTER TWENTY

Joan couldn't help herself. She had meant to leave things well enough alone after Alice's wedding, when Arthur had suffered that unfortunate fit, poor soul. Violet and Joe had both advised her never to see him again. Even Ernest, usually so sympathetic, had cautioned her against trying to see him before he was ready. But she couldn't simply let it slide. It had been nearly a week since the wedding and she could only imagine what he must be thinking, given that she hadn't been in touch. She didn't want Arthur to think she blamed him for what had happened. That would be too awful. No, she was determined to see him, even if he told her to go away.

On her afternoon off, she told Mrs Newton another little fib, that she wanted to take a cycle ride in the fine weather. Feeling awful about the necessity of lying just to see her friend, she crossed her fingers nonetheless and borrowed Mrs Newton's bike from outside the shop, calling out, 'Thank you,' through the open door.

She set out beyond the village, biking up the steep hill out of Porthcurno and along narrow shady lanes on the road to Trethewey until she reached the turn-off that led to the Greens' home. She'd never been there before but Arthur had described its location and it wasn't hard to find.

Once she was past the elegant beech trees that hid the house from view, Joan got off and walked the rest of the way, pushing the bike. It wasn't a large house but it was standing alone in well-maintained grounds. She didn't know much about the family, but Arthur had confided that Mr Green had inherited money from his grandfather, who'd been a successful businessman in Penzance.

Her heart thumping, Joan rang the bell and waited. When the door opened, a lady looked out at her with mild surprise. With soft fair hair cut simply about her face, she was dressed in a pretty summer frock and low heels. Joan could tell at once that this was Arthur's mother, for they looked startlingly similar, especially about the eyes. Besides, she'd spotted the same lady with Arthur at the opening of Mrs Newton's shop.

'Good afternoon, Mrs Green,' Joan said hesitantly. 'I'm sorry to disturb you but I was wondering if Arthur was at home.'

The woman's eyes widened. 'You know my son?'

'Yes, my name is Joan Fletcher. I live at Postbridge Farm.'

'I see.' The woman's face had hardened. 'It's good of you to call, Miss Fletcher, but I'm afraid my son is not up to seeing any visitors today. Or indeed for the foreseeable future.' She paused, and then added, 'He needs rest. And no excitement.' She looked Joan up and down, her look not particularly friendly. 'No excitement whatsoever. Do you understand?'

'Yes, of course,' Joan said miserably, and turned from the door, wheeling her bike away.

The front door closed behind her, and that seemed to be that. But she had not gone more than ten paces when she

244

heard a shout and turned back, startled. An upper window had opened and Arthur was leaning out, waving furiously at her.

'I say,' he shouted, 'where are you going? I'm up here. Come and see me.'

Joan bit her lip and returned to the house, leaning her bike against the wall. She peered up at the window, where Arthur was still leaning out. 'Your mother told me you weren't receiving visitors. She said you needed rest.'

'Did she?' Arthur looked aggrieved. 'Hang on, I'm coming down. Don't move a muscle.' And with that, he pulled the window shut.

Joan was surprised by his almost brusque manner. He'd never behaved like that when they'd met at the Grange. But she reminded herself that he was still unwell and probably not feeling himself.

When the front door was thrown open, Arthur stood there, looking surprisingly healthy. It was hard not to remember his tormented groans while he lay writhing on the filthy ground. But perhaps he was already on the mend, despite what his mother had said.

'You're looking b-better …' she stammered, and unaccountably blushed.

'I'm feeling better,' he agreed. 'It was very wrong of my mother to send you packing.'

'But if you need your rest—'

'I've had nothing but rest for days and I'm heartily bored now.' He gestured her inside. 'It's all the fault of that mangy doctor. He said I should stay in my room for the rest of eternity, but I've been champing at the bit to see you again.' He frowned when she still wouldn't budge. 'Won't you come in?'

Terrified of his mother coming back and spotting her, Joan shook her head. 'I'd rather not, thanks.'

'Oh, come on, don't be nervous,' he coaxed her, before grabbing Joan's hand and dragging her into the house. 'Here, we can sit in the kitchen and have coffee and biscuits, like civilised people. Do you like coffee?'

Joan, who'd only tasted coffee twice in her life, said truthfully, 'I'm not sure.'

'Let's find out, then,' he said with a grin.

Giving up, she followed him through his parents' house, which was a very comfortable home and not as grand as she'd feared at first sight. The kitchen itself was large and well lit by rows of windows overlooking a charming rose garden with a small ornamental pond beyond.

'There, isn't this nice?' He drew out a seat for her at the table and began making coffee, opening and closing cupboards noisily, and prising the lid off a biscuit tin. She thought he seemed almost manic, and wondered if he could be as well as he'd claimed. 'I haven't had coffee in ages either. Mother won't make it for me because she says it's bad for the nerves. But I'm sick of endless cups of tea. And never seeing anybody. I'm glad you came. I was beginning to think you'd never forgive me for what happened.'

'What *did* happen?'

'I made a fool of myself, that's all.'

'Of course you didn't. I only wish I could have helped more. But I didn't know what to do for the best,' she confessed. 'Besides, after Ernest and Joe took charge, I couldn't get near you. I'm truly sorry if you thought I deserted you, but I didn't.'

'There's no need to apologise,' Arthur said, frowning round at her. 'Though I did try to warn you. I told you we shouldn't keep seeing each other. And we shouldn't. But I was selfish ... The thing is, I like you and I think you like me. And I wanted so badly for it to work out. Now everything is ruined.' He bowed his head, the biscuit tin forgotten.

Jumping up, she took the tin from him and set out the biscuits on a plate. 'Don't be silly,' she said quietly, 'you haven't ruined a thing. I like you too, and I'm glad you like me. Yes, maybe you do have a few problems ... but you're not alone. Plenty of people are still suffering because of the war. There's no need to give up just because of that. We can sort things out, can't we? Ernest says you just need time to *heal*. Do you think that sounds right?'

Thrusting his hands into his pockets, Arthur shrugged. 'My parents think I'll never get better. They've given up on me. It's all rather wretched.'

The kettle was boiling, its whistle shrill. Hurriedly, Joan took it off the heat. 'Well, I haven't given up on you. And I'm sure there must be something that would help you get better. But let's start with this coffee, shall we? Everything else can wait. Now, what on earth is *this* and how does it work?' She was staring at the strange contraption that looked like a miniature mill, into which Arthur had stuffed a handful of coffee beans. 'Seems like an awful lot of work for one drink.'

He laughed, and patiently demonstrated how the coffee bean grinder worked.

Having laboriously made coffee together, they sat and drank it at the kitchen table. Joan was feeling shy and barely made eye contact with him, but Arthur looked at her intently the whole time.

At last, pushing aside his coffee cup, he leaned across the table and took her hand. 'I'm sorry,' he said deeply. 'I must have scared you the other night.'

'I was quite worried,' she admitted. 'Was it definitely the fireworks that made you unwell? Because I wasn't sure if I'd said or done something wrong.'

He looked horrified. 'You? Say something wrong?' He shook his head. 'It was nothing to do with you. It was those damn bangs and explosions. The blinding lights.' His gaze slipped away, his face abstracted. 'Hearing those noises, I forgot where I was for a while. Even who I was. I was completely taken over. I was back in the war, I think. Back in France.'

She nodded silently, for that account tallied with her memory of the event.

'I can't apologise enough for having frightened you, Joan.' He squeezed her hand gently, concern in his eyes. 'Can you ever forgive me? I hope you can. The thing is, I've never met a girl like you before ... Someone who *understands*.'

'You mean because we both like painting?' She was confused.

'That, yes, but me as well.' His thumb ran lightly across her knuckles. 'You see the real me. Not who they want you to see. The broken boy ...' He bared his teeth in self-mockery. 'The one who couldn't hack it on the front line and got himself sent home in disgrace.'

'Is that what happened?'

'Not entirely ... I'll tell you the whole damn thing one day. Not now though, eh? It wasn't my finest hour. Let's not spoil the moment.' Arthur lifted her hand to his lips, and she

shivered with delight. 'With you, I'm not broken anymore.'
He grimaced. 'Well, so long as nobody lights a firecracker.
Once that happens, all bets are off.'

As they were laughing and he was holding her hand, his
mother walked into the kitchen. Her eyes flashed, seeing
Joan there, but, with awful restraint, she said, 'I thought I
heard voices. What are you doing downstairs, Arthur? You
know what the doctor said. You should be resting. Not
entertaining.' Her disapproving gaze roved across Joan's
face. 'I thought I made myself clear that Arthur shouldn't be
disturbed. Doctor's orders.'

Arthur stiffened. 'It's not her fault. I saw her leaving and
called her back.' He released Joan's hand, looking flushed
and annoyed. 'Anyway, you can't keep me locked up in that
bedroom forever, you know. I'm not a child so stop treating
me like one. In fact, you should know, Joan is my girlfriend,'
he went on, this announcement shocking Joan rigid. 'And if
I want to see her, I will. I hope that's understood.'

His mother stared at him in horror. 'Your *girlfriend*?' She
almost shuddered. 'Your father will be home soon. We can
talk about it then.'

'There's nothing to talk about, Mother. It's none of your
business anyway. Dammit, I've been to war. I've fought for
my country. I'm not a boy anymore.' Arthur jumped up, a
muscle jerking in his jaw. 'I won't stand for it, do you hear?'
Joan had risen to her feet as well, embarrassed and unsure
what to do. Now he took her arm and steered her into the
hallway. 'We're going for a walk.'

'But you mustn't leave the house,' his mother insisted. 'The
doctor was very firm about what was permitted and what
wasn't. Total bedrest, he said.'

'Arthur,' Joan suggested nervously, 'perhaps your mother's right and we should go for a walk another day … I don't want to set your recovery back.'

'Oh, tosh!' he exclaimed, grabbing his jacket. He threw open the front door and ushered her out. 'It's all nonsense. Look at me, I'm as fit as a fiddle.' Then he saw Joan's face and stopped. The wild look in his eyes died away and he said more soberly, 'Of course, if you don't want to go for a walk with me … I just thought, since we can't get any privacy in the house …'

Seeing his chagrined expression, Joan felt awful. Now she'd made him feel bad, and in front of his mother too. 'No, I'd love to go for a walk. But only if you're well enough.'

'Well, staying cooped up indoors isn't going to help me,' he bit out, throwing his mother a furious look. 'You know, perhaps I ought to have taken a bullet and died on that damn battlefield. That's what *they* all think.'

'Arthur, no,' his mother cried, her face distressed.

Joan was horrified too.

'Sorry,' he said at once, looking at them both apologetically. 'I shouldn't have said that,' he admitted. 'But fresh air will do me good. Aren't you always saying that?' He held out a hand to Joan. 'Come with me?'

There didn't seem much point upsetting him further by arguing. Besides, she did want to speak to him alone. Taking his arm, Joan hurried down the garden path with him, leaving his mother looking after them in concern.

'You … You didn't really mean that, did you?' she asked once they were out of earshot, fearing the answer.

But Arthur shook his head, grimacing. 'Though I wonder sometimes if it wouldn't have been better for me to have died, rather than putting my parents through this.'

'That's not true and you know it. Look, you'll get better soon. You need plenty of rest, that's all.'

He said nothing to this.

The path they were following wound among leafy shrubs and trees, birds singing unseen in the branches above as they walked arm in arm. She breathed in the sweet fragrance, wishing she knew how to help him. But she suspected nothing but time would heal his wounds …

Then he said quietly, 'Can I tell you something? Something I've never told anyone else.'

'Of course.'

They had come to a halt beside a small pond edged with flowing ferns and flag irises. There was an old rustic bench in the shade of a willow, and Arthur sank down there, pulling him with her. His fingers curled about hers, warm and intimate, but the distant look in his eyes made her heart ache.

'It's hard to say this out loud,' he began, 'and I apologise in advance if it upsets you, but I … I killed a man once. Probably more than one, the way we were all scattering bullets about.' He drew a pained breath. 'But this one I'll never forget.'

She was surprised and a little uncertain but wanted to hear him out. 'Tell me.'

'We were going house-to-house in a French village, on the lookout for snipers and booby-traps. It was getting dark, the Germans had just left and the place seemed deserted. Then I caught a movement out of the corner of my eye, and this soldier appeared in a doorway. German uniform, funny little helmet. I could barely make out his face in the dusk …' He stopped, staring at nothing.

Joan shivered. 'Go on.'

'I was terrified, I don't mind telling you. I'd seen friends

251

shot dead in front of me, you know? Blood everywhere ...' He swallowed. 'I raised my rifle and shouted something, I don't know what. The German raised his rifle and shouted too. So I pulled the trigger. And at that very second, I realised what he was shouting in broken English. "I surrender! I surrender!"' A tear rolled silently down Arthur's cheek. 'He was just a boy like me ... Seventeen, eighteen years old. And I shot him dead while he was trying to surrender.'

Tears brimming in her own eyes, Joan put her arms around him. 'Oh, Arthur.'

'Next thing I knew, I was being bundled off to a field hospital, raving like a maniac. The doctors swore I'd recover in time, of course ... Bed rest, like the doctor here has prescribed. But every time I closed my eyes, all I could hear was that boy shouting, *I surrender, I surrender*! And the crack of my rifle.'

'I'm so sorry.'

'Now you know what kind of man I am, I expect you'll never want to see me again.' He buried his face in his hands, his groan despairing. 'Oh God, what's to become of me, Joan? What's the point of it all?'

She couldn't think of anything to say that wouldn't have sounded flat and hollow, so held him tight instead, waiting until he seemed calmer and more in control of himself before speaking. 'I know it's hard, but you can't let this thing get the better of you,' she told him softly. 'Because if you want us to be friends, you'll have to prove to your parents and the doctor that you're getting better. Otherwise they might lock you up for good and we'd probably never see each other again. And that would break my heart.'

He raised his head, his look bemused. 'It would?'

'Yes, silly.' She looked deep into his eyes. 'First though, you need to stop blaming yourself for that boy's death. Do you think you can do that?'

'But—'

'We were at war,' she pointed out, 'and you were a soldier. You did what any other soldier would have done.' She took a deep breath. 'Your duty.'

He closed his eyes and bent his head again. 'That's kind of you,' he muttered, 'but not true. If I'd listened to him properly, if I'd waited a few more seconds …'

Joan could see he still wasn't thinking straight. Besides, he needed to sort things out with his parents before their friendship could go any further. Her heart wrenched in agony as she released him. 'I can see why you'd think like that, but you really need to talk to your parents about it. And the doctor too. He might be able to help you.' She paused, not wanting to leave him alone in this dangerous mood. 'Shall we walk back together?'

To her relief he agreed without protest, and they walked in silence back to the house. A car had arrived while they were gone, she realised, and a man in a smart brown suit was waiting by the front door with Arthur's mother.

'Your father?'

Arthur nodded, hands in his pockets as he stared broodingly at his parents. 'You'd better go,' he said. 'I don't want you getting tangled up in this mess.'

Joan rather thought she was already tangled up in it. And she wished that she could stay. But it was better that he should speak to his parents alone. 'Thank you for telling me what happened in France,' she whispered as they parted. 'I understand now why you feel so awful about the war. And I

253

want to help, only I'm not sure how. But what you need is to see the doctor again and do whatever he tells you. That's the only way you'll get better.'

He let her go without comment, his head turned away.

Joan collected her bike and cycled home in a weepy, unsteady way. She hated having to leave Arthur where he was unhappy. But the last thing she wanted was for him to collapse again as he'd done during the firework display. It was time for him to get better and the experts would probably know best how to achieve that.

As for the suffering he'd witnessed during the war, and the boy he'd shot dead … His words, his bleak look, haunted her on the way home. She was no longer surprised by the strange things he'd said and done since they'd met. Because how could anyone keep such horrors locked up inside and not be driven out of their mind by them?

It was raining that evening when Joan trudged out to shut the hens up in their coop for the night. She'd left it quite late and it was already dusk, the sky a dull cloudy violet, the farmyard cobbles shimmering wet. Her head was full of seething doubts over the way she'd left Arthur like that, not staying to support him. But she wasn't a doctor – and it might have been dangerous to interfere …

All the same, she would go back tomorrow. Just to be sure he was all right. She would demand to see him, and refuse to go unless they let her in.

With a newspaper held over her head against the rain, she shooed the last reluctant hen into its coop, fastened the door, and began to dash back across the yard.

'Joan!'

The piercing whisper brought her up short and she stared about the farmyard in the gathering dusk, baffled and unsure. 'Hello?'

A shadow detached itself from an outbuilding and shuffled towards her. It was Arthur, she realised with a shock. He was not wearing a coat and looked soaked and bedraggled.

'I'm sorry,' he said, his voice shaking, 'tell me to go if you must, but I had to see you again … To explain if I can.'

Horrified, she grabbed his arm and dragged him into the shelter of the barn. 'What on earth are you doing here?' she demanded, looking him up and down. 'Goodness, Arthur, you're in a right state.' Her gaze dropped to his muddy trousers and she gasped. 'But where … where are your shoes? Your feet are bare … and they're covered in mud!'

'Who cares about that?'

She stared, wondering if he really had lost command of his senses. 'But why on earth—?'

He interrupted her impatiently, as if such details were unimportant. 'I tried to talk to my parents, but all they did was lock me in my bedroom while they waited for the doctor to come and see me again. They even took away my coat and shoes. So I climbed out of the window.'

'Oh for goodness' sake, Arthur.' She shook her head, unsure whether to laugh or cry.

'I couldn't rest until I'd had a chance to talk to you again.' He slicked back the wet fair hair flopping in his eyes. 'I should never have told you all that about my time in France. Will you promise to forget what I said?' He winced. 'I told my parents too. My father tore a strip off me for telling my mother such an awful thing, and for … for crying. He said I was a c-coward, that I'm … weak.'

'Your father was quite wrong to say that,' she said, angry on his behalf. 'Anyway, I'm glad you told me. *Glad*, do you hear?'

'Glad?' He was staring. 'I don't understand. It's such a horrible story. Deeply upsetting, my father said.'

'Not as upsetting as it was for you,' she pointed out hotly. 'In fact, as soon as you told me, it explained everything. I knew then what you'd been through.' She flung her arms about his still, unresponsive figure. 'You mustn't blame yourself for being unhappy. All it means is that you're a human being. That you care. Of course you reacted when he raised his gun. If you hadn't, you might have been the one lying dead. But it's only right and natural for you to regret his death. That boy could have been you. In a way, he *was* you.' She pulled back, seeing tears in his eyes again. 'Sorry, I'm bringing it all back, aren't I?'

'N-No,' he stammered, 'you're just the first person to say any of that. To understand what I'm feeling. And to say it's okay ...' He hit the side of his head. 'All the nightmares and mess in here.'

'Of course it's okay.' She swallowed, knowing it was time to admit the awful truth she'd held back from him before. 'You remember what I told you that day at the Grange ... That I suffered from bad dreams too?' When he nodded, she spoke falteringly of the night when the drunken soldier had assaulted her. Tears fell as she described that terrifying encounter and its aftermath, but afterwards she felt such a lightening of the heart, she knew she'd done the right thing. 'I used to be so afraid of men ... But since meeting you, everything's changed.' Standing on tiptoe, she set her lips to his. 'I ... I love you,' she whispered, heart thumping at this bold admission, for she'd only just realised how she felt herself. 'I love you, Arthur Green.'

And to her relief, instead of being horrified by this extra burden on his soul, he gave a deep, heartfelt sigh. His arms came about her too, and suddenly they were kissing in earnest …

Early next morning, Joan stirred in her sleep, hearing someone ponderously climbing a ladder nearby. She sat up, straw in her hair, to find herself staring into Violet's blank face.

Memories shot back into her head, and her cheeks flared with heat. Arthur's kisses becoming more demanding, her own needs soaring, and then the two of them climbing the rickety ladder into the hay loft above the barn, the floor still soft and musty with the remnants of last year's hay, grass-seeds everywhere in the warm, dark air.

'Joan? We've been looking for you everywhere,' Violet snapped, and then she stopped dead, glancing from Joan's scanty attire to Arthur, as he too sat up, drowsy and blinking, and barely decent. 'Oh, bloomin' hell,' she gasped. 'You silly, silly girl … What in gawd's name have you gone and done now?'

CHAPTER TWENTY-ONE

Caroline had been strangely quiet on their long drive through the Cornish lanes, only truly coming alive once they'd passed Bodmin. From there, she peered out from the cramped back seat of Cameron's car, exclaiming in delight at the beautiful, rugged landscape of the moors on either side. When they finally got out at Thornton Hall, she gave Selina's arm a squeeze, breathless with excitement. 'Oh, Selly … What a place! And you live here now. How lucky you are.'

'Lucky, you call it? I'd rather not live here and have my sister still alive,' Selina said, smarting at Caro's remark.

'Of course you would.' Her friend blenched. 'I'm sorry, that was a thoughtless thing to say. Please forgive me.'

Now Selina felt bad. 'There's nothing to forgive.' She turned to Cameron, who had been unloading their bags. 'Thank you ever so much for driving me home. And for agreeing to bring Caroline too. All I ever seem to do is ask favours of you. You must be heartily sick of it.'

He shook his head, smiling as he effortlessly carried their bags into the house for them, one under each arm. 'Not a bit.

You're very welcome, both of you. But I'd better get back to my sister's. We left Porthcurno rather later than I'd planned, and I imagine she'll be worrying where I've got to.' He turned and shook both their hands before adding, 'Goodbye.'

His manner was friendly, Selina had to admit, yet somehow cool and impersonal too, quite as though they'd never kissed at the farm. She wished Caroline wasn't there so she could talk to him properly. But she felt too awkward in front of her friend.

As he drove away, his tyres spitting gravel, there was a cry of 'Aunt Selly!' from upstairs, and Selina looked up to see three children descending the stairs. Peter came skipping down, his face lit up, clearly relieved to see her. By contrast, his sister Jemima seemed almost glum. She was holding Faith's hand, helping the little girl totter carefully down the broad staircase.

'Hello, children.' Selina shook Peter's hand, then Jemima's, and bent to embrace Faith. 'How have you been while I was away? Behaving yourselves, I hope.' She ruffled Faith's hair, noting uneasily that the youngest child also seemed unhappier than when she'd left. 'What's the matter? Has something happened?'

'Martha smacked Faith and made her cry,' Peter said at once, and an angry flush crept into his thin cheeks. 'All because she didn't want her bath yesterday evening. Martha said she had to take a bath every night, and when Faith refused, she smacked her hand.' He sucked in a breath. 'Twice.'

'She did *what*?' Selina was horrified. 'Tell me you're joking.'

But Jemima shook her head. 'It's true. We were both there, up in the nursery. Peter was reading a book out loud to us while Faith and I built a tower of bricks. Martha came in

259

and kicked the tower over. She was in a stinking m-m-mood,' she stammered, tears in her eyes. 'I don't know why, but she was. And when Faith said she wasn't ready for her bath yet, Martha grabbed her hand and smacked her.'

Faith pointed dolefully to her right hand. There was no mark on her fair skin, thank goodness, but her mouth turned upside-down and quivered as she too trembled on the point of tears. 'It hurt,' she whispered.

'Then the horrid beast dragged her away to her bath,' Jemima went on furiously, 'and all we could hear was Faith crying and crying in the bathroom until she was almost sick.'

'Good God.' Caroline's startled gaze met Selina's. 'Who on earth is this "Martha"? She sounds like a right tinpot tyrant.'

'She is,' Peter agreed, and promptly held out his hand, as they hadn't been introduced yet. 'I'm Peter March, by the way. Who are you?'

'Caroline,' she replied simply, and they shook hands. 'I'm your aunt's friend. I'm just here for a few days, then I'll be going back on the train.'

'Trains are spiffing,' Peter said enthusiastically.

'Yes, they are,' Caroline agreed with a grin before turning to shake Jemima's hand, and to say, 'Hello, pleased to meet you,' to Faith too. She stroked the little girl's hand gently. 'Though I'm sorry to hear this Martha was beastly to you. She sounds mean. I hope your hand's not still hurting.'

Faith shook her head dolefully.

Repressing the impulse to march upstairs and remonstrate with Martha straightaway, Selina suggested they should run and fetch Mrs Hawley for her, as her friend Miss Ponsby needed to be shown to a guest room.

While the children ran off gleefully in the direction of

the kitchen, she turned to Caroline for some much-needed advice. 'That awful woman … The children's nanny, you understand.'

'Yes, I guessed as much. What a horror she sounds.'

'I already had to speak to her recently about her behaviour. Now this … What on earth should I do, do you think? I can't allow her to get away with smacking the children. And Faith is such a dear. How on earth could anyone treat her so badly?'

'I don't know. But I'm afraid you'll have to sack her.'

Selina was aghast. 'Sack her?' she repeated, a cold feeling of dread in the pit of her stomach. She had never sacked anyone in her life. But Caroline was right. She had the children's welfare to think about. She was their guardian and couldn't let her sister down. 'Oh dear … Though it's what Bella would have done, I suppose. She doted on her babies.'

'And I'm sure you'll find a new nanny,' Caro said reassuringly.

'Yes.' Selina was filled with fresh determination. 'I shall go and speak to her at once. No point putting it off.' But inside, she was churning with anxiety.

She didn't much like Martha and was certain the nanny had never liked her in return. Now, she would have to confront her about this latest misdemeanour. After all, the girl could hardly be left alone with her nieces and nephew again.

As Caroline fell in beside her, she asked nervously, 'Should I turn her away at once or serve a notice?'

'She should leave straightaway.' Caroline sounded very certain. 'Smacking a child that young? She shouldn't be left in charge of them even a day longer.'

Selina was thrown by the idea of immediately looking

after the three children herself, but knew Caroline was right. And it was surprisingly hard to rein in her temper, especially when she saw Martha emerge from a side room and felt a surge of heat in her cheeks, thinking what the awful woman had done to little Faith.

'Will you be all right on your own for a few minutes?' she asked Caroline.

Her friend squeezed her hand. 'Of course, you do what needs to be done.' She leaned across, whispering in her ear, 'Do you want me to come with you?'

'No, but thank you,' Selina told her with more confidence than she felt. Then she turned to Martha. 'I need to speak to you alone,' she said sharply, indicating the study where she had spoken to the nanny before. On that occasion, they had seemed to come to an agreement about how to deal with the children going forward, but clearly the nanny had her own ideas.

Martha arched her brows in faint hauteur, but followed Selina into the study without protest. 'Is there a problem, Miss Tiptree?' she asked, her tone insolent.

Selina felt her hands tighten into fists, her heart thumping uncomfortably. 'Jemima tells me you smacked Faith while I was away. She wouldn't take her bath, apparently, so you physically chastised her.' She had meant to stay calm and professional, but now that she was face-to-face with the perpetrator of this crime, Selina found it hard to speak in a temperate manner. 'Well?' she demanded when Martha said nothing, merely tossing her head and pursing her lips. 'Is it true?' She heard her voice shake with an emotion she couldn't quite suppress. 'And if it is, what have you to say for yourself?'

'Miss?'

'Don't you *Miss* me!' Selina exploded, and saw the young woman's lips curl in derision. 'You smacked a four-year-old child!'

'She's nearly five. And not too young to be taught right from wrong,' Martha whipped back at her. 'I was busy and she was giving me the runaround. What did you expect me to do?'

'Busy? Looking after Faith is your job. And I certainly don't condone you smacking a child who's merely being a little difficult.' Selina drew a deep breath, trying to regain control of her temper. She could hardly claim the moral high ground when ranting at a member of staff. 'Besides, what do you expect of a girl her age who has just lost her mother? If she was being difficult, she has some excuse, don't you think?'

'That was weeks ago,' Martha said sullenly.

Selina stared at the nanny in amazement, wondering why on earth she'd taken on such work when she appeared to lack all empathy.

'I spoke to you once before about how you were handling the children, and it was clear to me on that occasion that you resented my interference. I hoped you would come to respect me as your new employer, given that my sister appointed me guardian to her children. But I can see that hope was useless. Also, you seem singularly unsuited to looking after a child as young as Faith.' She drew a deep breath. 'Therefore, I am relieving you of your duties. You are dismissed, and I would be grateful if you would pack your bags and leave Thornton Hall in the morning.' She paused as the girl stared at her, her mouth falling open in surprise. 'I shall ask Mr MacGregor to make sure your wages are paid to the end of the month. Given your behaviour, I feel that is more than generous.'

'You can't sack me!' Martha burst out.

'Yes, I can. My late sister left the care of her children entirely up to me, and I no longer require your services. You are dismissed.' She thrust her shaking hands behind her back and nodded to the study door. 'I suggest you go and pack.'

'But Mr MacGregor—'

'Mr MacGregor was left to oversee the estate, not the welfare of my nieces and nephew. He has already indicated that he will cede any family decisions to me. Which includes the hiring and firing of nannies, trust me.'

Martha stared at her another few seconds, bright red in the face, looking as though she'd been slapped. Then she stamped away, leaving the door wide open. 'We'll just see about that,' she threw back in a choking voice, and disappeared towards the servants' quarters.

'Oh Lord …' Selina bent her head, breathing shallow. All her life, she had spoken her mind freely – too freely, some might say – but she had not enjoyed that. Not one little bit.

Caroline hurried into the study, looking concerned. 'Selly? Are you all right?' She seized Selina's trembling hands and squeezed them. 'How did she take it? What did she say?'

'She wasn't very pleased,' Selina admitted with a hoarse laugh, but managed a smile as the three children ran into the room, with Mrs Hawley following. 'Hello, my darlings. Good news. I've spoken to the dreaded Martha about her smacking you, Faith, and we have agreed she doesn't suit us as a nanny anymore. She'll be leaving in the morning.'

Faith's eyes grew round as saucers. Peter cheered. Jemima gave a heartfelt sigh and smiled at her tremulously. 'Thank you, Aunt Selly,' the girl whispered, clutching her little sister's hand.

Mrs Hawley folded her arms at her waist and nodded. 'Very good, Miss Tiptree,' she said with an air of increased respect. 'I thought it might be time that good-for-nothing girl found a new position. Ever since the loss of your sister, she's been giving herself airs above her station.'

'What Mrs Hawley's trying to say is, good riddance to bad rubbish,' Peter said, and they all laughed.

Selina woke the next day full of trepidation. What had she done? Dismissing the nanny had been madness. What did she know about looking after children? But upon going down to breakfast, she found the children in high spirits and Mrs Hawley bustling about them, seemingly happy enough with the new situation. Caroline, who claimed to have passed a restful night in the guest room, came down in trousers rather than a skirt, and Peter looked at her with new approval.

'I don't know why girls are always wearing skirts and dresses anyway,' Peter remarked, buttering himself a second slice of toast. 'Pass the jam, would you, Aunt Selly?' He glanced out of the window. 'It makes it awfully hard to climb trees, and I like climbing trees.'

'You're a boy,' Jemima said scornfully. 'You'll never be forced to wear a skirt or dress. Unlike me.'

'Now, go easy on that jam, Master Peter,' Mrs Hawley warned him, carrying in the tea tray. 'We're running low. So many empty shelves in the shops these days, Miss,' she added to Selina. 'It's shocking. Though come summer's end, we'll have a dozen jars of home-made jam in the pantry, God willing.'

'Home-made jam is the best,' Jemima agreed, looking the

most cheerful Selina had seen her in a while. Perhaps she too was feeling better for the absence of the nanny.

'Peter has a treehouse,' Selina told Caroline, and winked at the boy across the table. 'Perhaps you could show our guest your lofty domain this morning, Peter.'

He studied Caroline dubiously. 'Mother never came to look at it. Do you climb trees?'

'I love climbing trees,' Caroline told him with a grin. 'So long as they're not too tall, that is. Besides, as you say, I'm dressed for it.'

Faith was kicking her feet back-and-forth, humming to herself as she ate her jammy mess of porridge.

'How are you feeling this morning, Faith?' Selina asked gently.

Faith looked up at her uncertainly, porridge dripping off her spoon onto the tablecloth.

'Would you like to see Peter's treehouse too?' Caroline asked her, bending forward.

Faith nodded enthusiastically. 'Yes, pweese.'

'What? She's too young to climb trees,' Peter exclaimed, looking horrified at the thought of his small sister invading his special place.

'Pweese, pweese,' Faith repeated, kicking her feet back and forth more violently.

Jemima frowned at her sister. 'Stop making such a racket, Faith.'

Faith kicked even harder, glaring at her sister.

'Faith, dearest,' Selina said diplomatically, 'I think that noise is giving Caroline a headache. And then she won't be able to take you to see the treehouse, will she?'

This ploy worked. Faith instantly stopped kicking and

returned to eating her porridge. And Caroline flashed her a quick secret smile that seemed to say, 'Well done.'

After breakfast, Selina and Caroline enjoyed a long gossipy chat in the morning room. Then she retrieved the children from the nursery where Peter and Jemima had been squabbling over the best way to teach Faith her letters, and the five of them trooped out into the woodlands to visit Peter's treehouse. Selina wasn't keen on climbing trees, so she stayed firmly at ground level. She sat with Faith on the green earth and watched while Caroline, Jemima and Peter climbed the tree with varying degrees of ease, and disappeared inside the treehouse, an elaborate affair of ropes and planks that creaked and shifted as the three of them moved about inside.

'Good morning,' a voice said coolly from behind her.

Selina jumped in surprise, seeing Helen and Cameron Bourne a few feet away. It was a fine day and Cameron's shirt sleeves were rolled up to the elbows and his tie loosened.

He looked rather handsome in a careless way and she found herself blushing as their eyes met. She had been trying to forget the kiss they'd shared the night of Alice's wedding, but it was difficult, and she knew she was in danger of developing a crush on her neighbour.

'Hello,' she replied awkwardly, getting up. 'Were you coming to see me?'

'We called at the house and Mrs Hawley told us where to find you.' Helen Bourne was gazing up at the treehouse. 'Goodness, how many people are up there? It looks awfully dangerous. Ought to have been torn down years ago, if you ask me.'

Cameron came forward to shake hands with Selina. 'Out

here on your own with the kids? That's brave of you. Where's the nanny?'

'I sacked her,' Selina admitted.

'Good God.' Helen Bourne gazed round at her blankly. 'Whatever for?'

'I didn't feel she was particularly good at her job,' Selina told them coolly. 'I wrote her a reference, of course, and advised her to be nicer in her next job. But she left before breakfast this morning. We'll all be happier without her, I'm sure.' As Jemima began to climb down from the treehouse, Selina hurried to stand beneath her in case the girl fell. 'Careful, Jemima. Take it slowly.'

Inevitably though, the girl's foot slipped and Selina only just caught her. She staggered back and was glad when Cameron steadied her.

'I hate to say I told you so,' Helen said icily, 'but I told you so. It's a miracle none of them have broken their necks yet.'

'Hey up there,' Cameron shouted, laughing when Peter poked his head down through the leafy branches. 'You'd better come down, I'm afraid. My sister won't be easy until she knows you're safely on the ground.'

Peter climbed down without mishap, landing in front of Helen and giving her a supercilious look. 'I was just showing my treehouse to Aunt Selly's friend,' he informed the Bournes. 'Caroline's a good sort. She's a Land Girl, did you know? Just like Aunt Selly was.'

'That's Miss Ponsby to you,' Selina corrected him swiftly.

With a shrug, Peter went on, 'Jemima says she'd like to be a Land Girl too. Though she can never get out of bed in the mornings, so she'd be no good at it, would she? *Miss Ponsby* says Land Girls have to get up ever so early. Before it's even light some days.'

At that moment, Caroline climbed down too, almost as agile as Peter. There was a smudge of green on one cheek, her fair hair in disarray. She said a cheery hello to Cameron, but encountered a hostile stare from Helen that made her stammer, 'How … How do you do? You must be Cameron's sister. I'm Caroline Ponsby.'

Looking her up and down with disgust, her gaze particularly lingering on Caroline's trousers, Helen ignored her outstretched hand and turned back to Selina. 'You know your own business, of course. But I'd advise you not to encourage the children in climbing such a tall tree. Jemima could have been seriously hurt just now. No doubt you think it's amusing, risking their lives, but I doubt Bella would have approved,' she finished.

Her spirits at a new low, Selina said nothing to that, but asked, 'Would you like to walk up to the house with us? It's nearly lunchtime. Perhaps you'd like to stay for something to eat?'

To her relief, Helen glanced at her watch and shook her head. 'I'm sorry but I've just remembered an appointment this afternoon. Perhaps another day?' She glanced at her brother. 'If you'd like to stay and have lunch, you must. I can walk back alone, don't worry about me.' Though her tone implied the opposite.

With a hesitant look at Selina, Cameron took the hint. 'No, of course I'll walk back with you.' He took his sister's arm and said a friendly goodbye to the rest of them.

Once they'd gone, Selina and Caroline strolled back to the house with the children, where the kids stampeded away, apparently returning to the nursery.

'Look after Faith, you two, and make sure you all wash your hands and faces before lunch,' Selina called after them and then trudged into the morning room where she collapsed onto the sofa. 'Good Lord … It's only been one morning and already I'm exhausted. What was I thinking, letting the nanny go? Those three have so much energy, I'll never keep up.'

Caroline came and sat beside her. 'You'll be fine,' she said firmly, and took her hand. 'I believe in you, Selly. You always achieve what you set out to do. You get things done.' Her face was glowing with a strange light. 'And seeing you with those kids just now … I think you'll make a wonderful mother.'

Touched, Selina felt tears springing to her eyes. 'Really? Because I don't have a clue what I'm doing. I'm just lurching from one day to the next, and hoping for the best.'

'But that's what everyone does,' Caroline pointed out. 'That's what we've all been doing since that awful day in the summer of '39 when we first heard we were at war. We muddled through and somehow our side won. Now we have to fix everything that got broken. But we can do it. Just as *you* can do this, even though it's hard work and you've never done it before.' She hesitated. 'You just have to let love guide you.'

'*Love*?'

'Of course.' Caroline nodded, watching her closely. 'You loved your sister, and now you'll love her children.' A tear trembled on one of her sandy lashes and she blinked it away, choking as she added, 'Oh, Selly, you are the most wonderful person.' She took a shuddering breath, then finished in a rush, 'I didn't mean to say anything, and I hope you won't hate me forever for this, but I … *I love you.*'

'Sorry?'

Caroline swallowed, then whispered, 'I said, I love you.'

Selina stared at her and didn't know how to respond. At first, she thought Caroline must be talking in general terms about friendship and sisterly affection. But that throb in her voice …

A numb shock ran through her and she sat very still, struggling for the right words. The words that wouldn't smash their friendship to bits. Was Caroline saying she was *in love* with her? The same way a woman fell in love with a man? She was, wasn't she? Selina blushed and didn't know where to look. Gently, not wanting to hurt her feelings, she disengaged her hand from Caroline's. She wanted them to stay friends but couldn't, in all conscience, give Caro the mistaken idea that she felt the same way. Because, much as she held her friend in warm affection, she didn't and never could love her *like that*.

But how best to say so without breaking her heart?

In the end, it was Caroline who broke the silence. 'Oh golly, I … I knew I shouldn't have said anything,' she admitted, stumbling over her words. 'But there's no point pretending anymore. I do love you, Selina, though I've tried ever so hard not to. I can't seem to shake it. And now you're falling in love with Cameron Bourne instead.' There was despair in her voice. 'I suppose you could do worse. But does he know who you are deep down inside, Selly? Will he ever know the real you?'

Unsure what on earth she meant by that, Selina said with difficulty, 'I'm not falling in love with Cameron Bourne … I don't think so, anyway. And I'll always be your friend, I hope you know that. But I can't feel the same way.' She touched her friend's hand. 'I'm so sorry.'

'Don't be,' Caroline said simply. 'I never thought you would. I just couldn't leave without telling you the truth.'

Feeling awful, Selina leaned over to give her a big hug. They held each other in silence for a moment, then she sat back with a wobbly smile. 'Honestly, I'm glad you did. It was very brave of you. And I hope one day you find someone who'll make you truly happy.' She gave a cracked laugh. 'Someone nicer than me.'

Caroline said nothing but looked away. There was a solitary tear running down her cheek.

Life, Selina thought, watching her guiltily, could be so cruel sometimes. But Caroline was right about one thing. The only way to get through the hard times was with love.

CHAPTER TWENTY-TWO

'Bit more to the left,' Sheila suggested, waving her hand vaguely. 'And a dab higher, maybe?' At last, she gave Margaret the thumbs-up. 'Stop right there, Maggie. That's bloomin' perfect.'

Having positioned the large poster on the inside of the shop window to Sheila's satisfaction, Margaret pressed hard to make sure the glue worked, and then stepped back, wiping sticky hands on her work apron.

'Well, your poster's gone up. Now to see if anyone fancies putting their hand in their pocket for a good cause.'

'I should hope so,' Sheila said frankly. 'Else I'm wasting my time with this council malarkey, ain't I?'

She nipped out of the shop and stood, hands on hips in the warm Cornish sunshine, to admire the poster. A bold pink with deep blue lettering, it invited villagers to donate clothing or contribute financially to the Porthcurno neighbourhood fund, a good cause that would benefit 'local people in need'. One of the councillors had arranged for posters and leaflets to be printed at minimal cost and displayed in a few prominent locations throughout the village and in some outlying areas too. The council, needless to say, was also contributing. Sheila had made sure of that at the very first committee meeting she'd attended.

'It does my heart good to see that there,' she told her sister, who'd also come out to admire her handiwork. 'Now let's hope I have time to deal with the donations, what with everything going on at the moment.'

'Hmm,' was all her sister said to that, clearly still sceptical that anyone would bother rooting through their old clothes for poorer folk. And maybe she was right. But Sheila refused to let doubt cast a pall over her plans for the village. She believed in the goodness of people's hearts and was sure donations would soon come rolling in …

'Right, back to work. That spilt flour won't sweep itself up.' Sheila smiled at an old lady approaching with a shopping basket over her arm. 'Morning, Mrs Padgett.'

Margaret obligingly fetched the broom. But as soon as the customer had left, she stopped work again, more keen to gossip than complete her chores. 'So you were telling me about that Land Girl … You weren't serious, were you? She didn't *really* spend last night in the hayloft with that young man of hers, did she?'

Sheila sighed, wishing she'd never mentioned the shocking episode with Joan and Arthur. But after hearing Violet's outraged shrieks that morning as she hurried out to work, it had still been on her mind when she reached the shop and found Maggie waiting for her. She'd let slip a few juicy details before realising she probably ought not to have said a word. Now it was obvious her sister wouldn't rest until she'd winkled the whole story out of her.

'Young people make mistakes, don't they?' she said awkwardly, for she liked Joan and didn't enjoy the idea of gossiping about her. 'Least said, soonest mended.'

'But Joan … It's true I've only seen her once or twice in the shop, but you've always said she's such a well-behaved, quiet little thing. I can't believe she'd do something like that.'

'They do say it's the quiet ones you need to watch though, don't they?' Sheila screwed the lid back onto the lemon sherbets and replaced the heavy glass jar on the shelf. 'Maggie, I've told you before, don't leave these jars open after weighing out sweets, it attracts the wasps. Mrs Pearson left twenty minutes ago. This should have been put away by now.'

'Sorry, Shee.' Her sister finished sweeping the floor where a flour sack had spilt before straightening up. 'I must have got distracted putting up that poster of yours.' She put away the broom in its cubby hole behind the counter. 'So, what's Violet going to do about Joan? I suppose she's told the girl to leave. Can't be having that kind of carry-on in a respectable household.'

Sheila threw her sister an irritated look. Maggie had always been a bit uptight, and Violet wasn't exactly relaxed about such doings herself. She'd been much more open-minded as a young woman, it was true, but now she was settled at the farm, a housewife and mother, she seemed to have changed her tune.

'Violet was all for throwing her out on her ear at once, but Joe stepped in. Thing is, they're desperately short-handed at the farm. It'll be harvest-time in a few weeks and he needs more help, not less.'

'She's staying on, then?' Maggie was amazed.

'I don't think anything's decided. But she's in the doghouse with Violet, for sure. Especially given that the young man had a funny turn after Alice's wedding, so heaven knows what problems he has.' Seeing a familiar figure looming in the doorway, Sheila felt an odd little flutter in her chest. Hoping it was silly girlish excitement rather than a heart problem, she patted her hair before hurrying forward. 'Hello, Bernard. How are you?'

The councillor shook her hand as though they were mere acquaintances. But his smile told a different story. 'Hello, Sheila. Very well, thank you. And look who I found in the street.' He nodded over his shoulder, and Sheila realised that George Cotterill was with him. 'An old friend of yours.'

'Hello, George,' she said quickly, shaking hands with him too and hoping he wouldn't notice how flustered she was. 'How are you? And Hazel and the kids?'

'Very well, thank you.'

'Dickie sleeping through the night yet?'

George gave a chuckle. 'Not even close. But we're coping. It's our next-door neighbours I feel sorry for,' he added, grimacing. 'He's got quite a pair of lungs on him.'

She introduced her sister, and they spoke for a while, exchanging pleasantries about their families and the weather, before Bernard said abruptly, 'Look, Mrs Newton, I've been telling George about your plans to tackle poverty in the area. And he's willing to lend a hand with the organisation.' He clapped George on the back. 'In fact, I've persuaded him to join our working group. Good news, eh?'

'Blimey, yes.' Sheila felt gratified that so many villagers were willing to volunteer. She had feared people might be snooty or resistant to the idea of helping the poor, preferring to keep things as they had been before the war. But times had changed since then, everyone more aware now of the need to pitch in and help their neighbours. 'Thank you, George.'

Outside the shop, she saw Mrs Treedy hurrying past with her family, the youngest ones looped together with string to stop them wandering off. 'Oh,' she exclaimed, and seized George by the sleeve, earning herself an amazed look from both him and Bernard. Standing on tiptoe, she whispered in his ear, "Ere, George, do you need a cleaning lady down at Eastern House? Because I know someone who's desperate for work. Got a large family to support all on her own, hard worker, nice lady …' She was overselling Mrs Treedy, perhaps. But she knew how it felt to need money, and she couldn't offer the woman a job herself, having only just enough work in-hand for her and Maggie. 'What do you say?'

George pushed back his hat and scratched his forehead. 'Cleaning lady? We already have one. But,' he added uncertainly, seeing her pleading expression, 'she's getting on a bit, it's true, and could probably do with an assistant. Who is this hard-working lady who's after a job, anyway?'

'I thought you'd never ask,' Sheila said promptly, and dived out of the shop. 'Mrs Treedy?' she called after the woman, who turned with a look of trepidation as though fearing someone was about to slap a Final Demand notice on her. 'Could you spare a minute, love?'

When Mrs Treedy came into the shop, Sheila introduced her to George, saying, 'This is Mr Cotterill, who runs Eastern House.' As they shook hands, she added, 'George is looking for a cleaning lady, and I recalled you saying you might be interested in work like that. Are you still free?'

'Yes,' Mrs Treedy said eagerly, and smoothed down her hair, turning to shoo her youngest children out of the shop.

'Wait for me outside, petal,' she told one tearful-looking girl, whose filthy smock was torn, the hem trailing. 'Now be a good girl for Mummy and stop blubbing, there's a dear.' She shot Sheila and George an embarrassed look. 'I'm ever so sorry … She's grazed her knee, poor thing.'

'Oh dear,' George said sympathetically.

Sheila went after the weeping child and scooped her up in her arms, carrying her into the shop and setting her on the counter. 'Maggie,' she told her sister, 'could you fetch us a bowl of warm water, a clean cloth and the bottle of TCP? It's under the sink.' She winked at the girl. 'Now, what's your name, poppet?'

'Eunice,' the girl whispered shyly, no doubt shocked out of her weeping fit by being snatched into a strange place by a strange lady. She glanced at her mother, who told her to behave herself, and seemed reassured by this instruction. 'Only I don't like antiseptic, if you please.'

'Stings, don't it?' Sheila said kindly, nodding. 'But it stops the germs getting into your blood. You wouldn't like germs in your blood, my love.' Margaret had returned with the bowl, cloth and antiseptic. Sheila cleaned the dirty knee as gently as she could while the girl sucked in her breath, wriggling. Then she shook the bottle of TCP and applied a dab to the cloth. The girl shrank back at the smell, her nose wrinkling. 'Sharp sting coming … But you'll get an aniseed ball if you sit very, very still,' she added, and swiftly pressed the cloth to the grazed knee.

Perhaps enticed by this exciting offer, Eunice obediently froze, though her face screwed up and her little hands balled into fists.

'Brave girl,' Bernard said approvingly, who had been

watching all this while Mrs Treedy and George were discussing the terms of the job at Eastern House. Sheila's daughter had done that same job herself, of course, on first coming down to Cornwall, so she had a good idea what it would entail. And she knew George would be a fair boss, understanding and tolerant.

She lifted the little girl down from the counter, fetched her an aniseed ball, and then one for each of her siblings too, taking them out of her own sweet ration for the week so the books would balance, and smiled as Eunice ran away with the paper bag of sweets clutched to her chest. Outside in the village street, the other kids gathered about her in wonder, to discover what had been done to her inside and exclaiming over the goodies she'd brought back with her. Even the pork pie thief, Jack, had been provided with an aniseed ball and was soon sucking on it ruefully, his hands in his pockets.

Now that Sheila knew *why* he'd taken the pork pie, and since he'd turned up as agreed to clean her shop windows until they gleamed, she didn't hold a grudge. If she could have found *him* work, she would have done. But there were limits. Besides, Jack would be needed to keep an eye on his younger brothers and sisters while their mother was down at Eastern House, cleaning out the big house and no doubt the tunnels behind it too, which still apparently housed the rows of fiendishly complicated machines used to intercept messages from friend and foe alike during the war.

Bernard had been standing outside, studying the poster in the window. After George had left, having agreed working hours with a gratified-looking Mrs Treedy, he wandered back into the shop. 'Impressive handiwork, and a worthy cause. I'm sure the villagers will soon respond with donations.'

'Thank you,' Sheila said, pleased that he approved.

'Mrs Newton,' he said, removing his hat and turning it in his hands, 'I was wondering if you were free to join me for lunch and a walk today? My car's parked just down the road. I could drive us into Penzance, perhaps. Or out along the coast road, if you prefer?'

'Do you have enough fuel for that?' she asked bluntly.

Bernard laughed. 'As a matter of fact, I do,' he said, and glanced at Margaret, who was serving a customer at the counter. 'If your sister can hold the fort for a few hours, that is?'

She was a working woman, Sheila told herself sternly, and ought to say no. Besides which, what did he mean by it, asking her out to lunch like they were a courting couple? Her heart thumped and she didn't know where to look, warmth in her cheeks as she struggled against the urge to say yes. It wasn't right to be going out to lunch with a gentleman when she'd only recently lost her Arnie.

'Oh yes,' Maggie said with a smile, having got rid of the customer as quickly as she could, 'you go, Sheila. I can run things here. And I'll cash up and lock the shop if you're not back before closing time.'

Sheila glared at her sister silently. But there seemed little point in resisting, so she soon found herself seated beside Bernard in his large white car – a Daimler, he told her proudly, as though this should mean something to her – as it bowled along the narrow lanes towards Penzance. It was a warm summer's day and all the windows were open. She wasn't wearing her best, only a workaday dress and a plain headscarf to keep her locks in place. But then she hadn't expected to be whisked away on an adventure with this man by her side, had she?

'Are you cross with me?' Bernard asked.

'Eh?' Sheila turned her head to stare at him, astonished. 'Why on earth would I be cross with you?'

'Putting you on the spot like that in front of your sister. It wasn't very polite of me, but, to tell the truth, I was worried you'd say no if I asked you out to lunch in private. And I know it's not been that long since … since you lost Arnold. The last thing I'd want to do is make you uncomfortable.'

Sheila's heart thundered. So, she hadn't imagined his interest in her. It was romantic, not just him being polite. She wasn't sure how she felt about it. But she didn't want him to know that either.

'Uncomfortable?' she repeated scornfully. 'I'm too old for all that nonsense. And a spot of lunch with an old mate from school days … What could be more natural? Blimey, no need to make a bloomin' mountain out of a molehill.'

She was fishing, of course. And reeled him in.

'*An old mate*? I'm hoping for rather more than that, my dear Sheila,' he said, his gaze on the road. 'Though I'll perfectly understand if you find anything more impossible. I count myself lucky to have met you again.' He paused, then added lightly, 'But I'll be a lucky fellow indeed if you consent to my courting you.'

Oh my gawd, Sheila thought, knitting her fingers together in her lap, completely thrown by his openness.

'One step at a time,' she replied, and pointed hurriedly out of the windscreen. 'Look at that … A peregrine falcon, ain't it?'

He smiled, letting her change the subject without protest. 'I believe so.'

'I do love Cornwall.' Sheila sucked in a lungful of fresh air. 'You know, much as I miss Dagenham at times, all them busy streets and me old neighbours, I'm not sure I could ever live there again. Not now I've put down roots in such a beautiful part of the world.'

His gaze rested on her face for a few seconds before he looked back at the road. 'I'm very glad to hear that,' he murmured. 'Now, lunch in Penzance, then a walk along the seafront?'

'Sounds like heaven,' she agreed.

They had a lovely afternoon together, eating lunch in a busy seafront restaurant in Penzance, followed by the promised walk along the prom. Bernard talked about his volunteer work as a fire warden during the war, and his long-standing friendship with George Cotterill – something they had in common – and Sheila nattered on about her family mostly, all the marriages and births they'd enjoyed in recent years, and how different all the babies were. He seemed interested, or at least politely pretended to be. The drive back went ever so quickly, but it was still gone closing time by the time they pulled back into the quiet village of Porthcurno.

'I'll drive you up to the farm,' Bernard said gallantly.

Checking along the street though, Sheila was amazed to see her sister only just locking up the village shop.

'Could you 'ang on a tick, Bernie?' she begged him, and jumped out of the car, running along to the shop. 'Maggie? Why are you so late closing up?' Then she saw her sister's tear-ravaged face and gasped. 'Oh gawd, what is it? What's the matter, love?'

Margaret put her hands to her cheeks, moaning, 'Oh, Shee … The worst possible thing …' Her chest was heaving. 'Stanley came to the shop while you were gone.'

'*Stanley*?' Sheila blew out an angry breath. Bernard had followed her from the car and was listening intently. 'Her husband's been round, causing trouble no doubt,' Sheila told him in an undertone before turning to hug her sister. 'What did he say to you? I swear, if Stanley's made a bloomin' nuisance of himself, I'll go round to Chellew Farm meself and give him what for.'

'He said he knows where I'm living. Yes, and that I'm working at the shop. And he's going to come round every day until I agree to … to go back to living with him.'

'Finally got sick of cooking and cleaning for himself, has he?' Sheila said shrewdly.

Bernard was frowning. 'Forgive me for interfering, Mrs Chellew, but are you planning to seek a divorce?'

'A divorce? I hadn't thought much about it,' Margaret admitted, looking embarrassed that he'd overheard her troubles, for like many women she didn't enjoy airing her dirty linen in public. 'Getting divorced, after all these years together … Oh, I don't know. It's such a big step.'

Sheila chewed on her lip. 'But it might be the only thing that'll stop the evil beggar from coming around bothering you,' she pointed out. 'Your friend … That lady who's letting you kip on her sofa, I doubt she'll want a nasty bloke like Stanley knocking at her door every five minutes, demanding his wife back.'

Margaret shook her head miserably. 'She already said if he comes around, kicking up a fuss, she'll have to show me the door. She doesn't want the neighbours talking.'

There was only one thing for it. 'Don't you fret, love,' Sheila said, giving her sister an impulsive hug. 'You can move in here.'

'*Here*?'

'There's a flat upstairs where Arnie lived before he moved up to the farm with me.' She gave her sister a wink. 'If you don't mind living above a shop, it's yours.'

'Oh, Shee …' Margaret burst into fresh tears, burying her face in her apron skirt. Her shoulders heaved with strong emotion. 'After everything I done wrong with Violet and Lily,' she choked, 'I … I don't deserve your kindness.'

'Don't get soppy too quick, Mags. You ain't seen how pokey it is up there,' Sheila told her frankly, but grinned. 'What are sisters for, eh?'

But she gave Bernard a worried look behind her sister's back, for she knew Stanley Chellew to be a cruel and persistent bully, and dogged at getting whatever he wanted.

It would take more than a broom and a few hard words to send a man like that on his way.

CHAPTER TWENTY-THREE

Joan felt as though she were walking on air. Yes, she could barely look Violet or Joe in the face now, but she didn't regret what she and Arthur had done. She had simply followed her instincts, realising herself to be in love with Arthur and knowing with every fibre of her being that he loved her back. So, she'd seen nothing wrong in consummating their love, even if finding them in the hayloft had shocked Violet to her bones.

After leaving the hayloft, Arthur had asked Joan with surprising calm, 'If you're all right staying here with the Postbridges, I'd better head home and face the music. No doubt my parents will be furious too that I was out all night.' His gaze had searched her face, worry in his eyes. 'But I'll come back soon. We're going to be married, I promise you that.' He'd hesitated. 'Assuming you can stomach me as a husband?'

Joan, who hadn't even thought as far as marriage, felt her heart swell with joy. 'I'll manage somehow,' she'd whispered, smiling at him. 'But your poor feet ...' She'd lent him an old pair of boots and a coat to get him home, since he'd come out with neither the night before, and stood at the gate to wave him off.

In the snug, the Postbridges had tried grilling her for information about her and Arthur, and Violet had even said a few harsh things about her morals.

Ruffled by some of Violet's remarks, Joan had resisted the urge to be rude in return, merely apologising for having shocked them before heading up to her room for a proper sleep. 'Anyway, I don't know what you two are so upset about,' she'd said defensively when they stared at her. 'You're not my parents.'

'That's as may be, but this is my property,' Joe had told her gruffly, banging his stick on the floor. 'You Land Girls are here to work. Not mess about with boys in my hayloft.' He'd shaken his head. 'And I thought you were such a nice girl too.'

Boys? There'd only ever been one boy, Joan had thought crossly.

'I *am* a nice girl,' she'd said through gritted teeth.

'Give over now, Joe,' Violet had said, perhaps seeing how dangerously close to tears Joan had become. 'It's probably best she takes the day off anyway. We can talk again after supper.'

Joan had sloped wearily off upstairs, meeting Tilly on her way down and saying, in response to the girl's look of blank astonishment, 'Please don't ask. I've had a long night. See you later.'

After a wash, she'd changed into her night clothes, and then slept heavily for hours. In fact, she probably would have slept all day, if it hadn't been for a sudden commotion outside in the farmyard late afternoon. She'd heard a vehicle coming

286

up the hill, its engine note unfamiliar, and sat up groggily, thinking it must be Arthur coming back with his parents.

Joan leapt out of bed, splashed her face with water, dragged a comb through her hair, and got dressed again before dashing downstairs.

In the kitchen, she found Violet Postbridge with little Sarah Jane tugging on her skirt. She was talking to a young man whose face Joan couldn't see, as he was facing the other way.

He was wearing an army uniform, so she knew at once it wasn't Arthur. But, having only just woken up, it took a few seconds of baffled staring to realise who she was looking at.

At that instant, the young man turned, smiling, and stretched out his arms to her. 'Hello, Joanie.'

She threw herself at him with a shriek. 'Graham. Oh, you're back from Europe at last! It's marvellous to see you.'

She hugged her brother tightly, and felt his strong arms close about her. She'd missed him so badly, and was so much in need of a friend at that moment, she felt almost as though he'd come to rescue her. As though she had somehow psychically communicated her need to him across the miles, and her younger brother had heard her plea and magically arrived at her door.

'Have you been demobbed?' She looked him up and down, noting his smart uniform. 'Or are you on official leave?'

He shook his head. 'Demobbed. I'm back for good. Though still in uniform for now.' He laughed when she squealed again with excitement. 'I should get my official papers through in a few weeks. I shipped over with a load of other chaps and thought I'd come see you first before heading back to London.' He held her by the shoulders, smiling into her eyes.

287

'Mrs Postbridge has just been telling me you've been in bed all day. Are you unwell? Though you look healthy enough to me. Look at the roses in those cheeks!'

Catching Violet's glare over his shoulder, Joan said hurriedly, 'Perhaps we could go for a walk and I'll explain properly,' she suggested. 'If that's all right with you, Mrs Postbridge?'

'You do what you want, love,' Violet said sharply, and turned to sit Sarah Jane down at the table again, where it seemed the little girl had been crayoning while her mother baked. 'I'm sure it's no concern of ours,' she added tartly, 'seeing as how I expect you'll be leaving us soon anyway.'

'Eh?' Graham glanced at Joan in surprise.

'Not here,' she whispered, pulling on her boots and dragging him outside with a tight smile.

In the farmyard, the light was a soft warm gold as afternoon tipped towards evening. Tilly and Joe were presumably still out in the fields, while Caroline had not yet returned from her trip to Bodmin, leaving Joe grumbling at her continued absence.

But how to explain everything to Graham?

They walked across some rough pasture and stopped under a tree for shade. Unable to hide her anguish, she sank down on the grass, fists clenched, and her brother threw himself down beside her, removing his cap.

'Now then, Joan, let's hear what's been going on,' he said easily. 'Whatever it is, I'm still your brother. I'll support you, no matter what.'

This was too much for her. Joan burst into tears and couldn't speak for several minutes. He waited patiently until her tears had slowed, and then squeezed her hand.

'Come on, spit it out, Joan. I'm worried about you now. All these tears ...'

Graham was so much more mature than Joan remembered. But then, he'd been away fighting in a war. It had been some years since she'd seen him. Small wonder he struck her as older and wiser. And right now, she valued that wisdom.

Rubbing damp cheeks with the back of her hand, she explained what had happened. How she'd met Arthur, how they had spent so much time together sorting out books at the Grange, his awful fit on the night of Alice's wedding, and how his parents had forbidden them to see each other ... Finally, between bouts of fresh tears, she touched on how she and Arthur had spent the night in the hayloft, and been discovered by Violet in the early morning.

Graham, having listened in silence, though with a gathering frown, gave a low whistle. 'Good God ... I had no idea it would be something so serious. You were always the sensible one, Joan. Now this ...' He didn't meet her eyes as he added, 'And he claims he wants to marry you, does he? He sounds like an odd fish to me, this Arthur chap. I don't like the idea of it, to be honest, you and this fellow ... Sounds like Mrs Postbridge was right when she told you he's not the full shilling. Do you really want to shackle yourself to him for the rest of your life?'

Joan stared at him in horror. Hadn't Graham heard a word she'd said? 'But I'm in love with him,' she stammered, 'and there's no question of being *shackled*. Yes, all right, we jumped the gun a bit. But this is 1946, for goodness' sake. We're not living in the dark ages.'

He shrugged. 'I suppose times have changed since before the war, you're right. But people are still judgemental. I wouldn't want you to be gossiped about. You need to be sensible.'

'That's my business though, isn't it? I love you dearly, Graham, but I'm still your big sister. You don't have the right to tell me how to live.' Perhaps she had expected too much from her brother, who had come home and walked slap bang into this dreadful situation. But he'd said he would support her, no matter what. Instead, he was siding with the Postbridges and Arthur's parents. 'I was so happy when I walked in and saw you. I was thrilled that you were back in one piece, that you'd survived. Please don't be horrid now ...'

She couldn't help it, she burst into tears again, and this time he sat up and drew her into his arms. 'Don't cry, Joanie ... I'm sorry. You're right. I said I wouldn't judge you. Now I have. But this chap, he'd better marry you straightaway. I mean, what if ... You know, what if you and he ...' He stopped, looking embarrassed.

'Sorry?'

'Come on, you're a woman of the world. Or you certainly are now. What if you've got a bun in the oven?'

'Oh!' Her cheeks flared with heat as she realised what he was trying to say. 'Yes, I see what you mean. But since we're getting married, nobody would know.'

'Only if it happens quickly,' Graham pointed out. 'His parents don't approve though. What if you never see him again? Then you'll be in a right pickle, my girl.'

She hadn't considered what would happen if she fell pregnant after last night. Perhaps he was right and she was being naïve. The thought filled her with trepidation. But she was still willing to give Arthur the benefit of the doubt. 'Shall we walk back? It's ever so warm ...'

They started back towards the farm at an unhurried pace.

'I didn't properly say,' she added, 'but I'm overjoyed that you're back, that you made it. I was so scared for you, Graham. I used to lie awake at night worrying about you.'

'So did I,' he said frankly, and they both laughed.

Then, suddenly, Joan stopped dead in the centre of the farmyard, at the sight of Arthur there with his parents, getting out of their car. Her heart thumped wildly and she felt almost faint, seeing the grim look on her beloved's face. Whatever had transpired between him and his parents, it hadn't been good.

Graham took in the scene with one quick glance. He said tensely, 'Is that him?'

'That's Arthur, yes,' she whispered.

To her surprise, her younger brother strode forward with a determined air until he came face-to-face with Arthur, who looked at him blankly.

Graham drew himself up to his full height, glaring into the other young man's face. 'I know what you did,' he said from between gritted teeth. 'You're damn lucky I don't smash your teeth down the back of your throat for it. How dare you? My sister's a good girl, you had no right to interfere with her like that. I hope you've come here to propose to her. Because otherwise—'

'Of course I want to marry her,' Arthur threw back at him, back straight, his hands clenched into fists, automatically standing up to this unknown opponent. 'But it's not that simple.'

'I knew it … You're backing out, aren't you? You snivelling coward.' Looking him up and down with contempt, he pushed Arthur backwards, so that he stumbled, almost falling. 'As soon as she told me about you, I knew what kind of man you were. Came home early from the war, did you? Couldn't handle it? I've known men like you. They'll do and say anything to get out of uniform.'

'What's going on here? Who is this young man?' Arthur's father came around the car in a hurry. He and Mrs Green had been speaking to Violet and Joe outside the farmhouse, but now he'd noticed the two men arguing, and there was a look of thunder on his face. 'Arthur, come here.'

But it was too late.

'I'm no c-coward,' Arthur was insisting, his voice fierce. 'You don't know what the hell you're talking about.'

'Yellow-bellied *coward*,' Graham said deliberately.

Arthur lurched forward, a hot flush in his cheeks, and slammed his fist into Graham's face, who fell backwards with a gasp.

Recovering, Graham rushed forward with fists raised. He thumped Arthur in the face, and Arthur thumped him back, following this up with a roaring charge, head down.

Joan shrieked, 'No! Stop it, both of you!'

Her shouts fell on deaf ears. The two of them were already on the ground, rolling about in the dirt of the cobbled farmyard, while chickens squawked and ran about hysterically. Joe's working dogs crouched in defensive mode, not quite daring to bark without permission but growling at these intruders with blood-curdling snarls.

'Do something, pull them off each other,' Mrs Green cried, clasping her cheeks in dismay.

'No, let them get it out of their systems. No point interfering.' Joe leaned on his stick, watching the fight with interest.

Mr Green ignored him and waded in, perhaps driven by his wife's shrieks, somehow managing to drag Arthur away. Joan felt sick, seeing that Arthur's nose was bleeding copiously, and his lip was badly split. Graham wasn't looking too good either, one eye partially closed and already swelling, where no doubt he'd soon be sporting a large shiner.

Joan loved both these men equally, but she was furious with them too. 'Couple of idiots,' she snapped, and strode into the farmhouse kitchen in search of something to clean their cuts.

Muttering something under her breath about men and fighting, Violet followed her and reached up to the medicine cupboard at the same time as Joan. 'Best let me do it, love,' she said, not unkindly. 'I've more experience of dealing with cuts and bruises than you.'

There was no arguing with that. Joan, desperate for something useful to do, took charge of Sarah Jane instead, fetching the little girl some orange squash and overseeing her colouring. Meanwhile, Violet dabbed TCP on the young men's faces and knuckles, which were badly cut and grazed. Joan wanted to launch into a tirade at them both, but since Mr and Mrs Green were doing all the talking, it was impossible to get a word in edgeways.

'Arthur's told us everything, and I think it's disgusting,' Mrs Green said in her well-modulated voice, arms folded, throwing a furious look at Joan. 'She clearly lured him in. Arthur's not the sort to do anything like this otherwise.'

'Don't you talk about our Joan like that,' Violet snapped over her shoulder, almost as though Joan were her own daughter. 'More likely your boy seduced her, not the other way round. He's a man, ain't he? It's always men who do the seducing.'

'That merely shows how few good men you know,' Mrs Green remarked in acid tones.

'Why, you …' Violet gasped, a flush in her cheeks.

'My dear,' Mr Green murmured in mild reproof, casting a wary glance at Joe.

He needn't have worried that Joe would be offended. The farmer, having sent his dogs outside, was more focused on keeping the peace. 'Now, ladies,' Joe said uneasily, 'let's try to keep things civil, eh? There's a lot of bad feeling in this room. And this is where it's led. To a bunch of bruises.'

Joan didn't know what to say. But she felt grateful towards Violet for standing up for her. She'd seen Tilly looking out of the kitchen window during the fight, but there was no sign of her now. The other Land Girl must have gone up to her room to stay discreetly out of the way. For that she was thankful, as Joan was certain Tilly had no idea that she and Arthur had spent the night together. Mrs Newton had been around when Violet and Joe had cornered her that morning, demanding answers. But the fewer people who knew, the better.

Arthur, slumped on a kitchen chair while Violet dabbed at his cuts, caught her eye and said thickly, 'I don't care what they say, Joan. I still want to marry you.'

'Don't worry, mate, you're going to bloody marry her,' Graham told him crisply, ignoring Violet's pursed lip at his coarse language.

'Not if we send him away, he's not.' Mrs Green was looking coldly triumphant.

'Excuse me?' Graham shot back at her, his frown ferocious.

'That's what I was trying to tell you outside,' Arthur threw in bitterly, 'when you thumped me in the face.'

'I pushed you, in fact.' Graham glared at him. 'You thumped me first.'

'Oh, shut up, for goodness' sake, both of you,' Joan exclaimed, and everyone looked round at her in surprise as though they'd forgotten she was still in the room. 'There's no question of anyone sending Arthur away. We're getting married, and that's an end to it. Though where we're going to live afterwards, I have no idea.'

The Greens looked at each other uncomfortably, saying nothing.

'Where on earth were you planning to send your boy?' Violet demanded, straightening to stare at the couple.

'To a sanatorium,' Arthur admitted through gritted teeth. 'They were talking about having me committed. Like I'm mad. All to stop me marrying Joan.'

'Nobody's sending you to a sanatorium, Arthur.' Joan decided it was time to nip this nonsense in the bud. 'Once we're married, I'll look after you. Though I don't think there's anything wrong with you that a few months away from your parents wouldn't cure.'

'Excuse me?' Mrs Green was glaring at her.

Joan took Arthur's hand. 'Well?'

Their eyes met, and he nodded. 'I'll do whatever you say, Joan.'

Violet merely shrugged, putting away the medicaments in a brusque manner. Joe tapped his stick on the floor approvingly.

Mr Green laid a hand on his son's shoulder. 'Son, you've made your bed and now you have to lie in it. I hope you and this … this girl can make a go of things. And I suppose you can live with us once you're wed.' His wife made an angry noise but Mr Green shook his head. 'No, I've decided. We'll have to make the best of a bad job. No more arguing.'

Graham got up and came to stand over them. He touched Joan's cheek. 'You sure about this, Joanie? I know I lost my temper earlier but I was just caught off guard, that's all. If you'd rather not marry him, we'll find a way to hush it up.'

Joan almost laughed. 'You silly thing,' she said affectionately, not bothering to answer that. 'And since we missed out the introductions earlier, what with you two being too busy punching each other in the face, Graham, I'd like you to meet my fiancé, Arthur.' She smiled as the two men eyed each other uncertainly. 'Arthur, this is my little brother, Graham. Now, please shake hands and stop being so utterly ridiculous.'

Graham laughed and stuck out his hand. Arthur shook it, smiling ruefully.

'Welcome to the family then, I suppose,' Graham said, and slapped his assailant on the back. 'Just don't treat her badly, that's all.' He paused. 'You've not got a bad right hook,' her brother added grudgingly. 'Though you've a lot to learn about defence.'

'Maybe you could teach me,' Arthur suggested. 'For next time.'

The two men grinned at each other.

The introductions over, Arthur pulled Joan irreverently onto his knee, an act which silenced everyone in the room for a moment, including Joan herself. But to her surprise it seemed to break the ice too, even Mrs Green looking amused at last.

'We'd better set a date, I suppose,' Arthur remarked, an arm about her waist. 'And, erm, the sooner the better.' He leaned forward and whispered in her ear, 'Just in case.'

Joan blushed.

CHAPTER TWENTY-FOUR

It was harder than Selina had expected to say goodbye to Caroline. But the Land Girl didn't dare delay her return to Porthcurno any longer, having already overstayed her official leave by several days and being too afraid of Joe's righteous wrath to push it any further. Despite the awkwardness between them since Caroline's declaration, she still felt the loss of her friend keenly, and waving her off at the train station reduced her to tears.

'Write to me,' she joked, while Caroline nodded and waved frantically from the window until the train was out of sight.

Cameron had kindly driven them to the station, and Selina sat beside him in silence most of the way back to Thornton Hall.

'Missing your friend already?' he asked as they drove through the entrance gates.

'It's certainly been lovely having her at the hall these past few days, but she was needed back in Porthcurno.' Selina shot him an apologetic smile. 'I'm sorry. I've been poor company today, haven't I?'

'Not at all,' he said politely.

She asked on impulse, 'Would you like to go riding with me tomorrow? I've been intending to take Bella's horse out for ages now, and Mrs Hawley says she's hoping to gather some late gooseberries with the kids tomorrow morning, for jams and preserves. That should allow me a few hours' freedom from the nursery.'

'Of course. I'll ride over first thing in the morning. But surely you intend hiring a new nanny soon? You can't think Bella intended you to look after those rowdy three on your own?' He was frowning. 'She certainly never did.'

This was the first time she'd ever heard him speak of Bella and her children with anything other than deep respect, and it left her feeling uneasy.

'I don't mind their rowdiness.' She paused. 'Besides, I would dislike spending much time apart from the children when they've only recently lost their mother.'

'Quite so,' he agreed at once. 'I hadn't considered that. Sorry, you must think me a regular brute.' He drew up in front of the house. 'Nine o'clock tomorrow?'

She agreed, waiting until he'd driven away before going inside the big house. The three children were in the kitchen with Mrs Hawley again, making a racket as Jemima and Faith danced around the table while Peter played a series of pots and pans with a wooden spoon. Talk about rowdy, she thought, rather glad that Cameron hadn't walked in on that scene.

Mrs Hawley, rolling out dough, was looking harassed, and threw her a grateful smile when Selina suggested a family walk in the grounds before tea-time.

While the children dashed away to put on their outdoor

shoes, Selina said, 'Mrs Hawley, thank you for looking after the children this week. I'm sorry to keep lumbering you with them.'

'They're no trouble, Miss,' Mrs Hawley insisted, generously flouring her rolling pin and returning to the dough. 'Anyway, I daresay a new nanny will soon settle them down.'

Selina said nothing but went away with a frown. Must she engage a new nanny, then? Everyone seemed to think it the right thing to do. Yet surely Faith and Jemima would do better with a family member looking after them, given their vulnerable state?

And Peter didn't need a nanny at his age. His tutor had been pleased with his progress this year and was already talking about sending him back to Marlborough School, the exclusive boarding school he'd attended before Bella's illness. She didn't have the heart to tell Peter there likely wasn't enough money in the estate for such an expense. Mr MacGregor had kindly suggested several less expensive boys' schools in the West Country, and she certainly preferred the idea of him being nearer to home. He might be nearly a grown-up but she could see he was still hurting after the loss of his mother.

As promised, she spent the afternoon exploring the lush summer gardens with the children, then joined Jemima and Peter for dinner and a couple of raucous hours of board games after Faith had gone to bed.

Later, once all three children were safely tucked up in bed, Selina finally retreated to her own bedroom, curling up with a mug of cocoa and her sister's journals.

The house felt quiet and far emptier now that Caroline had gone, and Selina had to admit to feeling lonely. However, when she recalled their difficult conversation, she experienced again that peculiar shock of realisation, still struggling to accept that Caroline's feelings were not simply those of a good friend …

She also found her thoughts returning to Cameron as she restlessly flicked through the pages of the journal she was reading, looking out for mentions of his name.

Now and then her sister had written a short passage involving her closest neighbours, the Bourne family, most usually referencing Helen, with whom she seemed to have spent a great deal of time in her first few years at Thornton Hall. Clearly Bella had been good friends with Helen at one stage, having managed to heal the breach between the two families, even if the two women had grown further apart in later years. She wondered what had happened to interfere with their friendship. It was strange and uncomfortable to read such private reminiscences, hearing them in her sister's voice, and Selina was aching with grief by the time it was bedtime, wishing she'd stayed closer to Bella after her marriage.

Cameron was rarely mentioned in those early journal entries, except as a close friend of Bella's husband. Perhaps, Selina thought, wearily closing the journal and replacing it on her bedside table, Cameron might feature more frequently in her sister's later journals, especially in the period after Sebastian's death.

The next morning, a gardening boy who also served as stable hand saddled Bella's horse and brought it out into the yard for nine o'clock. Cameron came trotting around the back of the house just as Selina was mounting, and raised a hand in greeting. 'Good morning,' he called, handsome on the back of a fine black gelding, his bearing stiff and military, though his hands were relaxed on the reins, suggestive of a long acquaintance with riding. 'Isn't this a glorious morning? Perfect for a morning ride over the moors. I can't wait to show you the best bridle paths.'

They rode out of the estate through woodlands and were soon following a well-beaten track into the heart of Bodmin Moor. The rolling green-brown slopes were steeped in sunshine and shadow, light glittering off bullrush-shrouded bodies of water dotted here and there across the wild expanse.

Slowing to a walk, Cameron pointed at a craggy peak, rising hazy blue-grey in the distance. 'That's Rough Tor up there, the odd-shaped hill.' He told her the Cornish pronounced it 'Rowter', adding, 'The place has quite a reputation hereabouts. Ghostly doings and so on. It's just a good climb, if you ask me. But legend says a girl was murdered there once, so the locals are superstitious about it.'

His remarks surprised her. 'You were born here, weren't you? Yet you don't consider yourself a local?'

He laughed. 'My family's not native Cornish. That's all I meant.'

They rode on together, increasing to a brisk trot as the track gradually broadened between thick sweeps of bracken and springy heather.

'Where are your family from, then?'

'From the North of England, originally,' he admitted, 'though that's going back several generations now. All the same, I doubt the Cornish would consider me a native. My way of speaking is too different, I suppose.'

'Yes, we Land Girls had a little trouble fitting in with the locals in Porthcurno at times,' she admitted. 'What did you think of Caroline, by the way?'

He shot her a thoughtful glance. 'A very emotional woman. She was deeply upset when she had to return to Porthcurno without you. She misses you, that's obvious. I was surprised, to be honest, that you didn't ask her to stay on at Thornton Hall.'

'You think I should have asked her to stay for good?'

'Absolutely not,' he replied, brows raised. 'I've always said you should look forward in life, never back.' When she looked at him, puzzled by his cryptic words, he added more forcefully, 'Sometimes people have to be left behind, and that's all there is to it.'

'What are you saying? That you … you don't think Caro's any good for me as a friend?'

'Forgive me for speaking bluntly, but I suspect she'd like to be more than a friend to you. And you don't share that wish, do you?'

Selina flushed, horribly embarrassed. She looked straight ahead between the horse's pricked ears, and swallowed, unsure how to reply. Well, she'd asked for his opinion of Caroline, hadn't she? She could hardly complain now, simply because she wasn't happy with what he'd said. She found herself uncomfortable though, taken aback by how closely he'd observed the friendship between her and Caroline.

'Goodness, this is glorious country. I don't know why I didn't come out riding earlier,' she said, abruptly changing tack. 'I've been reading Bella's journals lately. My sister used to ride over the moors with Sebastian when they were first married. Did you ever ride with them in those days?'

'Frequently, yes. And I went riding with her after Sebastian died too, to keep her company, and also for protection.'

'Protection?'

He looked at her sombrely. 'The weather can change rapidly on the moors. And this terrain can be treacherous too, especially after rain. It's rarely a good idea to go out riding alone here, unless you know the ground well. I know Sebastian would never have wanted Bella to ride out on her own, and after his death, I carried on that tradition.' He saw her expression and smiled. 'I suppose that sounds awfully chauvinistic. These days, they say women can do anything that men can, given how well you ladies managed during the war.'

Selina bit her tongue, not wanting to offend him with a sharp comment.

'But Bella knew as well as any of us how challenging the moors can be,' he went on, seeming oblivious to her silence. 'Once or twice, out riding together, even we fell foul of unpredictable weather ...' His voice trailed off and he looked away into the distance, as though in reverie.

'But on a day like this,' she said, glancing up at the blue skies, 'surely there's little danger of rain?'

Smiling, Cameron drew his horse to a stop, and she did likewise. With his riding crop, he pointed behind them to a bank of dark clouds that she'd failed to notice gathering a fair distance away, around the Bodmin area. 'Those are rainclouds. Heavy too, by the look of them. They'll be here within the hour, depending on wind speed.' He studied her light outfit, for she'd not worn a coat, relying on a long-sleeved blouse and sleeveless jacket to keep her protected from the elements. 'We'll need to turn back soon, unless you enjoy getting soaked to the skin.'

He was laughing at her, Selina thought, and was suddenly annoyed. Cameron wasn't just chauvinistic but high-handed too. And she could imagine Bella secretly resenting his interference when he insisted on accompanying her on moorland rides. But some men could be like that, couldn't they? Always telling women what to do …

On a furious impulse, she dug her heels into the horse's flanks and the animal leapt forward, responding to her direction and rapidly shifting into a thundering canter. At once she realised her mistake. She hadn't ridden that fast in a long time, and found herself clinging desperately onto the horse's mane as well as the slipping reins, hoping she wasn't about to make a fool of herself by falling off in front of Cameron.

Hearing hooves behind her, she realised with an embarrassed sense of relief that he'd caught up with her.

Leaning across, their knees bumping, Cameron made a grab for the horse's bridle, calling 'Whoa there!' to the horse, trying to slow its headlong pace.

But the horse startled at his touch instead, tossing his head and breaking violently to the left, the reins dragged out of her hands. Seconds later, one of the horse's shoulders dipped as he stumbled badly in the bracken, perhaps catching his foot in a concealed rabbit hole, and the world turned about her in a sickening blur as she tumbled from the saddle.

Thankfully, it had rained in recent days, and the ground was soft enough to cushion her fall. She landed in bracken and a few thorny shrubs, and sat up at once, feeling ridiculous.

Cameron, having caught her horse, dismounted and walked back to her with both animals in tow. He looked concerned. 'Good God, Selina, are you all right? Can you stand?'

Still dizzy from her fall, she struggled to her feet, relieved to find both ankles sound. 'I haven't seriously hurt anything,' she said, flushed and breathless. 'I … I think he put his foot in a rabbit hole.'

'Yes, I saw what happened,' he said curtly, 'and you may not have sprained anything, but the horse has. We'll have to walk back. Hopefully, the vet will be able to put a poultice on it to reduce the swelling, but you won't be able to ride him again for some time, I'm afraid.'

'Oh no, poor thing.' She stroked the horse's soft nose, and peered apologetically into large velvety dark eyes. 'I'm so sorry you got hurt.'

'Why on earth did you dash off like that?'

'I thought the horse needed at least one good gallop before heading home,' she lied awkwardly, avoiding his gaze. 'We'd better head off straightaway or we'll get caught in the rain.'

They set off along the track, weaving their way at a slow walk through clumps of heather and granite outcrops of rock. Before they had cleared the moor, however, rainclouds swept in exactly as Cameron had predicted and the deluge began. Great fat droplets of rain sploshed onto their faces and backs, and they were soon sodden.

'There!' Cameron pointed to a barren outcrop of rock with an overhang, where they could shelter. There wasn't quite room for the horses, but he seemed to think they wouldn't mind a little rain, so they hurried up the slope, secured the horses to a thorn bush, and huddled together under the overhang of rock, waiting for the rainstorm to pass. 'Sebastian used to call this Dead Man's Bluff,' he told her, removing his cap and shaking raindrops off it. 'I'm not sure why. He made up names for lots of local landmarks. The way his mind worked, I suppose.'

Now that they were no longer moving, Selina began to shiver violently, perhaps in response to the sudden change in temperature. 'Well, this is m-marvellous,' she muttered.

With her sleeveless jacket, she had no way of warming herself up. But of course Cameron was wearing a coat and shrugged out of it at once. He slung it about her shoulders, saying, 'No, I insist,' when she protested. 'I rarely feel the cold. But you're soaked through. Plus, you've had a shock. Falling off a horse like that … It's never pleasant.' He rubbed the tops of her arms, looking into her face. 'How are you feeling? Better?'

She tried but couldn't answer, pricklingly aware of his proximity. Rain drummed frantically on the moorland around them and dripped off the rock overhang. There was no room to move without exposing herself to the rain, so she just stood there, gazing into his face in silence.

Without a word, he bent his head to kiss her.

In a trance, she wound both arms about his neck, and kissed him back. In that shadowy space, his hands moulded her body, and she felt almost faint, clinging to him as the kiss deepened and grew hotter.

At last, she must have made a sound under her breath, for he drew back abruptly, and apologised, running a hand through dishevelled hair.

'I'm sorry, I shouldn't have done that … Look, the rain's stopping already.' He stuck his head out to study the sky. 'What did I say? The clouds have almost passed and I expect the sun will be out again soon. We'd better get going before the horses catch cold.'

Cameron had been so confident when he'd kissed her at the farm, she was surprised by his new uncertainty. Still, he'd gone a little further this time and was maybe shocked that she hadn't pushed him away. But the truth was, she'd let Johnny take liberties like that a few times, and so hadn't been fazed by his actions. No doubt that made her appear 'fast' in his eyes … The possibility annoyed her.

After he'd seen her horse stabled and left instructions with the stable hand to contact the vet about a possible sprain, Cameron parted from her with a polite handshake, once again as though he'd never kissed her at all. He was rather too good at blowing hot and cold, she thought with a flash of impatience, watching him ride away before she hurried inside to change her damp clothes.

Late that night, sleepily reading her sister's journal in bed, Selina came across a poorly scrawled passage that made her freeze in shock.

Caught Sebastian with Helen today. They were in the garden room. I couldn't see what was going on but heard the way Helen was speaking, and my stomach turned. I knew it! All those times he swore they were just old friends … After she and Cam had ridden home, I confronted him about it, but he denied everything. Said they'd been discussing his brother James and how heartbroken Helen had been at his death. I felt sick, more at his lies than his adultery. But they say men often look to other women when their wives are pregnant, and this is my second pregnancy now, so perhaps he's bored and simply amusing himself elsewhere. And Helen is young and fresh-faced. I can only hope he remembers his duty as a husband and a father in time, and drops this little game.

* * *

Fatigue falling away, Selina sat up in shock.

What on earth …?

Her brother-in-law Sebastian had dared have an *affair* with his next-door neighbour, Helen Bourne? And while she was still quite a young woman too …

That would certainly explain the woman's lofty behaviour about the house and her barely disguised contempt for Selina. She'd previously assumed it was because Helen had once been in love with Sebastian's brother, the heir to Thornton Hall, but this changed everything.

Though, if true, why had Bella seemingly forgiven such a gross betrayal of her trust? She had introduced Helen and Cameron as good friends and neighbours, and given no inkling of a dark past between them, apart from that odd remark about Helen having been a 'bitter spinster' in Sebastian's eyes. Had she been trying to protect her late husband's reputation by hiding the truth, even from her own sister?

Though of course Helen would have been bitter, Selina thought, catching her breath at the thought. Bitter that her lover was married to another woman …

Her sister must have been a veritable saint, Selina decided. Far from saintlike herself, she felt furious on Bella's behalf. Next time she saw Helen, she would surely not be able to hide her rage.

Turning down the page edge to mark it, she read on, scanning the pages ahead for Helen's name. But what she found was even more horrifying, and her heart thumped violently as she read and re-read the passage in disbelief. It was dated nine years previously, still before the war but well after Sebastian's affair with Helen.

Cam tried it on with me today while Seb was away in London. We were out riding and it came on to rain, so we sheltered at Dead Man's Bluff. That's when he kissed me. I don't feel even remotely romantic towards him, plus I am a married woman. I wrestled with whether I should tell Seb on his return but decided against it. What the eye doesn't see, the heart can't grieve over, and I'd hate such a long-standing friendship as theirs to be ruined by one stupid mistake.

Dead Man's Bluff?

But that was where they'd taken shelter from the rain too. And he had kissed her there just as he'd kissed her sister too, all those years ago.

Reading on, she found further references to Cameron and Helen Bourne, and one telling comment where her sister wondered if the pair were trying to split her and Sebastian up, so they could get their hands on his large estate, presumably through Helen marrying Sebastian afterwards. But then Bella had decided she was being mean and paranoid and imagining things …

Was it possible that Cameron had wrongly assumed Selina had inherited money or a sizeable share of the estate on her sister's death? Or perhaps that by getting close to her, he might be able to influence young Peter into selling him part of the estate at a reduced sum once the boy reached his majority?

Selina's face hardened. 'Oh, Bella,' she muttered, 'you were always far too nice to suspect when you were being duped.' She closed the journal with a snap. 'I'm not going to make the same mistake.'

* * *

309

The next day, sitting outside with the children under the shade of a large parasol, she heard a car, and five minutes later, Cameron Bourne strolled around the corner with his sister Helen.

'Hello,' he said cheerfully as the kids ran to greet him, 'what are you three doing? Sketching the rose garden? I say, Peter, that's pretty good … You've got a keen eye.'

Helen came to sit beside Selina on the bench. 'Cameron told me about your little adventure on the moors yesterday. Feel all right now? And how's Bella's horse?'

'I'm fine, thank you,' Selina replied stiffly. 'The vet called yesterday evening. He said it's not a bad sprain, just minor swelling, and should pass off soon enough, given the right treatment.'

Inside, she wanted to scream at the Bournes to go away and never come back. But she couldn't do it. There were rules of etiquette that still had to be followed, and the children were listening to their conversation. Besides, she didn't want them to know she'd uncovered their secrets.

But that didn't mean she had to encourage their visits.

'That's excellent news.' Cameron smiled, thrusting his hands into his pockets. 'By the way, we called round with an invitation. A select dinner party at our house this Saturday night. Do say you can make it, Selina.'

'Yes, please,' Helen agreed. 'You absolutely must come.'

Suspicious of their motives, Selina pulled Faith onto her lap, pulling a few grass blades out of the little girl's hair. 'Erm … Saturday night? I'm afraid not, sorry.'

'Oh, that's a shame,' Helen cried.

'Another evening, then.' Cameron was still smiling but his friendliness no longer felt genuine.

'Perhaps,' she said.

Yes, the Bournes had behaved abominably towards her sister, and even if Bella hadn't felt able to defend herself against this scheming pair, Selina had no such qualms. She was starting to come into her own at Thornton Hall, and to see where she could most be useful to Bella's children, and she certainly didn't need or want a romantic attachment, especially one that seemed so eerily constructed out of *déjà-vu* and memories of her dead sister. Perhaps she was imagining sinister undercurrents where none existed, but she wasn't willing to take the chance. Not after reading her sister's journals.

'I was just about to take the children inside for juice and biscuits,' she went on, getting to her feet and perching Faith on her hip, despite the child's weight. 'So if you'll excuse me?' And with a cool nod to her astonished neighbours, she called the children to come back indoors.

'Biscuits? Yes, please.' Jemima skipped and hummed ahead of them, clapping her hands.

It was the first time Selina had seen the girl look so carefree since the horror of her mother's death, and she recalled with a pang why she had come here to Bodmin in the first place, to ease Bella through her final weeks and to care for her children once she'd gone.

Bella's children had to be her number one priority. And they were. Indeed, it was no hardship, for she already loved these three like her very own.

'I've never much liked the Bournes,' Peter muttered once they were out of earshot, and Selina had put a wriggling Faith down to toddle eagerly after her sister.

She beamed at the boy, amused by this almost adult show of solidarity. 'Me neither,' she said, and put an arm about his shoulders, hugging him close.

CHAPTER TWENTY-FIVE

The man in the shop doorway stopped and cleared his throat. 'Morning, Mrs Newton. The wife asked me to drop this off,' he said awkwardly, holding out a bulging sack. 'Donations for the needy, she said. Where do you want it?'

'Morning.' Sheila bustled forward. 'You can give that to me, sir.' Taking the sack, she loosened the neck and peeked inside. Mostly children's clothing, and a few pairs of scuffed shoes minus their laces. Exactly what was needed, she thought with a burst of pleasure. 'Tell your wife thank you, it's much appreciated, and these will soon find their way to a good home.'

With an embarrassed nod, the man continued on his way along the sunlit village street. It was late summer and she could hear Joe's tractor droning back and forth in the fields above the village, as he and the Land Girls brought in the harvest. It had been good to welcome Caroline back to the farm after her short holiday. The girl had come back from Bodmin slightly subdued, but that was only to be expected, still pining for her friend as she was, and she'd soon got back into the swing of farmwork without complaints.

Sheila turned, holding out the sack of clothing. 'Margaret, could you—?'

'Stow it upstairs with the rest?' Her sister gave a crooked smile. 'Yes, though I won't hardly have room to move up there soon, the number of donations you've had recently.'

Maggie went off grumbling but Sheila could tell she was secretly enjoying their collection request having received so many donations. Many of the women who'd come in with unwanted items had stopped to exchange a few words of commiseration with Margaret about the failure of her marriage, for word had gone around the village about Stanley's brutish ways. Although people disapproved of divorce in the general way, when it was the case of a wifebeater, most were inclined to see that as a special case.

Sheila would have taken the sack upstairs herself, but she badly needed to catch up on her paperwork, and Margaret had only been sweeping the front step, which was always dirty, not surprisingly, given how many farmers wandered in and out during the day, trailing mud, and often kids too, with dirty faces and even dirtier boots.

As she returned to studying the ledgers with a distracted frown, an elderly lady in a plain brown hat limped slowly into the shop, leaning on a cane.

'Good morning, Mrs Downing,' Sheila said in a cheery fashion, glad to be interrupted again. Sums were not her strong suit. Indeed, poring over rows of figures as she struggled to make them add up was giving her a headache. 'Nice to see you again so soon. Did you forget something?'

'Erm, yes.' Mrs Downing had already come in once that morning for her usual ration of meat and veg. Now she stopped before the counter, biting her lip. 'This collection of unwanted clothing … Does anyone need to know if a person were to ask for, say, a cardigan? I mean, you don't make a list of recipients?'

'Bless me, no.' Sheila understood at once, and her heart squeezed in pain for the frail old lady. 'It would just be between you and me.'

'I'm not in need, as such,' Mrs Downing said with an embarrassed smile. 'It's just I like to use my clothing ration to help my daughter. She lost her husband in the war and her son's growing so quickly …'

'No need to explain, love.' Sheila came out from behind the counter, adding conspiratorially, 'I've a nice pile of cardigans upstairs. Did you have a particular colour in mind, or should I just bring them all down?'

Mrs Downing hesitated, glancing about the empty shop, then whispered, 'Blue, if you have it. Or lilac at a pinch.'

Going to the base of the stairs, Sheila called up to her sister, 'Mags, could you bring down any blue cardigans for ladies? I think we've two or three in the woollens pile.'

She took the lady into the back room and left her there to try on the cardigans Margaret had brought down. Once she'd chosen one, Sheila bagged it up for discretion, and waved away her mumbled thanks.

'No need, love, it's my pleasure,' she insisted. 'Do come back if you need anything else. Always happy to help and no questions asked.' She gave Mrs Downing a wink. 'And tell your daughter we've plenty of boys' clothing as well as ladies'. Also, there's a council fund for people who need a bit of help with their bills. Just let me know.'

Smiling, she and Margaret stood in the doorway and watched the old lady head happily off down the street.

'It does my heart good to think we're able to help a few people out in these hard times,' she told her sister, who had fetched out the broom but was leaning on it rather than doing anything useful.

'It's a pity they're shy about accepting help though,' Margaret said. 'I was proud like that once. Didn't like other people knowing my private business. Now I know better. Sometimes you need a helping hand, and that's all there is to it. No shame in admitting it.'

'Oh, Mags.' Surprised and touched, Sheila gave her a quick hug. 'You and I had our differences in the past, no point denying it. But I'm happy we've made this work.'

Briefly, her sister beamed. Then she bent to sweeping and her face settled back into its usual dour expression. Sheila supposed it was hard to change the frown of a lifetime. 'So you were saying earlier that they're getting married,' Margaret remarked, squeezing the broomhead under the counter in case any dirt might have got under there too.

'Eh?' Sheila blinked. 'Joan and Arthur, you mean?' They'd been chatting about the Land Girl and her beau before that new donation had arrived, interrupting their cosy gossip. 'Of course they are, bless 'em. And a lovely couple they make too. So, all's well that ends well.'

Sheila reopened Arnie's old ledger and began running her finger down columns of figures, comparing them to her own recent takings. By her estimate, she was making more money than Arnie ever used to do. But then, the war was beginning to recede in people's memories, and although most rationing was still in place, some of the wealthier folk now had change to spare when they came shopping.

It was a pity the same wasn't true of the poorer folk, she

thought. But her community fund should start to help them soon, if people could get past their embarrassment at asking for help.

'And what about you?' her sister asked, shooting her a sly look. 'Don't think I haven't seen you and Bernard together. First, he only came into the shop a few times a week. Now he's here every day, regular as clockwork. The two of you are inseparable.'

Sheila felt guilt-stricken again, though it was silly to feel that way. Arnie wouldn't have wanted her to never look at another man again … Would he?

'It's no secret that we're stepping out,' she replied cautiously, 'but I told him straight, I loved my Arnie to bits, and I ain't ready to love nobody else.' Sheila hesitated, her gaze moving over the figures in the ledger without really seeing them. 'Still, I could do worse. Bernard's a nice bloke. Bit posh, perhaps. But maybe it's time I moved up in the world. Running a shop, seat on the council—'

'Rich boyfriend,' her sister threw in.

Sheila chuckled. 'He may have money and a nice car, but Bernard's no toff.' And it was true. Deep down, he was still the boy she'd been to school with. And she felt comfortable with him. They were never at a loss for something to talk about, where she'd often struggled to get Arnie to talk about anything. And she did like a good old natter …

'Does Violet know about him?'

'She knows we're good friends,' Sheila told her defensively. 'I don't think Violet approves, if that's what you're asking. But it ain't none of her business, is it?'

To her relief, Margaret dropped the subject. 'How about

that other Land Girl? The one who went swanning off to Bodmin for her holidays. She back yet?'

'Caroline? Lord, yes. And just in time, else Joe might have driven his tractor all the way there to drag her home.' She shook her head. 'He's been beside himself, wondering how he'll manage once Joan's left us to get married. Land Girls are bloomin' hard to come by now the war's over. It's back-breaking work and not as many girls are being recruited these days. All the same, he's asked Violet to write to Mrs Topping, the Women's Land Army coordinator—'

'Talk of the devil,' Margaret gasped, promptly disappearing into the back of the shop.

Seconds later, Violet herself appeared in the doorway. 'Afternoon, Mum,' she said, her eyes narrowed on the back of the shop. 'Was that Aunty Margaret I just saw scuttling off like a badger into its hole?' She still hadn't quite reconciled herself to Margaret being one of the family again. But maybe in time …

Sheila rolled her eyes. 'Give over, would you, love? We've been through all that before. My sister is welcome here, so don't bother getting on your high horse over it.' She closed the ledger and slid it back under the counter. 'What can I do you for? Or is this just a social call?'

Violet set her wicker shopping basket on the counter. She asked for a few pounds of potatoes and carrots, wrestling with ration books as she also ordered tobacco for the men, though Joe rarely smoked his pipe these days, and their weekly allowance of sweets. 'Joe's got such a sweet tooth,' she grumbled, pointing to the jar of Black Jacks. 'He'll regret it if he loses any more teeth. When we still had the evacuee kids with us, he used to give them most of his ration. Now he eats the sweets himself and wonders why he gets the toothache. Silly sausage …'

While Sheila was tearing out the coupon stamps from the ration book, another woman hurried briskly into the shop. It was Mrs Treedy.

'I hope you don't mind me dropping by again,' she said, placing a small greaseproof parcel on the counter in front of Sheila. 'But I had some pasty left over and thought you might like it. It's proper Cornish, my old mum's recipe. Just a little thank you for your help the other day,' she finished, with a wary glance at Violet.

'This is my daughter, Mrs Postbridge,' Sheila said, introducing them. 'Vi, this is Mrs Treedy. George just gave her a cleaning job at Eastern House.' She gave Mrs Treedy an encouraging smile. 'Violet used to clean there herself, when she first came to Porthcurno. She's an expert with a mop.'

Violet didn't seem to find her joke very amusing. She shook hands with Mrs Treedy. 'Nice to meet you, Mrs Treedy, I'm sure,' she said in her best village voice, the one she used when she didn't want people to know she came from Dagenham. 'Yes, we took what work we could, back in the early years of the war. Difficult times … But we're out the other side now, and everything's looking up.'

Mrs Treedy gave her a thin smile. 'For some, maybe,' was all she said.

Violet said something about the weather, and while they were arguing over whether there'd be more rain that week or if the fine weather would hold, the bell over the door jangled and a man shuffled into the shop.

The three women fell silent, looking round at him.

It was Stanley Chellew.

Sheila's heart thumped. She knew at once what he was there for. To cause as much bloomin' trouble as he could before dragging Margaret back to his farm.

Her brother-in-law's appearance shocked her though. He looked twenty years older than when she'd seen him during the war. His shoulders were slumped, and he walked with a stoop, his hair was white and shaggy, his beard unkempt, his cloth cap grimy. He was wearing a thick jacket despite the heat and shabby brown trousers, held up by a wide belt that was shiny with age. His cheeks were craggy and deeply pitted, his nose a bulbous red, the surest sign of a drinker.

Stanley recognised her at once and growled, 'Where's my wife? I know she's here so don't beat about the bush. Just fetch her or else!'

Mrs Treedy had shrunk back against the counter when Stanley glanced her way, but stayed where she was, staring at him fixedly.

Sheila hurried out from behind the counter, wishing either Joe or Ernest were on hand. 'Now, Stanley,' she began placatingly, but was interrupted by her daughter.

'I beg your bleedin' pardon?' Her posh air forgotten, Violet was suddenly shrill, arms folded, chin up. 'I think you'd best leave, Stanley Chellew, before you get what's coming to you.' She looked him up and down with contempt. 'Don't think I've forgotten what you done to our Lily, when she was barely out of school. How you dared lay hands on her …' She choked on the words, no doubt recalling Mrs Treedy's presence in the shop, and finished thickly, 'Go on, sling your hook.'

'I'm not moving 'till I've seen my wife,' Stanley snarled, and took a lurching step towards Violet, who bridled and drew herself up as though about to do battle.

Hurriedly, Sheila stepped between them, hoping to goodness he wouldn't dare thump a woman of her years. 'You heard what Violet said. You can't just come barging in here, throwing your weight about. This is a respectable establishment. So unless you want me to report you to the police, you'd best leave.'

'Report me to the police?' Stanley repeated with hoarse laughter. 'There's only one bobby between here and Penzance, you silly cow, and he's in my pocket. In fact, maybe I'll send him round here myself, to ask where you got all this stuff.' He gestured to the produce on the shop shelves. 'Who's to say you didn't get it on the black market, eh? You'd best be careful threatening me with the police, Sheila. You're not in Dagenham now. This is *my* place.'

'Why, you scabby little ...' Sheila only just stopped herself in time from swearing, recalling belatedly that she was a councillor now. 'Maybe once I might have let you push me around, Stan. But not anymore. And you won't push my sister around either.'

Sheila moved to usher him out of the shop, but the brute caught her arm and twisted it behind her back, his foul breath in her face.

As she struggled to free herself, with Violet pitching in, there was a shriek behind them, and Margaret rushed out from the back of the shop, a rolling pin in her hand, which she laid about his head and shoulders, screaming, 'Get out, you nasty, good-for-nothing old ...' And she used a few choice words on top that made Violet grin appreciatively at her aunt.

Protecting his head, Stanley stumbled sideways, also swearing fit to turn the air blue. 'That's assault, that is,' he yelled, wincing. 'I'll see you in prison for this, Maggie.'

'Go on, then … call the police,' Margaret spat. 'I'll gladly tell them what you've done to me, you bully. Bruises, broken bones … Yes, and locking me in the cellar to stop me going to the doctor.' She surged forward again, rolling pin raised, clearly intending to do him a serious mischief. Her eyes were blazing and her face was flushed. 'If anyone deserves prison, it's you.'

Crouched in the doorway, determined not to be driven out, Stanley grabbed up a crate of fruit to protect himself. 'You're mad, you are. You *need* to be locked up. And I'll see that you are.'

Scared by the look on her sister's face, Sheila wrenched the rolling pin from her. 'Calm down, Maggie. We'll deal with this idiot.' She glanced at her daughter. 'Take her down the back, would you?'

Dazed and shaking, Margaret reluctantly allowed Violet to steer her away.

'You're still my wife, Margaret Chellew,' Stanley yelled after her, and put down the crate of fruit, which was thankfully still in one piece. 'I'm not giving up until you're back where you belong, cooking my dinner and cleaning my house. Do you hear?'

Sheila and Mrs Treedy looked at each other, then grabbed Stanley between them and propelled him swiftly into the street. He was so shocked, he didn't even resist.

'And don't bother coming back. Or next time, I swear to God, I'll finish you off with the rolling pin myself,' Sheila snapped before slamming the door in his face, drawing the bolt across, and turning the 'Open' sign to 'Closed'. Then she watched as he staggered away, making sure he wasn't loitering about in hopes of sneaking back in later.

'Your sister's husband, is he?' Mrs Treedy nodded grimly without waiting for an answer. 'There's only one way to deal with men like that, and it don't involve the police.'

Sheila, deeply shaken, set her hairnet straight again. 'I don't intend going to prison for that fool,' she said shortly. 'I expect my two sons-in-law will be having a word with him after this. That should do the trick.'

Violet returned at that moment, a high flush in her cheeks. 'What a nasty piece of work. You managed to get rid of him, then?'

'Of course, and he'll think twice before bothering us again,' Sheila said, with more hope than confidence. 'All that bluster about the police … He wouldn't dare. We've got more on him than he has on us.'

Someone rapped at the shop door, and she looked round sharply to see Bernard Bailey peering in at them, a look of surprise on his face.

Relief flooding her, Sheila hurried to unlock the door and flip the shop sign back to 'Open'. 'Sorry about that,' she told him breathlessly, 'we had a bit o' trouble, that's all. My sister's husband turned up again. We had to ask him to leave.'

'More than once,' Violet added grimly.

'Mr Chellew? Yes, I saw him getting into his van up the road. He didn't look in great shape, to be honest.' Bernard raised his brows, looking round at them all. 'What did you ladies do to him?'

With a benign smile, Sheila passed Violet the rolling pin, who tucked it placidly under her arm. 'Oh, nothing much. But I don't think he'll be back in a hurry.'

And the three women laughed, while Bernard looked on in bemusement.

When Mrs Treedy had gone, Violet excused herself, hurrying into the back room to make a nice cup of tea for poor Margaret, whose nerves were shot. That left Sheila and Bernard alone together in the shop, and for once she felt unaccountably nervous, unsure where to look. What had her sister said? *The two of you are inseparable.* Hardly true, but she found herself blushing as they stood looking at each other in silence …

'I hear congratulations are in order,' Bernard said at last. 'One of your Land Girls is engaged to be married to Arthur Green, is that right?'

'Good news travels fast.'

He grinned. 'He's had some troubles, that boy, but settling down with a wife is the best thing that can happen to a man.'

'Tell that to Stanley Chellew.'

'Point taken.'

He pulled off his cap and ran a hand through silver hair. Not that it needed tidying. He was such a dapper gent, Sheila thought, suppressing a flutter of excitement at the thought that they were courting. She'd told Margaret it wasn't serious between them, and she'd meant it. They were just having a bit of fun, weren't they? Shooting him a sideways look though, she felt a surge of something more than simple affection, and knew she'd fibbed to her sister. Which left her more confused than ever.

'It's always nice to have a wedding in the village though,' he went on slowly, holding her gaze. 'It's lovely to see folk getting married and the men not having to go away to war afterwards. It's a cause for celebration, and a sign that things are finally getting back to normal.'

Sheila gave a tremulous smile. 'I hope to goodness you're right, Bernard, and I wish them two young people all the happiness in the world.' She wished every happiness for herself and her family too, if that weren't too much trouble for Him upstairs to arrange.

Bernard reached for her and she sensed that he meant to kiss her. Suddenly unsure, she slipped behind the counter, out of his reach, saying hurriedly, 'I … I expect you'd like your weekly sweet ration before you go.'

'Sheila …'

'It's no trouble. Now, what would you like?'

But she felt so guilty and confused. And, turning to the glass jars on the shelf, Sheila almost choked as the dearest memory swept over her: Arnie in his apron, standing behind this same counter, weighing out sweets for her when they were first courting and handing them over with a mischievous wink.

'Oh …' Her heart ached.

'Are you all right?' Bernard asked, his voice deep with concern.

'Yes … Yes, of course.' Sheila threw him a quick reassuring smile over her shoulder, for he wasn't to blame for her shilly-shallying. 'Just my back playing up.'

But she'd finally come to a decision. It was time to stop living in the past. She would visit Arnie in the churchyard again, and this time make a full confession about Bernard. And she'd ask for his blessing too, for a sign that she wasn't doing the wrong thing by stepping out with another man. No doubt Margaret would say she didn't need to, and that she was being silly, worrying what her dead husband would think about all this. But Sheila knew she wouldn't be able to rest until she'd admitted everything to Arnie.

'Now,' she went on, her voice steady again, 'what can I get you, my love? We've these new Sherbet Pips fresh in,' she told him cheerfully, transferring the heavy jar to the counter and fetching the scoop. 'Bit sharp, mebbe, but sweet enough to please,' she added with a wink, knowing she could almost have been talking about herself.

'Sounds perfect,' he said.

EPILOGUE

Joan rinsed out the wine glass she'd been drinking from and set it upside down on the draining board. Then, with a sudden tremor, she stared out of the window across the darkening yard at Postbridge Farm and thought, *I'll never stand here again to wash up or fill a kettle. Or not as a single woman. I'll certainly never* live *under this roof again. Never be a Land Girl again. This is the last time I'll do any of this …*

'You not gone to bed yet, love?' Mrs Newton asked, interrupting Joan's thoughts as she came bustling in from the snug with a tray laden down with dirty glasses.

The whole household had spent a long, riotous evening celebrating the night before her wedding and talking of old times together, and Joan doubted there was a single clean glass left in the place. Except the one she'd just washed up, of course.

'I'm heading upstairs now,' Joan told her, quickly drying her hands. 'Caro and Selly have already gone up, and I think Tilly's in the bathroom.'

'It's been like old times, having Selina back at the farm with us,' Mrs Newton told her, smiling. 'She and Caroline were the first to come here as Land Girls, you know … I was just saying to Vi how much I miss them three evacuee kids too. Lovely Janice and Eustace, of course, and little Timothy, bless his heart. The house was so busy in them days. Now Selina's moved away, and you'll be gone tomorrow. I don't know how Joe's going to manage the farm with only two Land Girls to help out.' She kissed Joan on the cheek. 'Good luck, love. Being a housewife is a full-time job, as you're about to find out. All the cooking and cleaning, and the bloomin' ironing …' She pulled a face. 'I do envy you though, starting out on your married life, young as you are … It warms my heart to see you and Arthur so happy and in love.'

'Thank you, Mrs Newton.'

Joan felt a pang for the older lady, knowing how much she must be missing her late husband. Although, judging by the gossip flying about the village about her and Mr Bailey, it seemed unlikely Mrs Newton would stay a widow much longer.

'Call me Sheila, love.' She sighed, her eyes brimming with tears. 'You know, some folk say you're never too old to fall in love, but it ain't the same when you're older. At least, not to my mind. When you're young, everything's so new and magical … But once you're a bit longer in the tooth, you go into these things with your blinkers off, I can tell you.' Sheila gave a self-conscious laugh. 'Well, you must've heard about me and Bernard by now.'

'Not much,' Joan fibbed kindly. 'Except that the two of you are … friends.'

Sheila gave her a wink. 'I'll tell you a little secret, shall

I?' she said, lowering her voice. 'I went to visit Arnie's grave the other day. I go regular, you know, to say hello to the ol' fella, put down fresh flowers and clear the leaves off his grave. Only this time, I had a confession to make.' She hesitated, looking almost guilty. 'I didn't think it was right not to let Arnie know I'm courting again. It sounds superstitious, but I couldn't rest easy, not without having told him about me and Bernard. Anyway,' she went on with a sweet smile, 'after I'd made my confession, a little white blossom fell into my lap. No idea where it came from. It just bloomin' fell from the sky. And I thought to myself, that's Arnie, that is. Giving me his blessing to be happy again.' She looked at Joan anxiously. 'Do you think I'm soft in the head for thinking that?'

'No, it's a lovely thought … Sheila,' Joan said softly, holding her hands. 'Really, really lovely.'

'Aw, bless your heart.'

'And what you've been doing for folk in the village … That's wonderful too,' Joan told her earnestly. 'Arthur and I saw the poster in the shop window. He's asked his mother to donate some of his old clothes, and she said she'd sort out some good pots and pans too, ones she rarely uses. I believe his father's already donated some money to the fund.'

'Yes, the Greens have been very generous.' Mrs Newton looked pleased. 'I wasn't sure how people would take it at first … But not a day goes by that someone doesn't turn up with a bag of clothing or bric-a-brac for those in need. Why, only last week, my supplier dropped off a box of kiddy toys that his sister's family don't need anymore, along with the usual crates of fruit and veg. I've been bowled over by the response, I won't pretend otherwise.'

'People can surprise you, can't they?' Joan agreed, smiling. 'Sometimes you just need to ask.'

Ernest Fisher interrupted this cosy chat, calling through the open door of the snug, 'Sheila, are you bringing another bottle of that home-made gin or what? We're dying of thirst in here.'

'You'd better not be knocking it back on your own out there, Mum,' Violet shouted, but the rest of whatever she said was drowned out as everyone in the snug fell about laughing.

Sheila's sister Margaret appeared in the doorway with a shy smile. 'Need any help, Shee?' Having overheard a few arguments recently, Joan knew she'd been shunned by the family for the past few years, but she'd accompanied her sister up to the farm that afternoon and spent a good hour talking to Lily in the snug, who'd very kindly come over from Penzance for the wedding. Lily had wept, and so had Margaret, and Mrs Newton had bustled in and out of the snug while the two women cried and talked, fetching clean hankies and endless pots of tea. Now it seemed there was a truce of sorts between them all.

'You can carry the nuts and pickled herrings, Maggie,' Mrs Newton said, and handed a tray to her sister with a wink. 'I'll keep hold of the bottle, ta.'

Grinning, Joan said goodnight to them all, left the hardened drinkers to enjoy yet more of Mrs Newton's infamous home-made concoctions, and climbed wearily up the stairs to bed.

That is, her physical body was tired, but her mind was on fire with excitement. She was getting *married* in the morning, finally able to show off the beautiful cream dress she'd bought new from a boutique in Penzance, despite the extravagance and all the coupon stamps it had cost her. But 'you only get married once', as the shop assistant had told her. And thank goodness for that, she thought, as she'd been run off her feet getting ready for the big event. At last, there was nothing left to organise. Everything was prepared for her wedding day. All she needed now was her beauty sleep.

But on the threshold of the bedroom she was to share with Tilly that night, she found Caroline and Selina camped out, still drinking and chatting.

She stopped in amazement on seeing them, not quite sure she could manage more fun and chatter that night. 'I thought you rowdy lot were going to bed early.' She gave an extravagant yawn. 'I don't know about you, but I can barely keep my eyes open. I've been so busy these past few days, getting everything ready ... Now I'm shattered.'

'We won't keep you up much longer,' Selina promised, coming to kiss her on the cheek, which surprised Joan, for she and the other Land Girls had never been that close. 'I wish you all the best, Joan. I'm so glad I was able to come back for your wedding day. It's going to be marvellous. And you and Arthur will be ecstatically happy together, I'm sure of it.'

'Fortune teller, are you?' Joan said a little flippantly, for everyone had been saying the same thing over recent days, and she was beginning to worry they might be tempting fate.

'Well, you can't have a worse marriage than Selina's sister had,' Tilly remarked, standing before the mirror as she brushed her hair before bed.

Joan frowned. 'What do you mean?'

'I was just telling these two about my late sister, Bella. I've been reading her journals,' Selina explained reluctantly, 'and it seems her husband Sebastian had an affair with one of their neighbours once, a woman called Helen.'

'How awful!' Joan was horrified.

'He was much older than her, so I suppose he probably seduced her. Though if you ask me, she's exactly the kind of woman who would deliberately try to steal another woman's husband.'

'That won't happen to you though, Joan,' Tilly hurried to assure her. 'I wasn't saying that at all. Quite the opposite. You and Arthur will be deliriously happy.'

'I'm not sure how deliriously happy we can be,' she admitted, 'living so near his parents. The cottage they've given us is practically at the bottom of their garden. Though I'm thrilled and grateful to have a home of my very own, of course. We've been so lucky.'

Actually, she was secretly in love with the ramshackle cottage. It was tiny and needed a great deal of work, but, in her mind's eye, she already saw it drenched in white roses in the summertime, with fragrant jasmine and red-hot pokers in a charming cottage garden, and it seemed to her a perfect haven of happiness.

'Arthur's the lucky one, to be marrying you,' Caroline said firmly, and also surprised her with a hug. 'But listen to this … You remember Cameron? He's the brother of the woman who had the affair with Selina's brother-in-law … He made a pass at her sister Bella too, years ago, and recently tried it on with Selina herself. She sent him off with a flea in his ear, of course. But he and his sister sound like a pretty horrid pair, don't you agree?'

'Yes.' Astonished, Joan stared at Selina. 'How dreadful for

you. Gosh, and he was so kind towards Arthur too. I'm sorry you've been stuck there on your own with them.'

'It was quite unpleasant for a while,' Selina agreed, a little pale. 'But Caro's been very supportive,' she added, shooting the other girl a grateful look, 'and the children have been keeping me so busy lately, I've had no time to brood.'

'Yes, Caroline told us you'd sacked the nanny. She sounded *awful*. I don't blame you at all. Have you found a replacement yet?'

'No … In fact, I've decided to look after the kids myself.'

'*Yourself*?' Perhaps unfairly, Joan had always thought of Selina as rather superficial and boy-mad, not someone who would easily take on such a heavy burden as child-rearing. She even recalled Selina mocking her once for being a 'maternal' type around children, rejecting that instinct as a bad thing. But losing her sister and gaining an instant family must have changed her. 'Goodness me.'

'Honestly, it's not so hard once you get used to their routines.' Selina looked round at their astonished faces, and grimaced. 'Though it can have its drawbacks. The housekeeper volunteered to mind the kids while I came to the wedding, but I'll have to dash back right after the wedding tomorrow, I'm afraid.'

Caroline's eyes were sad, though she said quickly, 'Of course. We understand. They need their aunty.'

'Yes.' Selina smiled, her face lighting up. 'You know, I don't think I've ever been so content as these past few weeks without the nanny, just being a mum to them … They're such lovely children. And little Faith is an absolute darling.' She took Joan's hands, her look pleading. 'You and Arthur must come and meet them. Please say you will. It's a lovely big house and I'd be thrilled to have your company.'

'I'll mention it to Arthur,' Joan promised her. 'Though we'll be heading off ourselves straight after the wedding reception.' She stopped, shocked to her core as reality struck her. 'Gosh, I'm going on my honeymoon tomorrow … How strange that sounds.' She giggled, and the other girls laughed with her. 'I'm going to be *a married woman*. It's hard to believe.'

'I can believe it,' Tilly said, beaming at her, 'and I'm glad you're going to be happy at last. Everything has been so hard these past few years. I'd started to believe nobody would *ever* be happy again. Then the war ended and everyone was beside themselves. People jumping into fountains fully clothed, getting drunk and dancing in the streets … Well, we all saw the photographs and read the stories. Only all that joy didn't last, did it? Things just got harder and drearier. I sometimes think it'll never end. The rationing, the hardships, slaving away all hours as a Land Girl …'

'Tilly, you've barely been a Land Girl for five minutes,' Caroline exclaimed, and they all laughed. 'Wait until you've spent a whole winter trudging out in the dark at five in the morning to dig for mouldy potatoes or throw turnips at sheep. Then you can complain about *hardship*.'

'Or when the pigs get out in a rainstorm, and you have to dash about the yard trying to catch them, and they're so quick and slippery, and you end up covered in mud …' Joan added, and they all laughed so hard they cried. Wiping tears from her own eyes, she said with a gasp, 'Oh, I'm going to miss you all so much. Miss this farm, miss Violet and Joe, miss working on the land. I'm even going to miss the pigs.' She shook her head, bemused. 'I'm going to miss all of it, and I never thought for a moment that I would.'

'What tosh!' Selina burst out. 'You'll be far too busy being in love to spare a thought for us girls, and especially not for those muddy pigs.' Selina gave her a hug, surprising Joan once again with her unexpected warmth. It seemed she really had changed since leaving the farm. 'Now, get to bed and dream of your beloved,' she whispered in Joan's ear, 'because tomorrow you're going to marry him.'

The next day, Joan floated down the aisle on her brother's arm in a sea of fragrance, clusters of white flowers everywhere, incense on the air mingling with the musty smell of hymnals, sunlight dazzling her eyes, and the organ playing so loudly, she could almost feel it in her bones.

Ahead of her, Arthur waited before the altar, his face aglow and yet sombre too, aware of the solemnity of the occasion.

His parents were seated in the front row, not happy that their son was getting married, but clearly determined to make the best of the situation. His cousins and aunt and uncle had turned up as well, and beamed at her from the next pew back, a friendly bunch whom she looked forward to getting to know better.

On the other side of the church, Mrs Newton – *Sheila*, Joan reminded herself – sat primly with her friend Bernard Bailey, with Violet and Joe alongside them, Margaret too, and the other Land Girls, Tilly, Caroline and Selina. Their heads all turned as she drifted down the aisle in her lovely frock, and she smiled back at them tremulously, her heart thudding. Behind them sat Lily and Tristan, who'd brought

Morris with them, the little boy solemnly pointing out saints in the stained-glass windows. Alice wasn't there, alas, too busy in London with her new husband to travel such a long way, but Penny had come on the train from Bude, and even dragged her husband John along too, the two of them winking as Joan sailed happily past.

A few feet ahead of her, Sarah Jane scattered fistfuls of rose petals over the stone flags, more confident in the role of flower girl since Alice's wedding. The Reverend Clewson was frowning at Violet's daughter in a vengeful manner, for he'd warned her most explicitly at the rehearsal not to strew rose petals in his church. Sarah Jane had ignored him, of course, being only tiny and most likely not knowing what 'strew' meant, and too mesmerised by the tufts of hair growing out of his ears to listen to what the vicar was saying to her anyway.

It was so beautiful, Joan thought, such a perfect moment. It was breathtaking to look about the church and see all these people who'd turned out for her wedding day, some of them like family to her in the absence of her blood relatives – except for Graham, of course, who was patting her arm with a reassuring smile – and she was simply overwhelmed.

She was also deliriously happy, exactly as her friends had claimed she would be. And to think, not so long ago, she'd thought the other Land Girls distant and hard to talk to, that they had little in common. Now she was sad to be leaving the farm and her dear friends behind.

But as her gaze returned to her husband-to-be, so handsome and full of love, a man who had suffered and come through it all to find her, everything else fell away and

Joan couldn't wait for them to be alone together at last, as man and wife …

'Dearly beloved,' the vicar began, and Arthur took her hand and smiled.

THE END

ACKNOWLEDGEMENTS

It's my pleasure as always to thank my wonderful agent Alison Bonomi for everything you so tirelessly do for me. It's much appreciated! Also to everyone at LBA for your support and hard work.

My thanks also to the totally amazing team at Avon Books. I can't believe we're already at Book 7 in the Cornish Girls series! And it's all gone so smoothly, thanks to the hard-working and knowledgeable publishing team behind me. Especial thanks go to my editors for *A New Hope*, Sarah Bauer and Emma Grundy Haigh, and also to the marvellous Amy Baxter and Rachel Hart, as well as Maddie Dunne Kirby, Raphaella Demetris, Ella Young, Jess Zahra, and everyone else who's helped pull these books together in recent years. I couldn't have done this without you!

Thank you also to my readers, who continue to amaze me by knowing far more about my characters than I seem to do – my head is always in the latest book, alas! – and whose affection for the Cornish Girls keeps me going from book to book. Thank you all from the bottom of my heart.

Lastly, a massive thank you to my three youngest who still live at home – Dylan, Morris and Indigo – for doing all the housework and cooking whenever I'm late with a deadline, and to my beloved husband Steve for not minding that he married a novelist with her head always in the clouds. He was made Mayor of our town this year, which sort of makes me Lady Mayoress. I shall endeavour to live up to the title, and not spend any important occasions scribbling furtively in my trusty notebook, honest!

Betty x

Go back to where it all began – don't miss the first book in the glorious Cornish Girls series …

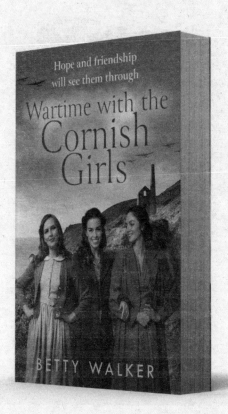

Available now in paperback, eBook and audiobook.

Follow up with some festive fun for the
Cornish Girls …

Available now in paperback,
eBook and audiobook.

Enemy gunfire on Penzance beach brings
the Cornish Girls rushing to the rescue …

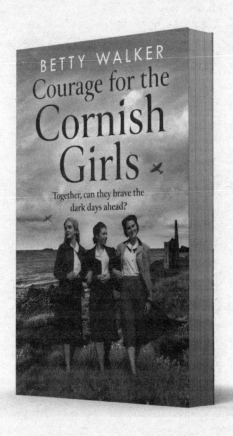

Available now in paperback,
eBook and audiobook.

Can the bonds of motherhood give them the strength they'll need to get through the war? ...

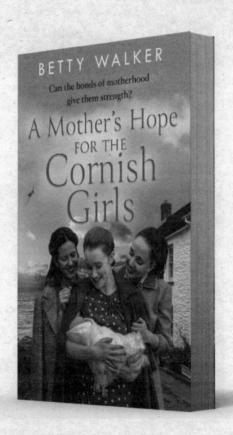

Available now in paperback,
eBook and audiobook.

Can love still thrive in the uncertainty of war?

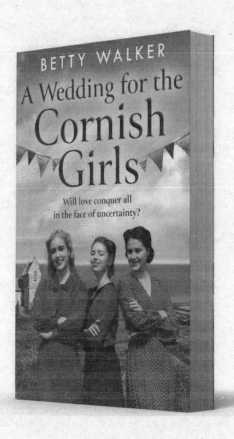

Available now in paperback, eBook and audiobook.